D0399162

DREAM CITY

A NOVEL BY BRENDAN SHORT

DREAM CITY

A NOVEL BY BRENDAN SHORT

MACADAM CAGE

MacAdam/Cage
155 Sansome Street, Suite 550
San Francisco, CA 94104
www.MacAdamCage.com

Short, Brendan, 1969-
Dream city / by Brendan Short.
p. cm.
ISBN 978-1-59692-318-8
1. Boys—Fiction. 2. Collectors and collecting—Fiction.
3. Big little books—Collectors and collecting—Fiction.
4. Chicago (Ill.)—Fiction. I. Title.
PS3619.H6685D74 2008
813'.6—dc22
2008029413

Grateful acknowledgment is made to The Dille Family Trust for
permission to reprint excerpts from *Buck Rogers in the City Below the
Sea* by H. Dick Calkins and Phil Nowlan (originally published by
Whitman Publishing Company). Copyright 1934 and renewed 1961 by
John F. Dille Co.; copyright assigned 1980 to The Dille Family Trust.
Buck Rogers is a registered trademark and copyright owned exclusively
by The Dille Family Trust.

Grateful acknowledgment is also made to Northwestern University Press
for permission to reprint an excerpt from *What Saves Us* by Bruce Weigl
(originally published by TriQuarterly Books, Northwestern University).
Copyright © 1992 Bruce Weigl. Reprinted by permission of Northwestern
University Press.

For Stephanie and my parents,
with gratitude and love

WHAT IS THE MEANING OF IT ALL?

MILLIONS ARE EXPENDED—A MAGIC CITY CREATED—THRONGS COME—
THE WORLD WATCHES—THEN IT VANISHES—WHY?

...A little while ago this site was placid lake. Now, shimmering beside the water, a dream city is risen. It lights the sky with splendor, yet soon will disappear and be merely a memory.

A Century of Progress World's Fair Guidebook, 1933

We are not always right
About what we think will save us.

—Bruce Weigl, "What Saves Us"

THE SHADOW OF ST. ROSE OF LIMA

1932–1934

1.

WHEN MICHAEL HALLIGAN WAS NEARLY SIX YEARS OLD, THE PICTURES IN the funny papers made more sense to him than the words. There in color, spread out on his bed, was Dick Tracy; stoic and keen-jawed, he waited in an alley with his elbow resting on a wooden crate. And there was a typical villain; unshaven and burly, he smacked around a poor disheveled boy until Tracy leaped from the shadows, delivered a right cross to his jaw and a left jab to his kisser, and lifted him high for a dramatic body slam. In the final frame, Dick Tracy shook hands with the boy he'd saved. Word balloons rose from their mouths, but Michael understood only bits of what was said: *kid, me, I'm, you, help, who, why*. He needed his mother to tell him the rest.

Michael leaned back, satisfied with the *Chicago Tribune* funnies, their pages lurid against his drab blanket and gray-papered wall. In the next room, his father snored. In the kitchen, his mother slapped the floor with a mop. A few minutes later, she opened his door. Her hair had a way of changing color from red to russet to brown, depending on what she wore and how the light hit her; this morning, beneath a 40-watt bulb, it was somewhere near rust.

When she told him to shove over, Michael scooted to the edge of the bed. He was small for his age but not slight; serious but rarely sullen. His skin was prone to sunburn, windburn, and blushing, and in his mouth a gap marked the spot where a tooth had recently wiggled free. He had chapped lips, the exhausted gray eyes of someone who had relaxed too little or squinted too much, and teeth that chattered when he was cold, which was seldom, or anxious, which was often. From his father he had inherited a poker face. The freckles had come from his mother. She squeezed in between him and the wall, her gingham dress damp in patches with sweat and washing water, and she spread the comics across her lap. Beginning with *The Gumps* and *Old Doc Yak* on page one and working her way to *Moon Mullins* and *Kitty Higgins* on page eight, she read aloud from the word balloons, using a different voice for each character. Michael corrected her when Winnie Winkle sounded too much like Maw Green and Harold Teen had a hint of Kayo. After she finished reading, she carefully tore along the newspaper's fold until four sheets of funnies lay on the bed. She held up the first sheet and asked, "Which side?"

She flipped the sheet from back to front, front to back. *The Gumps* or *Gasoline Alley*? The paper rustled, and the comics on one side showed faintly through to the other. When Michael chose *Gasoline Alley*, she set aside the first sheet and picked up the second, which she flipped back and forth until Michael made up his mind: *Little Orphan Annie* over a combination of *Smitty*, *Herby*, and *Little Folks*. The next choice was easiest of all; even though Michael wasn't wild about *Harold Teen* or *Looie Blooie*, they were better than a full-page advertisement for Ovaltine.

Michael's mother held up the last sheet. As usual, Michael found this final decision difficult, bordering on impossible. It was unfair that earlier he'd had to decide between strips he didn't like, but now he had to choose between *Dick Tracy* and *Moon Mullins*. Eventually he made his selection, and his mother reached across him to the bedside table, where she pushed aside cast-iron cars and Lincoln Logs until she found the masking tape. Kneeling on the mattress, she taped the four sheets of funnies to the wall. On the last one, Dick Tracy stared out, hand in pocket, ready to spring into the bedroom if a rescue was required.

Michael's mother lay down. Michael nestled into her side, rested his head on her breast, and draped his arm across her body. He gazed at the four sheets of newspaper: windows onto a brilliant world, different in every way from the window on the opposite wall, which revealed nothing but the neighbors' brick façade. They settled into silence then, his cheek on her chest, and she brushed his fine red hair with her fingers. It was mid-September, eleven o'clock. They had been up for several hours already—worshipping, working, just now relaxing. When she yawned, he yawned. In the next room, Michael's father stirred but then stopped stirring. He had been awake earlier, too, but only long enough to eat breakfast and relieve himself; like God, he spent the seventh day resting.

"Can someone forget how to sleep?" Michael asked.

His mother stopped caressing his hair. "What do you mean?"

"Can a person forget how to sleep?"

"Like you'd forget someone's name?"

"I guess."

"Or where you left something?"

"I think so."

"Have you had trouble sleeping?"

"No," Michael lied. "I was just wondering."

His mother smelled of scrambled eggs and bacon. Against his head, he felt her breastbone and the beating of her heart. Under his arm, her ribs rose and fell.

"So can you?" he asked.

She roused. He could tell she had fallen asleep.

"Can I what? What do you need?"

"Can you forget how to sleep?"

Again she said nothing and was soon breathing in the slow, raspy way of a deep and easy dreamer. With her hand as snug as a cap on his head, Michael tried but failed to ride her breath toward sleep.

Eventually they rose and, with Michael's father, ate a wordless lunch of chicken soup and bread and butter. His father left in the afternoon and returned for dinner, after which he and Michael sprawled on the living-room rug and aligned tin armies against each other. They shouted commands to their soldiers and imitated the sounds of feet marching, guns firing, men dying. The muscles in his father's forearms were strong ropes, tightening knots. A platoon vanished in his grip. Soldiers advanced and retreated, then fell with mortal wounds; they returned from the dead just to fight and die again. As the smell of toil and blood from his father's job at Armour permeated the battlefield, the carnage continued until Michael's seven-thirty bedtime.

That night, alone and restless in the dark, Michael again lay awake in bed. He heard no streetcars, no factory sounds. The birds and bums must have been asleep in McKinley Park. He closed his eyes, rested his hands beneath his cheek as comic-strip characters did, palms together, and conceived a trail of *ZZZZZ*s rising from his head. He counted sheep, something he had heard people speak of, but he only knew the numbers up to twenty, and in his imagination there were many more sheep than that. They dangled like those in Casey's butcher shop, their bodies drained of blood and stripped to the sinew. He returned to the front and again counted those he could, but the stillness of the sheep now frightened him, and the struggle to sleep only made him less sleepy.

He tossed aside his covers, knelt on his bed, and with his eyes closed ran his fingers over the funnies, pretending the word balloons were lassos that might rope him into another world. There were worlds within worlds, he sensed, and worlds beneath the ones he knew. Voices crackled inside radio sets. On movie screens, people became giants or vanished into black. At the bottom of the river sat arrowheads and animal guts, and inside the earth, dead people lived with worms and ants and slugs and rocks and roots and snails and creatures no one had ever seen. Michael was glad it wasn't Saturday, when his mother would throw away his comics, leaving him to consider the marks where tape had taken off a little more of the wallpaper. On nights without his funnies, he would grow frightened thinking that the torn patches were the eyes of a devil who watched only him. He'd pray to Dick Tracy to protect him, but his hero would be gone with the rest, crumpled in the garbage can.

Tonight, however, Dick Tracy was with him, as were Skeezix, Texas Slim, and the rest of his friends, living flat beneath his fingertips. In his head he heard his mother's deep Dick Tracy voice say, *What's the matter, kid?*

"I can't sleep," Michael whispered.

Why not?

"I don't know. I just can't."

You know what you should do?

Michael shook his head. He imagined Dick Tracy in profile—a crescent creased into his cheek, a dent in his tan fedora.

You oughta pee. Then get a glass of water and come back to bed.

"But I'm afraid."

Of what? Peeing?

"Of being out there alone."

Don't be such a baby. If anything bad happens, all you gotta do is run back to us. We'll be here.

Michael hesitated but then stepped onto the floor. With his eyes closed, he inched into and along the hallway, touching the walls for guidance, listening to the creaks and hums of the house. He was the star of an action strip, groping from tree to tree in a night-dark jungle, eventually reaching the carpet of twigs and slithering bugs that was the bathroom's cool linoleum. Out of habit, he turned on the overhead light, letting the chain clatter, but he still didn't open his eyes. He peed but decided not to flush, for fear of waking whatever worlds lurked beneath the flooring.

A brave and blind explorer, he trekked farther down the hallway—now a desert, now the moon—finding his way as much with his hands as with his feet. As he groped for and finally flicked the kitchen light switch, keys jingled at the back door. He froze, eyes still shut, as the door rattled open. A cold gust struck him. A man hummed, closed the door, and laughed.

"You asleep?"

Michael usually saw his father only at breakfast and dinner, before bedtime, and on Sundays. But late at night and in the early morning, while lying in bed, he often heard his father's slow and impatient voice, its long pauses set like snares.

"You awake?"

His father—all tobacco smoke, stale sweat, dead flesh—stood before him. Blindfolded and shackled, Michael nodded.

"Then why don't you open your eyes?"

Michael stood silently in his father's pause, waiting for the trap to spring, for his father to smack him across the head, or shove him, or shout, "I've had about enough out of you." He wondered if Dick Tracy was supposed to rescue him, or if he would have to save himself.

"What's wrong? You scared?"

Michael shook his head. He knew his father was not the kind of man to be on Dick Tracy's good side. He knew it from the severed dog's head that had appeared one morning on their porch, from the bullet that had shattered the kitchen window and tunneled into the wall, and from the woman who had shouldered his mother at the National Tea store, sending her tumbling into a display of Post Toasties. *That's for that son-of-a-bitch husband of yours.* He knew it whenever his father went out at night and appeared the next day with a black eye or bloodied knuckles. But mostly he knew it from the air he breathed: a stockyard stench that bit his eyes and whispered insistently that the world was filled with villains.

"You plan on being scared your whole life?"

Michael shrugged and then flinched when a coarse hand patted his cheek.

"What if I just open your eyes for you, then? You'll see there's nothing to be afraid of."

A heavy arm wrapped around Michael's back and yanked him forward. The thumb of his father's other hand landed hard on his eyelid. With his chest and chin pressed against his father and his head tilted back, Michael stood only because his father held him. When the thumb started to lift his upper lid, Michael squeezed his eyes shut and scrunched his face. He squirmed and looked down as far as he could, feeling dizzy from his muscles' strain and his father's force. Against the back of his eyelid, veins formed a neon web. His father laughed and released him. Michael stumbled, then steadied himself.

"You're like some statue in a park, you know that? Like one of those generals with a sword. All you need is some pigeon shit on your shoulders." He poked Michael's chest. "If you remember anything I tell you, remember this. Ready, kiddo?"

Michael stayed where he was—a statue.

"When you fear, you lose. It's best to forget your fear and charge ahead with life. Don't pay any attention to what scares you, because if you do, the world will eat you alive." His father slapped his back. "You got it? You understand what I'm telling you?"

Michael nodded.

"Now go to bed, kiddo. Get some sleep."

His father headed down the hallway, then opened and closed the bedroom door. The bed creaked as he settled into it.

Still willfully blind and now so sleepy he stumbled, Michael found a glass in the cupboard. As he filled the glass with water, he remembered that when he was three, nearly four, he had chewed his tin soldiers; they'd tasted like pennies and left paint on his teeth and metal on his breath, and he'd given them up only when his father rapped his forehead with a spoon and told him to quit being such a goddamn baby. Searching for the light switch, he ran his fingers along the wall and felt the little bump, as soft and slight as one of his nipples, where the bullet was still buried. His father had stuffed the hole with putty and painted over it, and afterward he'd acted as if nothing had happened, but Michael knew what was hidden there. He switched off the light and shuffled down the hallway, doing his best to imagine the walls and floor exactly as they were in real life.

As Michael pushed open his door, he pictured Dick Tracy standing in profile in the middle of the bedroom, hands in his pockets. Michael shut the door quietly and made his way toward the bed. After setting the glass atop his bedside table, he yawned and let his body flop onto the mattress. Dick Tracy's desk and water cooler were in the corner of the room, where the dresser usually stood. The narrow window that looked onto the neighbors' bricks was now wide and filled with skyscrapers, a cathedral's spire, a quarter moon.

Were you afraid, kid?

Michael shook his head and slipped under the covers. "When you fear, you lose," he said, falling asleep as the last syllable left his lips.

2.

ELIZABETH HALLIGAN WALKED WITH MICHAEL PAST BRICK BUNGALOWS like her own and two-flats the color of strong coffee. With their breath vanishing before them, they strolled along empty sidewalks where, later in the day, children would run and roller-skate, their parents and grandparents shouting in a mixture of Polish and English for them to avoid the flower beds. In the sky a full moon faded. A few blocks ahead, sunlight framed a warehouse in a smoky violet glow. They passed the shell of a four-story apartment house that had never been fully built. On the first floor, just past the empty window frame, people gathered around a bonfire. At all hours, squatters came and went from the building, and occasionally one or two would knock on the Halligans' back door, offering to sweep the steps in exchange for a sandwich or a bowl of soup. Elizabeth always turned them away, afraid that kindness would only encourage them.

Elizabeth and Michael turned right onto Ashland and passed retailers, wholesalers, and Irish families on their way to Good Counsel. It would have been easier to go along with them and not walk the extra mile to St. Rose of Lima, but Elizabeth had gone to St. Rose her whole life, just as her mother and grandmother had, and it seemed pointless, possibly traitorous, to shed an old loyalty for a new one. They passed a furniture manufacturer, a tool and die, a candy factory, and a derelict warehouse with half its windows busted out and the other half covered with newspaper and grime. Michael tugged on her coat.

"We're gonna read the funnies when we get home, right?"

"Can you remember a Sunday we didn't read the funnies?" she said. "Can you remember a Sunday we didn't do the exact same thing?"

"No."

"Then why would today be any different?"

She quickened her pace, feeling an urge to leave Michael and the rest of her life on the sidewalk. This urge came on powerfully at times, and often she dreamed she was someone else: an heiress, a novelist, an aviator. She read serialized stories in the newspaper and listened to *Painted Dreams* on the radio when she was too bored to do anything better; she knew the many ways a woman could disappear—run off to Hollywood and change her name, join a convent, lose herself in the bed of another man—but none of these vanishings suited her or struck her as likely. Women who turned themselves into someone else were the glamorous kind or the fallen kind, and Elizabeth saw herself as nothing so extraordinary.

The street rose to span the Chicago River. At the crest, Elizabeth stopped and waited for Michael, who was hurrying toward her. Beneath her, dark water crept by, covered with an oily film, fringed with dying brush. During the week the tanneries and meatpackers dumped blood, bone, and guts into this patch of river, known locally as Bubbly Creek, turning it into a toxic witches' brew with bubbles rising to the surface. It was said that during the Great Fire the water had burned for three straight days, and that if you watched the fatty surface long enough, you'd see a rat skitter across it or a deformed fish turn belly-up. To the east lay miles of stockyards crowded with lowing livestock. Beside the pens stood meatpacking plants—those great rusting hulks—steel volcanoes seething above the flat, gray land. This morning, no smoke billowed from their stacks. The air was less brown and foul than usual; it smelled more of doomed life than of death, which was something of a comfort and made Sunday more bearable than the rest of the week. A little winded, Michael finally reached Elizabeth. She took his hand in hers and gave it an apologetic squeeze.

Elizabeth shouldered open the heavy wooden door of St. Rose of Lima and led Michael inside. They dipped their fingers into the font, blessed themselves, and entered the cool, creaking nave. Her family, as usual, took up an entire pew. Her father sat on the end closest to the center aisle, wearing his customary black suit and clenching his hat by the brim in case someone tried to sneak up and steal it. He faced forward, chin up and back rigid—a dog proud of the beatings he took. Next to him sat her brother Tommy, who winked and waved at friends like a chairman of his own little chamber of commerce, his wife and their three little girls beside him like props. Then came her brother Bill, who was getting fatter and balder with each week, and who stared blankly ahead, as if he might suddenly shake his head, look around, and wonder where the hell he was. His wife and two boys sat to his left. And last, as always, was her sister, Mae, the reluctant intermediary between Elizabeth and the rest of the family.

Elizabeth steered Michael into the pew and settled him next to Mae, who had freckles and a dimpled chin like her siblings but rarely seemed at ease with her features. She gave Michael a quick one-armed hug but then returned to her usual position: hunched forward, elbow on knee, hand on cheek, eyes down, apparently hoping nobody would notice her. Elizabeth looked down the row at the rest of her family, searching for an acknowledgment she knew would never come.

After the readings, Father Collins closed the Bible and took his place in the pulpit. He adjusted his thick glasses and smoothed down his thinning hair. He was a stout man with pockmarked cheeks and no sign of a neck— a former fullback under Knute Rockne at Notre Dame. In the past, he'd done his best to patch things up between Elizabeth and her family, but his efforts had failed.

"Pride," he said. The word echoed through the half-empty church. "Those of us who suit up in the game of religion throw around the word with great regularity and vigor, but for most people it means nothing. How often do we stop and ask ourselves: 'What is pride?' Do we know? Do we care? Will we recognize it as it grows like an infection inside us? Will we detect its symptoms before it's too late, or will it rot our souls like spiritual gangrene?"

Elizabeth's gaze wandered through the church, from the congregants she had known her whole life, to the vaulted ceiling with its plaster cracks and water damage, to the statues of saints in the walls. As a girl, she had been told that these figures were saints, and so she'd seen saints, but lately, when she studied their faces, she thought they were no different from anyone else. They had been the sculptor's friends, his family members, models he'd paid to sit for him. In stripping his subjects of themselves, he had bestowed upon them dramatic lives, horrific deaths, and flawless souls; he had made them holier and more important than they'd ever been in life.

"We encounter pride strutting across street corners and movie screens," Father Collins continued, "or leaping from magazines and radios, and we call it *dignity* or *success* or *confidence*. Or we call it *pride* as if it were a good thing instead of the deadliest of the seven deadly sins. We admire it in others, we welcome it into our homes, and we believe that by being in its presence or breathing its air, we will become better than everyone else. Better, even, than God. But that's when we should glance left and right and get ready to take a hit, because it is in those moments that pride blindsides us, drives us into the ground, and literally knocks the spiritual wind right out of us."

Father Collins was speaking with a poise he rarely displayed, rolling in the way an amateur musician can be a virtuoso for a measure or two, but then he stammered and lost his place, and his fleeting grace was gone. Struggling ahead, sweating and rushing through his sermon, he reminded the congregation that pride never sat out a down or stopped to catch its breath; a good game plan was required to defeat it, and if that game plan contained a surfeit of personal moral vigilance, then it was possible that the infection of pride would give way to another infection, a holy infection, which would suddenly be free to grow and spread and release God's love inside us. Father Collins cleared his throat, picked up a piece of paper, and read that the school's radiators would soon require fixing, the choir was in need of a tenor, and the Ladies' Auxiliary of the Defenders of St. Rose of Lima would be holding a bake sale to pay for a statue of St. Rose to replace the one in the parish house, which someone had accidentally knocked over and broken. Lastly, his face flushed and his voice trailing off, he thanked Mr. George Dunne for his generous financial assistance, which would enable the church to purchase new catechism books for children and converts.

Elizabeth looked down the pew at Tommy's tensed jaw and narrowed eyes. Her father and brothers had loved her husband, Paddy, when he was a young man working on their delivery trucks and beating George "Rabbit" Dunne in the ring, and they had almost been more excited about his marriage proposal than she'd been. But three years ago they had stopped speaking to her, and Mae had arrived with the message that as long as Paddy was around, the Fitzgerald men wanted nothing to do with Elizabeth. She didn't know the whole story because Paddy never told her anything about his business, her brothers and father refused to speak to her, Mae didn't know anything about anybody, and her mother, who would have known and would have told her, had died ten years earlier. The only things she knew for certain were that whatever Paddy did most evenings wasn't right, and that he did it for Rabbit Dunne.

The congregation stood, knelt, stood, and knelt again. Father Collins held the host above his head and recited in Latin the words that turned bread into flesh. *If only all changes were that easy*, Elizabeth thought.

The sun had risen and the moon had vanished from the sky, but the day was no warmer than before. Elizabeth walked a few steps behind Michael and side by side with Mae, who chattered about her new job at Marshall Field and Company.

"You never offer a perfume sample to a lady unless she has acknowledged your presence in a positive way."

"You don't?"

"No." Mae lit a cigarette, took a drag, and exhaled. She was bundled in a purple coat that had been Elizabeth's a decade ago. It had fit Elizabeth with style, but on Mae it was tight and outdated; the buttons were mismatched, the collar worn and faded. "And even then, you first present the bottle for her inspection. That's how you demonstrate that you're serving her—not trying to sell her something or tell her how to smell." Mae took another smoke and passed the cigarette to Elizabeth. "But with a man, it's the opposite."

"It is?"

"Of course it is," Mae said. "Even if he doesn't notice you, you approach him, offering your wrist, not the bottle, so he can get a sense of what the perfume will smell like on his wife or girlfriend."

Michael ran forward a few steps, stopped, and pulled an imaginary pistol from his coat pocket. He fired straight ahead, then to his left, then to his right, jerking his hand back with each shot. After firing what must have been twenty bullets without reloading, he slipped the pistol into his coat pocket and strutted ahead, stepping over a victim here, a victim there.

"They say men respect women who show them attention."

Elizabeth laughed and passed the cigarette back to her sister. "Who's *they*?" she asked. "And why should I believe them?"

When Mae blushed, guilt spilled inside Elizabeth. Her little sister's inflated words often put her in the mood to criticize.

"The scientists say it," said Mae, as if shocked by her sister's ignorance. "They call it 'the science of selling.' If a person does X, then he'll do Y, and then Z. They've done studies on it—first with rats, and then with actual people, I think. It's common knowledge."

"You don't say."

Mae flicked away the cigarette butt the way a person might send an ant flying across a room. It tumbled down the sidewalk and smoldered.

"I do say," she said.

A few blocks later, Mae went her own way. Elizabeth and Michael headed up Ashland, which was now bustling with people. From the candy factory came a scent so sweet, it hurt the senses: sugar burning at the bottom of a copper vat. Soon Paddy would wake, and there would be rooms to clean, meals to cook, funnies to stick to the wall. Her comfortable home awaited her with its Extra-A Washington red-cedar shingles, Number One yellow pine joists, hydraulic-creosoted wall plates, grained Georgia pine doors, and galvanized iron drain spouts. In the two years since he'd had the bungalow built, Paddy had insisted they keep the builder's brochure on the coffee table for guests to admire, but since visitors seldom came, the only one who ever flipped through it was Elizabeth.

Half a block down 36th Street, about forty people in their Sunday best gathered in front of the abandoned apartment house Elizabeth and Michael had passed earlier. On the stoop, at the center of the crowd's attention, towered a thin man with a shock of blond hair and a green suit. His head and shoulders arched forward, and his body swayed like a sunflower that had grown too tall and top-heavy. "Now, I'm not saying this building has a soul." His voice was that of a radio announcer praising cigarettes or shaving cream. Behind him, inside the building, a woman and four children leaned dully on the window ledge. "I'm not trying to peddle hocus-pocus here. What I'm saying is that in the heat of these flames," he said as he pointed at the fading bonfire inside the building, "people are trying to warm souls that have grown icy from ignorance, neglect, and abuse." He scanned his rapt audience. Elizabeth and Michael stopped at the back of the crowd. "The banker, businessman, and bilker will tell you otherwise. They'll say these people are destroying private property and need to be evicted and maybe even run off to prison—as though they themselves, as members of the international banking community, have not already turned this great, God-fearing country into one giant prison of greed, and poverty, and want, and need, and hunger, and thirst." The words tumbled more loudly and quickly from his mouth, and with a jab of his finger he emphasized each one. "And deprivation, and despair, and debauchery, and usury." Elizabeth's skin prickled at the rhythm in his voice. "And crime, and vice, and vindictiveness, and godlessness, and pride."

The crowd cheered. The man held up his hands for silence.

"When a good, God-fearing family owns something, that possession takes on their goodness the way damp sand accepts a footprint: it helps them nurture their souls. I don't care how old or inexpensive the possession is—it becomes sacred. As long as you've earned it, it's sacred."

Elizabeth thought of her home. No matter how hard she tried, she couldn't keep crumbs from the corners and scuffs from the walls forever, and by the time she scrubbed one room and moved to the next, dust was already settling in the former. Even if she could clean everything, she would never be able to rub away the fact that the house had been bought because of whatever Paddy did for Rabbit Dunne.

"But of course, this is something a banker doesn't understand as he sits there hunched behind his desk in his office—dark and cold, because that's the way vermin like it—figuring out the value of you and your family with the stroke of a pencil." He scrunched his face, bent forward, and made scribbling motions with his hand. "Can you see him with his greedy little fingers, beady little eyes, and a heart that beats less often than a stone? You better see him, brother, because he sees you. You better see him, sister, because he looks at you as nothing more than an amount of money, and he's constantly trying to figure out where he can stick his decimal point and separate you from your sacred possessions. If you have an automobile, he'll send someone to repossess it. If you have a house, he'll kick you and your children out into the street on a cold, rainy night. Or in this case," he said, turning to point to the apartment house and then swinging back to the crowd, "in this case, he'll decide to tear down a building he let rot for years, sending the poor families that call it home out to wander destitute, just like the holy family did before they found the warmth of a stable in Bethlehem."

The man wiped his brow, and the crowd cheered. Elizabeth wasn't sure what to make of his words, but the passion in his voice stirred something inside her. When a few people left, she stepped forward with Michael, then forward some more. Soon they were in the center of the crowd.

"When I talk about sacred possessions," the speaker said, "I mean things that are earned through thrift and hard work—not through usury, theft, or crime. I mean comforting objects that sustain our physical existence and foster moral behavior. They are what we need to navigate safely through this life and secure our place in the next. Man is nothing without these sacred possessions."

Elizabeth pictured her old apartment in a Canaryville two-flat, with its drafts and cheap wood and walls she could have broken through if she'd pushed hard enough. She had known her neighbors then, had grown up with them. They'd respected Paddy and admired her. They'd stopped by to chat and laugh. She hadn't felt compelled to battle time in Canaryville, to guard her possessions against every threat of dirt, to prevent each inevitable nick. With an old place like that, she just did the little she could and accepted her limitations. The scars were there, so what bother was one more? The one time she had voiced her frustration at trying to keep their bungalow looking new, Paddy had accused her first of ingratitude, then of negative thinking.

"Are you saying you're not going to clean anymore?"

"Of course not."

"Because we're not the Rockefellers. We can't just hire a maid."

"I'm just saying the house can't be spotless all the time."

"The oath of the lazy is 'I can't.'"

The speaker leaned toward the crowd. "And how do our esteemed city fathers respond? Do they house the homeless? Do they feed the hungry? No, they spend millions of dollars constructing shameful, extravagant edifices for the World's Fair next year—or the Century of Progress, as they obscenely call it. They decide to hold an orgy of sin and indulgence, enticing the masses to worship the gods of Goodyear and Ford and Studebaker, and then, when they are through, when every nickel has been extracted from the throng, they will tear down all those structures instead of providing them to those in need of shelter." He paced back and forth, then stopped and whispered, "I'm tired—sick and tired. These people," he said, raising his voice and sweeping his arm to again include those inside the building, "these poor, humble people are tired. And I know that many of you good, God-fearing people are tired, too. Am I right about this?" The crowd muttered agreement. "Show me your hand, brother. Lift yours up, sister. Who here is tired?" The man raised his hand and was quickly joined by most of the gathered.

Michael tugged on Elizabeth's coat, then tugged on it again. She watched the speaker's hand splayed against the sky. His fingers shot out from his palm like rays of light from a child's penciled rendition of the sun.

"Who here is tired of hardworking people losing their homes not because they're lazy or unwilling to work, but because they don't have the money to pay rent or meet the obligations of their mortgages?" More hands went up. Elizabeth kept hers at her side, afraid to draw attention to herself.

"Who here is just plain sick and tired of what has become of our great country and our sacred possessions?"

There were about twenty people left. With the exception of Elizabeth and Michael, each held a hand in the air. The speaker loomed in front of the crowd with both arms raised. Elizabeth had never seen someone with such conviction.

"Hold those hands up. Lift them heavenward."

The man smiled on the audience, then pointed at Elizabeth. He stared at her in the same penetrating way Paddy often used to stare at her, and sometimes still did, as if all of life came from her.

"Aren't you going to raise your hand?"

Elizabeth blushed. His finger was aimed at her heart.

"Aren't you sick and tired of this vicious world? Don't you get so angry sometimes that you just want to tear the whole place down?"

His hazel eyes flashed with zeal, but otherwise his expression seemed fatigued. Studying his smooth, handsome face, Elizabeth found it easy to imagine him as a boy.

"What is your name?"

"Elizabeth."

"Welcome, Elizabeth. My name is Eddie. You may think I don't know you, but I do. I know you wouldn't be here if you weren't angry at something or someone. You wouldn't be here if you were happy. But your fear prevents you from raising your hand." He stood so powerfully, so filled with purpose, yet his body seemed frail enough to collapse. He needed a hearty meal, a good night's sleep, someone to take care of him. "Would you like to become so courageous you won't recognize yourself anymore?"

Elizabeth sensed that he understood her in a way nobody, not even she, ever had. She nodded.

"Is that a yes?"

"Yes," she said.

"What my Society for Sacred Possessions offers is hope, Elizabeth. Hope for the salvation of this great land, our sacred possessions, and our souls. Hope for you and everyone else here. But you can't have it if you don't want it."

A few months ago, Paddy had told her, "You have to have hope." She'd just had a miscarriage, her third, and she knew that in her tears he had seen only her loss, not her relief. "With hope and hard work, newness is always possible."

Her husband bore bruises, scraped-raw skin, and a face that was aging too quickly. He smelled of the daily slaughter. Was that what hope looked like? Was that the scent it gave?

Elizabeth gazed at Eddie and the grin floating across his face. She felt exhausted by the thought of going home, of living out the rest of today, and tomorrow, and all the days that remained. She closed her eyes, and racing past her came Paddy and Michael, comic-strip heroes with perfect bodies and sturdy jaws, and the faces of saints, expressionless and still. She raised her hand, and as the crowd let out a cheer and Eddie shouted something about courage, she fell into their approval and let it lift her.

3.

TEN CARCASSES CAME DOWN THE LINE ON A PULLEY CHAIN, LIMBLESS AND headless, jostling one another like belligerent men. They stopped in front of Paddy Halligan, who steadied the first steer and with his knife slowly made a deep, clean cut down the backbone, pulling the blade through skin and muscle, rocking it at the gristle. What little blood remained in the body splattered onto his boots and dripped to the floor. He moved from the first steer to the second, to the next, on and on until each had been split. He flexed the stiff muscles in his hand, wiped the blade on his apron.

First, decide what your goal is to be, he recited in his mind. *Then make that goal a reality.* As the screeching machinery carried away the old bodies and brought on the new, Paddy imagined himself sitting contentedly on a long, shaded porch, smoking a Lucky Strike. The sun shone in a clean sky. A breeze came to him from across a calm lake. He pulled the knife through each animal, flexed his fingers, cleaned his blade. Steam rose from the slick floor and from the dozens of men working down the line. A dirty glow showed through windows that lined the walls, set too high to either look through or open.

The gears moved. The line advanced. Dead, dangling beasts traveled from man to man and lost more of themselves along the way. Paddy pictured a gas station with six pumps out front and a four-stall garage. *In envisioning one's dreams, one must make a point of staying within the bounds of reality, lest one renders one's dreams unachievable.* Automobiles entered the garage broken and drove out restored. Men in spiffy blue mechanic suits

pumped gas and repaired engines. Like a master on his plantation, Paddy
oversaw the action from the front porch of a neighboring house.

New bodies were before him: simple flesh, pure meat. By now, Red had
made the proposal to Rabbit Dunne, who would go along with it because,
despite his deficiencies as a man, Rabbit knew what was best for business.
Paddy got back to work and tried not to visualize his dream of building the
station and watching it grow, of hiring men, and of one day sitting back and
letting them do all the work. *Do not wallow in your dreams the way the
indolent pig wallows in his own filth and muck.* But his imagination was
tenacious, enticing. By the seventh steer, he was again on the porch in his
imagination, sucking down a Lucky, watching cars roll into his service
station, but then suddenly he was on the porch of Blessed Savior Orphanage
in Kinsman, Illinois, with the other boys, grinding ants into the splintery
boards with his thumb. When a *cha-chunk* and long, high whistle sounded
in the distance, the boys darted to the iron fence, grabbed the bars, and
gazed across the cornfield. "I see it," someone shouted. Above the stalks,
gray smoke bloomed and an engine's stack glided past like a periscope,
headed toward Chicago. "It's a Pullman," a boy said. "A cattle train," said
another. The stack passed by. The boys guessed, argued, lost interest, and
eventually wandered back to the porch, but Paddy stood alone at the fence,
praying to God to put him on the train. He'd go as a passenger. He'd go as
freight or huddle between cattle. And when the train had gone without him,
he squeezed the bars and prayed for the train to derail and for every living
thing inside it to die.

A carcass slipped in Paddy's hands and fell hard to the ground, just
inches from his feet. A few men rushed over, and together they hoisted the
steer back onto the hooks. Paddy punched the beast several times, then
picked up his knife and eagerly sliced it open.

As a boy he had longed to get back to Chicago. Now he couldn't wait to
leave. He wanted to be free of the packing plant, with its putrid air and
sudden dangers: the severed fingers and burned skin, the occasional animal
that fought and flailed against its inevitable death, disrupting the order of
things and trampling those who couldn't get out of its way. The insanity of

the world could take over quickly, Paddy knew; it could rush toward you and from you before you knew what was happening.

While it is best to think of "dos" in any successful enterprise, there are three "do nots" to keep in mind.

It was for Elizabeth and Michael that he did what he did, to buy things other men could not: a Harris & Company bungalow, new leather shoes, the choicest cuts of meat. That was why he did this work, and why he took care of the men Rabbit Dunne wanted taken care of; it was all for the sake of his family. Didn't Elizabeth understand that? Was she so goddamn blind she couldn't see it? For a slab of steak, a shot of whiskey, his mouth on her breast, her hand stroking him. For life's few comforts, he had to be cruel.

Do not falter.

Soon his hands would turn their attention to automobiles and a mechanic's life of taking up broken things and making them work again. They would mend pushrods and rockers, adjust throttles, pump gas. The lines of his palms would darken with oil, not blood. And soon after that, other hands would do his work for him.

Do not fear.

The line moved. Ten fresh carcasses appeared before him.

Do not fail.

Paddy steadied the first beast and made a quick stab into its back. He leaned his cheek against the body and smelled the new death there.

Later that day, in the dark, Paddy jogged down side streets and alleys, cut through gangways, and twice crossed Bubbly Creek. Each night, he met the others at a new location: in a boiler room or three-flat, at Guardian Angel Day Nursery or Florsheim Shoes, in a house basement or a pew at Good Counsel. Tonight, it was the Cracker Jack plant. He circled a block, circled another. He deliberately took wrong turns, glancing now and then to see if anyone was following.

The definition of a "man of accomplishment" is "he who takes charge of his life." Success is not so much gained as taken.

He knocked at a back entrance, as he'd been instructed to the previous night. A fidgety man answered the door and led him up a flight of metal stairs to a large executive office. A dozen of Rabbit's men were already there, smoking cigars, drinking beer, and leaning against shelves of leather-bound books. At the far end of the room, Rabbit sat behind a wide oak desk, flipping through sheets of paper with his thick fingers and breathing hard through his nostrils. He boasted a shiny bald head and a mouth filled with teeth that were little and uneven, like bits of broken china swept up from a kitchen floor.

Paddy made his way directly to Red Walsh, who sat reading a newspaper beside the desk, looking debonair in a tan linen suit, one leg crossed over the other in an aristocratic fashion, his auburn hair glistening with palm oil. When it came to blood, Paddy and Red were first cousins once removed. When it came to the law, they were brothers, Red's parents having adopted Paddy after he'd been in the orphanage a year.

Red looked up, grinned at Paddy, and stood. He was the tallest man in the room by at least three inches, and he stood a head higher than Paddy. He was the most handsome as well, with Douglas Fairbanks' jutting jaw and a hypnotist's pale blue eyes. He took Paddy by the elbow and guided him to a secluded corner.

"How's the job?" Red asked.

"How the hell do you think it is?" Red had spent only a few months in the packing plant, nearly two decades earlier. All of Rabbit's men had moved on from there, and Paddy knew they looked down on him for still toiling on the line. "You know it's no kind of job for a man."

Red put his arm around Paddy's shoulders. It was a gesture as familiar as any to Paddy. When he was eight and Red sixteen, his new brother had draped his arm around him and said, "If anyone picks on you, you tell me." A little more than a decade and a half later, just a few years ago, he had again leaned into Paddy and asked if he wanted to earn some extra cash.

"I talked to Rabbit this afternoon," Red said. The air reeked of Cracker Jack, was almost sticky with the stuff.

"And?"

"He agreed."

Paddy felt a quiver of joy, which he quickly suppressed. *Like money, hope must be accumulated and saved, not flaunted.*

"When do we get started?"

"It'll take time," Red said as he glanced past Paddy and waved to someone near the door. "Maybe a year. Maybe two."

"Two years?"

Red shrugged and held out his soft hands, those of a negotiator, a briber, a pimp. Rings adorned several of his slender, tapered fingers.

"And what am I supposed to do in the meantime?"

"You wait."

"I'm tired of waiting."

"And one more thing."

"What's that?"

"Keep doing whatever Rabbit tells you to do."

Red squeezed Paddy's upper arm and sauntered off to glad-hand some of the others. Paddy stood in the corner, arms crossed, and glowered at the rest of Rabbit's men. They lived in Bridgeport or Canaryville, and as members of the Emerald Athletic & Benevolence Society, they'd been known in their adolescence as Emerald Lads. They'd played football and taken Holy Communion together, shared whores and bottles of eighty-proof, and met their future wives at club-sponsored dances. They'd cornered Lithuanians and Poles in alleyways, dragged blacks and Italians into dank cellars, chased Mexicans over backyard fences. They'd hurled bricks and empty bottles, slammed heads into walls, kicked broken ribs, spit and pissed on the injured, and dumped the most unfortunate into the river. They spoke with reverence of their youthful indiscretions, which Paddy had been a decade too young to share in, and over the years they had moved on to city hall or law offices, been ordained into the priesthood, become either upstanding or disreputable businessmen, or settled for employment with the Chicago Police Department. Paddy had never been one of them, had never been more than Red's little bastard brother—kept around because of his hands. Though he sometimes picked up whiskey from a Joliet farmhouse and delivered it to speakeasies and rectories around 47th Street, he mostly repaired Rabbit's delivery trucks and fleet of Packards, or inflicted injury on the thieves and petty bootleggers (like Elizabeth's brothers) who interfered with the flow of profits. The money was good, and so were the perks: the liquor, the girls, the liberty to injure.

Rabbit called Paddy over to the desk and handed him a scrap of paper. An address was scrawled across it in pencil.

"First off is Stephen Barry," Rabbit said. "Be there at nine and wait out back. He'll come to you."

Paddy remembered Stephen Barry. Smug and stocky, with thick hair on his neck and forearms, he was the kind of man who thinks he's got the world either dazzled or beaten silly. He'd laughed at Paddy's warning to stop selling his gin.

"And then there's Kevin Kearns, or Old Kevin, as he's called," Rabbit said. "You know him well, I'm told."

Paddy pictured the lonely old drunk playing his harmonica for pennies, going door to door for table scraps.

"We need to make an example of Old Kevin," Rabbit said. "There's too many people taking a bottle here, a bottle there. It's a kind of behavior that needs to stop."

Paddy crumpled the piece of paper and buried it in his coat pocket. He searched the room for Red, but his brother was gone. "He's just a harmless old gink," Paddy said.

"Nobody's harmless."

"But Old Kevin—"

"I don't give a shit if he's the Blessed Virgin." Rabbit's voice silenced the chatter in the room.

"I'm just saying—"

"And I'm just saying that to get something in this world, you have to give something."

Paddy stared at Rabbit's tiny teeth and shiny head, and at the burly body beneath them. *Trust is a luxury item, bought only by fools.* Rabbit had never liked Paddy's quick hands and confidence, or at least he hadn't liked them since the 1923 Emerald Lads Boxing Tournament. Only eighteen, Paddy had taken the middleweight title that night from Rabbit, who at the time had been undefeated in forty-seven bouts. The second-round knockout had stunned the crowd. Paddy had smiled at their dumbfounded silence with his hands raised in victory.

Paddy nodded. *Knowing which battles to lose is how you win the war.*

"I want marks on him," Rabbit ordered. "I want people to know we're not fucking around."

Paddy weaved his way through Canaryville and hopped a fence into Stephen Barry's backyard, where he waited beside a distillery shed, his attention alternating between the man's house and a November sky with no visible stars. The plan was simple: Rabbit would build a service station outside the city, and Paddy would run the station, which, in addition to being a legitimate business, would serve as a front for whatever activities Rabbit wanted to undertake. Paddy would make monthly mortgage payments for roughly ten years, and then, when he had paid off his debt, he would own the property outright, with no further obligations.

Stephen Barry emerged from his back door and hurried to his shed, which he unlocked and entered. Paddy followed. When Barry started to say something, Paddy covered the offending mouth with his left hand and struck the man's temple with his right. He came in with two more rights and then both fists. Blood ran from Barry's nose and mouth. His eyes shut. His body fell.

In the ring, in his youth, Paddy had taken the advice of the priests and nuns at Blessed Savior, who had told him to look for Jesus in the faces of his enemies. Where others had found compassion in this instruction, Paddy had uncovered further reason for anger. It was Christ who had killed his mother, demanded too much goodness and selflessness, never answered his pleading childhood prayers, and spawned all those evil do-gooders who told him to forget about this world and prepare for the next. The priests and nuns had told him that his mother most likely had gone to hell, that his father surely would if he hadn't already, and that Paddy himself had only the slimmest hope of salvation. They had made him confess his sins and then dispensed the penance. They had watched him with Jesus eyes and chastised him with a Jesus tongue. And after striking him with a varnished paddle or cramming soap into his mouth, they'd smiled a Jesus smile.

With Stephen Barry at his feet, Paddy opened the spout of the still. Alcohol poured onto the ground and soaked the unconscious man's clothing. Paddy pictured the liquid flooding the backyard and coursing through the cobbled alley. Stray dogs would lap it up and stagger away blindly. Desperate men would hold bottles to the flow and gather the spirits they needed.

You must first see yourself as the man you want to be. Only then can you start to become that man. Your fate is up to you!

Paddy ran through the night, twice crossed the blood-dumped river, and walked past pool halls, secret saloons, and music clubs on Halsted Street until he found Old Kevin sitting on a milk crate on a street corner, playing his harmonica for nobody. The notes never came close to catching a melody.

With the promise of a smoke, Paddy led the old bum into an alley. Standing beside a garbage can, Paddy lit a cigarette for himself and one for Kevin.

"It's been a while," Paddy said. It had been months since he'd seen Old Kevin, years since they'd spoken to each other. "Not that I mind."

"I thought about saying hello one time, but—"

The old man stopped talking. He puffed his cigarette and coughed, phlegm rattling in his throat.

"Don't worry yourself about it," Paddy said.

"I still haven't met your boy," Old Kevin said with a drunken slur. "What's his name?"

"Michael."

"Is he a Kearns?"

Paddy shook his head and said, "He's the same as me."

"What are you, again?"

"A Halligan."

Paddy exhaled smoke and looked at Kevin Kearns, who was probably no older than sixty. Several of his teeth had rotted down to the gums, and his jowls were sunken from drink and decay. He was missing the tips of three fingers on his right hand. His left was a useless, paralyzed lump. Paddy found it hard to believe the old bum was his father.

"I've come about business, Kevin."

Paddy had never referred to the derelict as his father; in his opinion, the man's contribution to his life was minimal, even insignificant, nothing but a fateful spurt. Paddy stubbed his cigarette out on the brick wall and explained the problem to Old Kevin, who shivered and hacked.

"Can't you let me go?" Kevin bunched the collar of his tattered coat around his neck. Yellow hair splayed from his head and stuck out in tufts from his ears. "I know I'm worth nothing, but I don't deserve trouble."

"Sorry, Kevin, I have to."

Paddy grabbed Old Kevin's bony arm. *A man of success owes nothing.*

"You wouldn't hurt me, would you? Your very own father?"

Paddy came in swiftly with a right hook to the temple—a punch with no release of anger, no remorse, no guilt. No power. He expected Kevin to fall, but the old man stood straight, his expression changing from fear to anger.

"Damn you," Kevin said as he took an errant swing.

Paddy struck again. The old man did not go down, and instead landed a weak blow to Paddy's ear.

"Son of a bitch," he said. "Son of a whore."

With his left hand, Paddy slammed his father against the wall and held him there; with his right, he punched him again and again. He lost himself in the rage, in the blind pleasure and release he felt every time his fist struck something solid. His entire body surged and expanded. The Earth rotated his way. He was a boy again, naked and sobbing, locked in a dark coat closet. All he'd done was piss the bed. *Say "I'm sorry," and I'll let you out.* The priest left and came back, left and came back. *Just say it.* Paddy's stomach clenched at the scent of chicken soup from down the hall. His bladder felt as if it might rupture. *I'll let you starve, Halligan. Don't think I won't.* He strangled the sleeve of a scratchy wool coat and imagined it as the priest's neck. He punched himself in the head, stomach, and thighs again and again to prove his toughness to himself. *Say it, Halligan*. His body was raw and tender. Thirsty, he swallowed whatever spit he could muster. *Give up, Halligan. Give up*. Tears and piss raced from him. The priests dragged him out, but he never said a word of apology.

Old Kevin fell hard to the ground; his skull smacked the pavement. Chest heaving and blood raging, Paddy dug through his father's pockets until he found some change. He pocketed the money—Rabbit Dunne's money—and stared down at his sprawled father: a crippled old switchman, a tramp, a drunk. A rivulet of blood flowed from the back of Old Kevin's skull, another from his mouth; he breathed deeply and his eyes stayed shut. Paddy remembered the first time he'd met him, a few weeks after he'd left the orphanage to live with Red Walsh's family, when Kevin had staggered from a tavern and run right into him. Paddy had allowed his father to help him up and tousle his hair, call him a tough little fellow. This was years before accidents at the rail yard mangled Kevin's hands, years before Paddy confronted him about his identity. On the day they'd first met, Kevin Kearns had been a young man, happy with drink, drunk with life, and after picking up Paddy, he had wandered down the alley, singing to himself.

Paddy had hidden his heritage—the Kearns part of himself—from everyone but Elizabeth and Red, though he knew that gossip could swirl like mosquitoes above Bubbly Creek. He'd felt bitten several times by laughter and knowing glances, by broken-off sentences and innocent questions of lineage. As a boy he'd seen dimples like his own on his father's grinning cheeks, and he'd told himself to never smile again. It was the Halligan part of himself—his mother's—that he had claimed. It was the name he had been given and the name he had chosen to keep. It was a Halligan, not a Kearns, who had beaten Old Kevin. It was a Halligan who had shown loyalty to Rabbit Dunne and would ignore Red's possible complicity in it all. And it would be a Halligan who would make a new life for himself and his family.

The vanquished looks backward. The victor looks forward.

Paddy pulled two dollars of his own money from his wallet, crouched down, and slipped the bills into his father's shirt pocket. He stood, leaving Kevin Kearns in the alley, and walked to Rabbit's 35th Street warehouse. He nodded to Frank in the upstairs window and unlocked a series of locks. Once inside with the door closed, he turned on the overhead lights. Fourteen Packards, each one covered with a green blanket, stood before him. They were parked chronologically; the first seven were in a row, facing a line of the most recent seven. Rabbit had bought at least one a year since 1924, when he'd picked up a single-six runabout, cream with a crimson running board and broadcloth interior. Paddy walked past the boattail speedster and Cabriolet limousine on his left, the coupe and custom eight on his right. He pulled the blanket off the 1933 Dietrich convertible roadster, a machine that Rabbit had never driven, for fear of scratching or denting it. In the past, Rabbit had taken his Packards for a spin on quiet streets and Sunday mornings, but since a minor accident in the spring, he had stopped driving them altogether. Instead, he tooled around in a Studebaker.

Hurting people was Paddy's talent; fixing cars, his gift. He knew how automobiles worked in the same way some people can determine, through quiet observation, what others will say or do. He inspected the Dietrich's cherry-red chassis. There were no marks on the body, not even on the four whitewall tires or the spare on the running board. He sat in the driver's seat and started the car. The roar echoed throughout the cold garage. Each night, Paddy had to start one of the Packards and let it run for fifteen minutes. He went in order, so each car had a turn every two weeks. Since his days of working on his father-in-law's delivery trucks, he'd thought automobiles noble in structure and function. He closed his eyes and listened. For Paddy, it was a matter not of idling or running, but of how the vehicle breathed. With his hands between his thighs for warmth, and the car giving his body a soothing jostle, he leaned back and listened for any trouble that needed fixing.

As he drifted toward sleep, Paddy thought that his life could have turned out better if only he had kept boxing. After his victory in the Emerald Lads tournament, he had fought on the local professional circuit for a few months, winning twelve bouts and losing four. He'd not been happy with the losses, but he had been able to put them in perspective; with each fight he had improved, and his skills had drawn the interest of local trainers and promoters, at least until his last bout, when he was humiliated and knocked unconscious in the third round by a pretty boy named Oswald "Hard Knocks" Knoll, who punched as if he had four strong arms and seemed to know what Paddy was going to do before he did it. The defeat so discouraged Paddy that he never fought again. But sometimes he thought that if he had stuck with it, if he had gotten the breaks and training Hard Knocks and others had, things could have turned out differently. He could have ended up with a Packard of his own and men to follow his orders.

Paddy opened his eyes. *Stay awake! Stay busy! There will be ample time for rest once you are dead and buried in the ground.* He reached into the inner pocket of his coat and pulled out one of his booklets. On the cover, a cartoon man threw money into the air and danced beneath a smiling sun. *The Road to Unlimited Wealth & Happiness!* Paddy opened the booklet and read:

> What kind of man are you? Are you the kind who loves to be bossed around? Who is most happy saying, "Yes, dear" and, "Right away, sir"? If so, then this informative and motivational booklet is NOT for you!

> Then again, maybe you're the kind of man who dreams of better things, who has the guts to take on the challenges of life. If this sounds like you, then keep reading! UNLIMITED WEALTH & HAPPINESS are yours for the taking!

Paddy's attention wandered. His eyes blinked shut. He pictured Kevin Kearns unconscious on the ground and told himself that if beating the old man was what it took to make a future for himself, then so be it. He wouldn't feel guilty about it. The future was for the survivors, the fighters, like him— men willing to do whatever was necessary to succeed. The car breathed on.

It was a beauty, this Dietrich, a strong and elegant machine.

He considered Packard's slogan—*Ask the man who owns one*—and laughed at the thought of asking Rabbit anything about his cars. Rabbit knew what models he owned and simple facts about them: that the Dietrich had a 135-horsepower engine, for example, or that the Sport Phaeton had dual fan belts. He knew the value of each one, and what work Paddy had done on them. He could detect a scratch from across the garage. But he didn't really know the cars; he just examined them every few days and asked Paddy what they needed. Only Paddy truly knew the Packards.

Your knowledge is your power. Turn it into your gain.

Ask the man who repairs them, Paddy thought. *Ask the man whose ass is on the line if anything goes wrong, or who sits in a cold garage at midnight to keep the cars breathing. Ask the man who does what he's told.*

4.

FLAGPOLES FLANKED THE PROMENADE, TOWERING INTO THE HAZY SKY, their gigantic maroon flags rippling in the breeze off Lake Michigan. As Michael strolled between his parents, he imagined the flags were the sails of pirate ships, but this vision quickly dissolved amid all the distractions at the World's Fair. Hundreds of people walked along at the same stupefied pace: a troop of Boy Scouts, a gaggle of old ladies flicking paper fans before their faces, young couples arm in arm, and family after family after family. They passed a one-man band playing "Happy Days Are Here Again." They passed tap-dancing twin girls, a juggling clown, a woman in a bathing suit handing out balloons. High above them, the sky ride's two silver trams ran along parallel cables. Michael squinted until the wires disappeared, and in his eyes the cable cars became rocket ships.

"So, you're not gonna talk today?" Michael's father asked. His face was shadowed by the brim of his Panama hat. "Is that your plan?"

It was not quite noon, not quite ninety degrees.

"I'll talk when I want to talk," Michael's mother said. She wore a yellow sundress and bonnet. Her forearms were pink and peeling.

"Suit yourself. I'm not crying."

A crowd cheered, and Michael looked eagerly past his mother to the backside of a grandstand, beyond which, largely obscured by bodies and wooden bleachers, was a stage in the middle of a lagoon. A month earlier, Tarzan had swung onto the stage on a vine, beaten his chest, and given his famous call. Then he did an elaborate triple-somersault dive into the water and swam toward the other end of the lagoon, where Jane screamed, struggling to squirm free from a cannibal wearing a leopard-skin loincloth and a string of bones around his neck. He had white paint on his black face and chest, and he shouted all sorts of mumbo jumbo. Suddenly Tarzan leaped from the water, socked the cannibal in the jaw, and tore Jane away from him. The cannibal stumbled backward and into the water, where he flailed and squealed like a little girl. An older boy at school had crossed his heart and sworn on a rosary that he'd seen it. Michael looked now but saw nothing beyond the bleachers but nuggets of shimmering water.

"Well, if you're not gonna say anything, then I might as well read. That's almost like talking, isn't it?" His father opened the "Century of Progress" guidebook, cleared his throat, and read: "You have come here to see in epitome the great drama of man's struggle to lift himself in his weakness to the stars. The spectacle is enormous, for it includes all the manifestations of man's restless energies—"

"Gee," said Michael's mother, "ain't that swell."

"Nobody asked your opinion."

"Wouldn't be the first time."

"Won't be the last, either. You might as well get used to it."

In the courtyard of the Hall of Science, Michael stood a few feet away from his parents, close enough to know they were arguing, but too far to hear their words. He gaped up at the tall blue tower rising from an orange art-deco building that looked like the kind of place where Flash Gordon would pick up his next assignment. This was Michael's third visit to the World's Fair with both of his parents; he had attended eleven times already with just his mother. He had ridden on the Cyclone and the Ferris wheel, seen men build a Chrysler automobile and manufacture Miracle Whip, and walked through Japan, Sweden, and Czechoslovakia. There had been Indians and midgets, a tower of Nash automobiles, and a mechanical cow that chewed and blinked its eyes. A few weeks ago, his mother had let flyers fall from the window of one of the crowded sky-ride cars and float like confetti onto the Avenue of Flags. On each flyer was a picture of people sleeping in Grant Park and a message from Eddie and the Society for Sacred Possessions:

> Is this progress? While families throughout Chicago are robbed of their sacred possessions on a daily basis, the city throws an exhibition of indulgence and greed for industrialists. As a great Christian nation, we should hang our heads in shame.

When policemen greeted everyone at the end of the ride and asked who had dropped the papers, Michael's mother stood silent.

Michael fixed his gaze on a man in a brown suit eating an ice-cream cone, and tried to will the man into the air. He pictured him rising slowly, levitating, then flying this way and that, but no matter how vivid the scene was in his mind, Michael could not figure out how to transform the actual man, who was standing very much on the ground, running his tongue around the edge of his cone, into someone more worth watching.

"Come with me," Michael's mother said as she grabbed his hand. Michael looked back. His father vanished into a crowd.

The Transparent Man stood six feet tall on a rotating pedestal surrounded by a handrail, his arms and face lifted to the sky as though he were beseeching God for an end to some torment. His skin and muscle were layers of clear plastic, behind which, set puzzlelike, were synthetic internal organs that lit up one by one. Michael and his mother stood at the railing. Earlier in the summer, she had bought him a postcard with a photo of the Transparent Man on the front. He kept the postcard next to his bed, and on Saturdays, when his funnies were in the garbage, he would stare at the picture and imagine the Transparent Man mesmerizing criminals with his illuminated organs or running as fast as a train with his super-strong invisible muscles. Sometimes Michael carried the postcard with him, and sometimes he traced the Transparent Man with his finger.

Someone nudged him, and he stepped aside to let an older boy and girl settle in at the handrail. The boy pointed to the Transparent Man.

"He's got no wiener," he said.

A woman told the boy to be quiet, but most of the adults snickered. Michael eyed the Transparent Man with alarm. He'd never thought to notice this.

"I wonder what happened to it," the girl said.

"His wife took it," said a man.

"He used it so much, it dropped off," said another.

People laughed. Michael imagined the Transparent Man stepping down from the pedestal and tossing them aside one by one.

"I bet he never had one to begin with," the boy said.

Michael looked up at his mother for an ally, but her face seemed caught somewhere between a smile and a smirk. He stormed away, angry at everyone for laughing, furious at the Transparent Man and his nonexistent wiener. His mother followed, and together they made their way to Enchanted Island, where Michael climbed the fake rocks of Magic Mountain, crawled through the miniature castle at the summit, and slid down into a pile of children. Gradually his anger left him. He ate a hot dog and cotton candy, laughed at a trained monkey and a puppet show, and rode the merry-go-round. By the time he left Enchanted Island, his head was dizzy from sugar, heat, and excitement, as if the whole day were stuck to his brain and buzzing. He skipped and darted this way and that as he and his mother passed the Streets of Paris, where his father liked to watch naked women dance, and the building where twice before Michael had seen babies no bigger than kittens kept alive in incubators. They passed through an archway into Midget Village, which resembled Bavarian Village, except with smaller buildings, and stood at the back of a crowd watching midget couples perform a dance. The pigtailed women wore black skirts and flouncy white blouses. The men wore lederhosen and knee socks. They spun to the left, twirled to the right. They slapped their knees and stomped their feet. Restless, Michael drifted toward a cobbler fixing shoes in a doorway, a man selling pretzels at a stand, a woman milking a cow. Everywhere families wandered, and Michael imagined tagging along with them without their noticing. Maybe he could be folded into another life that easily. He stopped and looked around and realized he was lost.

He darted one way, then another, worried he'd never see his mother again. He was sunburned and slightly sick, and the buzzing in his head had worked its way into the rest of his body. Feeling tears start to form, he closed his eyes and pictured Dick Tracy. When the image was firm against the back of his lids, he opened his eyes, but his hero disappeared.

Michael took a deep breath and started to count to ten. By the time he reached eight, the flow of tears had stopped. He noticed a stone cottage with a half-open door. He approached the door and pushed his way into a dimly lit room. On the floor, beside a chair, were a turban, a stack of books, a mattress, and a lit candle rising from the mouth of a wine bottle. Michael looked at the far wall and gasped when he saw an old midget woman sitting there on a chair, filing her toenails.

"Who's there?" she asked. "Come closer."

Michael stepped forward into a small patch of light coming from the lone window. With its stone walls, shadows, and low ceiling, the room was like a dungeon. The woman put on her shoes.

"You lost?"

When Michael nodded, she told him to sit. She stood and dragged her chair across the room until she sat in front of him, her knees nearly touching his. Michael started to cry again.

"How old are you, young man?"

"Six."

When she smiled, her face collapsed into hundreds of little wrinkles. She looked as ancient as a few of the people who showed up at Eddie's apartment. As Michael played alone in the bedroom, they would sing and pray in the living room. Afterward, Michael's mother would say to him, "Remember that this is our little secret."

"I know," he'd say.

"And what do we do with secrets?"

"We keep them."

She would hold him to her hip and say, "Good boy."

Michael had never told anyone about the trips to Eddie's apartment, the adults holding hands in a circle, or his mother talking with Eddie after everyone else had left. If his father was angry today because of all this—if that was why his parents were fighting—it wasn't his fault. He'd kept his mouth shut.

The old woman took his hand between hers and patted it. Her skin was wrinkled and dry.

"Are you real?" he asked. He'd never been this close to a midget before. He'd never been touched by one.

"What do you mean?"

"Are you a real midget?"

The woman smiled. "Of course I'm real. Are you a real boy?"

Michael's tears were nearly gone, but he wasn't unafraid. He nodded.

"Would you like me to tell your fortune?"

Michael nodded again. The woman flipped his palm up and ran her fingertip along the lines there.

"Let's see," she said. "You are either from Chicago or visiting here with your family. Is that right?"

Michael nodded in amazement. How could she have known?

"And you love coming to the fair—especially Enchanted Island."

She held his palm close to her face and tilted her head. Her left eye fluttered constantly. Her right eye stared intently at his hand.

"According to what the gods reveal in these lines," she said, "you are a very special boy who will grow up to be a great man—perhaps the greatest who ever lived. Do you believe me? Do you believe you can be the greatest man who ever lived?"

Michael fought a smile that tried to bend his lips.

She squeezed his hand and leaned toward him. "Maybe you believe it a little?"

He grinned and nodded.

"Good. You should believe it." She patted and then released his hand. "Just look around at this fair—at all the amazing things that are happening in the world, all the progress, all the wonderful inventions. You must remember that there are no limits to what anyone can do."

Michael gazed at his hand as if it were a gift he'd just received.

A knock sounded on the half-closed door, and a full-size man stuck his head into the room. "What the hell, Dolores?" he said. "What's going on in here?"

"He's lost," she said. "He came in here."

"Well, I've got people for the next show, and you're already three minutes late."

The woman slowly picked up the turban and placed it on her head. She pressed her hands into the chair and pushed herself up. The man whistled a song from the doorway.

"We have to lock up, honey," she told Michael. When he stood, he realized that as small as she seemed sitting down, she was still a little taller than he was.

Outside, Michael watched the woman slowly climb steps leading to a stage. She sat in a chair, a microphone aimed at her mouth. The man stood at another microphone.

"Ladies and gentlemen," the man shouted, "thank you for your patience. Madam Zorenska—through the powers of extrasensory perception—will answer your questions about the future. Don't be afraid, folks—this 116-year-old midget mystic has predicted the assassination of President Lincoln, the great San Francisco earthquake, and the stock-market crash. So hand up your questions, ladies and gentlemen. Don't be shy. Madam Zorenska will divine your future."

People wrote on pieces of paper and handed them up to the man, who flipped from one to the next.

"Madam Zorenska, do you hear me?" he called.

She fluttered her eyelids and spoke in a breathy way: "Yes, I hear you." She had a foreign accent now, like that of Michael's neighbors.

"Madam Zorenska, this person asks: 'Will I find peace?'"

She inhaled dramatically, grimaced, and closed her eyes. Her left eyelid kept twitching. She tilted her head back, stroked her throat with her hand, and opened her mouth. "I see," she said as she lowered her head. "I see something—something that is faint but becoming clearer by the second."

Michael heard his mother shout his name. Her arms encircled him. She kissed his cheek and said he had no idea how happy she was to see him.

"I was so frightened," she whispered into his ear.

The crowd applauded Madam Zorenska's answer, which Michael had missed. He looked up to see his father watching the show, laughing and fanning himself with his hat.

As Michael walked with his parents past oversize buildings in orange, blue, red, and gold—the Sunday funnies come to life—he thought of Eddie's bedroom and the wooden blocks his mother had left there for him. They were various shapes and sizes, all sorts of colors, and with them Michael forged vast futuristic cities, in which he imagined Flash Gordon, Buck Rogers, and other, lesser heroes fight, fly, and cheat death until, feeling lonely and bored, almost imprisoned, Michael would destroy everything with a sweep of his arm. He hadn't mentioned a word of this to his father, nor had he talked about policemen coming to the apartment door, or how Eddie sometimes glowered at him with such disgust that Michael felt sick to his stomach. He hadn't talked about any of this to anyone, but his father was angry, and his mother was in trouble. It must have been his fault. He must have let something slip.

"You couldn't have asked what I thought?" Michael's mother said, as they descended a narrow staircase with black walls. She was a step in front of Michael and two behind his father. "I'm tired of you dragging me around like a suitcase."

Michael took a deep breath and counted from one to ten. His father stopped on the stairs and turned.

"You think this isn't for you, too?"

Michael held his great hand behind his back. Maybe he would knock his father out with it. Maybe he would seize him by the neck and lift him high into the air, warning him that things would be different now.

"Why the hell do you think I'm doing this? It's best for all of us."

She laughed. "You're so generous."

"Shut up." He took a step up toward her.

One two three four five six seven eight nine ten. He could kill her, Michael knew. He'd killed an old bum in an alley a few months ago—beat him and left him to die like a sick old dog. That's what boys at school had said.

"Working for Rabbit Dunne—is that part of your generosity, too?"

"You don't know my life."

"No kidding."

"When the hell did you get such a smart mouth, huh? You been taking courage pills lately?"

"Maybe I'm just wising up."

Michael hadn't told his father about handing out leaflets to hobos in the park, or cheering as Eddie broke down the door to a run-down old house, or watching his mother and Eddie sit close together on the couch, their hands entwined.

"Look," his father said in a sharp whisper, "I make the decisions for me and my family, and this is one of those decisions. If you don't like it, too bad. Tough luck. It's my goddamn family."

His mother shook her head.

"What do I have to do to make you happy? You hated Canaryville when we lived there. You hate McKinley Park. Now you hate a place you've never been. You used to be happy sometimes. Do you even remember that?"

"I used to have reasons to be happy."

"Well, that's what this is all about. It's a reason to be happy."

"Maybe for you it is, but not for me."

They headed down a long, dark hallway, the walls painted with menacing demons and human bodies writhing in agony. Skeletons leaped out with rattling bones. Screams and maniacal laughter blared from an overworked loudspeaker. Michael did his best to not let anything touch his great hand. The hallway turned twice to the right. At the end of the last stretch, Satan sat in a huge chair with flames painted along the sides and on the headrest, beckoning them by curling and uncurling his finger. Satan shook his pitchfork, tilted back his head and cackled, though the cackle was less than convincing. He sneered and tried to frighten them with a glare lifted from Bela Lugosi, but he seemed too tired to pull it off. Michael and his parents stopped in front of the large chair, ready for the admonishment that had cost a quarter. The Devil sneered, shoulder forward, his face red and glossy with makeup, his vermilion leotard bunched at his belly. He opened his mouth to speak, but instead let out a yawn.

"Welcome to hell," the Devil said at the end of his yawn. He spoke in a voice that was slightly sinister, but not sinister enough. Not twenty-five cents' worth of sinister. "Today you have tasted a mere sampling of what terrors the future might bring. Tomorrow your fate might be too hot for you to handle."

"When you say *terrors*, do you mean this little house of horrors down here, or all the money I had to drop on the midway?" Michael's father asked.

"Mere mortal, do not taunt Satan. I have powers you can never comprehend. I can crush puny human lives with my bare fingers." The Devil swept his arm with great histrionics, then reached his hand forward and slowly made a fist. "I can unleash evil upon the world in furious waves," he said, splaying his fingers like a gambler tossing dice, "turn man against man, wipe continents from the Earth."

"Yeah, yeah," Michael's father said. "It's real scary."

"You taunt me? You dare taunt me and my powers?"

"Not so much you. It's more the whole show down here. It's not hot. It sure as hell ain't scary. Those skeletons popping out back there were obviously fake. The World's Fair people could have done a better job of making this look like hell—that's what I'm saying."

Michael's mother crossed her arms in front of her chest. "For heaven's sake, Paddy, leave the man alone. He's just doing his job."

The Devil pointed his pitchfork at them, sneered, and started to say something, but then stopped and smiled at Michael's father. "Paddy?" he said. "Paddy Halligan?"

"Yeah."

"I'll be damned. I knew you looked familiar. Is that really you?"

"Who wants to know?"

The Devil introduced himself as Roy Coleman, an old grammar-school buddy. Michael's father snorted a laugh. Michael's mother repeated Roy's name. Their moods softened.

"I'm Elizabeth Halligan; used to be Elizabeth Fitzgerald."

"Son of a gun," Roy said. "Little Lizzy Fitzgerald."

"This is our son, Michael."

The Devil extended his hand and said, "Put her there, pal."

Michael held his great hand behind his back.

"Don't be rude," his father said. "Shake Mr. Coleman's hand."

Michael didn't budge. The man's red, sweaty hand hovered in the air before him.

"I can't," Michael mumbled.

"You can and you will." His father shoved him. "Shake his goddamn hand."

Reluctantly, Michael shook the Devil's hand.

"I'm a parent myself," Satan said as he released his grip. "Have a little girl named Alice." He pulled a photo from beneath the cushion of his chair and proudly showed it to them. "Sweetest little thing you ever saw."

Michael's fingers were greasy and smeared with red paint. He made a fist and felt his hand tense with power. It glowed with strength, became even greater than before. *Michael Halligan and the Hand of Justice.* He pictured the cover of a book: a mighty fist surrounded by bold letters.

Roy spoke about how he had been in the Hammond steel mills until the market crashed, and since then hadn't had much work, except to sing whenever he could get a gig. The devil thing had really been a godsend.

"And what about you?" he asked Michael's father. "What's in the cards for the Halligans?"

"We're getting out of the city."

"No kidding. Soon?"

"Next year sometime. Don't know when, exactly."

"Where you headed?"

"A town a few miles west, called La Grange. From what I hear, you can actually breathe the air out there."

"How you gonna pull that off? Magic?"

"I've been working on it for a while. A business partner just came through for me." He glanced at Michael's mother. "It's the chance of a lifetime, though not everyone sees it that way."

They chatted some more, mostly about the old neighborhood, and Michael struggled to make sense of what his father had said. Before now, he hadn't heard anything about moving.

Satan pointed down the hallway, where another family was approaching. "I gotta get back to work," he said, "but it was great seeing you." He grinned at Michael's father and said, "And you—you old so-and-so—we've gotta get the old gang together one of these days."

Michael's father nodded. "I'll tell them to look you up next time they're in hell."

Michael walked with his parents toward stairs that led up to sunlight and a sweltering afternoon. He looked back, and the Devil winked at him.

5

ELIZABETH SAT ON A PIANO BENCH IN EDDIE'S LIVING ROOM AND PICTURED policemen beating him in a dingy basement and leaving him handcuffed to the bars of a jail cell. They tied him to a chair, punched his face, clubbed his ribs, and later dumped him in some godforsaken cornfield. She tried to conjure hopeful scenes—Eddie standing on a chair in an abandoned warehouse this afternoon, winning over a crowd of fifty hungry people; Eddie telling her about growing up on a farm in Michigan before he had moved with his parents to Chicago; Eddie watching her in such a way that his attention felt like a modest sacrament—but visions of torture kept interrupting her memories. Officers blindfolded him, chained him to a wall, pressed lit cigarettes against his skin. She stood and paced the worn Oriental rug. She listened at the door for his footsteps on the stairs. The room, with its red velvet sofa, lace doilies, and tasseled lampshades, bore the prim style of a maiden aunt, yet in all of it was Eddie. His shoes lay beside the baby grand piano, his hats and coats hung on wall hooks, his liniment scent filled the air. Three hours ago, right before the policemen hauled him off from the warehouse, he had handed Elizabeth his keys and asked her to wait for him. Now dusk was coming, and miles away Paddy would soon leave work and head for home, expecting both his supper and his family. There was a crash, and Elizabeth gasped before realizing it was only Michael, knocking down blocks in the bedroom. She sat on the sofa, shut her eyes, and tried to settle her heart. If worry was a symptom of love, then what she felt for Eddie was the strongest, most worrisome love imaginable.

At first she had been reserved around him, but with each friendly touch, each earnest prayer, each rare smile and word of encouragement from him, she found herself more dedicated to his cause, more desirous of his presence. Sixteen months after their meeting, she now found it hard to know where his words ended and her thoughts began, and she felt emboldened and blessed by this transformation. In bed at night, she closed her eyes and imagined that Paddy's flesh was Eddie's flesh. Drifting down the aisles of the grocery store, numb with errands, she fantasized about running into him by chance. At times she became so engrossed in imaginary conversations or romance with Eddie that, in a panic, she would suddenly halt her daydream, fearful that she had spoken aloud, worried that people could read the blush on her face. It was schoolgirl stuff, with nothing more than occasional hand holding and professions of love, but it was risky nonetheless. Once, with Mae, she had accidentally referred to her husband by Eddie's name. The previous month, Paddy had found a flyer in her coat pocket. "Society for Sacred Possessions?" he said. "You turning into a radical?" He laughed. Reluctantly, she laughed too. "Oh, you know," she said, "some crackpot was handing them out." Since she'd joined it, the Society had grown from twenty members to one hundred. Eddie had been beaten twice, arrested four times, and received an anonymous note under his door, warning him to shut up or leave Chicago. There were more protests, more rallies, more hot meals handed out and buildings broken into, and even though she managed to attend only twice a week, at every prayer circle she was the one at Eddie's side.

When she heard heavy footsteps, she rushed to the front door and opened it. Trudging up the staircase was a young black woman.

"Can I talk to Mr. Kowal, please?"

"He isn't here," Elizabeth said.

"Are you his wife?"

"I'm one of his followers."

The woman stopped on the top step. She looked quizzically at Elizabeth, who pointed to the sign on the door and clarified that she was a member of the Society for Sacred Possessions, which was dedicated to transferring the nation's wealth from the pockets of the elite to the hands of the people so that the people—the good, God-fearing people who formed the backbone and the spine and, for that matter, the entire body of the United States— could reach a higher moral and spiritual state through—

The woman held up her hand like a traffic cop. "I know about your group," she said. "I hear your songs and prayers, and at night I hear your leader practicing his speeches. Everyone in the building hears him."

Elizabeth imagined Eddie preaching alone in his living room, and his tenants grumbling in the other five apartments. She had never paid much attention to them, except to know that white people were moving out and black people were moving in.

"I've come about the radiators," the woman said. "I've asked him before to turn them up, but he won't, and now there's frost on the inside of the windows and my little one's got the shivers. My husband and I pay for our heat, and I don't think it's too much to expect that we get some. I know everyone wants to save money, but this is too much."

"It's not about money," Elizabeth said. The property was Eddie's sole source of income, the reason he could devote his life to the Society, and if anything, he charged his tenants too little. At least, that was what he had said. "There must be some other explanation."

"Oh, he gave me an explanation, all right—said that radiator heat in a building was unnatural, that in olden days people wore animal skins and kept fires to stay warm, but that now we're all too dependent on modern conveniences. I'm not sure if this is part of what your group actually believes, but I'm not buying it."

Elizabeth wanted to explain that Eddie was an idealist and therefore prone to unorthodox opinions: that people with fair hair had greater intellectual capacities than those with dark hair, that the silver standard was the Christian antidote to the Jewish gold standard, that God had sent Elizabeth to him for a definite, yet still unrevealed, reason. His attitude about radiator heat, like many of his attitudes, might not have made sense in itself, but it was only a small part of a grand, true vision.

"I know you're just a follower," the woman said, "but would you mind telling Mr. Kowal what I said?"

"I'll tell him."

Elizabeth closed and locked the door. No black person had ever spoken to her in such a firm way before, and she felt for a moment that she should be offended by the woman's tone, especially as it pertained to Eddie, but she couldn't muster much indignation. The woman was poor and cold. She didn't know the real Eddie. She didn't know his truth. Elizabeth turned and saw Michael standing in the living room.

"Come sit with me," she said, forcing a smile. "We can wait for Eddie together."

Without a word, Michael walked back into the bedroom and shut the door. She heard him kick his blocks, and she feared he would tell his father everything.

Sometimes she looked at Michael and imagined that one day he would court a girl as intensely as Paddy had courted her. She worried he would dance only with the girl he wanted, and that he would hold her so tightly that for several minutes afterward, her left hand and waist would still feel the force of his lead. He would first kiss the girl in an alley, and would press his body hard against hers. He would propose, and if the girl remained as indecisive as Elizabeth had, he would wander past her house at all hours, and stare at her in church, and send her letters and gifts every day until she felt so scared and aroused and needed that she believed she had no choice but to accept his offer.

Elizabeth sat on the couch and thought of the move to La Grange, which was supposed to happen in the fall. Just before Christmas, only a month ago, Paddy had borrowed Red's car and driven her out to the vacant corner lot where the station would be built. Next door stood a bank. Across the street was a low stone train depot. La Grange was filled with towering oaks and grand Victorians, women with smooth skin and fur collars. Paddy said that until they saved up enough money for a place of their own, they would live in a few rooms in the back of the station. He claimed it would be like when they had first moved out of her parents' house and into that crappy little place in Canaryville. But back then there had been no Michael, no Eddie, and Paddy and Elizabeth had still had the time and energy and inclination to go to dances, host parties, and stay up late making love. In the middle of his empty lot, Paddy spoke of "opportunity," and whenever he said the word, it felt to Elizabeth like a jab to her heart.

Eddie had promised her courage, and he had given her enough of it that now she felt comfortable talking back to her husband and recruiting people at rallies, but whenever La Grange entered her mind, she became desperate and afraid, imagining herself sitting for hours behind the counter of Paddy's gas station while some other woman replaced her at Eddie's side.

"Whenever I think of your husband, I think of bankers and businessmen," Eddie had said when she had recently told him of the impending move. "Every day he steals you from me, the way they steal our homes and assets. But like the bankers and businessmen, he won't get away with it. I won't let him."

Elizabeth didn't move when she heard footsteps again. Someone tried the doorknob, then knocked. Elizabeth approached the door cautiously and asked who was there.

"It's me," said Eddie.

She opened the door and began sobbing when she saw his swollen right eye and torn collar. She wrapped her arms around him and kissed him, and to her surprise, he kissed her too. But within a few seconds, his body tensed. He stepped back.

She moved toward him, kissed his face, his neck, his tender eye. "You have no idea how worried I was."

"Elizabeth, no," he said as he squirmed free. He looked past her into his apartment. Elizabeth turned to see Michael watching them.

"Go back to the bedroom, sweetie," she said.

"Can we go?"

Elizabeth was no longer crying, but she hardly felt composed. "In a little bit," she said. "Not right now."

"But he's here. Why can't we go?"

"Listen to your mother," Eddie said in a weary voice. "And if you won't listen to her, listen to me. This is my home, and when you're here, you'll do as you're told."

Michael went back into the bedroom and slammed the door. Eddie hung up his overcoat and plopped onto the couch. He tilted his head back with his eyes closed and a hand on his forehead. Feeling as purposeful as a comic-strip hero and as necessary as a plaster saint, Elizabeth hurried to the kitchen, retrieved some ice, and wrapped it in a dish towel. She returned and handed Eddie the cold bundle, which he held against his eye. She knelt, removed his shoes, and sat beside him on the couch. When she rested her hand on his chest, he scooted away and said, "Elizabeth, please."

There were thousands, maybe millions, of women who dreaded their homes and regretted their marriages, but she was different from them. Eddie had plucked her from a mundane life and placed her at the center of something powerful and dangerous, something that grew bolder each day. She felt ashamed for the times she'd doubted his opinions or been less than appreciative of his attitudes. His beliefs were so strong that he had suffered for them. If that didn't prove his virtue, what could? She inched toward him and placed her hand on his shoulder.

He moved away from her again, almost to the end of the couch. "We need to control ourselves."

"I'm sorry," she said, though she wasn't sorry for anything.

He lowered the ice to his side. His eye would be bruised for days, but it would help him recruit more members. She pictured him pointing to it as evidence of what happens to those who stand up for the truth.

"Ever since you told me of your husband's plans, I've been asking God what to do," he said. "I've been praying about other developments, too— about what happens when our members stop coming here once everyone in the neighborhood is colored, and about the dropping property values and what it all means for the Society. I've been asking God every day for guidance. And on the way home from the police station just now, He spoke to me."

Eddie faced forward. For several seconds, neither he nor Elizabeth said a word.

"Did you hear a voice?" she asked finally.

"He didn't speak in words." Eddie gave her a fatherly smile. "He filled my heart with a feeling of deep certainty."

Elizabeth blushed. How was she to know what God sounded or didn't sound like? Eddie and Father Collins and others talked about hearing from God, but their claims made no sense to her. She had prayed ever since she was a girl, but God had never said a thing in response.

"He told me I should move to Washington, D.C., where I'll have the attention of policymakers and the international community. In Chicago, my words don't make it past a small group of people, but in Washington, influential people will hear what I have to say, and they'll spread my message around the nation and turn our truth into law." He cleared his throat and regarded his stocking feet. "But He also told me that I would succeed only if you went with me."

In her daydreams, whenever Eddie asked her to leave with him, Elizabeth's heart swelled with operatic passion. But now, in the wake of his words, her heart, though racing, hesitated.

"What about Paddy?" she said. "What about Michael?"

"Didn't you hear how your son just spoke to you? Didn't you see his disobedience? It's only going to get worse, you know. He's going to get older and more like his father, and you'll be stuck with them in a town where nobody knows you the way I do."

"But I can't just leave."

"And I can't wait forever for a decision." He stood and paced the room, dressed in the green suit he'd worn the first time she saw him and many times since then. She'd wanted so often to mend its fraying hems. After a minute, he sat beside her. He took her hand between his.

"If your husband and son weren't around, would you go with me?"

"Yes."

"And if we go, do you have faith that we can succeed?"

"Of course."

Her hand was nestled between his hands, warm and protected.

"Would you rather go with me or move to La Grange?"

"I'd rather go with you."

Eddie was so good to her, Elizabeth told herself. He helped her understand things she hadn't even noticed before, and he challenged her to be a better person, though sometimes she didn't realize this until after his words had broken her.

"God also told me that in order to prove our commitment, we must remain pure in spirit and flesh." Eddie squeezed her hand so hard, it started to feel numb. "We need to deny ourselves not only to each other, but also to anyone else who might feel entitled to enjoy our favors."

Elizabeth ran his words through her brain a few times, each time understanding a little more of what he wanted. He gazed at her with a simple, foolish grin, as though he expected her to thank him.

"God told you this?" she said, extracting her hand from his grip.

Eddie blushed and stood. He slipped his hands into his pockets. "It was something He led me to understand."

"Are you saying that God wants me to stop sleeping with my husband?"

He wrinkled his brow, as if smelling something rancid. He stood angled away from her. "He wants us to deny ourselves to everyone. He wants us to be pure."

"Did He tell you what specific things we should and shouldn't do?"

"I don't want to go into the sordid details."

"What sordid details? Tell me. I want to know what God wants of me."

When Eddie burst into sobs, Elizabeth flinched. She had never seen a man cry.

"If you choose your husband over me," he said, struggling to get the words out, "then let me know so I can make other plans."

"Eddie, please." She felt embarrassed. She wanted to usher him away from himself.

Elizabeth stood. When she touched Eddie's forearm, he turned away from her like an indignant lover in a silent movie. He took a deep breath and wiped the tears from his face.

"I wouldn't discuss such a thing if I hadn't felt that this was what God wanted of us. You know that, don't you?"

"It's all right," she said. "I understand."

"So, will you do it? Will you deny him? Will you go to Washington with me?"

She felt exhausted and bewildered. Michael wanted to be home, and for the first time in years, she wanted to be there too, alone in bed, buried beneath the covers, her body burrowed in a pocket of warmth.

"I'll do whatever you want me to do," she said.

Eddie gave her a curt nod and placed his hand awkwardly on her shoulder.

"I'm sorry I upset you," she said. "I didn't mean to."

"That's all right," he said, still not quite facing her, his chest rising and falling heavily. "I forgive you."

"Ladies and gentlemen, what you are about to witness is real, and therefore not for the faint of heart." The man wearing a white doctor's coat had a stethoscope around his neck and a pointer in his hand. He paced the bare stage in the dark, cramped auditorium. Audience members fanned themselves with hats and souvenir programs. "It is unsuitable for women, children, and those with nervous conditions. Anyone wishing to leave may do so now. Rest assured that you will receive a full refund upon exiting."

Elizabeth had not wanted to see the show in the first place, but Michael had insisted, and today, of all days, she wanted to placate him. He'd become an extortionist lately, hinting with little subtlety that he should receive baseball cards, candy, and ice cream in exchange for keeping her secrets, which he'd once kept for free.

"Very well," the doctor said when it became clear that nobody was going to leave. "Let's begin."

A nurse—or at least a woman who was as much a nurse as the man was a doctor—walked onstage, carrying a large bundle wrapped in a white blanket. People whispered and laughed nervously. They shifted in their seats.

"What we show you today is both a marvel and a monstrosity of nature." The doctor tapped the pointer against his leg. "The first thing I must say is that because of its shocking deformity, this baby died immediately at birth. No attempts could have saved it. No attempts were made."

With the flourish of a magician, he removed the blanket to reveal a large jar. People gasped and rose for a better view, and Elizabeth strained to see past them. The nurse walked back and forth at the front of the stage, and soon Elizabeth glimpsed the infant, floating in greenish liquid. It was scrawny, with a primary head that looked normal and a smaller one sticking out from the side of its neck. It was nothing like the baby on the sign outside, which was chubby, with two full-size, identical heads, both alert and grinning beneath the message: COME SEE THE TWO-HEADED BABY!

"Though we are not sure if this creature was the result of inferior breeding or simply a freak of nature," the doctor said, "we must be glad that God, in His infinite wisdom, chose the best course of action. And we must also be grateful that the medical community is working to ensure that hideously deformed beings such as the one you see before you are made a thing of the past."

The doctor tapped the jar with his pointer and explained that the baby had been a combination of twins: one dominant, one weak. In the womb, the weak one had tried to come to life, but the other had not let it, and so they'd ended up stuck this way, a mixture of people who couldn't live at all. The nurse cradled the jar. Beside Elizabeth, a man and a woman concluded that the baby undoubtedly had been a punishment from God, though they were not sure who had been punished. The baby's parents? Grandparents? The infant itself? The ways of God, the man claimed, were mysterious. Elizabeth watched the baby's scrunched-up faces and little fists, and she imagined it growing into a boy and then a man.

A few minutes later, as Elizabeth walked with Michael from the dim indoors to the bright, crowded midway, she felt that the world should have changed in some significant way because she'd seen the two-headed baby. The throng threatened to smother her, and the scent of popcorn, sweat, perfume, and aftershave turned her stomach. The sun's harsh rays made her feel sicker still. Tears in her eyes, she ushered Michael down a side path, where the crowd thinned. Her skin was hot in patches, cold in others; her legs felt on the verge of buckling. In her bag she carried flyers she was supposed to leave around the grounds. She briskly led Michael off the path, through a gate, and into Spanish gardens. Nearly hyperventilating, she hurried with him past leafy trees, fountains, and statues of nude men and women. She sat on a shaded bench beside a round reflecting pool, leaned forward, and breathed slowly, deeply. She prayed a Hail Mary in her head and asked God to help her, but she wasn't exactly sure what she wanted, and doubted that God would approve of her heart.

"Are you all right?" Michael asked.

"I'm fine, sweetie." She reached back and patted his knee. "Just feeling a little sick."

He pressed his head against her shoulder. If she ever left, if Eddie ever did take her away, Michael's forgiveness would be the only forgiveness she would pray for.

Her heartbeat calmed and the nausea left her. She sat up and let the wind play with her hair. It was so rare to see such a concentration of trees in the city, so uncommon to hear the rustle of leaves. She eyed the statuary: a pietà, a Venus de Milo, Michelangelo's David. There was a cubist sculpture that looked like a reclining woman, and another that may have been entwined bodies, and set amid ginkgos and birch trees was a toilet atop a stone pedestal. Confused, Elizabeth stood, and with Michael took the path to the toilet. Beneath it was a metal sign that read: THE "HOME PRIDE" MODEL—A TRUE WORK OF MODERN ART! COURTESY OF THE AMERICAN RADIATOR & STANDARD SANITARY COMPANY'S "GARDEN OF COMFORT."

"What's that doing here?" Michael asked. Elizabeth looked around and saw a space heater, a sink, and a radiator amid the trees and sculptures. "Why isn't it in a bathroom?"

Elizabeth sighed and glanced down at Michael. He already had bags under his eyes. Wrinkles stretched across his brow. He seemed more wary of the world than a child needed to be.

"Come on," she said. "We don't want to be late for Mrs. Twitchell."

They exited the gardens and made their way onto the hectic midway. All around were sweaty, imperfect bodies, laughing and shouting and throwing away their money and dignity for anything that promised a thrill. *Oriental beauties, gentlemen, we've got 'em right here in the exotic dance of the dragon! Let yourself be tantalized! Try your hand, young fella! Dunk the darkies!*

African dips—three balls a nickel! Relics and reenactment of the Fort Dearborn massacre—for your viewing pleasure! See our forefathers try to bravely hold back the ruthless, savage Indians! Elizabeth gripped Michael's hand and watched the crowd rush past. She hated Chicago. She hated the hustle and the taking, the wealth and the poverty, the cold winters and hot summers, the stockyard smells that had surrounded her every day of her life. If only Eddie would make good on his promise of taking her away; if only he would accept an offer on his building instead of complaining about property values—if only he would make a plan and act on it instead of talking endlessly, she would accept his offer and disappear, and disappear, and continue to disappear until there was no trace of who she'd been. But the only thing that had disappeared thus far was the vague and improbable hope of vanishing with Eddie before Paddy took her to La Grange. The baby inside her guaranteed that.

Waiting for Mrs. Twitchell, Elizabeth and Michael sat in the sparse shade of a young elm, which had been planted solely for the sake of the fair and would be pulled out when the whole spectacle was over. In front of them stood the Hall of Religion, which looked like a white Bakelite radio; from its roof rose an orange spire that more closely resembled an antenna than a steeple. Above the broad glass doors was a mural in which Jesus stood with his arms raised, surrounded by miniature versions of Muhammad, Buddha, and Zeus. Michael plucked grass from the ground and tossed the blades into the air. *He will survive without me,* Elizabeth thought.

A pickup truck approached slowly along the wide pedestrian walkway, honking its horn repeatedly, and then stopped a hundred feet from where Elizabeth and Michael sat. WHITMAN PUBLISHING—RACINE, WISCONSIN was printed on the door, and behind the wheel sat a heavyset, red-cheeked man. He climbed out of the cab, cupped his hands around his mouth, and shouted, "Gather 'round, gather 'round. Right here, right now, in the flesh, is that truest of true heroes, savior of the twenty-fifth century—the great Buck Rogers."

A man with a big, symmetrical smile and broad shoulders rose from the truck bed, waving excitedly. He was handsome and muscular in his skintight blue spacesuit with jodhpurlike pants. A yellow aviator helmet was strapped to his head. Red boots rose nearly to his knees. Children ran to him from all directions, their parents shouting for them to slow down, be careful, stay close. The driver caught the mayhem on a handheld movie camera. Michael hesitated a moment, but then sprinted toward the truck. Elizabeth followed, glancing backward to make sure she didn't miss Mrs. Twitchell.

"Hey, gang," shouted the man in the Buck Rogers outfit. "Is everybody having fun?"

The children, about forty in all, shouted, "Yes!"

"I'm sorry. I didn't quite hear you. I said, 'Is everybody having fun?'" When the children screamed their answer, he staggered back a step, pretending to be knocked off balance by their enthusiasm. "Boy, oh boy," he said, "you must be having one heck of a time to yell like that. But let me ask you something. Do want to have even more fun?"

When the children shouted again, he crouched down and smiled. His face and physique were so beautiful that Elizabeth thought he should be included in the mural on the Hall of Religion, or at least posed in the Garden of Comfort.

"As you probably know, I've had my share of adventures, and I hope you've been following all of them in the funny papers." As far as Elizabeth could tell, his only imperfection was a lazy eye. "Well, I'm here today to tell all of my friends that my very first exciting motion-picture adventure is going to be shown later today, at six o'clock, in the Hall of Science." He grinned. "How many of you want to see it?"

The kids raised their hands and shouted. Elizabeth glanced over her shoulder and saw Mrs. Twitchell standing in front of the Hall of Religion.

"Well, talk to your parents and tell them how much you want to see it. But if you miss it, don't worry. Pretty soon, you'll be seeing me at the picture show."

He reached down, picked up a few small books, and stood. Elizabeth made her way through the crowd to Michael.

"I have even more exciting news." The man held up one of the books, which was as big around as his palm, and about an inch thick. On the cover, a rocket ship soared through a cloudy wall dividing a dingy industrial city from a gleaming metropolis. "The latest Big Little Book should be in stores any day now. It's called *Trouble in the City of Dreams*, and it's set right here at the Century of Progress. You won't want to miss this spine-tingling adventure, which features some of your favorite comic heroes, joining forces for the first time ever in order to save the World's Fair."

Elizabeth placed her hand on Michael's shoulder. "We have to go," she said.

Michael shrugged off her hand. His eyes were on Buck Rogers, who said, "I'm afraid I have to be on my way."

The children begged their hero to stay.

"But before I go, I want to let you know that the good folks at Cocomalt have given me some copies to pass along to you. Would anyone like one?"

The children, Michael included, shouted and raised their hands. Elizabeth grabbed his upper arm and started to lead him away from the truck, but he squirmed free. She seized his arm again, but he slipped out of her grip, shouting for her to leave him alone. He pushed deeper into the crowd. She followed. Buck Rogers tossed a book into the crowd, then another, and another. Children leaped, lunged, squealed with pleasure. Michael shoved and tussled with three other boys. Elizabeth grabbed him by the collar and dragged him stumbling backward. A book flew from his hands. A blond boy snatched it up, raised it in triumph, and ran off. Michael cried and swung at Elizabeth. "It's all your fault!" he screamed. The truck roared to life and drove away. "You ruined everything!"

"What progress has been made?" Mrs. Twitchell asked, clutching her handbag to her chest. With her bulging eyes and scrawny neck, she resembled a baby bird, dependent on its mother for regurgitated worms.

"We recruited ten new members in the last month, handed out nearly a thousand meals, and opened up two warehouses and three apartment buildings that had been locked up. The people who are squatting there haven't been kicked out yet."

"This is success?"

"We do the best we can. You know that."

"But what good does it do for those who are unemployed? For those with no homes?"

"There's only so much we can do." Elizabeth looked at Michael, who sat pouting beneath the elm. She'd apologized and tried to hug him, but he'd wanted only to sit by himself.

"It just seems that more should have been accomplished by now."

Elizabeth had been foolish to think she could ask for help from Mrs. Twitchell, who did little more than write checks and complain; she had been foolish to think there was any way out of her predicament. She had tried her best to hold off Paddy, at least at times—most times, in fact, except when he forced himself on her, or when she couldn't help but reach for him in the night and imagine him as the tense and quiet young man who had tinkered with her father's delivery trucks and once told her, "I'd fix anything in the world for you." In those moments, when he would press himself against her, she would think how unfair and pitiful Eddie's request had been. Afterward, she would think how lonely both men made her feel.

She and Eddie had not spoken about his request since he'd uttered it seven months ago, except by implication, whenever he watched her leave his apartment, his face stony from his knowledge that he was sending her off to another man. At times she practically felt him sniffing for Paddy's scent on her skin, in her hair, and she'd feel determined to go home and let Paddy have his way with her.

Elizabeth sighed and looked at Michael, who yanked grass from the ground. She felt an urge to take him up in her arms and hug him, to apologize for causing him to lose the thing he wanted.

"I have to go," she said to Mrs. Twitchell. "I'm sorry we're not solving the problems of the world fast enough for you."

Elizabeth turned, but before she could walk away, Mrs. Twitchell grabbed her forearm and said, "Please wait. I'm sorry."

Every other week, a scene like this played out—in front of the Hall of

Religion, beneath the clock outside Marshall Field's, at a lunch counter in the Loop. On each subsequent occasion, Mrs. Twitchell's frustration and apology became more dramatic, her gestures more intimate, the amount of her donation larger. Then Elizabeth would take the check home and hide it somewhere—at the bottom of a drawer, folded up in the tip of a shoe, taped to the underside of a rug—until the next time she saw Eddie.

"I'm sorry I spoke to you that way," Mrs. Twitchell said. "I want to see things change so badly that I get frustrated when they don't. Sometimes I question whether Eddie has the best approach." She stared helplessly at Elizabeth. "Does he?"

"Does he what?"

"Does he have the best approach? I mean, is he right? Is his way the right one?"

Elizabeth wasn't sure how to reply. Like Mrs. Twitchell, she was merely a follower.

"You know these things," Mrs. Twitchell said. "You're a woman with a young child, like me—but you're different. You live these problems every day. I need to know what you think. I need to know how else I can help."

In Mrs. Twitchell's eyes was a desperate need for guidance. Elizabeth feared it was the same look she showed Eddie.

"You want to know how you can help?"

"Yes, I do," said Mrs. Twitchell. "Please tell me."

Elizabeth opened her mouth, but the words cowered inside her. Since their kiss, she and Eddie had had no intimate contact, much as she had wanted it then and maybe still wanted it now, but she had betrayed him many times by remaining faithful to her husband. The proof was inside her, known only to her, though soon it would be obvious to everyone. Eddie would never take her away with him.

Elizabeth looked up at the gods on the Hall of Religion. They were too cartoonish to help her, too foolish and arrogant to be any good to anyone. If someone didn't help soon, if something didn't change, in a month she would be stuck living in La Grange with Michael and Paddy and a baby on the way.

"Your husband is a doctor, isn't he?" she asked.

"Yes." Mrs. Twitchell frowned. "He grows rich on the sickness of others."

Elizabeth toed the ground. "I was hoping he could help me."

"Oh dear, are you sick?" Mrs. Twitchell rested her fingers on Elizabeth's forearm.

"Not really."

"Then what is it?"

"I'm pregnant."

"Oh, well, congratulations."

Elizabeth shook her head. She did not want to cry, especially in front of Mrs. Twitchell.

"What's wrong?" Mrs. Twitchell's fingers lingered on Elizabeth's skin for a few more seconds, then flew away.

"I was wondering," Elizabeth whispered, "if your husband knows someone who can help me. Another doctor, maybe?"

"I'm afraid I don't follow you."

"Does he know anyone who can help me take care of it?"

Mrs. Twitchell shook her head and said, "I still don't know what you mean."

"I can't have it. I just can't."

"Oh. I don't—I don't know what you're saying." Mrs. Twitchell twisted the strap of her handbag.

"Does your husband know someone safe?"

Mrs. Twitchell opened her handbag and pulled out a checkbook. "If this is about money, I'm sure I can figure out some way to help."

"It's not about money."

"Then I don't know what I can do. I could ask around, I suppose."

Elizabeth shook her head.

"My husband and I are not in a position to adopt, but I have friends who might be. I could talk to some people for you."

Elizabeth took a deep breath and released it slowly. "I'm sorry," she said. "I don't know what I was saying just then. I'll figure something out."

"I know you will. I know things will work out for the best."

Mrs. Twitchell wrote a check and handed it to Elizabeth, who smiled politely and walked toward Michael, who'd torn up a small patch of earth around himself. When Mrs. Twitchell called her name, Elizabeth turned.

"A baby." A smile strained Mrs. Twitchell's face. She held out her checkbook as though it could protect them both. "It's so wonderful. It's a blessing, even in these hard times. You'll see. You will."

Elizabeth and Michael walked in silence to the Garden of Comfort, where they sat on the same bench as before. She pondered Mrs. Twitchell's words and thought that all times were hard for someone, and blessings came only when you couldn't use them. She glanced absentmindedly at the check, which was for a hundred dollars, five times more than Mrs. Twitchell's largest check to date. Unlike her others, which had been made out to Eddie, this one was made out to "Cash." Elizabeth started to cry. With the check, she could go just about anywhere she wanted, change her name, start a life free of both Paddy and Eddie. Or she could care for the baby herself and tell Eddie, "Come with me if you want." One kind of woman would seduce Eddie, then tell him the baby was his. Another would see the pregnancy through, and commit herself to her husband. But Elizabeth wasn't sure what kind of woman she was, or what she was capable of doing. She needed a miracle, but there was no such thing. She felt she should pray, but prayer was just a pillow where you could rest your head awhile. She felt helplessly strong and hopelessly weak, more trapped and free than she'd ever felt.

"Let's go home," she said as she wiped her eyes. She stood, and when she rested her hand on Michael's shoulder, he seemed to soften to her. "Let's pretend this day never happened."

They passed the reflecting pool, the pietà, elms and oaks and maples, an icebox, a water heater, and a marble bust of George Washington with a laurel wreath around his head. At the Home Pride toilet, Elizabeth reached into her bag and pulled out the flyers Eddie had given her to distribute. *Do you like what you see of the future? The decadence? The greed? There is more to life than naked women and freak shows and never-ending thrills. Reclaim your sacred possessions! Reclaim your soul!* She opened the toilet lid, and without ceremony or a second thought she tossed the papers into the empty bowl.

7.

In his dream, he became Buck Rogers, dreaming of children clamoring for the books he'd tossed to them, and of the ring and the ropes and Sally Rand dancing nude with feathered fans, and of his fading youth and vague future and letters he'd not yet written, and of the vision that had vanished from his left eye. And when he awoke, he was a man of twenty-six named Oswald Knoll. He opened his eyes and with his one good one stared out the truck window. Night had fallen completely since he and Hank had left Chicago. Fireflies were the only lights across the prairie, stars and the waning moon the only ones above.

"You awake?"

Oswald turned ninety degrees to his left to look at his companion.

"You gotta stay awake, kid, and talk a little." Hank gripped the steering wheel hard, as if it might try to fly away from him. His jowls and gray hair shook along with the truck. "I'm not a young man anymore, and it's not always easy to keep the ol' peepers open on such a long drive. I need someone to keep me company. I need conversation. The mouth's a muscle, you know; you gotta exercise it now and then."

Oswald turned and faced the road. "I'm not much of a talker," he said.

Thirty times today and thirty times yesterday, he had jumped onto the truck bed and jabbered away at boys and girls. After each performance, he'd been stunned by his own enthusiasm.

"Or at least, I don't like talking when I don't have to."

They drove in silence for several minutes. Shortly after passing a sign that read, RACINE 20 MILES, Hank steered the truck off the highway and toward a gas station. An old man ambled toward them. His overalls were beat-up and baggy, as though he'd bought them as a younger, more substantial man.

"Excuse me, sir," Hank said once he was out of the truck, "would you happen to have a restroom on the premises?"

The man waved at the darkness all around them. "The whole place is my premises. You can do your business where you want, just as long as you kick dirt on it afterward."

Hank disappeared into the prairie, and the old man washed the windshield. Oswald climbed out of the truck. The Buck Rogers costume was bunched at his shoulders, knees, and crotch, so he pinched the fabric free and smoothed it into place.

"You going to some sort of costume party?"

Oswald turned to the man, who stood grinning and pumping gas.

"No, I'm not going to a costume party."

"What are you supposed to be, then?"

"I'm Buck Rogers. Don't you know Buck Rogers when you see him?"

"I'm not asking who you are. I'm asking what you're supposed to be."

"I'm not supposed to be anything," Oswald said. "I'm just doing my job."

Hank returned, bragging that he felt five pounds lighter, and as he asked the old man if any wild animals or ghosts haunted his property, Oswald slipped past them, crossed the highway, and trudged through waist-high grass. When he was far enough away that he could no longer hear Hank, he took a few bold steps forward and landed two quick jabs to the sky. He slid to his right and then boxed the sky into a neutral corner. The grass brushed against his legs and flattened underfoot. The earth sprang and gave like canvas-covered boards. Tomorrow morning he would drag himself out of bed and to his job in sales and promotion at Whitman Publishing, as he'd done each weekday for the past two weeks, and on his desk would be dozens of letters written by children, addressed to their comic-strip heroes; he would force himself to become the characters, whether the Lone Ranger or Mandrake the Magician, and answer their questions as best he could, but tonight, with Louise, he would need only to be himself. He took three steps back and let the sky come to him. He dodged its swift lunges, sensing its impatience and lack of courage. He was Oswald "Hard Knocks" Knoll again, undefeated and feared, though Hard Knocks no longer existed. He was Buck Rogers, yet there was no Buck Rogers. At times he felt as if a little bit of everything and everyone who'd ever lived or been imagined dwelt inside his soul, and that playing a part was not pretending. He had tried to explain this in a letter to Louise last night, their first apart since the wedding, but his thoughts had turned from his own words to tasting the sweat on her neck. The letter remained unwritten.

He'd first seen her between bouts at an Aurora, Illinois, arena. She stood in the middle of the ring in a dress the color of orange sherbet. Cigar smoke and catcalls surrounded her; browned bloodstains lay at her feet. She cleared her throat, lifted a microphone to her lips, and began to sing a cappella: "Over in Killarney many years ago, me mither sang a song to me in tones so sweet and low." Drunken men hooted and jeered at her beautiful fake brogue, and when the chorus arrived, they howled their accompaniment like dogs serenading a full moon. "Too-ra-loo-ra-loo-ral, too-ra-loo-ra-li. Too-ra-loo-ra-loo-ral, hush now, don't you cry." Sitting ringside, scouting his next fight, Oswald expected her confidence to falter or tears to overcome her, but instead her voice grew stronger. She waved her hands, inviting the jokers to join her. "Oft in dreams I wander to that cot again. I feel her arms a-hugging me as when she held me then." She aimed her microphone at them, smiling as though she'd trained them to act like fools. The men sang louder along with the verse and then another chorus, their mocking turning into admiration for her poise and good humor. And as she belted out, "That's an Irish lullaby," they erupted in a boisterous standing ovation. Oswald smiled and cheered along with the rest, and he knew that she was exceptional.

He stopped boxing and let the sky surround him. He closed his good eye but kept the blind one open. There was a difference between darkness and a void. There was no comparing night and nothingness; the former was so much less than the latter.

"I don't care if you want to box around the room in your drawers or just sit there and not say a word," Louise had told him at his lowest moment, right after his final bout. "I don't care that you can't fight anymore. I don't care that you can't see out of your left eye. I really don't, Oswald. I'm serious. This is something you need to understand."

"But you might care someday." He hadn't spoken in two days. His voice was as raw as split skin. "It might bother you that I never became who I could have been."

"I might care someday," she said, "but I don't now and probably never will, and I don't see how you can do any better than that."

He missed her when they were apart, and odds were good that he honestly loved her. She seemed wise and generous with her wisdom, but then again, she was only nineteen, and their marriage, just six months old, sometimes seemed like a whim that didn't know how to end. She could vanish like eyesight, like daylight or darkness, like everything that was living or trying to come to life.

"Hey, kid," Hank yelled. "Hey, Buck Rogers, or Oswald, or whoever you are. It's time to go."

Oswald opened his right eye and turned to face the gas station. Hank climbed into the truck and shut the door. There was no Buck Rogers, no Dick Tracy, no Lone Ranger, yet there needed to be. Somebody had to play them. And since he could no longer be who he'd been, since all his training and hard work were meaningless now, he figured he might as well let himself become the imaginary people that real people needed.

"Coming," Oswald shouted, and he ran across the prairie toward the sound of the engine turning over.

8.

JIMMY CROSS SAID THAT EVERYONE HAD TO PLAY HIS NEW GAME; THAT was rule number one. Rule number two was that the game could never have a name; it was too good to ever be called anything—except possibly The Game. Number three: he himself, and only he himself, could change the rules, and he could do so whenever he wanted. Richard Burke stepped forward from his spot beside Jimmy and asked if everyone understood. Everyone nodded.

The first- and second-grade boys, twenty-eight in all, were gathered after school in the dirt lot behind St. Rose of Lima. At the back of the group, Michael stood with his jacket bunched in the bend of his arm and his tie hanging loose and crooked from his neck. His satchel and cap lay at his feet. He pressed his fingers against the sandstone church and gazed up at the spire. Brown smoke from the stockyards tumbled past, making it appear as if the church were falling toward him.

"This is how the game works." Richard wiped snot from his nose. "When Jimmy says so, everyone lies down on the ground on their stomach. You can't move."

The previous year, Jimmy and Richard had pinched Michael's arms until his skin was dotted with bruises. They'd called him Runt and gotten the other boys and a few girls to call him that, too. Now, at the start of second grade, they had surprised Michael by inviting him to join their game.

"Me or Jimmy will shout a name," Richard said, "and then everyone gets up and beats on that guy until we yell, 'Stop.' Then everyone lies down again and we pick someone else." Richard coughed and coughed and then spit. "Any questions?"

The boys shook their heads.

"Good," Jimmy said. "Now, everyone on the ground."

As boys knelt and flopped their bodies onto the dirt, Michael stepped forward with flecks of the church on his fingertips. The sun peeked through the smoke for a moment, but the steeple blocked the rays from reaching him. At that morning's convocation, Father Collins had said, "Remember that the shadow of Saint Rose of Lima always covers you. Everything you do or think is a reflection of your faith and this school."

Michael lay prone and rested his cheek against a clump of dead grass. Pebbles and dull bits of glass poked his body. A thick root dug into his ribs. In the distance, a streetcar clanged and cattle lowed. Girls beat the sidewalk with their jump ropes.

"Halligan," Jimmy yelled.

Before Michael realized what his name meant, before he knew to stand, the other boys were on him with knees and fists and feet. They thwacked him with their coats and lashed him with their neckties. Michael curled up on his side until Jimmy yelled, "Stop!" With a few final slaps and kicks, the boys retreated. Michael rolled onto his stomach as laughter settled around him. His classmates lay nearby.

"Burns."

Michael stood and watched the boys chase Patrick Burns around the outside of the lot. They clawed at his arms, threw rocks and sticks. Michael took timid steps one way and then another, giddy at the hunt but unsure of where to run. When Burns tripped and fell, the boys pounced on him with yelps of pleasure. Michael lingered behind the mob, jittery to join them. Jimmy shouted for them to stop. As the boys backed away, Michael stepped forward. He swung his jacket and hit Burns on the head with it, kicked him in the back, and then scurried to the other side of the lot.

Michael lay on the ground. His body was sore, stinging in spots, but his blood thumped at the thought of another victim. He shivered with anticipation.

"Halligan," Jimmy yelled.

Michael stood but was immediately knocked down. Again, the boys were upon him with angry glee. Michael tried to stand and fight back, but the boys pushed him to the dirt. Someone kicked his stomach, and his breath left him.

Jimmy shouted for them to stop and then said with a laugh, "Sorry, Halligan. I forgot I already called your name."

The boys lay back on the ground. Michael wheezed and crawled toward the church.

"No quitters, Halligan," Richard yelled.

Michael stopped crawling and rested on his hands and knees, gasping for air. His breathing had nearly become steady when Jimmy screamed, "Halligan!"

The boys cheered and jumped on Michael.

"Halligan," Jimmy repeated.

Michael curled up on his side. He covered his head and bent his knees against his chest.

"Halligan," Richard yelled.

A belt struck Michael's back, a fist punched his leg, and soon all the individual pains became one. He curled up as tightly as a pill bug, protecting the math test in his pants pocket. He thought of his mother still in her robe that morning, her skin the scent of Gold Dust soap, and gradually he felt the boys being pulled off him by Moon Mullins, by Captain Easy, by Smilin' Jack.

"Break it up. Break it up, now."

His classmates flew through the air and crashed into the church, where they crumpled and fell dead to the ground. When he no longer felt anyone on top of him, Michael opened his eyes and unfurled his body. He reached into his pocket and felt the paper there. His classmates sprinted around the dusty lot, howling with joy. Father Collins lumbered this way and that on his bum leg, slashing his meaty hands through the air. He grasped at the students, but they were too quick for him to catch. When the boys had fled, Father Collins grabbed Michael's arm and pulled him to his feet.

"Look at you, Halligan. You're a mess." Father Collins brushed dirt and dead leaves from Michael. "Is this what you boys call fun?"

Michael shook his head. He was desperate for air.

Father Collins rested his hand on Michael's shoulder. "You all right, Halligan?"

Michael nodded. His back and head throbbed. He could practically feel new bruises forming.

"You need some toughening up." Father Collins mussed Michael's hair. "You're lucky to get away with just a few scrapes."

"Yes, Father."

The priest's face stiffened and eyes narrowed. "Now, whose idea was all of this?"

Michael shrugged. He wanted to build a huge world all his own and hide in a cave in the middle of it.

"You don't know?"

"No."

"Was it O'Brien? Was it Williams?"

Michael shook his head. "May I go now, Father?"

The priest straightened his black robe and nodded. "You can go," he said, "but I don't want to see any more of these games ever again. Is that clear?"

"Yes, Father."

"You can save yourself a lot of trouble by avoiding trouble."

With his satchel over his shoulder and his cap on his head, Michael trudged west on 47th Street past a five-and-dime, past a pharmacy, past poor men selling fruit and scraps of fabric. He crossed Ashland, Marshfield, Paulina. At Hermitage, he reached into his pants pocket and pulled out the test: *Excellent—100%!* He slipped the test back into his pocket and, as he did most days, crossed Damen Avenue to the city dump. Scraps of paper tumbled across muddy earth littered with every imaginable kind of trash. Rats scurried over and under the garbage. Flies swarmed low to the ground. The smell was awful, but Michael was used to it. Across the plain were shadowy figures of children and adults foraging through the waste.

He kicked bottles and cans. Nehi. Yoo-hoo. Atlas Prager. He did his best to avoid turds and dead pets, and he scanned the ground for baseball cards, books, and toys. He passed a gypsy woman and girl—probably mother and daughter—who bent down and examined snatches of cloth and chunks of wood. Despite the day's warmth, they wore scarves around their heads and shawls over their shoulders. Well beyond them, men with kerchiefs tied around their faces in the style of Old West bandits shoveled the remains of animals into the meatpackers' fire. The smoke from the flames rose as a gleaming white tower a hundred stories high, its windowless exterior made of marble. Airplanes, zeppelins, and spaceships circled its apex, upon which sat a red neon sign flashing Michael's name. More buildings appeared: a planetarium with an enormous telescope emerging from its gold dome, an all-glass laboratory with a landing deck on its roof, a gray metallic apartment house shaped like a robotic man, a black steel prison set on stilts so high, no convict could ever escape. A fountain shot water into the clouds. Michael looked at the ground, where a floor of ivory tiles stretched as far as he could see. His eyes followed the tiles until he noticed a tiny white hand sticking out from the earth. The tiles turned into mud and trash. He approached the hand, which was slightly curled, as though reaching for the hand that had recently let it go. With the discarded sole of a shoe, he dug into the dirt until he was able to pull out a porcelain doll: a little, pink-cheeked girl in a lacy white dress that was torn and badly soiled. One of its arms was missing, and its eyes were clogged with clay. Blond hair swirled from its head.

"Whatcha got there, son?" someone asked.

When Michael looked up, he saw a gangly man dressed in a pin-striped suit that was short in the sleeve and leg. His face was tanned a rich red color that reminded Michael of bricks; his silver hair was as wild as the branches of a half-dead tree. A fat man stood nearby with his hand on the handle of a wicker baby carriage. The gypsy mother and daughter came over to see what Michael had found.

When the scavenger asked if he could see the doll, Michael refused. The man took a dime from his pocket and held it up.

"I'll pay you for it."

The coin was dull and dirty, and Michael thought it might be counterfeit. But then he considered that ten cents would buy a second book to go along with *Trouble in the City of Dreams*, which his mother had promised him.

Michael felt something graze his arm and saw the gypsy girl's fingers making their way toward the doll. He lifted the doll away from her, but she kept reaching and soon took hold of its leg. When she smiled, Michael let her take the toy. She brushed dirt from the dress and adjusted the curls. After whispering to the girl, who shook her head and held her prize tightly, the woman grabbed the porcelain neck and lifted the doll higher and higher until the girl had to let go. The girl cried as the woman handed the doll to the scavenger.

The man scrutinized the doll from all angles, tried to scrape the clay from its eyes. He put the dime back in his pocket and took out a penny, which he tossed onto the ground near the woman.

"The price just dropped."

The woman cursed in words Michael didn't understand and spat at the man, who threw the doll to his partner. The fat man put the toy into the baby carriage with their other junk, and the two of them pushed onward. Michael watched the girl cry, her sobs coming from deep inside her. He wanted to dig up a better doll for her and put an end to her grief, though part of him loved her tears; he imagined she might sob and heave so hard that she'd grow wings or fangs or start to glow. Her mother grabbed her by the arm and led her away. As Michael strode north, he glanced back to see the woman and girl wandering through the dump, silhouetted against the flames of the meatpackers' fire.

Michael crossed Bubbly Creek, heading toward home. He pictured the book's cover—a rocket ship racing from a filthy city to a pristine one—and grew excited trying to imagine what comic-strip characters appeared in the adventure. Buck Rogers, of course. But who else? Dick Tracy? Brick Bradford? Joe Palooka? He had often envisioned various characters together, but had never seen it happen in the newspaper. He pictured himself reading the story at night, his mother's warm body beside his, her fingers stroking his hair. He would deliberately flub a few words as he always did, just so she would praise him when he said them correctly a few pages later. The pain from Jimmy Cross's game softened inside him. As he walked, he made swimming motions with his arms, imagining himself sinking into Bubbly Creek, but then rising and rising, breaking through the murky surface, through brown smoke, and into the clean blue sky. He flew above the smoke, above everything, but when he turned the corner onto 36th Street, he let himself descend to the sidewalk.

He pulled the test from his pocket and imagined his mother giving him a hug and saying how much she loved him. Michael smoothed the paper against his chest and cocked his cap. Polish kids wrestled and jumped rope in their yards. He swaggered by them and then hurried up the steps of his home. His mother would be cleaning or cooking, and when she asked how school was, he would hold out the test. Quietly, he opened the front door and entered the house. Grinning at his own stealth, he hung his cap and satchel on the coat rack. He listened for noises but heard nothing. With the test behind his back, he tiptoed down the hall but stopped when he heard a moan, followed by whispers coming from his parents' bedroom. He frowned. There was another moan and then a sharp cry. It had to be Aunt Mae. She was always complaining about something. He put the test in his back pocket and approached the bedroom's half-open door. The whispers grew louder. Michael heard a man's voice. He pushed the door open a few more inches and peeked into the room.

His mother lay motionless in bed, hair damp and swirled across the pillow, eyes wide and fixed on the ceiling. Dr. Shelley sat on the edge of the bed; beside him was a black leather bag. He unrolled his sleeves, took cuff links from his chest pocket, and affixed them to his shirt. Red-stained towels were bunched in a bucket on the floor.

"We need to get Paddy and Father Collins here," the doctor said.

Aunt Mae stood in the corner, wearing a gray dress, one hand flat against her stomach, the other rubbing the back of her neck. Against the beige wallpaper, in the dim light of afternoon, she was nearly invisible. Her eyes met Michael's. In a startled voice she called out Jesus' name and then his.

On the stoop, Aunt Mae explained that his mother was ill and needed time to rest. Michael understood this, remembered that she'd stayed in her robe this morning, which she did only when she was sick. Aunt Mae rested her hand on Michael's head and told him it might be best if he stayed outside until his father got home from work.

"I have something important to tell her," Michael said.

"It'll have to wait."

He stared at the splashes of red on his aunt's dress. He needed his mother to know about the test. His good news would help her recover.

"We're supposed to buy a book."

"What?"

"A book with Buck Rogers and others in it. I need to read it with her."

"What are you talking about, Michael? I don't understand what you're saying."

Michael showed Aunt Mae his test and explained the bargain his mother and he had struck: she'd promised to buy him the book he'd lost at the World's Fair as long as he did well on his next test. Aunt Mae took a deep breath and asked, "How much is it?"

After Michael told her the price, Aunt Mae reached into the pocket of her dress with a shaky hand and pulled out two nickels, which she placed in his palm. Her fingernails and knuckles were dark red. Her fingertips were sticky.

As he walked to the store, Michael remembered waking late one summer night to the sound of excited words somewhere in the house. At first he had tried to fall back asleep, but then, hearing Uncle Red's voice, he had risen from his bed and wandered into the living room, where his mother and father sat in their pajamas, and Red stood in an olive-green shirt and cream-colored pants. The air was sweltering and stagnant.

"Hey, Michael," said his uncle. "Look at this."

"Red, don't," Michael's mother said.

Michael's father laughed, and Red approached with one hand behind his back, the other fanning himself with his hat. Towering and grinning in front of Michael, he pulled a handkerchief from behind his back. It was mostly red, and rather than hanging loosely, it appeared stiff and wrinkled.

"Know what this is?"

Michael shook his head.

"John Dillinger's blood," Red said. "They killed him tonight. I was there right after it happened. His blood was still in the alley, so I dipped this in it. Wanna touch it?"

"Red, stop."

"Come on, Elizabeth," his father said. "This is historical."

Michael had heard about Dillinger on the radio and seen his face in newspapers and newsreels. He'd had his fingerprints erased and his face altered so nobody would recognize him. So how did everyone know he was dead, then? Maybe it was just some other man who had been killed. Michael reached out, took the handkerchief in his hand, and held the scratchy, hardened fabric. Before he left, Red snipped off two squares from the handkerchief, each the size of a postage stamp. He handed one to Michael's father and one to Michael, who placed his safely in the bottom of his underwear drawer.

As Michael turned up Ashland, he tried to imagine his comic-strip friends around him, but they kept dissolving into nothing. *That was blood*, Dick Tracy whispered in his head.

"Maybe she just cut herself," Michael whispered back.

Maybe. Maybe not.

Michael walked down an aisle of household cleaners, canned food, and pop bottles, wanting to show everyone his nickels. He made his way past greeting cards and magazines to a small rack of books. Everybody, he thought, had a few gallons of blood inside them. It was nothing to lose a little. At the bottom of the rack was a shelf of Big Little Books like the one he'd seen at the Century of Progress. He perused the titles and colorful covers. *Flash Gordon on the Planet Mongo* looked good, with Flash delivering an uppercut to Doctor Zarkov. Then there was *Chester Gump at Silver Creek*

Ranch, but Michael wasn't wild about Westerns. Book by book he proceeded until, finally, he reached the last one: *Buck Rogers in the City Below the Sea*. On the cover, Buck Rogers and his cohort, Wilma Deering, swam or fell or floated in water. Buck wore a green suit, and Wilma wore red. Confused, Michael went through the books again; he had never considered that *Trouble in the City of Dreams* wouldn't be here. When he reached *Buck Rogers in the City Below the Sea* again, he grabbed it, trying not to feel disappointed.

A few minutes later, he sat in the shaded gangway between his family's house and the neighbor's, below the open window of his parents' room. He hoped Aunt Mae had told his mother about his test. With his back against his house, he held the thick book in his hands and told himself that maybe this one was better than *Trouble in the City of Dreams*. Faint, indecipherable words came from the window above him.

It might have been him. Dick Tracy was still in his head, saying things he shouldn't have been saying. *He killed that bum, you know.*

"He wasn't here."

Maybe he found out about Eddie. Maybe he stabbed her and ran away.

"Stop it," Michael said. "You're wrong."

The voices above him grew louder. He still couldn't make out the words, but he recognized Aunt Mae's voice, and Father Collins's voice, and then his father's. Michael looked at his book. Buck Rogers seemed confused and in danger, but more than anything he appeared brave. Father Collins prayed in Latin. The words fell onto Michael, who held the book tightly, unable to open it. His mother would be overjoyed about the test, and she would love reading with him. He wouldn't even flub any words. He wouldn't do anything to make her feel worse. The back door opened and slammed shut, and Michael's father appeared at the far end of the gangway, his chest heaving, air huffing through his nostrils. He stormed back and forth, then punched himself in the temple. Then again. After several blows, he lowered his hands, closed his eyes, and tensed up, as though trying to make himself either explode or not explode—Michael couldn't tell which. After about a minute, he opened his eyes and turned toward Michael. Crying and worried whispers hovered in the air. His father had done nothing, Michael thought, nothing at all. She was just sick. Tomorrow she would be well. The book in his hands had practically become a part of him.

His father breathed hard, wiped sweat from his face. He dropped his arms to his sides and sat about ten feet away from Michael. He studied his hands and then glanced at Michael, who looked down at Buck Rogers and Wilma Deering.

"Michael," his father said.

"She's just a little sick."

"No."

"She'll be fine."

"No, Michael. She won't."

"She will."

His father banged the back of his head against the wall. "Mae," he shouted, "can you come out here and help me?"

Buck and Wilma seemed lost and helpless, and Michael wondered how they breathed underwater. He wished he was swimming in Bubbly Creek, plummeting through that awful water, but then rising into the sky, above the smoke and clouds, as high as he could go. Aunt Mae pressed him to her chest, held his face to her heartbeat. Michael closed his eyes. He felt himself falling, sprawling, sinking underwater. Fish darted by and plants swayed in the gentle current. He felt alone, afraid to breathe, until Buck and Wilma swam his way. They smiled, bubbles rising from their mouths, and they extended their hands to him. Michael reached out for them, and the book fell from his fingers.

9

MICHAEL'S MOTHER LAY IN A CASKET IN THE LIVING ROOM, IN THE SPOT where the sofa usually sat. Wooden chairs Michael had never seen before formed a crescent around her body, and a new crucifix hung crooked on the wall. In the arched entryway of the room, Aunt Mae crouched beside him.

"Pray for God to forgive her sins," she whispered. "Ask Him to accept her into heaven."

Michael stepped forward, fidgeting with the cuffs of his suit coat and watching the shiny black shoes Aunt Mae had brought him that morning. At the coffin, he saw that his mother's closed lips resembled a seam. Her face was dry and pale with some kind of white powder. *Flour on the kitchen counter*, Michael thought; *flour on bread dough*. He knelt on the padded kneeler and rested his folded hands against the casket. A few strands of his mother's hair quivered above the coffin's edge. Michael observed their slight movement and thought for a moment that she would sit up and smile at him. He made the sign of the cross—forehead, heart, shoulder, shoulder— and closed his eyes. *Hail Mary, full of grace*, he said in his head, *the Lord is with thee. Blessed art thou amongst women and blessed is the fruit of thy womb, Jesus.* He stopped praying. The words did not sound right. *Hail Mary, full of grace, the Lord is with thee. Blessed art thou...Hail Mary, Mother of God...*He'd recited the prayer thousands of times, but now, when he needed it to work, when he needed it to bring his mother back, the words were gone. He pictured Dick Tracy and Buck Rogers, thinking that if he imagined them well enough, they would appear for real in this world, or he would be transported to theirs. He opened his eyes. Nothing had changed.

An hour later, Michael walked down the hallway, across a borrowed rug that hid the blood stains. Adults swirled around him, told him how sorry they were, crouched and gave him hugs. They touched his head, his shoulders, his back, and when they'd finished touching him, he felt the ghosts of their hands upon him. He shut the door to his bedroom, knelt on the bed, and examined the funnies his mother had put up only a few days earlier. He saw how odd and unrealistic the characters were. Harold Teen's arms and legs were far too long for his body. Little Orphan Annie's eyes were nothing but full moons.

"Dead," he said as he ran his hands over the newspaper, then touched a piece of tape that bore a portion of his mother's inky fingerprint. "Dead."

There was a knock at the door. Uncle Red peeked into the room and asked if he could come in.

Michael nodded and sat on the edge of the bed. Red closed the door and sat next to him. He wore a black suit, not his usual white or tan, and in his hands was a metal fire engine.

"It's a gift," he said. He handed the toy to Michael, who raised and lowered the ladder and spun the wheels. Red turned his black hat over in his hands.

That evening, more hands made their way to Michael. It seemed that everyone needed to touch him. Words and laughter and cigarette smoke and perfume and crying and plates of food and rattling cups and saucers passed over him and curved around the corners of his family's home, which was cramped with bodies and warm breath. Half-eaten sandwiches sat on plates. Half-eaten cookies. Crumbs. Lipstick stained the lips of teacups like unwanted kisses. Women he didn't know stirred soup and scrubbed dishes. Men stopped by, shook his father's hand, and then left quickly. Michael sat on a sofa in the corner of the living room, his Buck Rogers book in his lap, and watched these men shake his father's hand and crack their knuckles behind their backs. He wondered if they went around the city killing people at night. He searched their expressions and gestures to see what secret messages they were passing—to see what they knew about his mother. He looked down at his book. *Albinos have appeared suddenly in several cities,* said Doctor Digby, who had a small pointed beard and tiny round glasses like a Russian in a movie. *But who they were and where they came from we didn't know.* Buck Rogers and Wilma Deering listened intently. Michael read the words slowly, understanding most, but not all. *We caught an albino girl and brought her here for questioning—but she refused to talk.* An old woman sat next to Michael. She pressed her scratchy cheek to his. "If there's anything we can do for you, just say the word." The albino girl looked like a beaten-up Jean Harlow. Doctor Digby and another man tied her to a chair in front of a small movie screen. They placed a lamp next to her head. *My assistant and I placed the girl in the mentaloscope and gave her a sleep ray. By tuning to her cerebral frequencies we were able to project her memory pictures on a screen.* Light from the lamp shone through the girl's skull and onto a wall, where it projected the image of a futuristic city of tall, sparkling towers. A man pinched Michael's ear. "Hang in there, kid." Michael didn't look up to see who it was. Maybe it was Dick Tracy; maybe it was a criminal. Projected next were beautiful blond women swimming underwater. They looked peaceful. "We love you, Michael." They seemed contented. "Get a good night's sleep." Doctor Digby threw the girl into a tank of water to see if she would breathe or drown. She breathed.

Soon everyone was gone except Aunt Mae and his father, who were in the kitchen. A plate shattered. "Dead," Michael whispered. "You knew about this, didn't you?" his father yelled. "Paddy, please," said Aunt Mae, but his father shouted her down. "You knew, and you tried to hide it." Michael stared at the book and told himself that nothing was happening and nothing had happened. There was a slap, then another. "Get out of my fucking house." Nothing was happening. Nothing would happen. The girl leaped from the laboratory and into the ocean to freedom. Aunt Mae ran weeping out the front door.

That night Michael lay awake in his bed and listened as his father paced the hallway, then unlatched and lifted the coffin lid. A minute later, the lid lowered and shut, and Michael heard more pacing. When his bedroom door opened, he held his breath and pretended to be dead.

"You awake, kiddo?" his father whispered.

He didn't kill her, Michael thought. It had been because of a miscarriage, which Father Collins had explained somewhat to him.

"Michael?"

The bed creaked as his father sat and then lay beside him. *Dead*, Michael thought.

"I want to tell you something, kiddo."

Michael let his breath slowly leave his body. He wondered why his father couldn't have died instead of his mother. Or why Michael himself couldn't have died with her. *Dead*. He considered his characters on his wall, but couldn't imagine how they could ever help him.

His father started to say something, but what came out was a choked sound. Michael released a little more breath, and then quietly inhaled through his nose. His father cleared his throat and sniffed. Two minutes passed, and neither of them spoke. Then, without a word, his father got up and walked out of the bedroom, then through the kitchen and out the back door.

Michael lay awake with his eyes closed. He held his breath, thinking he could die slowly and comfortably this way. He pictured the funnies on his wall and his mother in the living room, and he felt for a moment that he was dying. But soon dying became a struggle, and Michael, despite his best intentions and efforts, opened his mouth with a desperate gasp and sucked down as much air as he could.

THE WAY THINGS WORK
1940–1945

1

MICHAEL SAT AT THE KITCHEN TABLE WITH HIS EYES CLOSED, LISTENING as his father struck a match, then another. He smelled melting wax and chocolate frosting.

"All right," his father said. "Open 'em."

Michael opened his eyes and adjusted his glasses. In the glow of candle flames, his father set down a small square cake decorated with a message: *Happy 14th Birthday!* Michael frowned. He was thirteen today.

"Happy birthday and all that crap," his father said. "Make a wish."

Michael took a deep breath and blew out all but one of the candles.

"Almost got your wish, kiddo. Only missed one."

"No, I didn't."

His father grabbed two forks from the drawer and tossed them onto the table. "Don't be a jackass," he said, and then blew out the last candle.

Michael stuck his fork into one side of the cake. Sitting opposite him, his father did the same. When they had eaten nearly the entire thing, Michael realized he'd forgotten to make a wish. But since the things he wanted—to have his father disappear and his mother return, and to be someone other than himself—would never come true, there was no sense bothering with wishes.

"I've got an idea." His father aimed his fork at him. "Why don't you come with me to the White Crow tonight? No drinking, of course, but at least you'll get a taste of what you have to look forward to when you're older."

Michael shrugged.

His father shrugged mockingly in response. "You're fourteen. What else you gonna do? Sit around and read your little kiddie books all night?"

"I'm thirteen."

"What?"

"I'm thirteen."

"Come on, don't give me that bull." His father scooped up the last piece of cake and jabbed it into his mouth. "I'm your old man," he said as he chewed, his teeth and gums brown with chocolate. "I oughta know."

Michael and his father had moved to La Grange three weeks after the funeral, making the trip bundled up in a cold truck, hardly speaking along the way. Nothing of his mother accompanied them: no hairpins, no clothing, no photographs. Even her scent had been left behind.

"Here it is," Michael's father said as they rumbled over train tracks and pulled into the parking lot of a corner gas station. "Home sweet home."

Two shiny pumps stood in front of the green wooden building, which had red garage doors and a sign above them: UNION AUTO REPAIR & GAS.

"Where's our house?"

"In there," his father said, as he pointed at Union Auto.

Their tiny two-bedroom apartment in the back of the station had low ceilings and poor water pressure, and within less than a month, it reeked of gasoline and motor oil. Although the new quarters were cramped, La Grange was expansive in an entirely new way to Michael. The drugstores and markets had broad aisles and an overwhelming assortment of goods, including rack after rack of Big Little Books. The residential streets were wide, every tree towered, and even the smallest lawns were vast. Daytime was brighter than in Chicago, and night's darkness was deeper. When snow fell, it piled higher, stayed white longer.

Michael enrolled at St. Francis Xavier School, where he was not so much bullied as ignored, and he took on his mother's chores of cleaning the house and washing dishes. His father fixed meals, which usually consisted of sandwiches and canned soup, and most nights he worked late repairing automobiles. Every few days he exchanged briefcases and canvas bags with men sent by Rabbit Dunne.

"You know how to tie a tie?" his father asked after they had been in La Grange a month. He stood in front of the bathroom mirror, getting ready to leave for the night.

Standing in the doorway, Michael shook his head. He had worn only his clip-on since his mother's death.

"Your mother used to do that for you? For school?"

"Yeah."

"Well, she's not around anymore." His father slid the knot of his tie up to his Adam's apple. A cigarette jutted from the corner of his mouth. "So, you know what that means?"

Michael shook his head. Since his mother's death, he had become fascinated and a little frightened by how his father seemed to know what to do at any given moment, and by how fearless he was.

"Think." His father smoothed down his tie, removed the cigarette from his mouth, and flicked ash into the sink. "God gave you a brain to use, so use it."

Michael thought he knew what to say, but he wasn't certain. "It means I have to do it myself?" he asked.

"Are you asking me or telling me?"

"Telling?"

"Then tell me. Don't ask me."

"It means I have to do it myself."

"Bingo." Cigarette wedged between his lips, his father undid his tie and waved Michael toward him. "Watch me," he said, "because I'm only gonna show you once."

His father adjusted his tie until the thick end hung lower than the thin end. He slowly flipped and folded the ends over each other to form a knot, which he then tightened and straightened.

"You still got your own ties, right?"

Michael nodded.

"While I'm gone tonight, I want you to practice. When I get back, you should know how to do it yourself."

On his own in the apartment, Michael struggled to replicate his father's moves. He tossed one end of the necktie over the other, and the knot fell apart in his hands. He fumbled with the fabric and tangled it up into messy bows. Since the move, his father had shown him how to patch a tire and prepare a grilled cheese sandwich, and he had left him alone so frequently at night that Michael no longer cried upon hearing unexpected sounds. Eventually, almost miraculously, Michael perfected the movements. He smiled at himself in the mirror and raised and lowered the knot. He found his father's shaving kit and dabbed his face with the dry brush. He ran the dull end of the safety razor over his cheeks, chin, and neck, and then patted his face with a towel.

Shortly before dawn, his father came home drunk, stumbled past him, and flopped forward onto his bed. Standing in the doorway with the tie around his neck, giddy and nearly sick from lack of sleep, Michael watched his father, whose face was pressed into the pillow, a vein in his forehead throbbing. After a minute, his father opened his right eye and stared across the room at him.

"What is it?" he muttered.

Michael pointed to the tie around his neck. He couldn't keep from grinning.

"Yeah, so?"

"I tied it myself."

"So, what do you want?" His father closed his eye and wrapped his arms around his pillow. "A medal?"

By his thirteenth birthday, Michael had mastered the four-in-hand and the Windsor knot, and as he and his father walked from the car to the White Crow, his striped tie hung neat and straight. In his jacket pocket was *Tom Beatty, Ace of the Service, and the Big Brain Gang.*

Outside, the bar was little more than a cinder-block cube with a Hamm's beer sign flickering in the window. Inside, it was smoky, dark, and dank, crowded with petty hoods and ladies of the evening who had seen too many nights. A mahogany bar ran along the right side of the room, and on the left was a tabletop drum made of crisscrossing metal, like a miniature version of a cage that acrobats might scamper atop. Beside the drum was a table of tough-looking old women smoking cigarettes; in front of them were stacks of paper. As he stood beside his father just inside the entrance, Michael surveyed the room and imagined he was Mike Steele, special agent—a character he'd come up with during a daydream.

"Hey, everybody," his father shouted. Only a few people turned his way. "This is my son's fourteenth birthday. We're celebrating here tonight."

A woman winked at Michael, and an old boozer at the end of the bar raised his glass in a halfhearted salute. Mike Steele would have sized up the place quickly. He would have known where the money was stashed and who was carrying a gun, who was in charge and who knew the score. *This joint is dirtier than the city dump*, he would have said. *It's more crooked than a hockey stick.* Michael wondered briefly what his mother would have made of this place and his presence here, but then, as he'd forced himself to do countless times in the past six years, he stopped thinking about her.

Michael and his father walked to the far end of the bar and joined a group of men, who bought Michael a ginger ale and wished him happy birthday.

"Ask him some kind of math question," his father said.

"What the hell are you talking about?" one of the men asked.

"Ask him a math question. Like, what's two hundred and something times sixty-three?"

"Why?"

"Just ask him a goddamn question."

"All right, what's 519 times thirty-one?"

Michael closed his eyes and pictured white numbers against a black background. He set up the equation and quickly did the math, dropping a nine, one, and five, then a seven, five, and fifteen. As he added up the numbers, he wondered why the man had picked something so easy, and he thought about giving a wrong answer just to embarrass his father.

He opened his eyes. "Sixteen thousand eighty-nine," he said.

The men glanced at each other.

"Is he right?"

"The hell if I know."

A man with a lizard face grabbed a pen and notepad from his chest pocket and scribbled up the math. The group passed around the paper and confirmed the answer, then peppered Michael with equations, all of which he quickly solved. They slapped his back and called him a genius. Within a few minutes, however, they grew bored and moved on to discussions of baseball and horse racing, Nazis and cops. Before Michael knew what was happening, his father and a burly man were preparing to arm-wrestle at a table. They clasped their right hands, set their left arms behind their backs, and bent their knees. The lizard yelled, "Ready, set, go." After half a minute of struggle, Michael's father slammed his opponent's hand to the table. The men cheered, and the loser reluctantly ordered a round.

A buxom woman with a gap between her front teeth approached, and the group widened its circle for her. "Did I hear right?" she asked, grinning drunkenly at Michael. "Is today this handsome young gentleman's birthday?"

The men laughed and nudged Michael.

"Want a present you'll never forget?" one of them asked.

"If he takes after his old man," Michael's father said, "she'll be the one who won't forget it."

The men whooped and laughed. Michael felt terrified, not sure what was happening but certain he didn't like it.

The burly man pulled out his wallet. "I'll pitch in a buck," he said.

The others eagerly opened their wallets and pulled out dollar bills.

"Cut it out," Michael's father said. "He's just a goddamn kid."

He grabbed Michael by the arm and steered him to the other end of the bar. They sat there together for ten minutes, Michael with his ginger ale, his father with a beer, both restless and hardly talking. Finally his father said, "Look, I'm gonna be here awhile, so it's up to you whether you want to stick around or leave. You know the way home, right? It's only about three miles."

"I know the way."

"Great." Michael's father stood and drummed the bar with his knuckles.

"Happy birthday, kiddo."

Relieved to be alone, Michael took out his Big Little Book, which was only a little taller and wider than his palm, yet was so thick, he couldn't quite engulf it in his grasp. With the modest allowance his father gave him, he bought a new title every week or two. He opened the book in his lap and hovered over it, as though it were a guarded secret. As always, he focused so intently on the words on the left page and pictures on the right that he felt himself vanish from the world.

There was a clanging noise, like ball bearings being poured into a tin can. Michael turned toward the sound. A sweaty man cranked the handle of the metal drum for a few seconds. Then he opened a small hatch on the side and pulled out a ball. "Seventeen," he shouted. Michael knew that the numbers runners came by each Saturday with bags of cash and the lists of people playing that week, and he knew that occasionally someone won some money, but he'd never known how or where the numbers were chosen. The man closed the hatch and cranked the handle. The metallic slosh and drop began again and then ended. He pulled out another ball and called out the number. When he'd finished with all five numbers, the tough old ladies diligently flipped through their sheets of paper and crossed the losers off their lists.

Michael returned to the book in his lap, trying to ignore the laughter and cigarette smoke swirling in the air, the drink somebody spilled on his leg, the birthday wishes slurred his way. He felt a finger poke his shoulder, then poke it again and again. Michael looked to his left and saw a bald man leaning toward him.

"You're Paddy Halligan's kid, huh?" The man rested his elbow on the bar for balance. Slouched against him was a lazy-eyed redhead. "How old are you?"

"Fourteen," Michael lied.

"Fourteen?" The man turned to the woman. "That's old enough, ain't it? Why don't you show him the ropes?"

The woman looked with disgust at the man. Michael felt disgusted, too—at the man and at his father, and at the woman for being in a place like this.

"What do you say, kid? It's on me."

Michael stared down at his book. Mike Steele would have knocked out the man with one well-placed punch and said to the woman, *You oughta keep better company.*

The man poked Michael's shoulder.

"What's the matter? You scared?"

"Leave him alone, Jim."

Again he poked. "I guess being a coward runs in your family." He had onions and beer on his breath. Approximately half his teeth were missing. "Like father, like son, huh?"

Michael glanced across the room. His father grabbed the gap-toothed woman by the wrist and led her stumbling and giggling through a door beside the bar.

"Not a real man in the family."

"Cut it out, Jim."

The man quickly turned to the woman. "Don't tell me to cut it out. I'll cut *you* out. I'll cut you out, and then where will you be, huh? Back on the street, that's where."

The woman shouted at the man, the man shouted at the woman, and when she ran off crying, he turned his back to Michael and drank. Head down, Michael tried to read but soon grew distracted by the wallet sticking out of the man's back pocket. Michael read a little, then glanced at the wallet; read, then glanced again. He slipped the book into his jacket pocket and cased the place. He felt elated, larger than himself. No one was watching. *Crooks deserve their fate*, Mike Steele would have said. *Justice sets its own rules.*

Slowly, as casually as he could, Michael inched his hand toward the man, then quickly plucked the wallet from the pocket. But his fingers fumbled, and the wallet fell. As he reached for it, he bumped into the man, who spun toward him and yelled, "You got a problem?"

The man's eyes and breath were on him, and the wallet was on the floor, but Michael was no longer himself. He was Mike Steele, special agent.

"No," he said with a smirk. "I don't have a problem."

The man laughed and turned away. Michael stepped down from the barstool, crouched, and picked up the wallet. He slipped it into his pocket and slinked through the crowd toward the exit.

A block away from the White Crow, Michael dropped the man's driver's license down a sewer grate. Two blocks after that, he tossed the family photos and union card into a garbage can. By the time he was halfway home, all he had left were the wallet and seven dollars. He stopped beside the forest preserve, pocketed the cash, and hurled the wallet into the trees.

2.

A YEAR LATER, MICHAEL SAT WITH HIS BACK AGAINST ONE OF HIS FATHER'S gas pumps, wearing his blue mechanic uniform and reading *G-Man on the Crime Trail*. The sun was so brilliant that he squinted against the glare to read the words and scan the sketchy drawings: a hand firing a gun, a car taking a corner hard, a run-of-the-mill fistfight. G-Man was certainly no Secret Agent X-9, no Inspector Wade, no Radio Patrol. Eyes on the page, Michael reached into the copper bucket of ice water beside him. He fished out a piece of ice the size and shape of a bullet and popped it into his mouth. The cold rose sharply behind his eyes.

Business was slow, especially for a Saturday. Only two cars had filled up during the morning, and the lone vehicle in the garage was a Plymouth with a busted starter. Since noon, three numbers runners had shown up with their money and lists.

Michael set down his book and stood as a familiar black Ford coasted into the lot and stopped beside the pump. Harold Mason stepped from the car, hiked up his baggy blue pants, and adjusted his gold tie clip. His brown skin glistened with sweat and stuck to his white shirt. Directly above his lip, two thin wedges of hair formed a mustache. He placed his right foot on the car's front bumper and fanned himself with a wide-brimmed white hat. The stone of his pinkie ring glistened like water in a swimming pool.

"Fill 'er up?" Michael asked.

Mason nodded curtly. "Give her a good washing while you're at it."

As Michael pumped gas, Mason stretched and yawned and grabbed a piece of ice from the bucket. He rubbed the ice against his neck and said, "Look here, your old man in today?"

"He should be back about two-thirty."

Michael set the nozzle back on the pump and lifted the hood of Mason's car. His father was usually gone when the runners came; he was no good with numbers and didn't want to look stupid in front of men who were supposed to respect him.

"Well, I'm sure he's got no interest in seeing me. But then again, I've got no interest in seeing him." Mason dipped his hand into the bucket and splashed water on his face. "So it works out well that way."

After checking the oil and belts, Michael closed the hood and retrieved two rags—one dry, one wet—from the garage. On his way back to the car, he saw Mason leaning against the Ford with a mischievous grin. He pointed at Michael with his hat.

"Why is it, do you think, that your old man hates me but loves my money? Not that I'm criticizing, mind you, because I hate lots of people myself—your old man included—but I love their money. It's just that the situation intrigues me, and I was wondering what a boy genius such as yourself thought."

Michael wiped the fog light and imagined he was erasing the condescending smirk from Mason's face. Mike Steele would have known how to handle Mason. He would have pushed him against a wall and commanded, *Don't tell me what to do, boy*. He would have locked him up with the rest of the criminals.

"I thought it was other people's money," Michael said. "Not yours."

"When your old man accuses me of shorting him—which he does every damn week—then he is most definitely talking about *my* money."

"He likes everybody's money," Michael said as he scrubbed. "Doesn't matter whose it is."

"Oh, but it does." Mason crouched near Michael and aimed a finger at him. "Now, back when I was your age, I was a good student like you—memorized whatever mathematical law or theorem they threw at me and tossed it right back at them. But of all those teachers I had, not one ever taught me the most important law in the world, so I had to go make it up myself. I call it Mason's Law—named after yours truly, of course. Know what it says?"

"No."

"Mason's Law holds that the amount you hate a person is equal in intensity to how much you want what he has."

Michael considered this theory, but before he could get very far in his deliberation, Mason tapped his arm.

"A moment ago, I gave you the example of money. But now I'll give you a better one."

Mason rose and smoothed the potential wrinkles from his clothes. Michael stood and started washing the windows.

"What are you," Mason asked, "thirteen?"

"Fourteen," Michael said.

"Kind of little for fourteen, aren't you? Then again, your father's a little man. Little and insignificant." Mason chuckled. "Nonetheless, you are on the cusp, as they say, of manhood, as if manhood were the sort of thing that has a cusp. And believe it or not, and despite all evidence to the contrary, in the very near future, girls—or one or two of the more generous and less discerning ones—are going to be interested in you." He fanned himself with his hat. "What I mean to say is that at some point—and that point might be now for all I know—there will be a man you hate more than anyone else, and he will have something—a girl, let's say—that you want more than anything in the world. And you'll think it's love, so you'll act like a fool. And if you work hard enough at being a fool—which I believe you have within you to do—you might even take his girl away from him. And *that*, that whole experience, would be a prime example of Mason's Law."

Michael had no way to know if Mason was right. All the girls he liked, with the exception of two or three from his middle school, were either movie stars or pinups. So instead, his mind grabbed hold of what Mason had said about money. He considered the cash he'd recently been stealing from his father and thought that Mason might have a point.

"But in pondering Mason's Law, just make sure you don't indulge in the self-deception that the desire you feel is something like love, and thus cancels out your hate. Because chances are that any desire you feel is really just your revenge with good manners."

Michael stepped away from the car and strangled gray water from his rag.

Mason opened his car door and took out a large briefcase. "And that," he said as he slammed the door shut, "is your lesson for today." He grinned and patted his briefcase. "So, you ready for this?"

In the garage, they sat side by side behind the cash register, Harold Mason with a briefcase on his lap, Michael empty-handed. Tools littered the ground. Oil lay pooled in spots, like lakes on a map. Mason took two stacks of paper from his briefcase and handed them to Michael. The first set listed, in alphabetical order, the names of people in Mason's territory who had played during the week. Following each name was the series of five numbers that person had picked. The second set listed people by the lowest number they'd played. Later that night at the White Crow, after the numbers had been drawn from the drum, the old ladies could easily check the lists to determine who had won and what the winners were owed.

Mason took a large paper sack from his briefcase and handed it to Michael. "Before my twenty percent, the total was $570. Since you're the math whiz, why don't you tell me how much you've got there?"

Michael closed his eyes, imagined the equation, and did the math. He opened his eyes. "Four hundred fifty-six dollars."

Mason snapped his fingers and smiled. "Someday I'll stump you. You know that, don't you?"

Michael grinned. He almost said, "Thanks." But in the end, he didn't. He was dealing with a criminal, after all.

"And now I must take my leave, as they say. But you remember what I told you about Mason's Law, and make sure to credit me whenever you use it in conversation."

Mason paid for the gas and tipped Michael a quarter. As he walked away, he called back, "And please be sure to show your old man that my numbers add up."

A few minutes later, Michael placed the lists and money on the small kitchen table where he and his father ate silent meals, and where his father sat alone most nights, drinking scotch and listening to the radio. He tallied the numbers from one set of Mason's pages, then the other. The totals matched. Then, as he had earlier in the day, he picked a number at random and gently erased it, changing a bet from forty to thirty cents. He made the corresponding change on the other sheet and then to the totals. When he had finished his alterations, he took his cut from the money Harold Mason had delivered, bringing his take for the day up to a dollar.

Michael leaned back and smiled. Sixteen weeks in a row. Nearly thirteen dollars. The scheme was foolproof; the odds of the altered bets actually winning were negligible, and even if they did win, his father would blame the runners for the theft. Michael considered Mason's Law and thought that if a dollar was all he wanted, then he didn't hate his father nearly as much as he assumed he did. He frowned at the numbers. There was no reason he couldn't take more. It was illegal money, so no one was entitled to it. He changed a number, skimming a dime from the take. He changed another number. Then more. He trimmed twenty cents from one bet, a quarter from another. When he was done, he had three dollars for the day, which he slipped into his shoes, under the soles of his feet. Michael's heart raced. It was an act of heroism to steal from thieves.

Michael gathered everything Mason had brought and walked downstairs to the cellar. The walls were a mixture of concrete and rocks; stacked against them were old tires, scrap metal, and cans of motor oil. Michael went to the far corner and pulled two stones from the wall to reveal a dark space, about half the size of a dresser drawer, where his father kept both the station's money and whatever he collected for Rabbit Dunne. Michael slipped the cash and tally sheets into the space, replaced the rocks, and then bounded up the stairs as if sprung by the money in his shoes.

Michael sat back down in the sunlight and picked up his book. With *G-Man on the Crime Trail*, his collection of Big Little Books now stood at sixty-seven, and with the three dollars he'd made today, he could buy another twenty. He loved rearranging them: into alphabetical or chronological order, by author's name, by series. Once, he had set them in his bookcase in no order at all, but the chaos had made him fidget. Someday, he felt certain, he would own a complete collection.

As Michael opened his book, he heard his father call to him. Michael kept his eyes down, pretending to read. Within a few seconds, his old man's shadow slid across the page.

"Whatcha reading now?"

Michael held the book up to his father, who cradled a grocery bag at his hip.

"*G-Man on the Crime Trail?*" His father laughed. "The only reason they're on the crime trail is so they can get a cut of the action."

He squatted, fished some ice from the copper bucket, and stood. A year ago, Michael would have told him about Mason reaching into the bucket, but now he simply watched flecks of grime, evidence of his father's hand, swirl in the water.

"You restock the oil cans?"

"Yeah," Michael said.

He squinted up at his father, who rubbed the ice against his scalp, his shaded face nearly eclipsing the sun. Muscles and tendons showed taut in his forearm and neck, and grease darkened the lines of his forehead. His face and arms were coarse and suntanned. His chest was pale past the open collar of his shirt. Michael hated that their uniforms matched.

"Did you clean your room?"

"Yeah."

"That darkie come by this afternoon?"

Michael nodded.

"Did the numbers match up?"

"I checked them twice."

"Well, I'll tell you like I always tell you." His father squatted, grabbed another bit of ice from the bucket, and tossed it into his mouth. "All the runners try to nickel-and-dime us, but Mason's the worst because he thinks he's so damn smart."

His father stood.

"You hungry, kiddo?"

Michael shook his head. If he were Mike Steele, with a pistol behind his book, he'd have a clear shot.

"You need to eat to become a G-Man or Dick Tracy or whoever it is you want to be. You ever see one of those guys look like a twig?"

Michael shrugged.

"Well, I'm gonna make two baloney sandwiches, and if you haven't claimed yours by the time I'm done with mine, then I'm eating yours, too. Got it?"

Michael nodded.

"I said, got it?"

"Got it," Michael said.

As his father ambled toward the garage, Michael pulled out his hand, in the shape of a gun, from behind his book. He closed one eye, took aim at his father's skull, and fired.

Boom, just like that. And his father would drop down dead.

3.

Six weeks and twelve books later, on a muggy July afternoon, Michael again sat with his bucket of ice against the pump, this time reading *Gang Busters Step In*. When a horn honked, he looked up. Uncle Red waved from behind the wheel of his maroon Cadillac, its ragtop down and white leather glistening. Next to him, a young woman grinned and faced the sun with her eyes closed. Michael stood with his book as the car looped around the parking lot and came to a stop beside him.

"Look who grows into more of a man every time I see him," Red said. He wore a white linen suit. His tie and pocket handkerchief matched the peacock feather in the band of his white fedora.

"Now, pay attention, doll," he said as he turned to the woman beside him. "This young man is my nephew, Michael Halligan." He turned to Michael. "And this is Martha. She's a friend of mine."

The woman appeared much younger than Red, and although Michael found it nearly impossible to imagine, she was probably closer in age to him than to his uncle. She had scarlet lips and green eyes, and her tanned face was dusted with freckles. Her black hair hung in loose curls that seemed to wilt in the humidity. She put her bare feet on the seat, hugged her bent legs, and smiled sweetly at Michael, who gawked when the sundress slipped to reveal her naked thighs.

"Nice to meet you," she said.

Michael's eyes returned to Red, who asked, "Whatcha reading now?"

When Michael handed him the book, Red laughed and flipped through the pages.

"A crime story, huh? Wouldn't know a thing about it."

Michael put the nozzle into the gas tank.

Martha rested her chin on Red's shoulder and tapped the book. "I'd rather listen to the radio show than read about it."

"You would, wouldn't you?"

"What's that supposed to mean?"

"I mean, you want it handed to you easy like that. With a book, you have to rely on your imagination. You have to work at it."

Martha took the book from Red and held it firmly in front of her face.

"In the hand of the figure, glinting in the streetlight, was a pistol. It was a .38 caliber automatic," Martha read in the dry tone of a teacher. "A .38 caliber pistol is larger than a .36 caliber, but smaller than a .45. Of course, it is much larger than a .32, which is deadly enough. The caliber of this gun is important. That is why it must be remembered: a .38 caliber automatic." She closed the book and set it on her lap. "That's some pretty tough reading, all right."

"If you're so smart, Shakespeare, how come I never see you with a book?"

"Book, shmook." She waved her hand to dismiss Red's criticism. "Can you hear screeching tires or gunshots? No. It's just words and little pictures."

"You get all those sounds in your mind when you read."

Michael stopped pumping gas. Martha threw her head back and stretched her hands toward the sun. "I guess I just love the action," she said.

Red laughed as Martha turned to grin at him. He patted her thigh, stepped out of the car, and rested his hand on Michael's shoulder.

"Your pop in?"

"You want me to get him for you?"

"No, that's all right. I'll surprise him."

As Red disappeared into the dark garage, Michael washed splattered bugs from the windshield and surreptitiously watched Martha, who sat reading his book. He raised the hood, and as he checked the belts, she stepped out of the Cadillac and said, "So, your old man owns this station?"

"Yeah." Michael wished he was taller, and older, and muscular. He wished he didn't wear glasses.

"It's a nice place." She looked around and nodded as if trying to convince herself of this opinion. "Do you want to own it someday?"

As much as Michael wanted to say something suave, he couldn't think of a thing worth mentioning, and so he simply shrugged.

"How old are you?"

"Fifteen," Michael lied.

"Fifteen! Well, then, you must be dating girls."

A grin galumphed across Michael's face, and he felt the first pulse of an erection. He wondered if she was interested in him. Was this how it happened?

"I bet all the girls are crazy about you, and you don't even know it. That's always the way it is with you quiet ones."

Michael giggled, shook his head, and then slammed down the hood of the car. Martha brushed sagging curls from her forehead.

"Do you have anything cold to drink, Michael? I'm completely parched."

He thought about his bucket of ice, but water like that was unworthy of her.

"In the kitchen," he said.

"Would you mind getting me a glass?"

Michael hurried into the garage and then the house. When he reached the kitchen door and heard Red and his father talking, he stopped and waited for the right moment to interrupt them.

"He comes around here dressed up like he's going out for a night on the town," his father said. "Like he's head nigger or something."

"I bet."

"I've been itching to bust him good myself."

Michael ran his fingers over the coarse wood of the kitchen door and cursed when a splinter cut into his skin. He squeezed on each side of the white sliver in hopes of removing it.

"Well, don't jump to any conclusions," Red said. "I'm not sure what Rabbit's up to with this."

Michael peeked around the door. His father was sitting at the table.

Uncle Red leaned against the counter with his hat in his hand.

"So, you doing good?" Red said.

"Things could be worse. How about you?"

"Can't complain." Red grinned. "Got this little number out in the car you gotta see."

"One of yours?"

"Let's just say I'm breaking her in."

"I bet."

"Not that she needs much breaking in. She was basically semipro to begin with."

Michael's father chuckled. "I'm sure she'll go pro soon enough."

"I'm working on it."

Michael backed away from the doorway, feeling nauseated. He headed toward Martha.

"I thought you'd forgotten about me," she said as he approached her.

He stared at her in disgust. She was just like the whores at the White Crow, only somehow she still managed to look pretty.

"I couldn't get any water." He pointed at the copper bucket. "You can drink out of that if you want."

"I'm not picky, sweetie."

Martha lifted the bucket by its handle and sat down on the running board. She moved her legs apart, pushed her dress down between them, and placed the bucket between her feet. She cupped her hands, reached down, and drew water to her mouth. Michael squeezed his finger, hoping to push out the splinter. His fingertip turned purple.

"Something happen to your finger?" she asked.

Michael shook his head angrily.

Martha stood and walked toward him. "Come on. Let me see."

"It's just a splinter."

"Let's have a look."

She grabbed his hand. At her touch, his erection returned. When she ran her finger over the splinter, he winced.

"It's pretty deep," she said, "but I can get it."

She leaned over the car door and rummaged through her handbag. Her skirt rode up her legs, and her body shook as she searched. Even though he had a general concept about what she did with Uncle Red and other men, Michael wondered about the particulars. Sometimes, and with increasing frequency, he jerked off to newspaper pictures of Jean Arthur, Carole Lombard, and unnamed bathing beauties, but he never knew what to imagine other than the girl standing there with little or no clothing on, touching him, kissing him.

Martha sat down on the running board with a safety pin in her hand. She patted the space next to her. "Come on," she said. "Sit."

Michael sat. Martha held his hand and pricked gently at the splinter with the pin.

"Does that hurt?"

Michael shook his head and casually placed his free forearm over his groin, hoping she wouldn't notice his hard-on. He held his legs together and focused on the jab of the pin.

"My mother hated taking out splinters," Martha said as she concentrated on her work, "so I had to do it for everyone in the family. I kind of liked being in charge like that—except when it came to my father. He worked on the docks and sometimes went barefoot when his boots got soaked. Naturally, he'd come home with deep, deep splinters. And of course, because he worked on his feet all day, his soles were so thick, I could barely get the splinters out. I'd be sweating and sweating, digging in with the needle, and that lousy son of a bitch would be there reading his newspaper and drinking a beer, like I was his little slave."

Martha worked the needle a little deeper into Michael's skin. She furrowed her brow, then ran her tongue across her top lip. When her hair fell into her eyes, she blew it to the side. Michael's penis pressed hard against his forearm, which only added to the stimulation. He told himself that Red had been lying about Martha, the same way some boys at school lied about girls. She was good. She was pure.

"My mother," he said, surprised to find himself speaking, "used to hum a song to me when she'd take splinters out—to distract me."

"Did it work?"

Michael laughed. "Not really."

"What was the song?"

"I don't know the name of it."

"Hum it for me, then. Maybe I know it."

Michael could have hummed the song, and part of him wanted to hum it for Martha so she could hum it back to him, but instead he shook his head and looked at her face, her legs, the shape of her body inside her dress, trying to see all of her in detail, all at once.

"That's okay. You don't have to hum if you don't want to." She stopped, sighed, and wiped her brow. "Damn this splinter."

She hiked up her dress and clamped Michael's hand between her bare knees. She squeezed his finger. Feeling blood rush through his body, he pictured his books in his bookcase. He moved them around in his mind, ordering them one way and then another, but with his hand sweaty against Martha's skin, he was too distracted to achieve the calm that this mental exercise usually provided. He imagined moving his fingers up Martha's thighs, and having her smile and spread her legs.

"Red told me your mother's not around. I'm sorry about that."

"How about your mom?" he asked meekly, his voice cracking. He hoped her mother was dead; it would bind them in a profound way.

"Unfortunately, both my parents are still around. At least, that's the last I heard."

Suddenly, the splinter broke free from Michael's skin. Martha investigated the wound and said, "I think we got it." She washed his finger in the bucket of water and dried it on the hem of her dress. When she kissed the spot where the splinter had been, Michael felt a spasm in his groin. He tried to hold back, but then he let go as he stared at Martha, startled to see her so close to him.

"You okay?" she asked.

Michael nodded dumbly.

"It's just a splinter." She punched his shoulder playfully. "No need to look so surprised."

Michael's underwear felt wet and warm, then quickly grew cold. His body shivered, and his mind careened with the fear that Martha could tell what had happened. He leaned forward and focused on the ground, his arms across his lap.

"So, what do you do for fun?" she asked.

"I read," he said, refusing to face her.

"You're really a book person, aren't you?"

Michael nodded. "I collect them."

"I collect plates myself—nice china plates. I have ten different ones right now, and Red promised to buy me some more. They're so elegant, like something a queen would own, and just having them makes me feel more important than I know I am. I'd never, ever eat off them. I just look at them, and touch them, and think about how lucky I am to own such beautiful things."

Michael glanced at her. When she smiled, he blushed and turned away.

"What are your favorite books?" she asked. "You must have favorites."

He had favorites, but they changed from week to week, and ever since he'd written to Whitman Publishing about his intention to buy one copy of every available title, and a man there named Oswald Knoll had sent him promotional books that weren't available in stores, he had found it increasingly difficult to say which books he loved best.

"Do you have any with Superman or Captain America?"

Michael scowled and shook his head. Freaks like Superman weren't regular people thrown into dangerous worlds, like Buck Rogers or Captain Easy; they were merely gods who had every advantage they needed. It was no wonder they showed up only in cheap, flimsy comic books.

"Don't you like those guys who can fly or look through walls?"

"No," he said indignantly.

"Fine. Sorry I asked." After a few seconds, she said, "What do you do besides collecting books? When I was fifteen, we'd go out dancing and kiss in the alleys, smoke cigarettes, drink, and do stuff like that. What do you do for fun?"

"Nothing."

"Oh, come on." She nudged his side. "Tell me."

He wanted her to leave, or at least stop pestering him with questions. She was the one who'd done this to him. It was all her fault.

"I won't tell anyone," she said. "I promise."

Michael wasn't sure what to say. He had no friends, and the possibility of kissing a girl was as remote as anything he could imagine. When he heard his uncle angrily call his name, he looked up in a panic. Red and his father walked toward him.

"What's going on, Michael?" Red shouted, glaring at him. "I leave for a few minutes, and you start making cozy with my girl?"

Michael wanted to either run away or defend himself, but even standing, especially if the front of his pants was wet, would only make Red angrier.

"It's not like that, I swear," Michael tried to explain, but his father's and Red's laughter cut him off.

Martha mussed his hair and stood, and Red introduced her to Michael's father. As the three of them chatted, Michael stood with the bucket in front of his crotch.

Red wrapped one arm around Michael's shoulder and the other around Martha's.

"Here's the most important advice I can give you about girls, Michael." He pointed with his thumb to Martha. "They'll always get you into trouble. You try to do the right thing, but then you get mixed up with them and everything goes crazy."

Martha rolled her eyes and squirmed free from Red.

"Here's better advice," she said. "Don't assume you ever really know someone, because chances are, you don't."

She reached into the car, grabbed *Gang Busters Step In*, and returned it to Michael. He took it with one hand and continued to hold the bucket with the other.

You oughta keep better company, he wanted to tell her.

Red and Martha climbed into the car. With a tip of the hat from Red and a wink from Martha, they were gone. The convertible drove east and disappeared around a corner. Michael's father headed back to the garage.

Dust hovered in the air and settled slowly back to earth. Michael set down the bucket and saw no dampness on his pants. He sat on the ground and dunked both hands into the water, imagining something of Martha in it. He took a drink, then splashed water on his face. After drying his hands on his shirt, he leaned against the gas pump, opened his book, and found a crisp five-dollar bill stuck in the middle.

4.

AUNT MAE SET A CUP OF TEA AND A GLASS OF GRAPE JUICE ON THE TABLE and sat across from Michael, who eyed his ham sandwich and pickle wedge. It was almost noon. He hadn't eaten all day, but still, he made himself wait. Aunt Mae's sandwiches were skimpy concoctions: white bread, two thin slices of meat, no mayonnaise or mustard. After one of her lunches, on the train ride home, he was usually on the verge of fainting from hunger. He had to make the sandwich last a long time; he had to chew all the flavor he could out of it and then pretend it had filled him.

"So, how's school?" Aunt Mae lit up and set her matchbook and leather cigarette case beside her plate.

"It's fine." Michael took a drink. Aunt Mae had watered down the juice again.

"Are you enjoying it?"

On Michael's first day at Fenwick, a priest had paddled him for loosening his tie on school grounds. On the second day, he'd seen some older boys stuff a freshman into a gym locker. And just this week—only his third at the all-boys high school—he'd had the problem in the swimming pool.

"It's all right," Michael said.

"Doing well in Religion?"

Michael took a small bite of his sandwich and nodded.

Aunt Mae's apartment was a daunting place, the walls covered with sacred hearts, stigmatas, and Christs who watched everything at once. It was dim, too, with only one window overlooking the Oak Park El station and two lamps, which Aunt Mae rarely turned on. Even noontime in the apartment felt like dusk.

"Your mother would have wanted you to do well in Religion." Aunt Mae took a sip of tea and then a drag from her cigarette. An El train clattered into the station. Plates and cutlery rattled on the table. "You have a Saint Thomas Aquinas quality about you," she shouted above the racket.

Michael had no idea what she meant, but her comment terrified him nonetheless. He wanted nothing to do with saints or priests. At Mass that morning, he'd imagined Mike Steele nailing fat Father Walter to a cross.

"You're wise. Like me, you've suffered." Aunt Mae jabbed her cigarette toward him in emphasis, and ash fell into his grape juice. She stood, and as she headed to the kitchen, she said, "You don't talk much, but I can tell you're always thinking."

A few days earlier, Michael had been swimming in the pool with his classmates. He was used to being naked around the other boys now, though he still didn't understand why they were forbidden to wear trunks. As he rolled from crawl to backstroke, Michael was vaguely aware of Father Walter walking along the deck in his white clerical robe, twirling his whistle around his index finger. Michael inhaled and exhaled slowly, and his thoughts drifted to a woman on the bus who licked her thumb before turning the pages of her newspaper, and then to one on the train with the top two buttons of her blouse unfastened. He imagined high school girls, working girls, girls in stores, on sidewalks, and in the middle of the White Crow. He thought of Martha from that afternoon two months ago. She floated beside him in her sundress. The flimsy fabric swirled in the water. Her bare legs kicked. She was a ghost, a dream—vague, invisible, and real. Father Walter blew his whistle and shouted. Michael swam to the wall and realized he had an erection.

"Come here, Halligan," Father Walter shouted.

Without his glasses, Michael saw the priest as a hazy white blob.

"Come here this second, or you'll regret it."

Michael hesitated, trying to ignore the water's caress and turn his mind to the state capitals, the books of the New Testament, the formula for calculating the area of a rhombus.

"Don't try me, Halligan. Don't make this worse for you than it already is."

Michael climbed out of the pool and slouched toward Father Walter, trying to hide his shrinking hard-on with his hands. The boys laughed.

"What's this?" Father Walter asked, pointing at Michael's penis.

The boys laughed louder.

"What were you thinking about?"

"Nothing, Father." Water dripped from Michael's skin and pooled at his feet.

"Nothing?"

"I guess."

"It just happened?"

"Yes, Father."

"A miracle, was it?"

The boys laughed, and Father Walter shouted for them to shut up.

"How about those kids you boss around?" Mike Steele said. "What do you call that?"

"Mike Steele!" Father Walter exclaimed. "It's you!"

"In the flesh." There was a quick, efficient jab, and the priest fell hard.

"Get on the diving board," Father Walter said. "Hands behind your back."

Michael sulked to the end of the diving board like a mutineer walking a plank. He looked down at the pool and watched his classmates, who were indistinct in his sight.

"Let Halligan here be a warning to you," Father Walter shouted. "You need to control your sinful urges, because if you don't, your sinful urges will control you. They will rot your mind and turn your soul into a foul cesspool in which your better, godly selves will drown. They will turn you into weak creatures, susceptible to any lewd proposition or temptation, no matter how deviant and distasteful, and they will make you so disgusting in God's sight that He will refuse you a place in eternity, regardless of how worthy you might otherwise be."

Father Walter blew his whistle, and the boys went back to their laps. As he stood sacrificially on the diving board, Michael felt that sometimes life came down to two options: a person could obey an urge, or he could kill it. He lifted his chin and held back his tears. The boys swam. Father Walter walked the deck. All of them were nothing but smeared colors. Michael shivered so hard, the diving board bounced.

Aunt Mae returned from the kitchen with a clean teaspoon and an empty cup. Standing beside the table, she picked up his glass and reached the spoon into it.

"I feel you have a calling for the priesthood." She scooped out some juice dotted with ash and dumped it into the clean cup. "And don't think you're not good enough to become a priest." She spooned out more juice. Michael took a bite of his half-eaten sandwich and wondered what goodness had to do with the priesthood. "Or that you don't have the patience or holiness that priests need. Or that you're too selfish or petty or spend too much of your time looking at trivial and lurid stories instead of trying to better yourself." She held the glass up to the light and then set it in front of Michael.

She sat again and lit another cigarette. Since Michael's mother had died, Aunt Mae had withered into a shriveled little creature, with a face that made him think of shrunken heads. Her hands never rested. She was hardly ever without a cigarette, which had made her fingers and drapes turn yellow and the baby fat vanish from her body. She took a long drag and exhaled.

"In fact, not long before your mother died, she expressed to me her desire that you become a priest."

"She did?" Michael took another bite.

Aunt Mae held her cigarette in her right hand. With her left, she rotated the overloaded ashtray back and forth, as though loosening and tightening the lid of a jar.

"I can't remember where we were, but I distinctly remember her telling me how proud she would be if you devoted your life to Christ. She said it was her greatest hope." Aunt Mae puffed her cigarette emphatically, thoughtfully, as if smoking were her vocation. "I didn't want to tell you when you were younger, but I figure you're mature enough now to handle it. And for the most part, I think you're smart enough. You'll do the right thing." She reached across the table and patted his hand. "Now," she said, "how's your no-good bum of a father?"

"He's fine." Watching a few flecks of ash still floating in his juice, Michael tried to picture his mother telling Aunt Mae that he should become a priest.

"Is he still a criminal?"

"Yeah."

Michael hated learning things about his mother. Each new fact stabbed him with the feeling that he'd been too young to know her.

"You know what today is, don't you?" Aunt Mae asked. "Seven years ago."

Michael ate more of his sandwich. Of course he knew what today was. He'd been trying to forget it for the past month.

"We can never know God's plan," she said. "But He *does* have a plan. We have to believe that."

Michael didn't believe anything. It was ridiculous for a person to believe anything. His aunt was the most gullible jackass alive.

"I don't know why He took her, especially when He did, but He had a reason. I just know it."

Michael picked up the last bit of sandwich and popped it into his mouth.

"Did you remember to pray for her at Mass?"

Michael chewed and nodded. Aunt Mae always got around to these questions.

"What did you pray?"

The more he ate, the hungrier he became.

"I prayed for God to protect her and keep her."

Aunt Mae fidgeted with a charred match at the edge of the ashtray. "And that He forgive her?"

"Why should He forgive her? She didn't do anything but die. It wasn't her fault."

"Just answer me. Did you ask that He forgive her?"

Michael stared at the crumbs on his plate and said, "Of course I did."

"You remember to pray for her during the week, don't you?"

"I pray for her every morning and night."

"And at school?"

"We pray all the time at school."

"Good." Aunt Mae stubbed out her cigarette and fumbled through her leather case for her next one. "You can never be too safe when it comes to praying. You need to cover your bases with God."

Outside the window, people waited on the platform for an inbound train. Michael pictured his mother and he standing among them. If she were alive, would she still trust him with her secrets?

"What's the matter?" Aunt Mae asked, lighting her next cigarette. "You don't like your grape juice?"

Michael faced his watered-down juice and the ash on its surface. "No, it's fine."

"Then finish it," she said. "I don't want you leaving here less than full."

5.

SITTING ON A FOLDING CHAIR JUST INSIDE HIS GARAGE, PADDY WATCHED the autumn rain splatter against his gravel lot and spritz as far as his feet. All his life, he'd been waiting like this. Waiting for someone to show up and steal more of his time, or change his life for him. Waiting for his mother to stop coughing, get up from bed, and fix dinner; then waiting all night for her to move. Waiting for the deathly smell and flies to go away, and for the neighbors to stop knocking on the locked apartment door and asking if everything was all right. Waiting in the orphanage for bedtime and sunrise, for roll call and a turn at bat, for food, for second helpings, for the priests to say grace, for the priests to shut the hell up. Waiting on a train platform with other boys, shivering in the rain and wishing they weren't going to Blessed Savior. Paddy leaned back and pulled a cigarette and a match from his chest pocket. He hadn't thought about that morning in years, and remembered it now only because of the way the rain fell and brought up from the earth a familiar fertile odor, like nature working up a sweat. All the adults had had umbrellas that day, the boys only caps. When the caps got too wet, the boys took them off and got yelled at for doing so. "You'll catch cold. Put your hats back on," Father What's-his-name, the scrawny one, shouted. So back onto their heads they put their caps, which sat there as sodden and heavy as rain clouds. Paddy shook his head. The memory was Rabbit Dunne's fault, for making him wait like this, in this particular rain.

Paddy regarded the match and thought it had no business lighting with all this water around, but he struck it, and a flame appeared. Then he lit his cigarette, took a drag, and let the smoke out slowly.

He'd waited for Elizabeth, too. Waited for her to let him be alone with her, to kiss him back as though she meant it, to stop acting like a spoiled brat. Waited for her to accept his proposal. Waited with his back against a wall as she danced with boy after boy, occasionally glancing his way. She was trying to make him angry or jealous, to convince him to either give up or chase her; he wasn't sure which, and he wasn't about to do either, so he just waited for her against the wall. "Holding up the bricks," someone said. Other girls would come up to him and start to talk, but he'd ignore them, step aside, and watch Elizabeth. And gradually, as always happened whenever he waited, his motives changed. He'd start out wanting something simple and pure, like a kiss or a scoop of ice cream, but the more he had to wait, the more his desire would dry up and curl into something sharp and cruel, leaving him wanting the same thing as before—more than ever, in fact—but hating it as well. He'd no longer want to keep it like a kitten, but own and control it, like a dog. So when Elizabeth finally came up to him after Mass and said, "I've thought about your proposal and talked to my parents, and I think I'll say yes," he'd grinned and nodded, not so much because he wanted to marry her anymore, but because he'd won.

Paddy rested his elbows on his knees. His lot wasn't level. His store leaned slightly to the west. During the day and at night, trains raced past and whistled as if they were laughing at him. All of this was Rabbit's fault, too. He'd been the one to buy the land here and have his men construct the building on the cheap. Still, Paddy knew better than to complain. The station had been his idea, but it had required Rabbit's money, and that was the only fact that mattered. At least it wouldn't be long until Union Auto belonged to him—just two years and a few months. He was working hard, staying loyal, and paying Rabbit according to the terms of their contract. Putting the finger on Mason certainly wouldn't hurt his situation.

"We found some discrepancies," Rabbit had said over the phone the day before.

"I knew you would."

"We need to talk as soon as possible."

Each week Union Auto brought in a little more money than it had the week before. Each week it picked up another customer who once would have driven past in disgust. The people of La Grange were so moral that they complained to the police about Paddy's associates, but they were not so moral that they passed up great engine work and low prices for something as useless as principles. They had shed their reservations and integrity slowly, just as Paddy had shed parts of his past—his job, his house, his motivational booklets—and just as surely as he would shed Rabbit Dunne one day.

Paddy took a cigarette from his pocket, lit it off the other, and smoked them both until the first was dead and the second glowed with life. He watched the rain. What else could he do but wait?

An hour later, nearly ninety minutes late, Rabbit Dunne showed up in shirtsleeves with his son Georgie, a big, useless lunk in his twenties. In the garage, Georgie brushed raindrops from his pressed suit and Rabbit shook out his umbrella.

"You remember George," Rabbit said, as though all three of them had been pals many years ago.

"Sure, I remember Georgie," Paddy said. Rabbit's son was soft-handed and shifty, quick to step behind his father at the first sign of trouble. More than once, Paddy had had to scare off some young guy who'd said the wrong thing to one of Georgie's girlfriends.

"Do you have someplace we can talk?" Rabbit said with a grin that showed his tiny, ugly teeth. "We're gonna need to spread out some papers."

Paddy locked the garage and led them to the kitchen, where he set each of them up with a scotch and water. The rain had nearly stopped, but the sun had not yet returned. Water trickled from the gutters. Paddy smirked as Georgie pulled papers from his briefcase and stacked them on the table. Michael had no friends and spent most of his time reading ridiculous stories for boys, but at least he wasn't as spoiled and sneaky as Georgie had been at the same age. At least he didn't force others to fight his battles.

"This shouldn't take long," Rabbit said. "It's an amateur we're dealing with."

"Mason may be an amateur, but he's crafty. Didn't I tell you that?"

"You did."

Georgie finished pulling papers from his briefcase and sat with his hands folded on the table. When Rabbit gestured his way with an open hand, Georgie cleared his throat and said, "We looked at Mason's sheets for the past several months and discovered that on two occasions, the amount entered on a line was less than the amount the person actually paid. Not much, just a dime or quarter each time, but it made us wonder. Once could be a mistake, but twice seemed like someone trying to get away with something."

Paddy slapped the table. "Didn't I tell you?"

"So we checked with Mason."

"Oh yeah? What did that son of a bitch say?" Paddy laughed and looked at Rabbit, who picked up his drink and took a sip. Ice cubes clinked inside his tumbler.

"He makes a copy of every sheet he brings here," Georgie said, "and the amount he had for both those numbers was higher than on the sheets we had."

"So he's covering his ass."

"Shut up, Paddy." Rabbit set down his glass. "Let George finish."

Paddy remembered taking Rabbit out in the second round. Blood had run from Rabbit's mouth, and his eyes had shown no focus. Afterward, people said that Rabbit had been sick and past his prime, that Paddy had loaded his gloves or just been lucky. He clenched his fist beneath the table.

"We compared the sheets and noticed that for most weeks, a few amounts were lower on the sheets you provided us than on the ones Mason kept, and that the total always reflected these differences. So then we looked closely at these lower numbers and realized that the handwriting for them was a little different."

"What are you getting at?" Paddy said.

"Two weeks ago we made sure that Mason showed us his sheets before he gave them to you. They came out to $526. I verified it." He tapped the stack of papers nearest him. "The sheet you handed us showed a total of $524."

Paddy tried to understand what Georgie was saying, but it made no sense to him. How had Mason been able to change the numbers after he'd dropped them off? Or was this whole thing some sort of setup?

"Last week, we checked the sheets of all the runners before you got them. It ends up that somewhere between the sheets getting to you and coming to us, we were shorted five dollars."

"I don't understand."

"It's simple," Rabbit said. "You steal a little money here, a little money there, and hope nobody notices. Then, when we start snooping around, you blame the other guy. It's a loser's hustle, Paddy. You know that."

Paddy nodded. It made perfect sense to him now. Ever since the knockout, Rabbit had been seeking revenge, and now he had it. All it had taken were a few doctored numbers. Georgie was in on it. Mason and the other runners were in on it. Maybe even Red was in on it.

"Let me get this straight," Paddy said. "You're accusing me of changing the numbers and stealing the money?"

"Somebody did," Georgie said. When Paddy met his stare, Georgie didn't flinch as he once would have. "And it wasn't Mason."

Paddy leaned back and sneered. He was cornered, he knew, but not trapped. Sometimes you had to fight like hell, and sometimes you had to cover up until you regained your strength, but there was always a way out.

"Look, both of you," Paddy said, "why don't you just cut the bullshit and admit you're setting me up? At least that way we'll know where we stand."

Rabbit laughed. "First it's Mason, and now it's us. Who are you gonna blame next? Roosevelt? Hitler? Who was it, Paddy? Was it Red? Was it your son?"

Paddy felt as if he'd been suddenly, violently spun around and kicked in the chest. He recalled Michael sitting in the kitchen, in this very chair, working his way from sheet to sheet, then taking the money down to the basement. It was an insignificant memory that now seemed sinister. He imagined Michael erasing numbers, slipping dollars into his pocket.

"I don't know what you're trying to pull, but it's not worth all this trouble," Paddy said. "What are we talking about here? Twenty bucks? Thirty bucks?"

"How the hell do we know?" Georgie said. "You're the one who knows."

"Well, I don't know how much is missing, because I had nothing to do with this little scheme of yours, and you damn well know it." In Paddy's mind, Michael kept erasing numbers, stealing money. A dime here, a quarter there. "I don't have time for games, so add whatever you think is missing to whatever I owe on this place. I don't care if I have to wait an extra month to own it."

"Own it?" Rabbit laughed. "What are you talking about?"

"I'm talking about our deal."

"You mean our lease?"

"I mean our contract."

Georgie pulled out a few papers and pushed them across the table to Paddy. "You mean this? It's a thirty-year lease."

Paddy perused the small type, the notarized seal, the roman numerals, and the sentences that went on and on and never made sense. He had never seen the document before, didn't know what half the words meant. As Georgie rattled off page numbers and terms of the agreement, Paddy flipped numbly from page to page. Thirty years, starting today. A rent increase each year of no more than five percent. Default penalty. He flipped to the last page and saw three signatures: Rabbit's, Georgie's, and one that looked exactly like his.

"You sons of bitches," Paddy muttered. "It's a fucking forgery."

"Looks like your signature to me," Rabbit said.

"You can't get away with this."

"I'm afraid you're wrong there," Rabbit said. "The simple fact is that you can't get away with screwing me, but I can easily get away with screwing you. That's the way things work."

"But I have a contract. When I'm done making payments, the place is mine."

"Whatever you have, I never signed," Rabbit said. "Did you see me sign it?"

"Red gave it to me."

"Did he see me sign it?"

Paddy had never asked. He'd never seen any need to.

Rabbit took a pen from his pocket and a piece of paper from Georgie's stack. "You never did protect yourself well," he said as he signed the paper. "Just came out slugging. No finesse. No strategy." He slid the paper across to Paddy and stood. "You check the signature you have against this one. Then tell me I signed your so-called contract."

Georgie crammed his papers into his briefcase, then stood. Paddy remained seated. "You're not gonna get away with this," he said.

"Paddy, be reasonable. Who are you gonna turn to? The police? A judge? I'll just make sure they nab you for something. It wouldn't be hard." Rabbit picked up the lease from the table. He shook it at Paddy. "This isn't a bad deal if you really think about it. You're safe here for thirty years in your station, away from the city, away from me. All you have to do is pay the rent to George each month. He's in real estate now. Property development. Dunne & Company, he calls it." Rabbit looked at Georgie with a smile. "Tells me it's very lucrative."

Rabbit started to walk away with his son, but at the door he stopped and turned to Paddy.

"And in case it isn't clear, as of today, you no longer work for me. Our affiliation is over. No traffic comes through Union Auto. I assume this arrangement is agreeable to you." Rabbit grinned at Paddy. "And one more thing. If I were you, I wouldn't even think of breaking this lease. There are plenty of unsolved murders in Chicago—bums beaten to death in alleys, that sort of thing. I would hate to have to tell the cops what I know."

For several minutes after they'd left, Paddy sat staring at the tabletop. His thoughts wrestled with one another until it was hard to know what was real. Michael erased numbers in the kitchen. Red doctored the contract. Mason laughed. Rabbit oversaw them all. They were all in it together. Paddy picked up Rabbit's tumbler, spun, and fired it at the wall. Ice, liquid, and glass shot across the floor. He picked up Georgie's glass and threw it, too. Then he grabbed Rabbit's signature, stormed downstairs, pulled the rocks from the wall, and found the contract hidden in the back of his secret space. He flipped to the last page and compared the two signatures. They didn't match.

An hour later, Paddy stood drunk in Michael's bedroom. A notebook, a crucifix, and a lamp sat neatly on the desk. An alarm clock ticked on the bedside table. His son's cartoon books stood flush on their shelves. Paddy knew that Michael occasionally visited his Aunt Mae, which he had forbidden but pretended not to know, but otherwise there had been no indication that his son was a thief and a liar.

His thoughts crept to Elizabeth and that prolonged moment that had begun when he found the knitting needle in the garbage can and ended, if it ever ended at all, when Aunt Mae broke down and admitted that she'd found it beside Elizabeth in the bathroom, leaving him to always wonder but never know whether the child had been his or another man's. He'd never been sure which was the better truth.

Michael's bed was crisply made and free of wrinkles; its perfection infuriated Paddy. He grabbed the covers and yanked them off as hard as he could. The momentum sent him falling onto the bed, which slid into the wall. He lost his balance, slipped from the mattress, and landed on something that jutted into his tailbone. He cursed and looked down to see that he was seated in a large, low box filled with dozens of books. Beside the box was an identical one filled with more books. He picked up *Shooting Sheriffs* and tossed it aside, picked up *Jungle Jim* and did the same. He grabbed a folded piece of paper from between the pages of another book. It was a list that included book title after book title, in order of their purchase date. Most had been bought in the past three months.

Paddy knelt between the boxes, left hand raised above one, right hand above the other. He looked eagerly from box to box like a magician considering the halves of his beautiful assistant. He tilted the boxes forward, dumping their contents on the floor. The books thudded, flopped open, slid down one another. Then he picked up and flung aside book after book until a dollar bill fluttered down from one. He grabbed the bill, which was soft and a little oily, and pocketed it. He continued through the books, fanning their pages, ripping them in half. More dollars fell. When he was done, pages and torn covers lay scattered over the floor and the bed, and Paddy had eleven dollar bills and all the evidence he needed to know that his son, like Red and Rabbit and Elizabeth and everyone else in this miserable goddamn world, had betrayed him.

RIDING THE TRAIN HOME FROM SCHOOL, MICHAEL SAT CURLED UP IN A corner seat and read *Buck Rogers in the City Below the Sea*. The sun had nearly set. The day's heavy rain had turned to drizzle. Of all his Big Little Books, which, thanks to Oswald Knoll, now included 147 titles, this was the only one he'd not read from beginning to end. He would consider reading it from time to time and sometimes scan a few pages, but inevitably he would set it down, overwhelmed with the feeling that the book held some specter of his mother's death.

Strange and disturbing things began to happen in Atlantis. A man was assaulted and robbed of his clothing; a young woman reported that her boudoir had been ransacked; cases of food and chemicals began to disappear!

But this morning, Michael had thought that all around the world, people were being bombed, starved, and slaughtered; every day their misery came to him through the radio, and it sometimes seemed that evil would consume every living thing on Earth. He was fourteen, almost a man. It was childish to be afraid of a book.

The friendship of the Atlantians began to cool.

"Buck, they seem to be less friendly every day," complained Wilma.

"I guess they wonder if maybe we aren't the—the thieves!"

Feeling brave, Michael turned another page.

With his bag slung over his shoulder, Michael crossed Burlington Avenue, surprised to see Union Auto closed. It was just after five o'clock. There was still plenty of gas to pump. He walked around to the back of the house. A light was on in his bedroom; another was on in the kitchen. He unlocked the back door and stepped onto shattered glass and sticky linoleum. On the table stood a liquor bottle. After closing the back door slowly, he crept through the living room and stopped at the doorway of his bedroom. His father sat on the disheveled bed. Littering the floor were his books: torn, split, destroyed. Michael knew he should turn and run, but he couldn't help staring at what was left of his collection.

"How do I know?" his father asked.

"Know what?"

"If you're my son. How the hell would I know?"

Michael's attention turned from his books to his father, who squinted at him, slack-faced and sweaty.

"I'd never given it any thought before," his father said as he rose unsteadily from the bed, "but when I think about everything, I wonder if maybe you're somebody else's son. How would I ever know?"

Michael formed fists when his father stopped in front of him.

"Maybe I *am* someone else's son," Michael said. "It wouldn't bother me if I was."

His father shrugged. "Still, I hope you understand just how much you owe me."

"Why would I owe you anything?"

Only when he hit the floor did Michael feel his father's punch. Even then, it took a few seconds for him to understand why he lay sprawled in the doorway, his head ringing and his mouth filling with blood. He spat and tried to stand, but his father shoved him back down. Fists hammered his jaw, his temples, his ribs; pain exploded each time his father struck him. Michael flailed against each new sting until his mind collapsed in the same way his body had fallen. He felt himself hoisted, limbs flopping, and when he opened his eyes he was passing through the darkened garage. His father carried him into the damp twilight air, then dropped him onto the gravel.

Water lay in puddles all around Michael and dripped from eaves and streetlights. The garage door rattled shut. Beside him, his schoolbag was still looped around his arm. He struggled to his hands and knees, spat blood, and then, as pain flooded his body and his mind began to clear, he stood slowly and ran.

SUMMER NIGHTS. SOUTHERN BELLE. LOTUS BLOSSOM.

Mae Fitzgerald arranged the perfume bottles in the glass case, careful to make sure the names faced outward. The bottles were shaped like little hearts, pyramids, gift boxes, and elegant, slender women. The perfume inside them shone like liquid sunlight.

Passion. Amoré. Eternal Love.

Satisfied with the display, Mae locked the case and gazed out across Cosmetics, with its small, square counters set like islands in an archipelago. Tuesday afternoons were usually slow, but today was especially quiet. An elderly woman with thinning blue hair shuffled near Lipstick. A perky blond with false eyelashes powdered her face. A jowly businessman flirted with Elaine, the pixie of a girl in Rouge.

Mae lifted her right foot and stood like a wading bird. Then she alternated her feet. Employees were not allowed to sit, except during lunch and bathroom breaks. She made her way down the counter, leaned to her left, and looked out past Jewelry and Watches to the front doors. Wind and rain whipped around outside. People rushed up and down Lake Street with newspapers and umbrellas over their heads.

"It's still raining," a woman said, "if that's what you're wondering."

Ashamed that she'd been caught in a moment of personal curiosity, Mae stood up straight and faced the voice, ready to offer an apology and an explanation. Mrs. Warner—Mrs. Howard Warner—stood before her, drenched and smiling, shopping bags in both hands.

Mrs. Warner was no older than Mae, and was quite possibly a few years younger, but her wealth had a way of making her seem more mature. She did less to her appearance than most of Mae's customers, keeping her hair straight and brown and usually wearing the tamest of lipstick, yet she still managed to look more beautiful and composed than the others. Because she did not demand respect, Mae respected her without reservation.

"Mrs. Warner, hello. How are you today?"

"Wet," Mrs. Warner said, as she let her body flop back into the white vinyl chair reserved for customers. "And tired." She set her shopping bags on the floor and adjusted the rings on her fingers. "I told myself not to shop today. 'It's raining,' I said. 'Plus, there's the war effort to consider. You should save money, can some fruit, collect tin and paper, or do something equally honorable and patriotic. You should stay home and be a good little citizen.' But I just couldn't. I felt so restless. I felt that if I didn't get out into the world and buy something, I was going to slit my wrists, and what would that add to the war effort? Probably very little, was my conclusion. So here I am. I don't think I've ever shopped so much in my life."

Mrs. Warner unbuttoned her raincoat and shook it from her shoulders, revealing a silk blouse and tanned, athletic forearms that had been toned through sets of tennis and rounds of golf, which she often recounted for Mae's benefit. Mae found it difficult to look at Mrs. Warner's face for long without feeling flustered, so she focused instead on Mrs. Warner's arms, which flustered her, too, though not enough to make her avert her eyes.

"I wouldn't survive a week in a dreary climate—I'll tell you that right now. Howard and I went to Maine once for vacation. We sailed and watched the ocean and ate lobsters day after day—boiled lobster, lobster bisque, lobster salad…I'm surprised we didn't have malt o' lobster for breakfast— and by the fifth consecutive day of rain and clouds, I was ready to throw myself over the railing of a boat. Dead at the bottom of the sea—that's the way to go, if you ask me. Think of it—being down there with all those poor sailors and suicides and sunken treasure. There's such romantic doom in drowning." She seemed to think for a moment. Then she draped her arm across her forehead, rolled back her eyes, and said in a theatrical voice:

> O, what a noble mind is here o'erthrown!
> The courtier's, soldier's, scholar's, eye, tongue, sword;
> The expectancy and rose of the fair state,
> The glass of fashion and the mould of form,
> The observed of all observers, quite, quite down!

Mae didn't understand what Mrs. Warner was saying; nonetheless, she felt she should applaud. Mrs. Warner lowered her arm and stared at Mae. "Are you familiar with Ophelia?" she asked.

Mae rummaged through her brain for some object or anecdote that corresponded to Mrs. Warner's words, but she returned with nothing. She had never heard of a perfume called Ophelia. The name made no sense, but then again, in the world of perfume, little did. Customers often clamored for the most sulfuric odors, while the sweetest ones were sold on clearance.

"I think I'm familiar," Mae said, not wanting to disappoint or appear ignorant in front of Mrs. Warner, "but it's been a long time."

"It's been a long time for me too, Mae, but I could never forget:

> There's rosemary, that's for remembrance; pray,
> love, remember: and there is pansies. That's for thoughts."

Mrs. Warner looked solemnly at Mae, who more than anything wanted to pull a bottle of Ophelia from the display case and hand it to her.

"You understand, Mae, don't you?"

"Yes," said Mae, her voice a squeak.

"The tragic man, driving the tragedy of the woman who could save him. Only a genius like Shakespeare could have conceived Hamlet and Ophelia."

Mae felt needling heat rush to her skin. She had felt like a troll in front of Mrs. Warner on many occasions, but this time was the worst. As Mrs. Warner smiled, apparently thinking they had Shakespeare in common, Mae kept a tight grin plastered on her face.

One afternoon the year before, on a day off, Mae had walked two and a half miles to deliver a special order to the Warners' house, a massive colonial overlooking Thatcher Woods. She'd longed to see where Mrs. Warner lived, and maybe discover her first name on the letterbox. She had a habit of imagining her customers' lives as far more thrilling or tragic than hers—rich with sex and summers overseas, or cursed with murder and incest. As she trekked through River Forest, she fantasized about being invited in for a drink and lounging in luxury with Mrs. Warner, but no one was home, and no one came home in the hour and a half Mae waited on the porch.

"I need a bottle of perfume," Mrs. Warner said. "Something unique. Something new. What's come in lately?"

New and unique fragrances seldom arrived these days. The war had destroyed production in Europe and depressed demand in the United States. The prices kept rising while the scents mostly stayed the same.

Mae reached down, unlocked the cabinet, and pulled out the latest: Secret Admirer, Riviera, Rendezvous. She set the bottles on the counter.

"Tell me, Mae, do you have a sister?" Mrs. Warner opened the first bottle, sprayed her left wrist, and patted it against her right.

Mae watched Mrs. Warner's wrists, and in her mind darted images of Elizabeth on the bathroom floor, the knitting needle beside her hand, the blood. She thought she should tell the usual story of her sister dying as a result of a miscarriage, but then she thought better of it. Employees were encouraged to shy away from discussions of political, religious, or personal matters.

"No," Mae said. "I don't have a sister."

Mrs. Warner smirked. "Lucky you."

She held her left and then her right wrist up to her nose. She smelled the left again, and then the right. She slid the second bottle to Mae.

"Spray this on you," she said. "I don't want to mix them on me."

Mae sprayed the perfume on her left wrist, which she then began patting against her right.

"We're having dinner with my sister in Lake Forest tomorrow night. Her husband is an attorney for the Wrigley family—*very* wealthy. Every time we go there, she brags about the latest trip they've taken or the politicians and movie stars they've met. Obnoxious twaddle—that's all it is. No talk of art, no mention of politics, no literature, just gossip and name dropping. And then at some point she always shows me something she's bought on the black market: German chocolates, Italian silk, French wine. Inevitably she smells my neck and tells me what perfume I'm wearing. And the most awful thing about it is that she's always right." Mrs. Warner laughed and touched Mae's arm. "I think you can stop tapping your wrists together, dear."

Mae blushed and held her wrist up to Mrs. Warner, who took a whiff of the skin, then crinkled her nose.

"I want to surprise her with something new and wonderful. It would be a small victory, but a victory nonetheless."

Mae wanted to say something witty and sophisticated, something to convince them both that they were friends, but Mrs. Warner's elegance and poise intimidated her, made her nearly hyperventilate. On several occasions, on the hazy edge of sleep—but sometimes, she had to admit, while she was awake—Mae had imagined Mrs. Warner kissing and caressing her, and although she liked to believe she had erased these scenes quickly from her mind and shaken the tingling from her flesh, she knew she had indulged in them more often than not, and that the only reason she ultimately stopped any of them was out of fear that every sin she committed condemned her sister deeper into hell.

"Try this one." Mrs. Warner slid the third bottle to Mae. "Spray it on your neck."

Mae did as Mrs. Warner said. Letting the cool fragrance sink into her skin, she leaned across the counter and tilted her chin upward. When Mrs. Warner rose to inhale the scent, Mae closed her eyes, feeling the quickness and power of her own pulse. She waited for breath to touch her.

"That's the one," Mrs. Warner said. "I'll take two bottles of it, wrapped separately."

Mae opened her eyes, realizing she was still leaning across the counter like a cat lost in the bliss of a neck rub. She straightened, worried that some dark part of herself had been exposed to the world, and as she busied herself with gift boxes, tissue paper, and ribbons, she knew she should stop by church after work to ask God for forgiveness.

When she was finished wrapping, she placed the boxes in a bag and handed it to Mrs. Warner, who paid for the perfume and then held out one of the boxes to Mae.

"For you," she said. "For always being so helpful."

Mae stared in horror at the box. Employees were not allowed to accept gifts from customers; apart from theft, it was perhaps the worst thing they could do. Some of the finest employees, caught by undercover security agents, had been fired for doing so.

"I can't," she said.

"Of course you can. And you should. You deserve it, Mae."

"No, really." She kept her arms at her sides.

Mrs. Warner shook the box. "I insist."

Mae wondered why God was testing her. It was hard enough to know that her sister had killed her own baby, no doubt because of an adulterous affair; it was hard enough to bear that burden, and to financially and spiritually support Michael, and convince him to become a priest by lying about his mother's wishes, and to do her best not to be perverted by her weakest self. Over the years she had imagined Elizabeth committing adultery with men of all sizes, religions, and ethnicities. She never intended to let her mind degenerate into such scenes, but it did, just as it envisioned unimaginable encounters with Mrs. Warner.

"Here. Take it," Mrs. Warner said, placing the gift on the counter. "Return it, for all I care."

Panicked, Mae picked up the box and thrust it across the counter, accidentally striking Mrs. Warner's chest. For a moment Mae stared at Mrs. Warner, whose expression changed from shock to indignation to anger. Mae opened her mouth to apologize or at least explain, but no words emerged. Mrs. Warner grabbed the box from her and slammed it on the counter.

"It's a goddamn gift," she said before storming off. "Take it."

Half an hour later, at the start of her afternoon break, Mae locked herself in a bathroom stall and sat on the closed toilet lid. With her head in her hands, she wept. When her tears, but not their sting, were gone from her eyes, she leaned back. She didn't want to be a sinner, but she was, and sometimes she had to wade deeper through sin to reach her better self. She lifted the bottom of her blouse, reached for the waistband of her skirt, and pulled out the gift bottle of Rendezvous, which she had wedged between the fabric and her skin. She unscrewed the cap and the nozzle, put the bottle to her lips, and told herself that this time—this sip, this sin—would be the last.

8.

THE LETTERS CAME FROM ALL ACROSS THE UNITED STATES, ADDRESSED TO Captain Midnight, the Phantom, Don Winslow of the Navy, and the others. They were written in pencil, crayon, and ink, on monogrammed notepaper, butcher paper, the backs of old envelopes, the torn corners of grocery bags. Each afternoon, about ten arrived at Whitman Publishing in Racine, Wisconsin, and were routed to a desk in a cramped office nearest the emergency exit. Oswald Knoll answered them all. The children who wrote expressed enthusiasm for their hero's victories or concern over his latest cliffhanger, and some suggested elaborate methods for disposing of the most persistent villains. Although some of the children hinted that they would be more than willing to receive free toys or books in response to their words, and a smaller number were blunt in terms of what they wanted, most simply wrote out of a sense of appreciation or friendship, hoping to communicate with characters they admired and loved. Occasionally a child referred to a dead grandparent, a father at war, a missing mother. A letter might allude to illness, a violent uncle, a lack of food, or something else that would make Oswald want to gather up and protect all those who wrote to him.

Oswald promptly answered their questions, offered condolences or congratulations when appropriate, and always invited further correspondence. He sent them gifts they had not requested and advice he hoped they could use. Even though the majority of his time was taken up with planning promotional events, developing premium books for advertisers, designing retail displays, and dressing up as characters for war-bond drives, he always made time for the letters.

Oswald checked his watch. It was four-fifty. He opened the first envelope, which bore a postmark of Evansville, Indiana.

> Deer Captain Easy,
>   I lik Wash Tubbs but you ar my favrit. I lik wen you beet up bad giyz. You ar my best frend.
> From, Davy

It was tempting to weigh children's words too heavily or too lightly, to think that when a child claimed a character as his best friend, he either meant it too much or didn't mean it at all. Nonetheless, it was important to take them seriously. Oswald turned to the typewriter on the side table and typed:

> Dear Davy,
>   Thank you for your letter. It really made my day! Wash Tubbs and I are getting ready for an exciting new adventure, and we sure hope that you will keep reading. I'm glad that you like when I beat up bad guys, but I hope you know that I take no pleasure in such actions and only fight when it is absolutely necessary.
>   I'm throwing in a little book about our latest adventure on the high seas. I hope you enjoy it!
>   Write back real soon. I can't wait to hear from you again!
> Your friend,
> Captain Easy

Oswald was less than satisfied with the letter, especially with the repetition of the word *adventure*, but ever since the birth of his third child (and first son) a few years earlier, he'd put less pressure on himself to be perfect. During boxing matches, he used to have his corner man tally the number of punches his opponent had landed; after the fight, he'd examine the numbers and plan how to get hit less in the future. He'd brought this fastidiousness to Whitman nine years ago. Instead of filming and reviewing his fights, he filmed and reviewed his performances as fictional heroes. Instead of going from gym to gym to study other boxers, he rummaged through garbage cans around the publishing plant most evenings and saved the sketches, layout pages, and various documents that others failed to value. A few years after his arrival, his bosses, worried about the time he spent composing letters, told him to come up with a few standard responses—but he didn't listen to them. Then they told him to write no more than three sentences per letter, but he refused. Finally they told him to answer only two letters a day and throw away the rest, and he explained to them in a shaky voice that the letters had been written by children who found comfort in the books Whitman published, and to just ignore them was irresponsible and unethical, and if that was what they wanted, then he would have to quit. Since then, nobody had mentioned the letters to Oswald.

After packaging the letter and a book for Davy, Oswald replied to the next seven letters, struggling to say something original with each response. He looked at his watch. It was five-forty. He should have been home by now, but he prided himself on never allowing the letters to slide until the next day. He picked up the last envelope and was surprised to see a familiar return address in La Grange, Illinois. He hadn't heard from Michael Halligan—one of his favorites, one of the few he corresponded with under his own name—in a year and a half. He opened the letter and read:

March 12, 1943
Dear Jerk,

Who do you think you are sending all these goddamn books and garbage to my house and service station which I work hard to make a success huh? My son Michael doesn't live here anymore. He is gone and I don't know where he is or care for that matter. He is not welcome here and neither are your stupid letters or anything from you. In other words—STOP IT or you'll be sorry. If you don't stop I'll make you stop. Don't think I won't.

Yours truly,

Patrick Halligan

Proprietor, Union Auto Repair & Gas

P.S. And don't think I don't know who you are. I know. You can't fool me. Hard Knocks Knoll. I'm right aren't I? You bet I am. How many Oswald Knolls are there in the world anyhow? One is my guess and I bet I'm right. So it wasn't enough to KO me just because you were lucky enough to have good training and I wasn't? Now you have to keep sending crap to my house and taking away my time from important things? You had your good days and there's nothing I can do about that but I can make you stop bothering me. What that Mexican did to your one eye I can do to your other. Believe me I can!

Oswald had no idea who Patrick Halligan was, though the name sounded familiar. Since he'd had more than a hundred bouts as an amateur and a professional, it was quite possible they had met in the ring. But Oswald certainly knew Michael Halligan; he had filed carbon copies of all the letters he had sent the young man, and even though he assumed Michael had outgrown his books, he still mailed him something—premiums, title lists, original artwork—every few months.

The phone rang. It was Louise. She said that she was tired of taking care of Jane and Annemarie and Oswald Junior, and that all of them were too hungry to have even the slightest trace of patience left.

"If you don't get home in the next half hour," she said, "we're going to eat our dinners and then flush yours down the toilet."

He laughed. "Is that so?"

"Just try me, buster. If you're not here in half an hour, your pork and beans are toast."

"How about fifteen minutes?"

"If you make it home in fifteen minutes, I'll love you forever."

"How about ten?"

"Oh, honey, you can't even imagine that much love."

Oswald put on his coat and pulled out the drawer containing Michael Halligan's folder, which was thick with papers. It was a shame Michael had such a hothead for a father. It was a shame that no matter how much thought and feeling Oswald put into his letters, he couldn't really fix things. He was merely a spokesman for illusion, although there was something to be said for that.

9.

BARNEY TAYLOR PARKED HIS FATHER'S LINCOLN IN FRONT OF AN ENORMOUS pink Victorian. From the passenger seat, Michael looked out the window, feeling sick. The house must have been twenty times bigger than the apartment he and Aunt Mae had shared for the past three and a half years.

"Tonight's my best shot." Barney offered his flask to Michael, who shook his head. "I'm gonna score for sure."

Michael cleared his dry throat. "What's my date like?"

"Don't know." Barney took a swig. "But if she's anything like mine, you oughta be in like Flynn."

When Barney laughed, Michael laughed, though he didn't get the joke. He didn't know Barney well enough to understand his humor. He didn't know anybody all that well.

What he did know was that Barney was the only member of the math team who was worse at math than he was. He also knew that everyone hated Barney, who made a habit of bragging that he had been to the 1938 World Series, met several Chicago Bears, and had sex over Christmas break with a girl in Cuba. His family had a snooker table, a swimming pool, and a live-in maid named Ruby. Michael had been surprised when Barney had asked him on this double date.

"I know her from church, if you can believe it," Barney said. He had a mess of blond hair, fat lips, and chubby thighs that rubbed together when he lumbered like a circus bear through the halls of Fenwick. "My parents and her parents are friends."

Michael pictured Barney's date and his date getting ready, putting on lipstick and bows and brassieres and whatever else girls put on in such situations. He imagined himself entangled with this unknown girl, bundled in a coat in the backseat of a car. How would it even start? And once it did, what was he supposed to do?

"Jesus Christ, Halligan. You nervous?"

"I'm just not sure what to talk about with her."

"That's up to you, pal. Just as long as you don't talk about stupid things."

"Like what?"

"Like high school. Or math team. Whatever you do, don't do that queer thing you do with numbers." He took a sip from his flask. "What's the matter? Never been on a date before?"

"Of course I have," Michael lied. "Just never with a rich girl."

Barney closed up his flask and slid it under his seat. "Rich or poor, girls are all the same. Just ask her about herself and pretend to care when she talks." He pulled a stick of gum from his pocket and started chewing. "That works as well as anything."

A woman answered the front door, said Barney's name, and then shook Michael's hand. Her wrists were weighted down with bracelets, and her blue eyes were flawless and cold.

Barney and Michael sat in the vast living room, which was harshly lit by half a dozen lamps and decorated with figurines of sleek, tuxedoed gentlemen and willowy ladies in evening gowns. Above the fireplace, a tapestry depicted an upper-class hunt. A stuffed owl sat perched on the mantel.

Though less than a mile down the street, the place was a long way from Aunt Mae's one-bedroom apartment, which over the years had grown even more crowded with Catholic books and magazines, prayer candles, and paintings of Jesus Christ and the Virgin Mary. At night, on his cot in the living room, Michael sometimes thought that once he graduated from Fenwick, he would move into his own apartment. He wouldn't have to listen to his classmates call him Hard-on Halligan or let priests belittle him. He wouldn't have to attend Mass twice a week, or kneel on the floor with Aunt Mae and pray for his mother's soul, or sleep alone on a smelly old cot, or pretend to read booklets about the priesthood, or do homework as his aunt sipped whiskey at the table. He wouldn't have to carry her drunken, passed-out body to bed.

He heard footsteps on the stairs. When Barney stood, Michael stood. First came a girl with flushed cheeks and hair piled up like Betty Grable's. She wore saddle shoes, a pleated skirt, and a red sweater, and she reminded Michael of the silent beauties who populated movie backgrounds. He hoped she was his date, but then, in a panic, wished she wasn't. He had to start somewhere in terms of girls, and, like calculus to someone who hadn't learned long division, she was beyond his abilities and comprehension. The second girl came down the stairs: polished loafers, sagging socks, strong calves, thick waist. She was basic multiplication, simple fractions. Her face was as pale and pockmarked as a lump of raw dough; her eyes were as dark and inexpressive as raisins.

Barney's date was named Betty; Michael's was Ellen. Formal introductions were made, hands shaken, compliments batted awkwardly like balloons at a child's birthday party. Together they drove from Oak Park toward the La Grange Theater, which stood a few blocks from Union Auto. In the front seat, Betty and Barney talked quietly and passed the flask between them. Michael thought he'd like to work his way up to a girl like her, maybe in a couple of years, when, he imagined, his appearance would change: his jaw would become sharper, his skin clearer, his muscles bigger, and his vision repaired after a freak accident; he'd read about that kind of thing happening. He'd be tougher, too. Stronger. In command. Sometimes when he squinted at the mirror, he thought he was not all that different from Tyrone Power. With his features blurred, the similarities were there.

Betty turned toward the backseat and jiggled the flask. "Ellen? Michael? Care for a beverage?"

Michael shook his head. Ellen shook hers, too. When Betty winked at Ellen and laughed, Michael had no idea what to say.

Ellen turned to him. "So, you're graduating tomorrow?"

Michael nodded.

"I don't graduate until next year."

"Yeah?"

"Yeah."

He thought that a girl as homely as Ellen would want him to kiss her later in the night, or at the very least, she would be agreeable to it.

"I like to listen to *Meet Corliss Archer* and *Your Hit Parade*," she said, "and I'm thinking of becoming a stenographer or anthropologist after high school. What about you?"

"What about me, what?"

"What do you do? What do you want to do?"

Michael was not exactly sure what he did or wanted to do. He worked Saturdays and occasional evenings at a little service station in Berwyn, giving half his earnings to Aunt Mae and keeping the rest for himself. He could make chicken soup and mashed potatoes. He knew how to fry a pork chop. He enjoyed counting multiples in his head, masturbating, and imagining the suffering experienced by former bullies of his who had gone to war. He pictured them shivering in bunkers, alone and cold, running low on rations. He saw them captured by Japanese troops and locked up behind barbed wire, or plummeting toward the ocean in one-winged bombers. He worried about being drafted when he turned eighteen in a few weeks, and he hoped the fighting would be over by then.

Michael shrugged. "I listen to the war, I guess."

"Me too," Ellen said. "Which do you like better?"

"What do you mean?"

"Which part of the war do you like listening to better? Europe or Japan?"

"Europe, I guess, because it's over—though I liked it better right from the start."

"I like Japan myself, but that's because the Japs killed my cousin and the brother of one of my best friends, so I like hearing about how many of them we're blowing up."

Michael thought the conversation was going fairly well. They were talking, and that certainly was something—perhaps the most important part of conversation. But as he was thinking this, and as Betty and Barney giggled in the front seat, he realized that he and Ellen suddenly were not talking.

Ellen sighed. "Betty?" she said.

Betty turned around with a devilish smile, lipstick smeared on her teeth. She raised her eyebrows.

"Yes?" she said.

"Can I have that flask?"

"Yes, indeed. Here you are, mademoiselle."

Betty handed the flask to Ellen, looked at Michael, looked back at Ellen, winked, and then leaned, laughing, into Barney's shoulder. Ellen took a belt from the flask. Michael stared out the window. Mercifully, they arrived at the theater.

After a newsreel and a *Popeye* cartoon came *Laura*, which was about a dead girl who ended up not being dead, and the detective who falls in love with her and tries to figure out who killed the girl who everyone initially thought was the first girl, but who really wasn't her at all but was a second girl who had the misfortune of looking like the first girl. Betty snuggled against Barney and snored throughout the last half hour. Michael sat rigidly next to Ellen; he never moved his hands from his knees, but a few times he glanced at her staring at the screen, and he felt an urge to whisper to her about his mother and his father, about Aunt Mae and Uncle Red, and about his belief that his life, at any moment and without warning, could become as heroic as those he used to read about in his Big Little Books.

The film ended. The lights came on. Michael thought the movie was okay, Ellen found it marvelous, Barney said he knew all along that the old sissy guy was guilty, and Betty just groaned and held her head. She said she didn't feel too good.

In the bathroom, Barney washed his hands beside Michael, who looked up from the water rushing over his fingers to his reflection in the mirror. The light was horrible on his face, emphasizing every pore and pimple and making him wonder if he always looked so ugly.

"I'm going to drive around with Betty for a while," Barney said. "Why don't you and Ellen go to Woolworth's? We'll pick you up in an hour or two."

"Why?"

"Because this is it, Halligan. Betty and me. She's loosened up and good to go." Barney cupped water into his mouth, sloshed it around, and spat it into the sink. "Plus, I think Ellen likes you, and this will give you the opportunity to do something about it."

A couple of minutes later, Betty stumbled with Barney to the car, and Ellen protested, saying she wanted to stay with her friend. But Barney and Betty sped off, and soon Michael and Ellen were sitting together at a table. As he sipped his cream soda, hoping he came across as nonchalant and manly as Dana Andrews had in the movie, Michael concluded that he would be doing Ellen a favor if he kissed her. The only problem was that, for the time being, he couldn't think of a thing to say. Her feet nervously tapped the floor; her fingers twisted the strap of her handbag. She had just returned from making a phone call and visiting the ladies' room, where she must have stood before the mirror and wished she looked like Gene Tierney, who had played Laura, or like Betty or pretty much any of the girls in Woolworth's. If only he could think of the right thing to say, or at least something to say, he would be on his way to a kiss that would make her swoon.

Michael considered telling Ellen about how well he'd performed during his freshman and sophomore years on the math team, breezing through algebra and geometry and getting used to compliments and awards; about how he'd finished second or third at several meets; about how he'd loved it whenever the team won first place and they'd all cheer, "Secant, tangent, cosine, sine! Three point one four one five nine! Gooooooooooooo Fenwick!"

But if he told her the best parts about the math team, he should also tell her that he'd stopped winning or even doing well last year, that trigonometry and calculus baffled him, and that by the start of senior year he was nearly as inept as Barney. The theorems and formulas made no sense. Numbers didn't seem like numbers anymore; they were no longer solid and fixed, but variable. Their absoluteness had given way to uncertainty.

Sometimes in the middle of a test, he watched other boys scribbling away with confidence, and he wondered how they knew what they knew, especially when he knew so little.

Michael spied people chatting and laughing at other tables, and he hated them for making life look so easy. He glimpsed himself in the mirrored wall and knew that every detail of his appearance was wrong, and that overall he was a disaster. He was nothing like Dana Andrews. He and Tyrone Power were practically different species. He wanted to grab hold of Ellen, to squeeze her until she kissed him or cried in pain.

"Tell me when you were born," he blurted out.

She squinted at him. "Why?"

"Just tell me." It was a simple enough trick, just basic multiplication and addition, but still, it impressed people.

"Why? What are you going to do?"

"I'll tell you how many hours you've lived."

Based on her smirk, he knew he'd said the wrong thing.

"Why would I want to know how many hours I've lived?"

"Just tell me."

"You're trying to pull something, aren't you?"

"I'm not."

"Then why do you want to know?"

"Just tell me when you were born."

Two girls walked through the front door, and Ellen said, "Thank God." She stood, ran to them, and pointed at the table. When they looked at Michael, she grabbed their arms and shook her head. Then she returned and picked up her drink.

"I'm going to sit with my friends." When Michael started to follow her, she laughed and said, "Alone."

After paying the bill, Michael stepped into a thick fog and waited for Barney. Anger twisted him up, threatened to snap him or send him spinning. His muscles were taut, his insides tangled. About ten minutes later, Barney pulled up in his father's Lincoln.

"So, what happened?" Barney asked as Michael got into the car. "Did you kiss her?"

"No." Michael slammed the door. "I probably could have, but these friends of hers came in, and she felt she had to sit with them. How about you?"

"I probably could have scored." Barney pulled away from the curb. The car reeked of vomit. "Next time, definitely."

Barney drank from the flask and passed it to Michael, who closed his eyes, put the opening to his mouth, and pretended he was kissing Ellen. The liquid stung his throat and rose in vapors behind his eyes.

"Yeah," Michael said with a cough. "Next time I could kiss her."

He took another swig and imagined the liquor was poison. It tasted better that way.

"So, you gonna ask her out, then?"

"I don't think so," Michael said. "She wasn't all that good-looking."

A grin stretched across Barney's face until he spat out a laugh. "God, she was ugly."

"She was a dog," Michael said. "A disgusting dog."

Barney smacked the dashboard and howled in delight. His laughter was a mix of malice and glee; along with the booze, it undid the angry, frightened knots inside Michael, who closed his eyes and drank. He imagined kissing Ellen long and hard, a real movie kiss. Then he would push her away, call her a dog. She'd fall to her knees and weep.

The muscles in Michael's face slackened as they cruised around in the fog, and his body listed from side to side when Barney turned around in a dirt lot beside the forest preserve. They drove back into La Grange and passed Union Auto, which looked exactly as it had four years earlier. Michael felt an urge to walk through the back door and climb into his old bed. He wanted to wake up in his former room and have eggs and bacon with his father. Tomorrow was graduation, and nobody would be coming to see him receive his diploma. Aunt Mae had to work, and other than her, who was there? Michael felt disoriented from the alcohol and tense with frustration. He wanted to break himself from his past, snap his life at the present. He pictured two parts of his life in his hands: he'd throw the past to the ground, the future he'd hold like—like what? A sword? A torch?

"Did I ever tell you about the girl I screwed in Cuba?" Barney asked as they rumbled over the tracks. "She just lay there and let me do it to her, like it was no big deal. Didn't move. Didn't say a thing. Just lay there with her arms at her sides and her eyes on the ceiling—like she was some kind of doll."

"Yeah?"

Barney nodded. "It was great."

Michael tried to unlock the apartment door quietly, but he had trouble finding the right key, and then, when he tried to insert his key into the lock, the whole ring fell to the floor with a clatter. As he crouched to pick it up, the door opened. Aunt Mae stood before him wearing a terry-cloth robe, her eyes tired and bloodshot. She folded her arms in front of her chest.

Michael stumbled past her into the darkened apartment.

"You're drunk," Aunt Mae said as she closed the door.

"So what? You're drunk, too."

"I am not."

"Sure you are." He removed his jacket and let it fall to the floor. "You think I can't tell?"

He sat on the couch and kicked off his shoes. He wouldn't even change into pajamas tonight. He was a man; he could sleep in his clothes on the couch if he wanted. When he leaned back, the room spun. He sat up quickly.

"And what if I am drunk?" Aunt Mae said. "It's my right." She stood beside the couch. "I'm entitled to it, especially after all I've done for you, and considering the burden I bear."

Michael laughed as he propped up two pillows and leaned back slowly. The room didn't so much spin as sway. He closed his eyes. "I forgot about your great burden. I do apologize."

"And what would you know about it?"

He didn't answer. He wanted only to fall asleep and dream about Betty, or Gene Tierney, or Martha from years ago.

"It would be your burden, too, if I told you what it was." She nudged the couch with her leg. "If I told you about it, you wouldn't act so proud."

Michael shook his head and imagined Betty crawling in beside him.

"If I told you the truth about your mother, you'd have a sense of obligation. You wouldn't go off drinking all night. You would heed my advice and enter the priesthood."

He opened his eyes and studied his aunt. He saw and heard her as if from just beneath the surface of water.

"What are you talking about?"

"Nothing," Aunt Mae said as she turned away from him. Her body was shaking.

He closed his eyes and laughed. "You don't know what you're saying."

"I don't, huh? I'm the one who found her, remember?"

Michael opened his eyes again. He felt nauseated.

"Tell me," he said.

She shook her head.

He smirked. "It's probably just more of your goddamn bullshit."

She kicked the sofa. "How dare you." She kicked it again. "How dare you curse in my house."

"It's not a house. It's just a lousy apartment."

"I know it's just an apartment. I know it's nothing, but it's where I live, and it's all I have, and I refuse to let you or anybody else defile it by taking the Lord's name in vain."

She burst into tears, dropped down at the end of the couch, and hugged herself tightly.

"I didn't want to tell you, Michael. I didn't want you to have to bear the burden I've had to bear all these years—but I worry you're heading down the same path your father did. He was a good man once, or at least he wasn't all bad; he wasn't who he's become. And if you follow in his footsteps, I fear there will be no hope for your mother."

"What are you talking about?"

With her eyes fixed on her wringing hands, Aunt Mae talked about finding his mother and the knitting needle, and about understanding that her death and the baby's death had not been the result of a miscarriage, but had been caused by a deliberate and hideous act. She told Michael about cleaning up as best she could, calling Dr. Shelley, and hiding the knitting needle, only to have his father find it.

"I'm afraid she was an adulteress, Michael, and maybe with more than one man. There's no way to know." Aunt Mae shook violently. "I've tried for years to pretend this wasn't the case, but it's the only explanation I can come up with for why she would want to murder her own child."

"Maybe you're wrong."

"Oh, Michael, I'm not wrong. I wish I was, but I'm not."

Michael felt less drunk, but he hardly felt sober. When he thought about Eddie, he found it hard to breathe.

"Don't you see that we're the only ones who can save her?" Aunt Mae rested her hand on his knee. "Don't you see that it's our duty to make sure God forgives her?"

The image of Eddie raping his mother flashed in Michael's mind, followed by the picture of her as a willing participant in an affair.

"Will you consider the priesthood, Michael?" Aunt Mae edged close to him. She patted his chest. "Will you consider it—I mean, honestly consider it—for your mother's sake?"

When Michael nodded, Aunt Mae nestled into him, childlike, and rested her head on his sternum. He felt her shivers subside.

"I'm sorry you have to bear my burden now, too." She grinned weakly at him. "But you're strong, Michael. You're a man. I know you won't let your mother down—or me."

He held her gaze, which mirrored his confusion and loneliness, and he felt himself drawn to it. His face lowered and hers rose, and when their lips met, he pretended that he was no longer himself and that his aunt was Ellen, and then Betty, and finally Martha, and he knew that he would burn in hell forever. A couple of minutes later, Aunt Mae removed his hand from her breast and pulled away from him. She scooted to the end of the couch and adjusted her robe.

They sat in the dark, passing the inevitable, invisible moment when night gave way to morning. Aunt Mae sobbed. Michael tried his best to remain motionless, and as he stared at a painting of Jesus with blood on His hands, he knew he was irretrievably lost and undeserving of mercy. Eventually Aunt Mae closed her eyes. When Michael was certain she was asleep, he picked her up gently, imagining first that she was weightless and then that he was strong, and he carried her to her bedroom.

10.

THE NEXT MORNING, AS AUNT MAE GOT READY FOR WORK, MICHAEL LAY awake on the couch with his eyes closed. When she had gone, he rose, feeling groggy and cotton-mouthed. The previous night was murky, though clear enough that somewhere between eating breakfast and brushing his teeth, he decided to leave immediately. He stuffed his belongings into a duffel bag and made his way to his aunt's bedroom. Her vanity was covered with medicine bottles, makeup, and a small, dusty crèche. Stuck into the molding of the mirror were prayer cards and family snapshots, but none of his mother. He hadn't seen any photographs of her since her death, and this morning he wanted to search her face for clues about what had really happened eleven years earlier. He didn't want to believe his aunt's story, and, having spent the last few years doubting most of what she told him, he wasn't sure why he should believe her now, but he did. Carefully, he went through the vanity drawers but found nothing except bills, letters, rings, trinkets, rosary beads, and a few more photos of aunts, uncles, and cousins. He proceeded to the closet, rummaging through hatboxes, handbags, and suitcases, and then to the dresser, flipping aside blouses, handkerchiefs, and underwear, but the only things he found stashed beneath her clothing were several empty perfume bottles.

That afternoon, he skipped his graduation ceremony and checked into a decrepit hotel he'd passed hundreds of times on the bus ride to and from work. A bearded man with the feral look of a prophet sat behind the reception desk. He flipped open the guest registry and handed a pen to

Michael, who printed and then signed his name. Under the column headed "Transient or Permanent," he wrote "Transient." The man scrutinized Michael's entry and shut the ledger. Handing over the key, he said, "Deviant behavior is neither welcome nor tolerated."

Within a month after checking into the Hotel Alban, which smelled of urine and bacon grease and was infested with silverfish, Michael was promoted to full-time at the service station, was declared 4-F by the draft board for his faulty eyesight, and signed up for accounting classes at Morton Junior College. He kept waiting for his solitude to resemble freedom, or at least independence, but instead he felt more trapped than before. Everywhere he went, he felt Aunt Mae's breast and tasted her tongue; everywhere he saw Eddie pin his mother to the couch. The more he thought about his mother, the more clearly he remembered her holding Eddie's hand and kissing him in a doorway.

One Sunday, feeling more like a Permanent than a Transient, Michael rode an El train to the corner of 63rd and Cottage Grove, where his mother had dragged him dozens of times to meet with the Society for Sacred Possessions. He headed east on 63rd among people walking in and out of a grocery store, a butcher shop, a five-and-dime. Nothing looked familiar. High-schoolers kidded each other on stoops and street corners, street vendors hawked kielbasa and elephant ears, and in the upper windows of the three-story buildings were signs for dentists, music lessons, and fortune tellers. As Michael searched the crowds for Eddie and examined the architecture for a familiar detail that would tell him which way to go, he suddenly remembered that Eddie's neighborhood had been mostly black. With only white faces around him, Michael turned and headed in the opposite direction.

The neighborhood changed immediately west of Cottage Grove, as if a line separating the races had been drawn down the middle of the street. The sidewalks were just as crowded as they were in the white area, but the stores looked poorer and were interspersed with boarded-up businesses. An El train rattled on the tracks overhead.

"You looking for someone?"

Michael flinched. Beside him stood a man with a wrestler's compact body and the suave face of a bandleader. He had sharp cheekbones and skin the color of wet sand.

"I'm not looking for anybody," Michael said.

The man laughed. "Of course you are. You wouldn't have crossed the street otherwise."

Michael scanned the neighborhood as though the man wasn't there.

"What's the matter—don't like Negroes?"

"No."

"No, you don't like Negroes?"

"No. I mean, no, that's not it."

"Then how come you're ignoring me?"

"I'm not ignoring you."

"Look, I'm just trying to perform a community service. You're looking for something, and I can make sure you get it. You looking to get high? You looking for a girl?"

"No," Michael said indignantly.

"Don't get so upset. That's usually what boys like you want."

"I'm looking for a man named Eddie."

"Eddie?"

"He's white," Michael said. "Used to run a group around here about ten years ago. It was religious."

The man smiled. "Of course. I should have known. You're looking for religion." He made the sign of the cross and laughed. "Well, if you can't find your Eddie, then you come and find me. The name's Pete. I'm usually around."

He extended his hand to Michael, who hesitated to shake it.

"Something wrong?"

Michael shook his head and then shook Pete's hand.

"See, that wasn't so bad, now was it?"

Michael walked farther west, then back east to the train station, all the while eyeing the odd white face in hopes that it would be Eddie's.

*

Michael returned to 63rd and Cottage Grove the next Sunday and the Sunday after that. By the end of July, his trips to Eddie's old neighborhood felt as obligatory and unrewarding as Mass. He doubted that Eddie lived there anymore, but he still felt compelled to wander the streets, letting his eyes linger on the faces of the few white men he passed.

In August, a few days after the war's end, Michael moved from the Hotel Alban to a furnished efficiency on the upper floor of an eight-unit building just off the main drag in Lyons, with unobstructed views of two nightclubs and six taverns, including the White Crow. The apartment was dingy and cramped, with a kitchen that boasted nothing more than a hot plate, counter, and sink, and a mattress that felt like a burlap sack of tennis balls and broken springs. The coffee table stood on three wooden legs and a cinder block. The upholstered chair leaned precariously to one side. His first night there, Michael heard a man snore loudly next door and another across the hall threaten to beat his wife. When sleep seemed impossible, Michael left the apartment and wandered Ogden Avenue, feeling lonely among love-struck couples, drunken men, and occasional streetwalkers, and wondering if he would come across his father. The next morning, he rode the El to Cottage Grove.

"You looking for someone?"

Michael turned to see Pete beside him.

"Of course you are," Pete said. "You wouldn't be here otherwise."

"I'm still looking for Eddie."

"Were you looking for him before?"

"I talked to you a couple of months ago."

"I talk to lots of white boys. You know what they're usually looking for?"

Michael shook his head. Pete leaned in close and pointed to a girl in a sundress, sitting on the stoop of an apartment house with a burgundy awning. One of her slender brown legs was crossed over the other.

"Five dollars, and she's yours."

The girl chatted and laughed with an old man wearing suspenders.

"I'm looking for a man named Eddie."

"Eddie, right," Pete said with a laugh. "I know a guy who could be your Eddie for you, if that's what you want. I don't mind. I'm not here to judge."

"He ran a group about ten years ago—called the Society for Sacred Possessions."

Pete laughed. "The Society for Sacred Possessions, huh?" He shook his head. "Can't help you there, friend." He ambled away with his hands in his pockets, then spun around to face Michael. "Five bucks," he said as he held up his right hand, all five fingers extended.

Michael ogled the girl and imagined her caressing him and whispering, "Save me." He would rescue her, take her to his new apartment, buy her fancy clothes, and tell her that what she was doing was wrong, and every night thereafter she would express her appreciation to him. She noticed him watching her and winked. Michael blushed and turned away. Five dollars was a bargain, he thought, but he wasn't like his father; he wasn't the kind of man who visited whores. Out of the corner of his eye, Michael saw a tall white man pass by on the other side of the street. Wearing a gray fisherman's cap and a faded green suit, he carried a paper grocery bag in each hand, and he strode purposefully west on 63rd Street. Michael followed, jogging at times to keep pace with the man's long strides. The crowds and businesses thinned the farther west they headed; what people and stores remained looked broken down and abandoned. The man turned left on Rhodes and approached a small apartment building halfway down the block.

"Excuse me," Michael called to the man, who hurriedly unlocked the door and pushed inside. Michael rushed after him and stuck his foot between the doorframe and the door. "Is your name Eddie?"

The man pushed against the door. "What do you want?"

"I want to ask you something."

"Go away."

"Is your name Eddie?"

"Leave me alone."

"Did you used to run the Society for Sacred Possessions?"

"I don't know what you're talking about."

"My mother was Elizabeth Halligan."

The man stopped pushing but still leaned his body against the door. Through the small opening, weary eyes inspected Michael.

"I used to come here with her."

"I know," the man said.

"Can I come in?"

"Step back."

Michael backed up several feet. The door opened wide to reveal Eddie with his grocery bags in his hands. "All right," he said after a few seconds, "come on."

Michael entered the building. Eddie was halfway up the stairs. "Lock the door behind you," he called over his shoulder. "You can't be too careful around here."

Michael locked the door and headed up the familiar stairs, which leaned to the right and seemed to creak in anticipation of his steps. He followed Eddie into the third-floor apartment, which was warm and stuffy with the odor of unwashed clothing, and he immediately recognized the red velvet couch against the window and the baby grand in the corner.

"Sit down," Eddie called from the kitchen, where he was opening and closing cabinet doors.

Michael sat on the couch and surveyed the apartment, which was smaller and more cluttered with knickknacks and newspapers than he remembered. He rubbed his palm against the worn armrest and wondered if something of his mother—an eyelash, a hair, the ghost of a scent—was still here. Was her voice still echoing somewhere in the corner, so quietly he couldn't hear it? His pulse quickened. His throat constricted.

"Michael, right?" Eddie said as he walked into the room.

Michael nodded.

"A great leader realizes early on that he must remember names." Eddie sat on the piano bench. "You can forget a lot of things, but if you forget someone's name, you've lost him forever."

Michael had envisioned this encounter countless times over the past two months, and each time he'd imagined himself as braver, angrier, and clearer of purpose than he now felt. He'd pictured himself threatening Eddie to tell him the truth about his mother, or beating him senseless, but since he had never actually believed he would find the man, he wasn't sure what he should do now.

"So, what do you want?" Eddie asked.

Michael glimpsed his feet on the Oriental rug. His mother had set her feet here in the past. She'd breathed the air he was breathing. He looked up and cleared his throat. "I was just in the neighborhood," he said.

Eddie laughed. "Why? You enjoy depravity? You like to see people destroy beautiful places?" He folded his arms across his chest. He stared at Michael, his eyes like slits. "When my family moved to the city, we had nothing. We slept in parks and bathed in the lake. But my parents worked hard, and they prayed and went to church, and within ten years God blessed them with this building. We lived in this very apartment and made sure the other five were safe and comfortable, and if a tenant couldn't make rent now and then, my parents gave him a pass. But my father died, and then my mother died, and soon the neighborhood changed. So here I am, caught between colored tenants who don't pay me enough, and Jewish bankers who always want more."

Eddie blathered on, his condemnations aimed at the ceiling, the sofa, the silent grandfather clock with hands several hours off. Michael remembered sitting in the bedroom alone as the man's muffled speeches reverberated in the walls. He had always wanted Eddie to shut up, or disappear, or die.

"My mother's dead," Michael said.

Eddie turned to the window. The sunlight made him blink.

"Do you know what it's like to devote your life to others and then have them abandon you, steal from you, spy on you?" he said. "Have the authorities call you a demagogue? A communist? A fascist? Investigate your finances and then throw you in prison in an attempt to destroy you? Do you know about any of that? Can you even begin to imagine?"

"She died eleven years ago."

Eddie stood and paced and railed against the world, his Adam's apple working like a piston, his voice and gestures emphatic, theatrical. Michael remembered the man's speeches in parks and abandoned buildings, and the devoted look on his mother's face. Now Eddie was at it again, pounding the floor with his feet, striking the air with his fists.

Michael felt cold. He started to shiver. "Didn't you hear what I said?"

"Of course I heard you." Eddie stopped and glared at Michael. "People die all the time. It's not news."

Anger rose inside Michael. It filled him completely, stunned him into stillness.

Eddie looked away and vigorously rubbed the nape of his neck. "I saw the death notice back then," he said. "I was shocked. We all were." He looked at Michael. "It was your father, wasn't it? He killed her, didn't he?"

The hammering in Michael's heart rushed to his head and stomach. He felt dizzy. "She tried to get rid of the baby inside her," he said, the words snagging on their way out. "She bled to death."

Eddie's jaw clenched. "Is that what you came to tell me? Is that why you tracked me down?"

"I came because I wanted to know about you and her."

"You want to know about *me* and her?" Eddie's back stiffened. He stood erect, as if he thought the whole world had been built around him. "Why don't you ask your father about *him* and her? Why don't you ask yourself about *you* and her? I think those are better questions."

"What do you mean?"

"You think she liked dragging you all over the place? Why do you think she always closed you off in the bedroom? It wasn't because she enjoyed having you around—I know that for a fact. And now you come around, wanting to know about *me* and her? Well, go ahead and ask whatever you want. I'll tell you the truth."

Michael met Eddie's stare and held it.

"Was the baby yours?" he asked.

The question exploded in the room, and in its dust Michael felt overwhelmed by the realization that he had not known his mother as well as Eddie, or his father, or Aunt Mae, or countless others had.

"No," Eddie said, "the baby wasn't mine. The baby couldn't have been mine. I never would have done that to her."

The words Michael had hoped to hear had been spoken, yet he felt no peace. His mother's absence was everywhere.

"You know what your mother once told me?"

Again a chill came to Michael, made his body feel bloodless.

"You were in the bedroom, and we were out here. She was there, in fact, right where you're sitting. She turned to me with tears in her eyes, and she gave me the most grievous of looks. 'They're killing me,' she said, meaning you and your father. 'They're killing me. I have to get away from them.' And she was going to leave you. There was a plan, and I was going to help her. But she lacked faith, and so in the end she gave in to him and you and suffered the consequences."

Michael shook as though some great force was trying to break free from him. "Shut up," he said.

"You may think it was bleeding to death that killed her, but it wasn't. It was you and your father."

Michael charged Eddie and knocked him to the floor. On his back, Eddie raised his arms in defense. Michael glowered at him, his hands formed into fists. "You didn't know her," he said. "You never did."

"Go ahead," Eddie said. He was either laughing or crying; Michael couldn't tell which. "The bankers haven't destroyed me yet. The government hasn't. You think you can? You think you can ruin my life any more than you already have?"

Michael's body was hunched forward, ready to lunge but not lunging. He told himself to do it, to attack, but his body would not obey.

Eddie lowered his arms to his side. "Resist not evil," he said, "but whosoever shall smite thee on thy right cheek, turn to him the other also."

Michael lowered his hands, unclenched his fists.

"Don't be a coward," Eddie said. "Make your father proud, and kill me if you want to. You think it matters to me?"

Michael glared at Eddie for another few seconds and then stormed out of the apartment, down the stairs, and onto the sidewalk. He turned right, then right again, and hurried down 63rd toward the El station, growing short of breath as he passed boys playing war in the rubble of a vacant lot, a mother rocking a baby on a stoop, an old man hobbling with a cane. The sidewalks grew crowded. He felt as if he were both drowning and burning up in the warm afternoon. When he sensed someone beside him, he stopped and turned quickly, his hands ready to defend himself if necessary.

Pete smiled. "Relax, man. It's just me."

Michael continued toward the station.

"Where's the fire?" Pete kept pace with him. "Did you find your white man, white boy?"

"Leave me alone."

"Hey now, no need for anger. I'm merely asking as a concerned citizen."

When he got home, he would punch a pillow or a wall, or he would wander for hours, letting himself be tempted by the girls who loitered along Ogden Avenue. He would eat dinner alone, and as he fell asleep in his lonely, run-down apartment, he would try to forget the day and all his failings. The next day he would do the same thing.

"Have you thought any more about my proposition?" Pete asked. "Five dollars is all I'm asking. It would do you good."

Michael stopped. He had six bucks and some change, and he didn't care what happened to him. Pete could rob him blind and beat him senseless. When he reached into his wallet, Pete gripped his arm.

"What the hell? Were you born yesterday?"

Pete stared incredulously at Michael, then waved him toward an alley. When Michael had handed over the cash, Pete pointed to the apartment building with the burgundy awning.

"Head on up to number thirty-two," he said.

Michael entered the building, ignoring the asides of two men in the lobby. On the third floor he followed the narrow hallway until he arrived at the right door. He knocked.

"Come in," a female voice called.

Michael opened the door. In bed was a girl, but not the one he had seen sitting outside earlier in the day. This girl was just barely in high school, maybe even younger, her dark face round with baby fat. She wore a white cotton nightgown and sat up in a shadowed bed, reading the funny pages.

"You gonna close that door?"

Michael stepped all the way into the tiny room and shut the door behind him. The heavy lavender drapes were rimmed with thwarted sunlight.

"There must be some mistake," he said.

The girl flipped through the funnies. "You paid Pete, right?"

"Yeah."

"Then there's no mistake."

Michael watched her fold up her newspaper. He knew he should leave.

"Look, do you want to do this or not?" she said. "I've got things to do."

Michael undressed quickly, nervously, his body shaking and his teeth chattering. When the girl yawned and then sighed, he felt anger rush along with his blood. He'd make her lose that indifference, he thought. He'd show her he was someone to be respected. Naked except for his glasses and socks, he climbed into bed and on top of her. She hiked up her nightgown and gazed at the ceiling. He looked down at her breast beneath the cotton, and he placed his palm there. She took him in her hand. Her touch felt better and more alarming than anything he'd ever felt, and before he could hold back his response, he'd spent himself. He stayed where he was, on his hands and knees, as the girl reached over, grabbed a rag from the dresser, and wiped away the mess on her leg. Michael squeezed his eyes shut and thought for a moment that if he never opened them again, maybe he would disappear. The girl tapped his shoulder and told him he was done.

THE GREAT-MEN CLUB
1957–1961

SARA MALONE FELT LIKE AN OPERATOR RUNNING A SHELL GAME AS SHE reconfigured the stapler, tape dispenser, and mug of pencils on her desk, hand over hand, for what felt like an hour but was actually a minute and a half. For the third time that morning, she picked up her nameplate, brushed it with the cuff of her blouse, and set it down facing the large, rectangular room, which had the floor space of a school gymnasium and was crowded with row upon row of accountants working busily in the sputtering fluorescence. On the typing table to her left were a Smith-Corona Royal Quiet DeLuxe; shelves containing plain white paper, personal stationery for Fenton J. Appleby, and letterhead for Edwards, Appleby, Whitaker & Sloan; and yesterday's newspaper. She glanced at the half-completed crossword puzzle. *Amour of Eros*. Six letters. Blank, S, blank, blank, H, E. She grabbed a handful of pencils from her mug and stepped on them one by one, until she had snapped off each perfectly functional tip.

On her first day, just two weeks earlier, Sara had counted the accountants. Six across and ten deep, with one opening in the fourth row— a sea of men with their sleeves rolled up to their elbows. By her second day, she had done the addition and division and had figured out the ratio. Fifty-nine accountants, four partners, three office boys, a mail clerk, and three more whose jobs remained a mystery to her. Four secretaries.

Seventeen and a half men for each woman.

"Half a man is better than no man," her sister Michelle had said.

"Depends on the man," said Sara, "or on which half you get."

Pencils in hand, she strolled beside a long series of windows overlooking the Loop. Several stories below, an El train passed behind the Pittsfield Building and then reappeared. She imagined it jumping the tracks, breaking through an office window at *Man of Leisure*, and smashing Art Malone against the wall—a fitting gift on the six-month anniversary of their divorce.

"Good morning, beautiful."

Sara knew the voice belonged to Ricky before she saw him swivel in his chair, smiling and smoothing his hair over his bald spot. He bordered on handsome, in a prehistoric way: thick limbs and forehead, hairy neck and ears, and a wild shrubbery of eyebrows.

"So, is today the day I finally take you to lunch?"

She had used up all her excuses on him, and had thus eaten egg salad alone in the cafeteria every afternoon. She pictured the Berghoff, the Palmer House. Prime rib and heaping Caesar salads. The affluent *ping* of silver on china. Art used to take her to those places, and each time she had worn the clothes he'd wanted her to wear because showing her off, she knew, made him feel successful.

"Today's fine," she told Ricky and then continued on amid the clicking of adding machines and the glances of accountants. She enjoyed the attention of one here, one there, but when she noticed several watching her, she picked up the pace. In men's eyes she was used to seeing infatuation and lust, which were often hard to tell apart, but recently she'd sensed something new: bemusement, pity, derision. Since divorcing Art, she'd put on ten pounds and not slept well. The strain of living in her parents' garage apartment and trying to rebuild her life was wearying, and she feared that others saw her—and that sometimes she saw herself—as little more than a divorcée in decline, rapidly approaching the cliff of her thirtieth birthday.

She reached the pencil sharpener, where a redheaded accountant with thick glasses was attending to his dull tips. The shavings fluttered down to a garbage can.

"You can cut in front of me," he said.

She noticed he wore no wedding band, then felt pathetic for having checked.

When he stepped away from the sharpener and told her to go ahead, she rested her hand on his sinewy forearm. "I'm killing time," she whispered. "I'd rather wait."

He was more handsome than most of the accountants, although that wasn't saying much. Several years ago, with a wider and deeper pool of suitors, she would have waited for him to impress her and thus prove he was worth her attention, but now, as he meticulously sharpened his pencils and blew dust from each new tip, she felt like the one who had to stand out.

When he had finished, she smiled and said, "I'm Sara Malone, by the way."

"Michael Halligan." He was the same height as she was, and she told herself that was fine. With a slight bow, he headed back to his desk.

Sara ground each of her pencils to a point and tried to ignore the knot of sickness in her stomach when, in the churn of the sharpener, she heard the whir of Art's camera as he advanced the film. In her mind, she woke again to a winking aperture and frantically covered her naked body with a sheet.

"What are you doing?"

"Practicing my composition." He took a last shot. "Don't worry, there's no film."

"Stop it."

"I can't help myself. You look so beautiful."

Back at her desk, Sara grabbed her newspaper and looked at the crossword puzzle. *Psyche.* She printed the letters in the squares, then glanced at the clock. It was only noon. She wished Mr. Appleby would actually come to the office and assign her a task. Other than his daily phone call and the occasional Dictaphone tape left overnight on her chair, she had little interaction with him and therefore virtually no work. He was a gentle old man with impeccable manners, always dressed in a fashion that would have been called dapper in the twenties, with a gold watch chain on the outside of his vest and a pocket handkerchief to match his tie. Based on her limited contact with him, Sara concluded that if she ever came to know him, he would provide wise counsel on her life.

At one o'clock, Ricky stopped by Sara's desk, and together they took a cab to the Pump Room, where tuxedoed waiters served them martinis and

shish kebab. Ricky said that before the war he'd considered becoming a
fireman, like his brothers, but the horrors of combat, which he'd not
experienced but easily could have, had made him crave a job that was secure
and free of danger—hence, accounting. He explained the advantages and
disadvantages of both pork bellies and President Eisenhower, and Sara
ordered a second drink, then a third. He asked what her goals in life were,
and when she said being someone's secretary certainly wasn't one of them,
he interrupted to declare that setting goals was almost as important as
achieving them; in fact, if a person thought long and hard about it, he would
realize that setting a goal *was* achieving a goal. He proceeded to describe
the goals he'd achieved by setting them, and the goals he'd achieved twice
by setting and then achieving them. Two hours after they had left the office,
Ricky helped Sara put her coat on and whispered, "You are so beautiful."
His breath on her neck felt like groping fingers.

In the cab back to work, as Ricky sat too close and regaled her with
stories of the sailboat he'd bought in the spring, Sara tensed and remembered
raiding Art's desk but only coming across bills, bank statements, matchbooks,
and the articles, book reviews, and dirty jokes he wrote for *Man of Leisure*.
There was nothing under the bed or in the closet. Nothing in his suitcase. She
picked the lock on his footlocker, and, after tossing aside more clippings, she
found a cardboard box filled with black-and-white snapshots of women
wearing negligees or nothing at all. They lounged in rec rooms and on
unmade beds with eager grins, unsure smiles, or faces slack with sleep. She
flipped through the photos, feeling light-headed, and soon found four naked
pictures of her sleeping self, paper-clipped to a piece of paper bearing a
message: *For Bob*. Another set and a note: *For Andy*. Another, for James. A
fourth, for Mitchell. She knew the names but not the men: members of Art's
camera club, a seemingly harmless group that snapped pictures of wrestling
matches and neighborhood dogs. Sara tore the photographs of herself, but
always there was something to be seen: a nipple, bare flesh, bits of her
oblivious face. She gathered up the scraps and the other photos in the box,
then ran down the stairs and onto the sidewalk, where she buried everything
in the first trash can she could find.

*

After lunch, a little more than moderately drunk, Sara commiserated for half an hour on the phone with her sister, at first stapling blank pieces of paper together in an attempt to appear busy, but eventually leaning back and resting her feet on her desk. She was staring absentmindedly at her typewriter, the receiver warm against her ear, when she heard Mr. Appleby's rattling cough from across the room. She lowered her legs, muttered a quick goodbye to Michelle, and hung up the phone. She did her best to smile soberly as he approached and asked to see her in his office.

Sitting behind his broad oak desk, looking tidy and composed, Mr. Appleby explained to Sara that each human being had a value, a particular amount in dollars and cents assigned to each hour of her life. Her time could be bought or sold, bargained with or bartered, but it had a finite value. It was worth no more than that. And once she entered into a hiring agreement, her body and mind became vessels for the employer's spirit.

"The value of the company's time, on the other hand, is incalculable," he said as he rapped his neat little knuckles on his desk. "It is precious and irretrievable—like the value of the ocean or the air. You may try to assign it a specific value, but you will fail."

In between coughing fits, he told Sara of his valiant attempts to reach her by telephone. For an hour he had received no answer. Then, for another twelve minutes, he had been subjected to a busy signal. She started to apologize, but he silenced her by raising his index finger.

"If you were an Olympian training for the decathlon," he said, "would you waste your time on activities that hindered your training? Of course you wouldn't. You would realize that you had been called to serve a high athletic purpose, and that it was thus your moral obligation to surrender to the truth that your very body and mind and spirit belonged to a force outside yourself. And just as the Olympian has the moral duty to serve this unseen force, you are morally obligated to serve Edwards, Appleby, Whitaker & Sloan—and in this simple calling, you have failed utterly. You have failed me and you have failed yourself, and this organization cannot build its destiny on a foundation of failure. Therefore, it is with absolutely no reservation that I must inform you that effective immediately, your employment at this firm is terminated."

Sara hurried out of Mr. Appleby's office, grabbed her purse and coat, and shoved open the door to the stairwell. The door struck something, and Sara heard a curse and a clatter. As she cautiously opened the door all the way, she saw Michael Halligan stumble backward down the stairs. He grabbed the railing and steadied himself, but not before stepping on his glasses.

"Are you all right?" she asked.

He scowled at her, knelt, and picked up his glasses by one of their stems, as if he were holding a dead mouse by its tail. A bit of glass fell to the floor.

She crouched down a few steps higher than him. "I'm so sorry," she said. "I really am."

"A lot of good that does me. I can't see without them."

Sara continued to apologize for several seconds, and even insisted on paying for a new pair. Michael silently gathered up what he could of his lenses and put the pieces in his coat pocket.

"Look," he said as he stood, "don't worry about it. I have an old pair at home."

"Please let me pay for them."

He held up his hand. "It's all right, really. Just leave me alone."

"At least let me help you get home. How can you get home if you can't see?"

Together they walked south on Wabash, then west on Jackson toward Union Depot. Sara led the way, holding Michael's arm. They discussed his inferior vision and how long he had worked at the firm, they agreed that winter appeared to be coming early and that it was indeed odd that they both lived on the Burlington Northern line, and Sara let herself consider that maybe her miserable afternoon was part of an inscrutable plan God had laid out for her life, a plan that required her to wade through absurdity and annoyance to secure the rewards of true companionship and love. This prospect pleased her because it was pleasant in itself and because it far surpassed her other consideration, which was that her life was not only pointless and without reward, but worsening every day. Michael was polite and shy, friendly enough, and not at all bad-looking. She imagined him growing more handsome and distinguished with age, possessing talents he kept hidden out of modesty, singing lullabies to babies, and bringing her breakfast in bed, but then she stumbled on a sidewalk crack and remembered she was still a little drunk.

As they crossed the Chicago River, he asked if she had sharpened her pencils.

"I did," she said. "But then I got fired."

He glanced at her and said, "I'm sorry."

"Why are you sorry?" She squeezed his arm and shouldered him playfully. "Mr. Appleby's the one who should be sorry. That stupid mummy doesn't know what's good for him."

Michael stopped and turned to her. His nose was a little bigger than it should have been and his hairline seemed to be receding, but his eyes looked honest.

"Tell me when you were born," he said.

She laughed at his earnestness. "What are you talking about?"

"Tell me the date you were born, and I'll tell you how many hours you've been alive."

"Are you serious?"

"Come on," he said. "Tell me when you were born."

She told him her birth date, and he closed his eyes and faced the sky. Seeing his concentration, she suddenly felt like kissing him. She hardly knew him, and all around them commuters were rushing by. This was neither the time nor the place for a kiss, even though it would have improved her day dramatically, and his day dramatically, and thus most likely the days of everybody they would have subsequently met. He opened his eyes and looked at her.

"Two hundred fifty-six thousand, four hundred and forty hours." A shy grin shimmered on his face. "Approximately."

Michael turned and headed toward the station. Sara caught up with him and took hold of his arm.

"How did you do that?"

He shrugged. "It's just basic math."

"Yeah, right, it's just basic math. It's amazing."

"I could be wrong."

"But you're not, are you?"

"No."

They found facing seats on the upper deck of the Burlington Northern, which soon pulled out of the station. In the rail yard, tracks ran parallel to each other, then crossed or merged; some ended abruptly, which to Sara, in her inebriated state, seemed irredeemably sad. She stared at Michael, who faced her without expression. When he didn't look away, she continued to watch him, happy to have a man gaze at her and not say she was beautiful. A smile stretched across her face, even though she felt more like crying than she had all day. The train stopped at Cicero, Berwyn, Harlem Avenue.

"You know what the highlight of my life has been?" she said.

Commuters hopped down from the last step and plodded along the platform. Michael shook his head.

"When I was a sophomore in high school, I was named the war-bond queen." The train jolted forward and then accelerated toward the next stop. "I was up there onstage with three juniors and three seniors, who I thought were the most beautiful girls I'd ever seen—all of them like Veronica Lake or Rita Hayworth. I was terrified about being in front of the whole school, having everyone compare me with the other girls, but I'd been nominated, so I didn't have a choice in the matter. It was an assembly that went on for two hours or so, with speakers talking about war bonds in between sections of the contest. For the first part, we each had to sing a patriotic song. During the second part, a man from the USO asked us questions about the importance of supporting the boys overseas. Then we did the part with the bathing suits, and I remember walking around the stage in red high heels as all the boys clapped and whistled like mad and the USO man said, 'This is what we're fighting for, men.' My feet ached and my legs were cold, but they'd told us how important it was to smile, so I kept smiling."

Her grin was gone, along with the urge to cry. She felt calm, as though this moment had no cause and would have no consequence. The train stopped, and the doors opened.

"At the end of the contest, all of us girls sat in a row, facing the audience. The announcer named the third-place winner and then second place. There were five of us left. I figured I didn't have a shot, but then he called my name. Everyone stood and applauded and I walked around like I was the most important person in the world, like there was no way something more exciting could ever happen to anyone, and at that moment I honestly believed it."

The doors closed. Sara looked out the window and saw a sign for the Riverside station. She turned quickly to Michael.

"I'm sorry," she said, as the train started off again. "Wasn't that your stop?"

"It's all right," he said. "I'll take the train back from your station."

The Burlington Northern raced onward. The farther west it headed, the more stately the homes and trees became, as if greater beauty and a richer life were always just a little farther down the line.

"What about you, Michael? What's been the highlight of your life so far?"

"I don't know."

"Come on," she said, "think of something."

"I guess getting my associate's degree in accounting. Or landing the job at Edwards Appleby."

"That's the highlight of your life?"

He shrugged. "I'm proud of those things. I had to work hard at them."

It wasn't the answer she had hoped for, but there was something to be said for practical men. Art Malone had been impractical and dashing, after all. Michael was undoubtedly the reliable kind—steady, simple, no filet mignon, but no potted meat, either. Just good-quality cold cuts, night after night.

At Hinsdale they stepped down from the train and crossed the tracks to the opposite platform. In the distance shone the headlight of a train coming east from Aurora.

"Are you sure you can get home without your glasses? Are you sure you don't need my help?"

"I know the way by heart."

"You could at least let me pay for the pair I broke."

"Don't worry about it," he said. "I really don't mind."

Sara envisioned eating dinner with her parents in front of the television for yet another night. There was always a program to distract her from her unhappiness or shield her from her mother's Pollyanna suggestions that maybe Art deserved one last chance because wasn't he so terribly handsome and fun, and didn't they make a lovely couple, and besides, didn't she know that all men were animals? Sara had hoped to be stronger and more resilient by now, but every night she dreaded the after-dinner walk to her tiny garage apartment, which looked anonymous and cold whenever she switched on the light.

"Isn't it funny how we never talked to each other until today," she said, "but in the last hour and a half we've spent every second together? Isn't it strange how things like that can happen to people? Nothing, and then—" She stopped talking. She didn't know what came after nothing. Maybe something, maybe not. "Do you ever think about things like that? About how so much of life is predictable, but the only parts that really matter are the ones that are completely unexpected?"

Michael stammered, then grew silent. Sara watched the approaching train. She had lowered her expectations for him, and now he wasn't even going to ask her out on a date? Didn't he realize how easy she was making this? Didn't he realize that if he asked her out, she would say yes and they would fall in love and marry and have babies, and decades later one of them would die peacefully in the other's presence? Didn't he understand that love was more about will than about destiny, and that she had enough will for them both?

"To tell you the truth, the beauty contest wasn't all that great," she said, her eyes on the arriving train. "Afterward, some of the stitching on the sash came undone, and the tiara was just a piece of tin. The boys and a couple of the teachers told me how great I looked in a bathing suit, how I didn't look fifteen at all, and would I want to go for a drive sometime? The girls used to shoulder me into lockers and never invited me to anything."

She expected him to say something, but for several seconds he didn't. Then, as she buttoned up her coat, he cleared his throat and said, "The unexpected things don't really matter."

She turned to him, surprised he had spoken.

"What do you mean?"

"They don't matter—or at least, you shouldn't let them matter." His hair was fine. So were his lips. "You have to stay the same no matter what happens to you, good or bad. If you can maintain order and self-discipline and act like nothing happened, you'll have no trouble finding another job."

The gates clanged. The train slowed into the station. Sara knew she would find another job. Couldn't he tell that unemployment wasn't her problem? It was loneliness.

"So, unexpected things don't matter?" she said.

"Not unless you let them."

She watched him watching her, and she wondered how well he saw her without his glasses. If they passed each other on the street a month from now, would he recognize her? She stepped toward him. Falling in love was easy; any idiot could do it. All it took was willpower and a willingness to look foolish. Michael squinted at her, and she thought that if he told her she was beautiful, she would turn and walk away. She moved closer and shut her eyes. His kisses weren't great—they alternated between desperate and passive—but they were sweet in spite of themselves, and besides, they were kisses, which had been hard to come by lately. The train arrived and left without Michael. Maybe she was lowering her expectations, but wasn't that the best way to endure disappointment? Each year, you lowered your expectations a little more. Each year, you learned to stop chasing the things you used to crave and start yearning for what you had overlooked. Like love, maybe desire was more a matter of the mind than of the heart.

2.

EVEN THOUGH HE HAD LIVED IN LYONS FOR TWELVE YEARS, MICHAEL moved through the town like a stranger. He rarely visited the taverns and nightclubs, and when he did, he never stayed long enough to settle into conversation with anyone except the B-girls hustling drinks. In the grocery store he uttered the barest of pleasantries, and with waitresses his chitchat was minimal. His neighbors came and went with little more than "hello" and "so long" and curt nods of acknowledgment, which was more than fine with Michael. If he was known at all, it was by the prostitutes who plied their wares in the back rooms, upstairs apartments, and side-street houses that served as informal brothels. To them, if they bothered to ask, he was Mike Steele. To him, they were Lily and Blaze, Belle and Marilyn. Natasha, Roxy, and Reva. Ill-fitting pseudonyms stolen from films and other fantasies, donned with pride, and then worn until tattered.

Michael retrieved his notebook from between his mattress and box spring and opened to a random page:

> #131. September 13, 1951. 1:30 a.m. Eva. 3 stars. $5. Approx. 20 minutes. Red dress, red high heels, no nylons. 5 ft. 3 in. 125 lbs. Prob. early 20s. Prob. Polish (poss. immigrant, war?). V. little English. Brown hair, brown eyes, v. pale skin, mole on forehead, bruises on arms, small breasts, scar over lip, goose bumps. Upstairs—Larry's Lounge.

He flipped from page to page, and as he perused some of the 268 entries, beginning with the girl near 63rd and Cottage Grove and ending with one last month, he realized how few of them he recalled.

He shoved the notebook into a paper trash bag filled with old magazines, torn socks, and years' worth of dust from under the bed. Until today, he had never bothered to decorate his apartment beyond the shabby furnishings included in the rent, but now he had a pair of Naugahyde easy chairs, an Oriental rug, a radio, a floor lamp, and a bookcase filled with biographies and action novels he'd read over the years. His place was orderly, cozy, not the kind of home a person would expect of a man with 268 trips to whores under his belt. He dwelled on that number, let it lie in his mind like a cadaver cut open for autopsy. It certainly wasn't an inconsequential statistic, and it didn't exactly fill him with pride, but the very fact that it embarrassed him made him better than men who would have bragged about a number that high, or men like his father who flaunted their sins. Michael had his shortcomings, but at least he had the decency to not parade them around for others.

He again considered 268, divided it by twelve years, and came up with 22.33 visits annually, which further broke down to .43 visits per week, which seemed pretty low and may even have indicated he was less perverted than a lot of people. Not that he was proud of his past, but at least his life was changing. His three months with Sara had shaken him from predictability and made him consider the prospect that he could love someone without misfortune. For more than a decade, he had woken most days at six o'clock, done fifty push-ups and fifty sit-ups, read the newspaper on the train downtown, worked eight-plus hours, eaten alone, wound down with a book, bathed, shaved, and then climbed into bed, where he slept long and well, despite the incessant clamor outside his window. His time was ruled by order, which was liberating after the chaos of his father's world and the oddness of his aunt's, and he generally felt confident that no surprises were stalking him, muggerlike, waiting for the right moment to strike. On Saturday evenings, he ate out and sometimes stopped by a bar, and on Sundays, he didn't attend Mass, because nobody was around to make him go. Only about once every two weeks would a stubborn unease infect his body and rouse him in the middle of the night, causing him to pace the apartment floor, feeling tormented by lust and guilty about his inability to suppress it. He would curse himself for having such cravings, for being so weak, and he would sense his mother watching him, counting on him to do right. When his agitation became too great, he would head out and pay for the newest girl he could find, all the while trying to act as gentlemanly as possible under the circumstances, and believing that the whore he'd chosen was lucky to have him and not one of the many lowlifes prowling around Lyons. Later, no longer restless, he would sit at his table and jot down the details before kneeling beside his bed and praying perfunctorily for forgiveness. At first, each encounter had felt like a momentary vice he could banish by indulging once, or twice, or once a year, once a month, just once more, but over the years he came to see his need as a persistent part of him. One girl blurred into the next, one night into another, and eventually he came to enjoy writing and reading about his encounters more than the actual encounters themselves. The real pleasure—the calm he sought— came whenever he compiled the data: how many blonds, how many brunettes, their average price and rating, the percentage with blue eyes, the number with a noticeable birthmark or scar.

Michael reached into his pants pocket and felt the engagement ring he had bought in a burst of hopefulness a month ago but had not yet had the courage to offer to Sara. Whenever his heart or gut felt bold enough to propose, his head would show him all the ways she could break his heart or leave him or die, or it would remind him of how badly he had screwed up last month. The image of that final, gray-eyed girl, whom he had visited one panicked night shortly after buying the ring, was already vanishing from his mind, but the vague memory of her was always there—a warning of how unworthy and incapable he was of redemption.

A car honked, and Michael looked out the frosty window to see Sara in her father's Coupe de Ville. She had insisted on finally seeing his apartment and treating him to dinner tonight. He picked up the garbage bag and started to leave, but at the door he thought he should hold on to the notebook for a week longer, or maybe even a month, which would give him enough time to compile final, authoritative numbers and break down the data in such a way that he would be able to quantify, if not comprehend, the period of his life that had officially and undoubtedly ended last month. He slipped the notebook between the mattress and box spring and headed downstairs with the trash.

"I hope you didn't clean up just for me," Sara said as Michael sat in the passenger seat.

"Only a little."

He directed her around the block and into a parking lot behind his building. When she jokingly complained that she could have found the spot by herself, he told her she needed to be more careful. There were a lot of creeps in Lyons.

Since meeting Sara, Michael had mastered a rudimentary version of the fox-trot and discovered he was not half bad at waltzing, as long as the tempo was slow. He had eaten fondue and Indian food, played badminton and canasta. And just the other week, riding the South Shore train, he had crossed the Illinois border for the first time. At the Brookfield Zoo, watching animals he had previously seen only in books and movies, he became a child discovering life. Tackling Sara playfully in the snow, he felt like a teenager in love. And now, as she became the first woman to enter his apartment, he imagined himself the suave bachelor he had never been.

"Your place is nice." She removed her coat and draped it over her arm.

Michael glanced at the new furniture and decorations; at his new style, his new life, the price tag he'd accidentally left hanging from the lampshade.

"It's not much," he said.

"What's not much is this neighborhood." Sara stood at the window and looked down at the nightlife. She was a divorcée, and therefore not a virgin, but she had been virginal thus far with him, which both perturbed and pleased him. He didn't want her just giving it away to a guy like him, but then again, he really wanted it. If only he could have it, he would no longer feel driven to visit prostitutes. His lust would become love; his vice, virtue. "How can you live here with all that going on outside your window?"

"The apartment's cheap," Michael said, taking her coat and hat. "It's convenient."

Michael hung up her things, and as he returned from the closet, he watched her inspect his books and thought she should be in a elegant supper club, laughing over cocktails with a wealthy man in a snazzy suit, instead of running her finger over the spine of a Mickey Spillane book in a crappy efficiency apartment, alone with a man who had run around once with a whore behind her back—or twice, he had to admit, if he counted that time during their first week of dating, when he wasn't yet sure whether to consider her his girlfriend. Sara was far more beautiful and fun than any of the admittedly few women he had dated; she made him feel significant and adventurous, and sometimes, as when he had told her that his mother had died as the result of a miscarriage, she hugged him with such affection that his teeth chattered. He had developed such a need for her presence that he found it nearly impossible not to worry he was one word, one foolish action, one revealed truth away from her leaving him or admitting she had worked in burlesque, or had posed for *Man of Leisure*, or had had relations with many men. How had she met a man who worked for *Man of Leisure*, anyhow? And who, and how many, had there been before that?

Sara pulled *Buck Rogers in the City Below the Sea* from the bookcase.

"Is this yours from when you were a kid?"

"Yeah."

She flipped through the pages. "What were you like as a boy?"

"I don't know," he said. "I try not to think about back then."

"Because of your mom?"

Michael shrugged and said, "I guess."

He asked if she wanted a drink, and when she said yes, just water, he went to the kitchenette and filled a glass from the faucet. He could change. It wasn't impossible. On the road to Damascus, Saul had become Paul. After five centuries of suspended animation, Buck Rogers had become a hero. Sara deserved someone more handsome, confident, and decent than he was, yet in his better moments Michael felt he could become that man, but only with her help.

When Michael returned, Sara was sitting on the bed with his book. He handed her the drink and sat in one of his new easy chairs. The springs were too stiff, the stuffing too firm.

"I used to collect them," he said.

"What?"

"Big Little Books." He pointed to the copy on her lap. "I had nearly two hundred by the time I was fourteen."

She took a sip of her drink and kicked off her shoes. Michael put his hand in his pocket, slipped the tip of his finger into the ring. He wouldn't fail her. She wouldn't leave him or die young. Together they would buy a little house far away from Lyons.

"What happened to the rest of your books?"

Michael shrugged. "I don't know."

"How can you not know?"

"I just don't. Do you remember everything you ever lost?"

"If it was important to me, I do."

Then again, the time and place weren't right for a proposal, and he wasn't the marrying kind, as they said in songs. In the end it was probably wisest, and certainly safest, to forget about Sara and return to his old life, which, though lonely, at least wasn't so worrisome.

"My dad ripped up my collection and kicked me out of the house," Michael said. "That's the only book I have left."

Sara folded one leg under the other. A siren blared outside the window.

"You never talk about your dad. What's he like?"

Nervously, Michael flipped the ring from fingertip to fingertip. Memories churned darkly inside his chest.

"He was a real son of a bitch," Michael said.

"Whatever happened to him?"

"He died a few years back."

"I'm sorry."

"I'm not."

Picturing his father's face, Michael quickly, unthinkingly removed his hand from his pocket. The ring flew across the room and clattered under the bed.

"What was that?" Sara asked.

"What was what?"

"Something flew out of your pocket."

"Really?" Michael felt his face flush. "I didn't see it."

"It was in your pocket."

"I don't think so."

"It was, Michael. I swear to God it was."

She knelt on the floor and peered under the bed.

Michael stood and said, "It's probably just a penny."

"It's not a penny."

"I think it's a penny."

"Michael, I saw it. I know it's a ring."

Michael studied his feet. Two weeks earlier, a little loose on wine, he and Sara had kissed and pawed each other in the backseat of her father's car. She didn't offer the expected gentle resistance, and when he slipped his finger inside her, she dug her knuckles into his skin and released a sharp sigh. Her face was filled with such abandon that Michael pulled back from her. Her expression evaporated into embarrassment, and soon they were silently driving west, Michael wondering if he was capable of whatever feeling had produced such a look and such a sound, and proud for having elicited a response so desirous.

Michael looked from his feet to Sara, who knelt beside his bed and eyed him quizzically. He knew he was opening himself up to ruin with what he was about to do, but for the moment he didn't care. All he wanted was to see that abandon on Sara's face and hear her rapturous sigh over and over throughout his life, as though that expression and that sigh could save him.

"I was planning to ask you later," Michael said with a crooked grin.

"Ask me what?"

"If you want to get married."

She turned away from him and rested her hands on the bed as if she was praying. Michael feared she was preparing her rejection, but then she turned back to him and smiled.

"Well, then," she said as she stood, "we'd better find it."

She tried to shove aside the bed, which she didn't realize was bolted to the floor. Instead of pushing the frame, she sent the mattress halfway off the box spring.

"What's this?" Sara said as she picked up the notebook.

Hurriedly Michael took it from her and remade the bed so the notebook was hidden once more. "It's nothing," he said. "Sometimes I jot down my dreams in there."

"Really?" She grabbed his arm and squeezed it. "What do you dream, Michael?"

His back and chest now sweaty, he told her that actually, in all honesty, he rarely had dreams—in fact, he hardly ever did—so it was ridiculous to keep a notebook for them, especially when he basically never wrote anything in it, and he would probably get rid of it very soon, probably tomorrow, and anyway, wasn't there a ring they needed to find? Together they crawled on the floor, searching under the bed, until Sara shouted, "Eureka!"

They would marry four months later, on May 24, 1958. After a Minnesota honeymoon they would move into a recently constructed four-bedroom house in Western Springs, a suburb just west of La Grange that billed itself as both Queen of the Suburbs and Investor Town, USA, and, fittingly, their oversize home would be an outstanding investment, with aluminum siding, air-conditioning, two and a half bathrooms, and the municipal swimming pool across the street. "Your life won't be perfect here," the realtor would tell them, "but it'll be pretty darn close."

But at the moment, Sara and Michael were still in Lyons—a town that knew how to squeeze profit from misery—reaching under the bed, the engagement ring just beyond their grasp. Michael retrieved a fork from the kitchen, lay on the floor, and extended the utensil until he hooked the ring on a tine.

Michael knelt on one knee and placed the ring on Sara's finger. Crying, she looked down at the diamond, which was filigreed with dust and hair, and declared it beautiful.

3.

The boat struck the waves and Tom cast off. Slowly the great bulk of the "Revenge" slipped away, leaving the boy alone on the vast ocean.

At first Tom was afraid that his little craft might capsize.

Michael stopped caressing his testicles and turned the page of *Black Silver and His Pirate Crew, with Tom Trojan*. He stood naked in the bathroom, the alarm clock ticking atop the toilet. He resumed his delicate massage.

Even if it did not, he would surely die of starvation or thirst.

Night fell and he could not see through the blackness. Having no choice, he decided to trust to luck, and since it would do no good to row in the dark, he lay down in the bottom of the boat to sleep till morning.

Michael reread the sentence twice and wondered if it should have read: *Having no choice, he decided to trust* his *luck*. As much as he loved Big Little Books, and as satisfied as he felt to have amassed 112 titles over the last year and a half, he had to admit the books could be sloppy concoctions, with typos, grammatical errors, and drawings that had been awkwardly cropped from daily comic strips. He glanced at the clock and then down at his hand on his balls, and he wondered what kind of quack this Dr. Wallace was.

When he awoke, he was surrounded by water. Under the broiling sun, he rowed for a time, but did not know in which direction to go, so didn't outdo himself.

When night fell he was very tired, what with fits of rowing and all the worry about his fate. His sleep was filled with bad dreams, and the night was ages long.

The alarm clock rang, and Michael slapped it silent. He hoped his sperm appreciated all he'd done for them. He hoped they were, in the words of Dr. Wallace, "stimulated and raring to go."

Michael walked down the long hallway, his feet sinking into the plush carpeting—past the room Sara had decorated with a crib and stuffed animals, past the one now occupied by his books, past the empty one with the door closed, and into the master bedroom, where Sara waited for him beneath the covers. He lay beside her, and they kissed and touched for a couple of minutes before Michael suddenly stopped.

"What's wrong?" she said.

"You know."

She draped her arm across her forehead and sighed. "Yeah, I know."

Michael could practically feel Dr. Wallace in the room, exhorting them to screw, reminding them that conception sometimes required patience and careful strategy. It was chess, not tiddlywinks; *War and Peace*, not *The Little Engine That Could*. In the past he'd prescribed caffeine before intercourse, warm compresses right afterward, boxer shorts to increase Michael's sperm count, and, most recently, sex each morning for two straight weeks. At first Michael and Sara had been happy to follow the doctor's orders, but lately sex had begun to feel like a chore.

Michael faced the ceiling and listened to Sara's slow, rhythmic breathing. Since marrying, he had calmed, but there were still times at night when anxiety clawed inside him, scratching out new worries, ripping apart old ones. He had vague, terrifying dreams of his mother or Sara, dreams in which he couldn't run or scream or hit the brakes. Upon waking, he would rush to his Big Littles, which he would read and classify and reorder until he felt soothed. But mostly, as now, he marveled at his good fortune and felt satisfied with life. He turned and kissed Sara's forehead, her cheeks, her neck, and in response she sleepily ran her hand along his arm and then his thigh. Within five minutes, he was on top of her. Had Dr. Wallace been in the room, he would have cheered.

An hour later, Sara and Michael stood on the train platform surrounded by quaint shops, saplings in sidewalk planters, and immaculate families, every inch of Western Springs sparkling as if it had been lovingly polished overnight. Although Michael had reached a point where he could banter about kitchen tiles and gutters in the hardware store or chat with his neighbors about those Go-Go White Sox, he still felt like an interloper in the village.

"Where should we go?" Sara asked.

It was Saturday morning, and they should have been working around the house or shopping, but since the sky was clear and the temperature was supposed to hit eighty, they were on their way downtown.

"I don't know," Michael said.

Sara smiled. "Sounds like a plan to me."

The Burlington Northern arrived. Sara and Michael stepped into the last car and found facing seats on the upper level. The train started off, quickly gaining but soon losing speed as it approached the Stone Avenue station. When the train stopped, Michael glanced at Union Auto, which appeared green, murky, and slightly curved through the Plexiglas, like something on a television set or in a fish tank. In the gravel parking lot stood his father, who glowered at the train for a few seconds before crouching and picking up his newspaper. Every weekday, from the train window, Michael took a look at Union Auto, and every week or two he spotted his old man, who had grown leaner and gray-haired over the last eighteen years, with a jaw that probably hadn't unclenched in all that time.

"He looks like the most miserable man in the world," Sara said. When Michael turned to her, she said, "That guy at the gas station," and tapped the window. "I wonder if he was born looking that angry, or if something made him that way."

"Nothing made him that way," Michael said, not quite remembering why he had told Sara his father was dead, not exactly wanting his old man alive.

"You don't think so?"

The doors closed and the train inched forward. Michael felt a desire to stand in front of Union Auto with Sara and shout that he had just had sex with this beautiful woman in his spacious house. His father had never started his day like that. He had never owned a backyard that took him more than an hour to mow, and undoubtedly he'd never slept with a former beauty queen.

"I bet he just decided to be like that so he could make life miserable for everyone else," Michael said, watching his father slog back to the garage like a man who'd just been shot but was determined to keep the wound a secret.

Sara and Michael wandered into a used bookshop downtown and searched for Big Littles. A year and a half earlier, a few days after Michael's marriage proposal, Sara had bought him a copy of *Buck Rogers in the War with the Planet Venus* at a bookshop near her parents' house. She then took Michael to the store, where he found twenty more Big Littles stuck here and there in the children's section. "I've created a monster, haven't I?" she joked when she saw all he intended to buy. After that, his collection grew steadily. Either on his own or with Sara, he discovered books at rummage sales, church bazaars, and estate sales; through classified ads; and in junk stores and curiosity shops. *Doctor Doom and the Ghost Submarine. Blaze Brandon with the Foreign Legion. Smilin' Jack and the Stratosphere Ascent.* He remembered them all and sometimes wondered if the copies he bought now had been his as a boy.

They left the bookshop empty-handed and headed north on State Street, guided by crowds of people who seemed as aimless as they. Hand in hand, they strolled alongside the river on Wacker and then up the Magnificent Mile, stopping at display windows to gawk at clothes and jewelry, and when Michigan Avenue merged with Lake Shore Drive, Michael and Sara took a tunnel under the traffic to Oak Street Beach, where sunbathers lay out on towels and children squealed in the waves. The sun burned the back of Michael's neck and the tops of his ears, and a blister was forming on his heel. The glare made his eyes squint and his head throb, and as he and Sara followed the coastline's curvature, he imagined hiking thirsty and delirious across a desert in search of rescue. But then a breeze came to him, and with a start Michael realized he was in need of nothing.

"Look," Sara exclaimed.

Michael shielded his eyes and looked up. A mile ahead, on the Navy Pier campus of the University of Illinois, stood white tents, a roller coaster, and a Ferris wheel, like a mirage in the haze. None of it had been there a few days earlier.

"I've never been to a carnival," Sara said as they hastened toward the pier. "My parents thought they were low-class."

"They *are* low-class," Michael said.

They rode the Ferris wheel and carousel, took spins on the tilt-a-whirl and bumper cars, and got soaked on the log flume. They downed hot dogs and peanut brittle, tossed rings and balls, and paid a man on stilts to twist a balloon into a bear for them. Michael told Sara about Enchanted Island, the Transparent Man, and Buck Rogers shouting from a truck bed, and as he spoke, memories of the World's Fair rushed at him so quickly, he couldn't catch them all.

"It's nice," Sara said as they passed the Skee-Ball tent, "hearing you talk so much."

Away from the crowds, they encountered a fortune-telling mannequin encased in a booth. She wore a purple gown and flowery head scarf, and her finger pointed to tarot cards fanned out before her. Michael dropped a dime into the machine, and in response the fortune teller raised and lowered her mechanical eyes as lights blinked and eerie music played. The machine shut off and, almost as an afterthought, produced a small gray card, which bore a cartoon of a terrified man being chased by a devil with a pitchfork. Beneath the drawing was the message:

Has the Devil been chasing you?
Is that what makes you so blue?
Cheer up, cheer up, my own dear one,
For your fight against him has been won.

Yes, you've been up against it at times, and Fate in the form of the Devil has been at the bottom of it all. Now you can look ahead to better times. You will dream about the sun and that will be the beginning of a bright future.

Drop another coin in the slot and I will tell you more.

Sara wanted a prophecy for herself, but she had no dimes in her purse and Michael was out of change, so they decided that his fortune was their fortune, and together they dissolved into the thickening crowd. It became harder to move, and for a few seconds Michael felt they would never escape.

Their pace was somnolent as they headed back down Michigan Avenue and through the Loop. Outside his office building, Michael removed his glasses.

"Remember?" he asked.

"Of course I remember."

"That day we walked to the train, I didn't know what you were after."

"What do you mean, 'what I was after'?"

"I assumed you had some motive for being interested in me," Michael said as Sara led him home through the blurry city.

"Other than just being interested in you? Or hoping we'd fall in love?"

"I figured you were after money or leading me on. Or that there was something wrong with you."

"Maybe there was." She laughed. "Maybe there still is."

Heading toward the train station, they reminisced about their time together as though two years had been twenty. In front of the Rookery Building, Sara suddenly stopped. "You know I wasn't after anything then," she said, "and that I'm not after anything now, don't you?"

"Of course."

"How about you, Michael? What are you after?"

Michael considered Sara's question, uncertain of what to say, except "love" or "calm" or the basic things anyone would have said—none of which seemed sufficient or entirely true. He stopped and kissed her, and when she asked why, he didn't have an answer.

As usual, they sat upstairs on the Burlington Northern. The train crept through the darkened station and into the light of the rail yard. When Sara asked if he could tell what she was doing, Michael put on his glasses and saw that she was crossing her eyes and sticking out her tongue. He laughed but then stopped when he noticed his father sitting a few seats behind her, staring stoically out the window.

Sara asked what was wrong, peeked over her shoulder, and then turned back to Michael with her hand over her mouth, a face of mock horror. "Oh my God, it's him," she whispered. "Maybe he's been following us all day."

Michael removed his prophecy from his shirt pocket, pointed to the picture of the Devil, and then surreptitiously gestured toward his father with his thumb. Sara stifled a laugh.

"You think he's the Devil?" she whispered.

Michael shrugged. "I wouldn't be surprised."

"You'd think the Devil would have a better job than working on cars," Sara said. "He should be running a big company or something."

"Maybe working at a gas station is just a front." Michael glanced at his father, who was now staring right at him. He wore a dress shirt and tie, and his hair was combed and slick with grease.

"So, he runs all of his operations from a gas station in La Grange—is that it?"

"Without a doubt," Michael said, and then smirked as he imagined his father as anything more than a man.

Sara smiled and rested her head against the window. Soon her eyes were shut. Trying to ignore his father's presence, Michael stared at her. He didn't want a child, and the very thought of one often made his breath shorten with fear of what might happen to Sara or the baby, of what kind of father he would be, of how a child would mess up their marriage. But he wanted to keep her happy, didn't want her looking for someone better, so they would keep following Dr. Wallace's orders, and Michael would keep worrying that all his years in Lyons, and all he'd done there, had left him infected with some disease that made fatherhood physically impossible. Michael sensed his father watching him, recognizing him, and, like a boy drawn to the sun despite warnings of blindness, he glanced briefly again at his old man, whose eyes burned right through him. Immediately Michael turned to the window.

He imagined that the warehouses, smoke stacks, and industrial water towers he saw were the inked landscape of a Dick Tracy world.

As the train neared Stone Avenue, Michael watched his father rise and walk toward him, listing from the swaying of the journey. When the train suddenly jerked hard to the right, his father fell onto Sara. She woke, startled, and as his father removed himself slowly from her, Michael did nothing but watch.

"It was my pleasure," his father told Sara with a leer. Then he slapped Michael hard on the shoulder. "Looks like you've done well for yourself."

The train stopped at the station, then started toward Western Springs. Michael imagined the ways he might have been a hero: dragging his father from Sara, punching his old man's face, hurling him down the stairs.

"That was strange," Sara said as they stood to leave. "He acted like he knew you."

"It *was* strange," Michael said, his father's blow reverberating in his shoulder.

4.

Michael listened as Barney Taylor talked about his wife, his two kids, his split-level in Indian Head Park, and his eleven years teaching American history and civics at Lyons Township High School.

"How about you, Halligan?" he asked. "Any kids yet?"

They sat in a red vinyl booth. On the table were two mugs of coffee. Condiments stood off to the side, like a group of children hoping to be noticed.

"One's on the way," Michael said.

"Really? How far along is the missus?"

"Five months."

"How is she taking it?"

"Just fine," Michael said, though he didn't believe it. Sara had spent much of the first month vomiting—until Dr. Wallace started plying her with sample packets of Kevadon, which hadn't been so much experimental as miraculous in eliminating the nausea. She was fine for the second month, but in the third came anxiety and restlessness, with stretches of sleep lasting no longer than two hours. For this the doctor prescribed Miltown, which sedated Sara so successfully that lately she had been spending half the day in bed and the other half in a mild stupor. Dr. Wallace explained that any personality changes were temporary, and the most important thing was that her body provide a safe, healthy haven for the baby.

"You know, the concept of legacy has made its way down through the ages, from the primitives to today, although I fear we're getting so modern

that we've lost some of the natural wisdom the natives had," Barney said. In
the past fifteen years, his hair had thinned but the rest of him had thickened.
"Being closer in evolution to monkeys and easily smitten with superstitious
gobbledygook, I think they understood simple things we don't, like that
man lives on after death through his progeny."

The waitress set their plates on the table. Michael winced at the greenish
tint of his scrambled eggs and the wrinkle of his sausage links.

"Now, you're probably wondering why I called you out of the blue. You
probably thought to yourself, *Barney Taylor—wasn't he that spoiled rich kid
who liked to hear himself talk?*" Michael started to say something, though he
wasn't exactly going to disagree, but Barney held up his hand. "In high
school all I cared about was sports and boozing and scoring with girls, and
even though all of those things are essential appetites of man, they are not
everything. There comes a time when a man has to take a long, hard look
at himself and wonder, *What greatness have I achieved?* Have you ever asked
yourself that question, Halligan?"

Michael had been expending too much time and energy working at
Edwards Appleby, worrying about Sara and the baby, and building up his
collection to concern himself with greatness. "You're steady, even-keeled,"
Mr. Appleby had said right before promoting him to senior accountant,
"and that's about as good as one can hope for in this day and age."

"I guess I've never really thought about greatness," Michael said.

Barney shook ketchup onto his plate. He set the bottle back in its spot,
then lay the cap on top, unscrewed. "Well, don't worry. It's never too late to
think about it." He cut up his eggs, meat, and potatoes, and then stirred up
all of his food with the ketchup. "For me, it started when I was a sophomore
at the University of Illinois, taking a course about Ralph Waldo Emerson."
He crammed a forkful of the slop into his mouth. As he chewed, he spoke:
"I was basically majoring in anatomy—*female* anatomy—and partying, so
I rarely made it to class. I was getting a D, bordering on an F, when my dad
told me I was distantly related to Emerson on his side of the family. I guess
this news embarrassed me, because gradually I started reading the
assignments and actually became impressed with how insightful Emerson

was. Pretty soon he became like a god to me—or at least a 'god in ruins.'"

When Barney chuckled, Michael wasn't sure why. Others' words and gestures often perplexed him. He had come to rely on Sara as his guide through the thickets of sociability, but lately she had become as asocial as he was, a predicament that left him feeling lost and alone, his sleep more ragged, his left eyelid a little twitchy.

"My epiphany came during my junior year. I was in the bathroom of my fraternity house, and all around me, my brothers were shaving, snapping towels, and cracking jokes. As I put the razor to my face, someone accidentally bumped me from behind, and I gashed my cheek." Barney pointed to his face, but Michael saw no scar. "Blood was coming out and mixing with shaving cream, and it hit me just how mortal I was. If I had been bumped in a different way, or if I had been shaving my neck, the razor could have sliced open my carotid artery. And as I pictured all of this, I realized I had been spared because some hidden force, maybe God, was trying to communicate an important message to me." As Barney spoke, Michael kept glancing at the ketchup bottle and its loose cap. "I finished shaving and left the bathroom, and once I was back in my room, I asked myself what Emerson would have said about what I was experiencing. I went to my books and read and read for what must have been an hour, and then I found what I was looking for. Emerson said, 'All that Adam had, all that Caesar could, you have and can do,' and then he said some more stuff in there, and then the important part: 'Build, therefore, your own world.'"

Barney rambled on about writing down his philosophies, theories, and advice à la Emerson in search of the world he had been called upon to build, but all Michael could think about was the ketchup bottle. He told himself to relax, it was only a condiment, but his muscles grew increasingly agitated with an urge to screw the cap into place.

"I recently started a group of elite leaders I call the Great-Men Club." Barney let his sentence hover in the air for a moment, during which time Michael picked up the ketchup, shook a dollop he didn't even want onto his plate, and then firmly screwed on the cap and set the bottle where it belonged. Immediately, he felt relieved. "We have only eight members right now, but they are some of the finest men in the western suburbs. Once a month we meet to talk about the works and lives of great men of the past: Emerson, Lincoln, Jefferson, and their ilk; it doesn't matter who, as long as he was great. Then we discuss ways we can apply what they've written or done to make sense of the world's problems and to become better men ourselves." Like a beggar at a spigot, Barney cupped his hands. He gazed at them as if they held something that would cease to be a mystery in his capable grasp. "With the H-bomb and the Russians and Negroes and women, there are so many important problems out there that we've got to solve; they're not just going to go away, as much as we would like them to. And if you're like me, you want to whittle down all that confuses you into something so simplistic that you can hold and consider it."

Michael stared at Barney's empty hands and imagined Sara's expanding body and the smaller body inside it, and all that could go wrong, and all the responsibility that awaited him. This nesting of bodies made him feel desirous of his wife one minute and put off, nearly repulsed and resentful, the next. On several occasions he had wished, and even prayed, for Sara to have a miscarriage so that they could return to the life they had had after their wedding. He hoped Barney was right; he hoped mysteries could shrink and simplify.

Barney removed a small stack of postcards from his pocket and placed them on the table. Printed on the top postcard was a message:

You are cordially invited to the official inaugural meeting of the
GREAT-MEN CLUB
an exclusive fraternity of businessmen and civic leaders
in the western suburbs.

Please come to our meeting at the
York Tavern in Oak Brook, Illinois,
on Friday, May 20, 1960, beginning at 7:30 p.m., and learn how
YOU can achieve the GREATNESS inside you!

Our special guest and speaker for the evening will be
OSWALD "HARD KNOCKS" KNOLL,
local boxing legend and one of the greatest middleweights
of all time—undefeated and untied!

As Michael read the words before him, Barney explained that he was asking associates and friends to mail out postcards to the great (and potentially great) men they knew. The event was two months away—plenty of time to build up an audience.

"So, what do you think, Halligan? You want to help spread the good news?"

Michael tapped the stack of postcards. "This Oswald Knoll," he said. "Where does he live?"

"Racine, Wisconsin," Barney said. "How come? You know him?"

"No, I don't know him," Michael lied. "I've just heard of him, that's all."

"He's not a big name," Barney said with a shrug, "but he's the uncle of one of the great men, and the best we could do on short notice."

The waitress set down the bill, a little paper pup tent. Both men pulled dollars from their wallets and coins from their pockets.

"Can I get a commitment from you?" Barney asked as they pooled their money. "Will you come to the meeting? Will you send out these twenty postcards?"

"Sure," said Michael, his head racing with all he should ask Oswald Knoll. "I'd be glad to."

"Thanks, Halligan." Barney looked earnestly at Michael. "Remember that the search after the great man is the dream of youth and the most serious occupation of manhood."

He gave the table a firm pat.

"Emerson?" Michael asked.

Barney smiled. "Who else?"

5.

MICHAEL WATCHED HIS FEET PACE THE SCUFFED TILES, AND IN HIS HEAD he counted his steps. Two other men wandered nervously around the waiting room, and four more sat in hard plastic chairs, smoking, fidgeting, cracking their knuckles, and waiting for a nurse to open the wooden door marked: DO NOT ENTER. Michael stopped at plate-glass double doors and looked out at a phone booth at the edge of the parking lot. He knew he should call Sara's parents, but what would he say to them? After a minute he walked into the moonlight and entered the booth. He opened the phone book and flipped through its pages in search of his in-laws' entry: Harris, Robert of Hinsdale. He passed name after name. Fuller. Geraci. Gruber. Gupta. Hale. Hall. His eyes caught his own name and, right beneath it, his father's. The only Halligans in the book. After a moment's hesitation, and with little thought about why, he popped a dime into the phone and dialed. After four rings, his father picked up and in a groggy voice asked who was there.

Michael tried to think of what to say, but nothing came to him.

"I know you're there, pal." His father's breathing was hard and shallow. "I can hear you on the other end."

Michael cleared his throat and opened his mouth, hoping words would come of their own volition.

"Well, you know what?" his father said. "I hope you die, you son of a bitch, because who the fuck are you to wake me in the middle of the night?"

Michael hung up the phone, his heart jumping. He stared at the wide hospital window and thought of the other expectant fathers, whose wives likely had not gone into labor three months early and woken in the middle of the night, bleeding and crying. Disoriented, he returned to the waiting room with its hissing radiator, rattling pocket change, and nervous breath, wishing he had one of his books. He tried to run titles through his head, but they flew away before he could pin them down. The clock moved slowly, ticked loudly. Michael prayed wordlessly to God, Jesus, the Virgin Mary, assorted saints, and the Holy Spirit, asking them to forgive his previous prayer for a miscarriage.

An hour later, a nurse opened the DO NOT ENTER door and asked Michael to please follow her. In front of a nursery window, she asked him to please wait where he was, and when she left, he waited. On the other side of the glass, under harsh light, a dozen babies were laid out like pastries in a bakery case, some decorated in pink, some in blue. A little girl in the front row grew purple from her cries, which Michael could barely hear through the window.

Dr. Wallace strode toward Michael in pale blue garb, looking as well groomed as a television surgeon. He ushered Michael into a small, windowless room down the hallway.

"I'm sorry to have to tell you this," the doctor said as he sat in a silver chair behind a white desk. "Your wife is fine; she's resting well. But your son was born with various birth defects. Severe deformities, I'm afraid. Internal and external, affecting the heart, lungs, brain, eyes, and all four limbs. I've never seen anything like it, quite frankly." Dr. Wallace removed a stick of Juicy Fruit from the desk, unwrapped it, and placed it in his mouth. "He could die today, or he could die tomorrow or one week from now, but he won't make it much longer than that." The doctor chewed and smacked his gum. "He's alive right now only because we're keeping him alive. I'm sorry, Mr. Halligan, but it's best if you let him go in peace. I'm asking your permission for this."

Michael ran the doctor's words though his mind, struggling to envision his son. "Can I see him?" he asked.

Dr. Wallace vigorously chewed some more, then removed his gum and tossed it into a garbage can beside the desk. "Of course you can," he said.

The doctor stood, walked past Michael, and opened the door. With a straight arm and flat palm, he ushered Michael down the hallway. The room they walked to was dark and cold, with three incubators in the back and a nurse sitting sentry by the door. Michael followed Dr. Wallace past two empty incubators to the third. Inside it was a boy with only fleshy nubs for limbs. Wires and tubes stretched from his chest and nose, and a plastic mask covered his mouth. His face was red and wrinkled, with tender indentations of skin where his eyes should have been. Dr. Wallace spoke, but Michael barely heard him. He watched for movement in his son's body but saw none except for the labored rise and fall of his torso.

"The best thing to do would be to end his suffering," said the doctor, "and let him pass on in peace. If there were any hope, I would recommend otherwise, but there is no hope, I'm afraid. Just making it this far could be considered a miracle."

Michael nodded and studied his son, pondering Dr. Wallace's choice of words. He felt numb and responsible, and it seemed to him that all of his shameful actions had led to this moment.

"We prefer not to get mothers involved in such sensitive decisions," said the doctor. "We've found that they're usually too irrational to make the right choice."

There was no movement from his son except for faint, fatal breaths. Michael knew all of this was his fault—or his mother's fault, or his father's. Someone had to shoulder the blame.

"I'll give you a few minutes to think about it."

As Dr. Wallace passed through the doorway, Michael turned toward him and, without thinking, said, "Thanks."

6.

When the mail arrived, Willie Chambers set it beside the cash register and called out to Paddy, who was working under a jacked-up Bel Air. Paddy slid out from under the car, wiped his hands on a rag, and stood. Since he had kicked Michael out of the house nearly two decades ago, he had gone through fifteen assistants, most of whom he had eventually fired for insubordination, incompetence, theft, laziness, or some combination thereof. All had been white until Willie, none had lasted as long, and Paddy felt shrewd for having hired him. Willie was a wizard with automobiles, and he had polite country manners. *Yes, sir. No, sir. Thank you, sir.* He was in his early forties, with a wife and four children to support; he wasn't likely to walk off the job or develop a smart mouth anytime soon. Paddy picked up the stack of mail. When he saw a familiar brown wrapper, he told Willie to hold down the fort.

In the kitchen, Paddy opened a can of chicken noodle soup and dumped its contents into a pot. He turned the burner on low, sat at the table, and tore open the brown wrapper to reveal the latest issue of *Man of Leisure*. He flipped immediately to the photo in the center: a girl lying prone and nude on a couch. She smiled, her tongue barely touching her upper teeth, her chin in her hands. One foot pointed playfully toward the ceiling, and she arched her back just enough to show some nipple. Paddy sized up her beauty and eyed her for flaws, and then he turned to pictures of her lounging in a rec room, swimming in a pool, kneeling topless on a beach. She was from San Diego. She measured 34–24–36. Her hobbies included

swimming, tennis, and fast cars. Paddy laughed, thinking he could teach
her a thing or two about fast cars.

As he ate, he looked at the rest of his mail: a phone bill, an electric bill,
and a reminder from Dunne & Company that his rent was scheduled to
increase at the end of the lease year. At the bottom of the pile was a white
postcard with his name handwritten on the front, and a printed message
on the back inviting him to a meeting of something called the Great-Men
Club. The evening's speaker was to be Oswald "Hard Knocks" Knoll. Paddy
looked around the kitchen, almost expecting that joker from *Candid
Camera* to pop out of the oven and tell him to smile. He read the postcard
again and then paced angrily in the kitchen. The meeting was tonight. He
tried to understand why he had been invited and, more important, why he
had been invited so late, and then he wondered if Michael had sent him the
card. Paddy had seen his son around town a few times with that pretty wife
of his, and it had been a year since the encounter on the train. He didn't
like thinking that other people ever thought of him. It made him worry they
were plotting against him. He tore the postcard in half and tossed it into
the garbage can. He sat down, finished his soup, and returned to his naked
women, but even as his eyes roamed over their bodies, his mind imagined
a group of men cheering for Hard Knocks Knoll. If admiring an aging pretty
boy made a man great, then Paddy wanted nothing to do with this
ridiculous group. After all, what kind of organization called itself the Great-
Men Club and did not include him as a charter member? He set his dishes
in the sink and returned to the garage. Half an hour later he was back in
the kitchen, holding the two halves of the postcard together. He would not
go, he told himself. He refused to grant the Great-Men Club the pleasure of
his company. He refused to walk into whatever trap they had set for him.

Paddy hadn't been in a bar in years, and he'd never been in one like the York
Tavern, which struck him as the kind of place where Rotarians and Elks
made backroom business deals and college boys bragged about the coeds
they'd given it to. There were pennants, paintings, and animal heads on the
walls, but only six men sitting around, talking and drinking. The bartender

asked if he was there for the meeting. When Paddy nodded, the bartender
pointed to a door against the far wall.

Paddy opened the door and walked down a short, narrow hallway to a
large, smoky room crowded with men gathered around tables. There must
have been a hundred of them, most in their twenties or thirties, and not a
single one looked great. At best they seemed mediocre—the kind of men
who couldn't or wouldn't change their own motor oil. Grinning like a
buffoon, a chunky blond man came up to Paddy and introduced himself as
Barney Taylor.

"Who are you," Paddy asked, "king of the great men?"

"You could say that," Barney said with a laugh. He pointed to an empty
chair at a nearby table. "We're having everyone talk about a man they think
is great."

Paddy pulled out the chair and draped his coat over its back. He sat,
tossing his hat onto the table.

"My great man would have to be P. T. Barnum," said a sweaty slob on
Paddy's left, "because he made people want something and then told them
they needed it. And then, when they were worked up to have it, he charged
them an arm and a leg."

As the slob rambled on about suckers being born every minute, Paddy
surveyed the room. He didn't see Oswald Knoll anywhere, though he
doubted he would recognize him. He didn't see Michael, either. The slob
finished talking and turned to the beanpole beside him, who said his great
man was Charles Lindbergh.

Paddy eyed the empty pitcher and three empty glasses in the center of
the table, and he thought he could really go for a beer and a cigarette. A
waitress swished by, and the Casper Milquetoast on Paddy's right tapped
her arm and ordered another pitcher. Paddy watched the waitress scoot away
from the table, and thought he could really go for a woman, too. For the
last five years, he'd gotten by without alcohol and women and Lucky Strikes,
not so much because he'd wanted to quit them, but because he still wanted
to own his own station someday and blowing his money on pleasure was no
way to build up savings. Georgie Dunne couldn't hold on to the property

forever, and whenever he was ready to sell, Paddy would swoop in with enough cash to buy it. And if Georgie wouldn't sell the place, then Paddy would find another building when his lease ended in eleven years. The only indulgence he allowed himself was *Man of Leisure*, which was cheaper than screwing whores or going out on dates, and ultimately more pleasurable because it involved nobody but him.

The waitress set the pitcher on the table, and Casper Milquetoast paid her. After pouring his own drink, Milquetoast grabbed an empty glass from the center of the table and poured one for Paddy, who immediately downed half and gestured for more.

As Beanpole babbled about Charles Lindbergh's courageous passage, Paddy asked Casper Milquetoast for a cigarette. Milquetoast set the pack on the table and said, "Help yourself." As Paddy smoked, lovingly inhaling and exhaling, the men continued to go around the table, naming their great men. The greaseball picked Joe DiMaggio. The fatso, Franklin Roosevelt. The sad sack, J. Edgar Hoover. The sissy, General MacArthur. Paddy remembered that he had been naïve when he was the same age as these men, mailing off his hard-earned money for motivational booklets, trusting Rabbit and Red and Elizabeth and Michael not to deceive him. Casper Milquetoast said his great man was Norman Vincent Peale, who had shown him that positive thinking was the key to success in any situation, and that complaining, although a great temptation and a short-term salve, accomplished nothing. From Mr. Peale, he had learned that if he stopped fuming and fretting and started to trust himself, he could make his own happiness, be a winner, and get what he expected out of life. When he finished talking, the men turned to Paddy, who said nothing.

"How about you?" Sad Sack finally asked. "Who's your great man?"

Paddy took a gulp of beer, then another. He picked up the pack of cigarettes, shook one loose, lit it, took a drag, and said, "You know what your goddamn problem is, all of you?" He sensed the men wavering between confusion and fear. He had seen the same expression countless times, and he knew that a man who showed it would surrender almost anything for safety. "You wouldn't know a great man if he came up and bit you on the ass.

I mean, how great does a person have to be to fly a plane or hit a baseball or tell other men to die in some war?" He poured himself another beer. "When I was your age, I went around looking for advice and paying others to tell me what to think and do. When you're young and dumb and full of cum, that's just the way it is; you don't know any better." With the exception of Fatso, the men laughed nervously. "But I'll tell you something. Nobody knew what the hell they were talking about thirty years ago, and nobody knows what the hell they're talking about today. In another thirty years, it'll be the exact same thing. The world spins around, we all get thrown into it, and some people are lucky enough to land someplace good. Then they stand up, dust themselves off, and start talking about how all that spinning around and landing where they did was part of some great plan of theirs—but of course, that's bullshit, and deep down they know it. So these men you just mentioned, and this Barney clown over there—don't listen to them. Don't listen to anybody. Don't even listen to me." Paddy took another drink, feeling buoyed by the beer inside him.

"So, you don't have a great man, then?" Fatso said.

"I'll tell you who my great man is." Paddy stubbed out the cigarette. "I am," he said, pointing to his face. "Me. I'm my own great man. In fact, that's the sign of a great man—being your own great man. That's the whole point of being great."

After a few seconds, Casper Milquetoast turned to Paddy and asked, "Are you Hard Knocks Knoll?"

Paddy removed a cigarette from the packet. "I'll do you a favor," he said, "and pretend you didn't just ask me that."

Barney rapped his knuckles on a table for half a minute. When he finally had everyone's attention, he said, "As you've probably just discovered by talking amongst yourselves, there are many ways a man can become great. He can be a war hero or an athlete, or he can come up with an invention that betters mankind. Others, like Ralph Waldo Emerson, my great man, are profound thinkers who spend a lifetime sitting alone and examining themselves. But whatever form their greatness takes, great men share a core trait. And that trait, my fellow great men and potential great men, if I may be so blunt, is balls. And when it comes to having balls, you'd be hard pressed to find a man with more balls than our special guest for this evening: Oswald 'Hard Knocks' Knoll."

A trim man in a black sport coat and blue tie stood and shook Barney's hand. His hair was gray, but he was youthfully handsome. Paddy remembered his face—that of an actor or a prince, not a fighter: no crooked nose, no cauliflower ears. All of the men cheered except for Paddy, who looked around at their insipid grins. None of them had seen Hard Knocks fight. None of them had been punched silly by him for two and a half rounds and then woken up hours later on a training table with a ringing in their ears and the faintest memory of how badly they'd been beaten.

After a few remarks about his career as a middleweight contender, Hard Knocks said, "But tonight I'm not going to talk about boxing. I want to tell you a different story, one that I think demonstrates how hard it is to be a great man."

Paddy poured himself another beer, held up the empty pitcher, and let out a quick, piercing whistle for the waitress. A few men shot him glances, and someone shushed him. Grinning like a class clown, Paddy handed the pitcher to the waitress.

"I work for a publishing company that makes children's books, and over the years we've produced titles featuring some of the greatest comic-strip heroes of all time," said Knoll. "In my three decades there, I've had the opportunity to hear stories about the men and women who created these characters, and among the stories that have stuck with me is one concerning a man who was the original artist of one of the most famous strips of all time. Now, out of respect for privacy, I'm not going to name the man, or the character he helped create, but it's safe to say you've all seen this artist's drawings, and you most likely grew up as a fan of his character. Anyway, the artist's style had an innocent charm that few possessed, but it was less technically proficient than most of the competition's, by which I mean that their drawings were more detailed and realistic—though I think far less distinct and inviting—than his were. Over the years, the talent pool around him became deeper, and the trend continued toward cluttered, soulless panels that were easy to admire but hard to enjoy or remember. Eventually the syndicate that produced the strip decided it had to find a new artist. So, after nearly twenty years of drawing a legendary hero, of having his work cherished by millions every day, the artist was fired. Angry and helpless, he felt he had to do something. Unfortunately, what he did was go out into his backyard one night, start a bonfire, and throw into the flames everything he owned that was associated with the character—all the artwork he had done, all his notebooks, all his sketches. Every last thing was reduced to ash."

Paddy yawned histrionically and said, "Blah blah blah" under his breath. The waitress set down the pitcher, and when she told him the price, Paddy pointed to Casper Milquetoast and said, "He'll pay for it."

Milquetoast turned from watching Oswald Knoll and explained that he had already paid for a pitcher. Paddy said it didn't matter. The other men at the table whispered for them to be quiet, and Paddy told *them* to be quiet. Then Paddy suggested to Milquetoast that they arm-wrestle, and that the loser would buy the pitcher.

Paddy set his right arm in position to wrestle, elbow on the table, hand up and open. "I'm old enough to be your old man, for Christ's sake. Don't be such a coward."

Paddy could tell that Milquetoast felt uncomfortable and then anxious when Sad Sack, Beanpole, and the slob whispered for him to accept Paddy's challenge. Milquetoast placed his elbow on the table and grabbed Paddy's hand. The slob quietly counted to three, and almost immediately Paddy lowered Milquetoast's hand to the table. As Milquetoast dug a dollar out of his wallet, Paddy slapped him on the back. "You're a good sport, pal," he said. "No hard feelings."

"I'm not the person to be talking about greatness," Oswald Knoll said, "but I do think it's important to remember that fate can't be predicted or controlled, and that even if you excel at what you do, at some point all the personal qualities that made you great will fail you. Something unexpected will happen, and you'll try to face it like you faced other challenges, but nothing you do will work. To succeed, you'll have to see yourself and the world differently than before. And maybe you'll succeed, but even if you don't, you'll at least fail gracefully, which is sometimes the best you can hope for."

Oswald sat down. For a few seconds, nobody applauded. Then Barney and a few other men near the front cheered, and soon everyone except for Paddy was clapping politely. Barney stood, and as he talked about the camaraderie he saw throughout the room and mused on what Emerson would have said about it, the crowd grew restless. The waitress brought another pitcher to the table, and Fatso challenged the slob to arm-wrestle him for it. Then Beanpole challenged Sad Sack, and the greaseball challenged the sissy, and soon the table was engaged in an impromptu tournament. For the championship, Paddy finished off Fatso after a minute of struggling. Paddy leaned back, exhausted, his tablemates slapping his shoulders excitedly. He scanned the room and realized that men at other tables were arm-wrestling. There was laughter, cheering, arguing; the room was filled with life. Barney shouted about great men taking the initiative and being competitive by nature, and that there would be a contest among them all, with the winner getting a shot at Oswald Knoll and earning one year of dues-free membership in the Great-Men Club. Soon the winner from another table—a bulldog of a man—sat beside Paddy, who took the man's hand and within a minute was victorious.

Paddy shook out his arm, accepting his tablemates' praise. They were inferior to him, weak and pathetic, yet he needed their encouragement as much as they needed someone to cheer; that was what the weak and the strong gave each other. "Here they come," the slob said. Paddy looked up to see his son being led through the crowd, like a prisoner at a sentencing.

"I figured you were one of these great men," Paddy said.

"I guess you were right."

Michael sat down, looking exhausted. Paddy guessed that the little woman must have been keeping him up late every night with screwing or nagging.

"You think you can beat me?" Paddy asked.

"Not really."

They set their arms in position and grabbed hands. The slob counted to three. Neither Michael nor Paddy moved.

"Go ahead and win," Paddy said. He had memorized his son's address and phone number, and a couple of times had sat in a parked car outside his large house, wondering how Michael had come to afford a place like that. "I won't fight you for it."

"I don't want to win."

Paddy saw a little bit of Elizabeth in Michael's stubborn face. "Of course you want to win. Everyone wants to win."

Michael tried to let go, but Paddy held on and tilted his own arm backward until his knuckles were about six inches above the table. "Come on, beat me," he said, lowering his hand even more. "It's my gift to you."

The moment Paddy felt Michael try to win, he whipped his arm all the way around and drove his son's hand to the table. The crowd erupted in cheers. Michael stood and tried to loosen his grip, but Paddy wouldn't let go.

"Everything you have is because of me." Paddy released Michael's hand. "Someday you'll realize that. Someday you'll thank me."

"Why should I thank you?" Michael was red-faced, his eyed narrowed on Paddy. "If it wasn't for you, she'd still be around. She wouldn't have done what she did."

"And what the hell do you know about anything?"

"I know the secrets she kept from you. I know where she went and who she saw when you were at work."

Paddy stood quickly and walked away from Michael and his lies. "Bring on the next victim," he told the slob.

After defeating his next two opponents, Paddy walked to the front of the room amid the cheers of the great men. Barney congratulated him and told him to rest his arm for a few minutes. Paddy sat in a chair against the wall, facing the room of men, and as he listened to Barney talk about annual dues and the responsibilities of membership, he thought of Old Kevin, whom time and worms had no doubt whittled down to a skeleton. If Michael wanted to see a father who'd given his son less than nothing, he should have met Kevin Kearns; if he had, maybe he would have turned out a little more grateful.

Standing before the crowd, Barney asked Hard Knocks to entertain everyone with some humorous boxing anecdotes.

"I'm afraid I don't know any stories like that," Knoll said.

Barney prodded him, saying he must have some old tales or a few good jokes. "Boxers always have the best stories," he said. "Everybody knows that." Knoll kept claiming he had no such material, and Barney kept insisting he must. Finally Hard Knocks said, "You want a boxing story? All right, I'll give you a boxing story."

As much as he tried to ignore Michael's words, Paddy kept running them through his head. He gazed out at the great men, not seeing his son among them, and longed to be in his garage with his head down and his hands busy.

"I fought a man by the name of Martinez once," Knoll said. "He was a young guy, quick but without much power. I didn't know him all that well, but I'd heard he was a good guy, with a wife and two little kids. We were fighting, just doing our jobs, each of us trying to beat the hell out of the other, and in the fourth round I got him into trouble. He was just about to go down when I landed an uppercut that sent him through the ropes and to the floor, where he cracked his head on the cement. He was in a coma for three days but eventually went home. From what I heard, his brain never quite worked right after that. He couldn't write his name anymore, couldn't read, didn't do much at all except drink and yell at his family. After a few months of that, his wife put him in an asylum and went back to Mexico with their kids. As I trained for my next fight, I kept thinking about Martinez and what I'd done to him. I'd had him beat, and it wouldn't have taken much to knock him out, but instead I went for the kill. It was what I was supposed to do, what I'd trained my whole life to do, and so I did it. People told me it wasn't my fault, that when a man climbs into the ring, he assumes certain risks, but I couldn't blame Martinez for what had happened to him because I knew what my intentions had been."

The slob appeared beside Paddy and crouched next to his chair. "You ready, champ?" he whispered. "Ready for your big match?"

Paddy's mind darted from one dark place to another: seeing his mother dead in her bed, finding the knitting needle in the trash, hearing about Red's murder a few years back. He experienced these scenes impassively, as if daring his memory to hurt him.

"My next fight was a tune-up against a guy named de Macio, who happened to be one of Martinez's friends. Before the bout I got it into my head that I deserved to be punished for what had happened to Martinez, and that de Macio should be the one to punish me. I wanted to suffer and thought that my suffering could make up for what had happened to Martinez. Since de Macio had a decent jab, I figured I'd let him land it all night, which is what I did. I let him pop my eye a few times in the first round, and it felt good to feel pain. So I kept offering my eye, and he kept taking shots at it. By the sixth round, I'd been hit so much that the pain went away, and by the ninth my eye was so swollen and bloody, I couldn't see out of it. De Macio was winning, and I felt satisfied about that for a while, but then, around the twelfth, I panicked. I'd never lost before, never had a draw, and unless something changed, I was going to lose to a guy I should have done away with in the third or fourth round. I thought about all the work I had done for a title shot, and how much I wanted that belt, and with all that on the line, it became easy to convince myself that Martinez had only himself to blame for what had happened to him. He'd had no business being in the ring with me. He'd had no business not going down earlier. It was his own fault he was in an asylum and his wife and kids had left him. The thought of losing suddenly terrified me the way nothing had before, and so I started covering up better and going hard at de Macio. In the fourteenth round I put him down twice, and the second time he stayed down. I won the bout but lost sight in my eye. So there you have it. There's your boxing story—about how I didn't have the guts to lose."

Oswald Knoll sat, and the great men stared at him with disappointed expressions. Barney stood and clapped, and nobody joined him. But when he announced the arm-wrestling match, all of the great men cheered.

Paddy stood with no fight inside him.

"You can take this guy," the slob said. "Did you hear him talk? He doesn't have that killer instinct. He's weak. He's a coward."

Paddy turned to the slob. "A coward? You don't know a fucking thing about anything, do you?"

The slob gave Paddy a wounded look. "I'm just trying to help."

"You have no goddamn idea how great Oswald Knoll was, do you? Did you ever see him fight? Did you ever throw a punch and have him disappear on you, or have him drill you so hard with a hook, you thought he'd sent your rib into your heart?"

"Of course not."

"Then shut the hell up."

Paddy approached Oswald Knoll, knowing he had no chance of winning. Even if their positions were reversed and Hard Knocks was the one who had just arm-wrestled several men, he would still win. Paddy didn't care. He would get his fight back soon enough.

Oswald shook Paddy's hand and congratulated him on winning the arm-wrestling contest. Paddy looked into Knoll's damaged eye and said, "Let's get this over with."

Paddy and Hard Knocks sat down and clasped hands. Barney shouted to three, and Paddy's knuckles struck the table so hard and so fast, he barely felt his defeat.

7.

SARA GAZED OUT THE LODGE WINDOW AT THE VACANT SHUFFLEBOARD court and the dewy woods behind it. There was something about summertime that always made her blue. In the winter she never felt compelled to get outside and enjoy herself, so she seldom felt disappointed when fun failed to arrive. But in the summer she found it impossible to squeeze as much pleasure from the day as she thought she should; every second she spent inside was a second she could be outside, and every second outside never satisfied her as much as she thought it should. She looked at the early-morning sunshine on the grass, at the swimming pool, and at Michael sitting poolside with one of his damn books, and she thought she should take up gardening, which she had read was therapeutic for grieving people, but then she considered how much she hated dirt and bugs and had absolutely no interest in uncut flowers or vegetables that didn't come from a can, and she quickly decided that gardening was out of the question.

She knew she should go to Michael, but she didn't feel like pulling words from him like old roots from the ground. She wasn't eager to sit in his weighty silence or have him respond "uh-huh" to whatever she said.

On the other side of the pool stood a statue of Paul Bunyan with an ax on his shoulder. The lodge manager was proud of the statue, even though it was only six feet tall and bore a constipated expression. While showing Sara and Michael around the grounds yesterday, he had stopped and pressed a button on the ax handle. From a speaker in Paul Bunyan's beard came a whirring sound, followed by a deep voice saying, "Hello, I'm Paul Bunyan.

Maybe you've heard of me and all my adventures forging this great country of ours. Well, whether you have or you haven't, why don't you sit a spell and listen to my tale?" What followed was three minutes of grade-A hokum: of how he had yanked a maple from the ground when he was one month old, formed Wisconsin's lakes with his footsteps, and paved the way for glorious progress with swing after swing of his mammoth ax.

Sara took a deep breath and forced her face to smile. She went outside and ran her hand through Michael's hair. This was supposed to be a romantic trip—five days in Wisconsin with nothing to do but relax.

"Ready for breakfast?" she asked as cheerily as she could muster.

Michael lugged his eyes away from his book and stared up at her as though she were the sole cause of disappointment in the world. "Uh-huh," he said.

They had never named their son, and had refused the hospital's request that they donate the body to science. The grave, which they had visited twice in the sixteen months since the baby's death, was marked with a headstone that simply read: HALLIGAN. At home, the nursery was still furnished. Sara passed by its closed door several times a day, but she never opened it.

The first six months had been filled with too many afternoons crying in the kitchen or staring blankly at *Ladies' Home Journal*, too many Miltown tablets, more pounds she couldn't shed, a fear of leaving the house, pressure in her breasts from undrunk milk, and her son coming to her in dreams and unexpected daytime moments, his malformed face quietly accusatory. The next six months were a little better, propelled as they were by her faith that once she had made it through a year, she would be fine, but the few months after that anniversary were darkened with fleeting, unformed urges to drive off a bridge or leap in front of a train. But she gradually started sleeping better and crying less, stopped taking her pills, took long morning walks through Spring Rock Park, and thought that maybe it wasn't wrong or selfish to feel thankful that her son had died instead of living in misery. In the spring she decided she was ready to try again—to have another child, to save what was left of her stagnant marriage. As for what Michael felt, she wasn't sure.

He had lost weight and looked drawn, but otherwise offered no hints of distress. He went to work each weekday morning and returned home in the evening, and on Saturdays and occasional nights he went out for hours in search of Big Little Books. Sometimes he surprised her by stroking her back or buying her flowers for no particular reason, but when she brought up the baby or her hopes for another one, he usually said he didn't want to talk about it. So they didn't, though there wasn't much else to talk about, and in sixteen months they had slept together only a few times.

After a breakfast of pancakes and bacon, they walked past the pool, where kids were now splashing and diving, despite the rules, and pelting Paul Bunyan with beach balls. Every so often, a boy would slap the speaker button as hard as he could, and the recorded voice would say "hello," like a man walking eagerly, stupidly, into a party where he wasn't welcome. Sara and Michael went into their room and washed up. When they went back outside, people stood gathered around the statue, trying to figure out how to stop the recording, which kept repeating itself.

They drove alongside Lake Michigan north from Kenosha, through Racine and Wind Point, headed inland just before Milwaukee, and came back around via Big Muskego Lake. Small talk popped to the surface like feeding fish, then quickly disappeared, leaving the faintest of ripples. Sara felt relaxed, but not romantic.

"Look," she said as they passed yet another lake, "Paul Bunyan's footprint."

Michael was expressionless, focused on the road ahead.

"Remember what that statue said?" She cleared her throat and in a low voice said, "Those lakes you see are my steps as I strode proudly across the great state of Wisconsin."

"Uh-huh."

Around them were stands of cedar and pine and green, rolling farmland. It was both heartbreaking and beautiful how people had so thoroughly cleared away something majestic and replaced it with something equally, though differently, lovely. Sara rolled down her window and let the wind whip around her hair.

"It's no fun being divorced," she said as she closed her eyes. "At first you think it'll be like being alone, but it's more like being empty."

She held her hand out the window, felt the air force it backward. A tree falling, time passing.

"Who's talking about divorce?"

"We are, Michael. We just haven't used words until now."

Sara opened her eyes. They exited a scenic road and headed back onto the highway.

Michael hit fifty miles an hour and said, "I don't want a divorce."

"I'm sorry," she said. "I'm just in a mood."

She scooted toward him and leaned into his side. To her surprise, he wrapped his arm around her shoulder and held her tightly to him.

They ate Swedish meatballs and egg noodles at Ole Anderson's Family Restaurant, and they laughed about the goats grazing on the grass-covered roof. Afterward, they parked in the lodge's parking lot and strolled to their room in silence, but hand in hand. Paul Bunyan kept gibbering beside the crowded pool, his voice now weakened and warbled, as though he were constantly on the verge of tears as he told the story of his life—and who could blame him? How had he ever fit in?

"The manager isn't around to shut it off," a woman told Sara. "A Friday in August, and he's not here. What if something happens? What if someone drowns? That would teach him a lesson."

In their room, they closed the drapes and locked the door, but sound and sunlight found them. They lay in bed facing the ceiling, Michael still wearing his shoes. Sara heard every delighted child's squeal, every parental reprimand, Paul Bunyan lamenting his life, and she felt hopeful. She rolled to her side and began to unbutton Michael's shirt. He held her hand and kissed it, then kept holding it in a way that told her not to bother. Maybe her mother had been right years earlier when she had told Sara that men were like coconuts: hard and hairy and useless until broken open. If only she could crack Michael open just a little, as she used to, something sweet would pour out. Sara rolled on top of him, straddled his hips. When she started to again unbutton his shirt, he grabbed both of her hands.

"Michael, please," she whispered.

His eyes were closed and bespectacled, which made him look absurd. "Not now," he said.

"Then when?"

He didn't answer. Slowly, she rocked her hips back and forth.

"Quit trying so hard," he said, rolling out from under her.

"At least I'm trying."

"Well, stop it," he said. "It's embarrassing."

Sara rose from the bed and rushed to the bathroom. Her tears came from deep inside her; they burst forth, coursed mascara down her cheeks. After a minute she looked at her red, puffy eyes in the mirror. "Nobody loves an unhappy girl," her mother used to say. Then, with the heels of her hands, she would rub life into Sara's cheeks until they were red from friction. "Now show the world how happy you can be." Mother and daughter would stare at themselves in the mirror, ear to ear, hair mingled. Sara would see flakes of dry skin and makeup on her mother's face, wrinkles around her eyes. She would smile, and as her mother squeezed her tighter, her smile would grow and grow until she had convinced herself she was happy, though often her face hurt from the effort.

Michael knocked on the door. "Sara," he said. "I'm sorry." A few minutes later, he knocked again and said, "I'm going out for a little while. I'll be back for dinner." Then he left.

Sara continued to focus on the reflection of her face: a round, splotched, clownish thing; a horrible mask. If she could have her younger face back for a day, she would adore it and apologize for ever having criticized it in the past; she would appreciate it in a way she never had. She hated the way she looked and the way she felt now, hated Wisconsin and Paul Bunyan, hated Michael and herself and what had happened to their son. She washed and dried her face, then opened the bathroom door. Through the front window, she watched fathers tossing their children into the water, throwing balls to them, looking wonderfully chubby and unstylish in lounge chairs. For a moment, she imagined seducing one of them, bringing him back to this room out of spite, but then she closed the drapes, reached into her purse, and popped a Miltown tablet. Exhausted from crying, she lay down on her side and hugged a pillow to her chest. She grabbed another pillow, and another, and covered her head until she heard nothing but her own breathing. She fell asleep and dreamed she was watching herself scream, and gradually she realized that the scream was beyond her sleep, outside her, filling the room. Groggy and damp with sweat, she tossed aside the pillows, sat up, and listened. The sound came from outside, and it was as loud and piercing as the grinding brakes of a train. Michael was nowhere. The room was more shadow than light.

She opened the door and saw people gathered around Paul Bunyan, most covering their ears, a boy slapping the statue with a kickboard. She wandered outside, barefoot and a little drugged, not fully awake. The scream was coming from the speaker; it grew louder as she neared it. One of the fathers, dressed in baggy trunks and a flowing robe, marched toward Paul Bunyan with a tire iron. When he struck the speaker, the crowd cheered. He struck it and struck it, then passed the tire iron to another man, who continued the assault. From hand to hand the gathered passed the tire iron and took turns striking Paul Bunyan. But the sound grew louder.

Sara glanced at the parking lot and the vacant spot where she and Michael had parked earlier. The sun was just about to hide behind the tallest trees. Someone offered her the tire iron, and Sara took it, felt its warmth, and then weakly struck Paul Bunyan's dented face. "Come on," a woman shouted. "You can do better than that." She hit it again. Pain vibrated up her arm, wakened her. People cheered. She cracked Paul Bunyan again, then again and again, crying now, sensing she was causing a scene, and again and again until she dropped the tire iron and ran back to the room, where she sat on the edge of the bed, eventually calming, steadying her breath, and listening as the others struck and struck at the scream until, with a mighty cheer, they killed it.

8.

MICHAEL GRIPPED THE STEERING WHEEL TIGHTLY AS HE DROVE NORTH. He cursed himself for saying what he'd said to Sara, instead of just saying he wasn't in the mood for her, or instead of actually being in the mood. *Ace Drummond. The Adventures of Dick Tracy, Detective. The Arizona Kid on the Bandit Trail. Betty Boop in Snow White. Big Chief Wahoo.* He ran down some of his 184 titles in his mind, envisioning their names written on a page. A year earlier, he had assumed his collection was nearly complete, but then he had written to Oswald Knoll, who had mailed back a list of the 657 different Big Little Books published from 1932 to 1949, including rare premiums, slight variations from printing to printing, and the book Michael had seen at the World's Fair: *Trouble in the City of Dreams*, which Oswald had described as "rarest of the rare, withdrawn and destroyed due to proprietary issues, probably only a few in existence." Michael had felt dejected upon first glimpsing the list, but soon he had thrilled at the thought of all there was to discover. His grip on the steering wheel eased as he passed a sign welcoming him to Racine. He stopped at a stoplight, looked at the ranch homes around him, and wondered where he might find Oswald Knoll.

Through correspondence, Michael had learned that Whitman Publishing was a steadily shrinking division of Western Publishing, which had long ago forsaken Big Littles for Little Golden Books, which were fine for three- and four-year-olds, Oswald wrote, but not for older children, whose parents were abandoning them to television with alarming indifference. Michael stopped at a gas station and found the address for

Western Publishing in a phone book, stopped at another station to ask for directions, and then stopped at a third when he realized he was lost. Around six o'clock, he pulled into the vast, mostly empty parking lot of a large, gray industrial plant glimmering in the sunlight. After tugging on the locked front doors, Michael walked alongside the building until he reached an orange metal door marked: ADMINISTRATIVE PERSONNEL ONLY. He turned the knob and pushed open the door into a narrow hallway with white cinder-block walls. He closed the door behind him quietly and listened for evidence of another human being, but all he heard was the electrical hum and buzz of the building. The walls were scuffed and chipped, decorated with framed covers of *The Jolly Barnyard*, *I Can Fly!*, and other Little Golden Books. Someone coughed. Michael followed the echo down the hallway, around a corner, and to a room where a typewriter clicked out one labored letter at a time. When Michael knocked, a man told him to enter.

The office was windowless and not much larger than a walk-in closet, crammed with filing cabinets and a metal desk cluttered with papers, an oscillating fan, and a black manual typewriter. In the middle of the mess, a young man sat in a tilted-back chair, a coffee mug between his thighs.

"Can I help you?" he asked, glancing up from the typewriter. He wore horn-rimmed glasses, and a cigarette dangled from his mouth, the tube of ash as long as the unburned section. His white short-sleeved dress shirt was soaked at the armpits. His cheeks were red with acne.

"I'm looking for Oswald Knoll," Michael said.

Focused on the paper scrolled in the typewriter, the young man said, "That's me." Then he jabbed the keys as if they'd insulted him one too many times.

Michael felt confused. His mind darted around for an explanation until the man stopped typing, looked at Michael, and laughed.

"Oswald Knoll, Junior," he said as he leaned back in his chair. "Everyone calls me Junior, despite the fact it's not my name." He flicked ash into his mug. "I assume you're looking for my father."

Michael nodded.

"He should be back any minute now."

Junior returned to his keys, and Michael thought it impossible that someone so unhealthy-looking had been fathered by Oswald Knoll.

"I collect Big Little Books," Michael said. "Your father has helped me out a lot, so I figured I'd drop by to say thanks."

"You collect Big Little Books?"

"Yeah."

"Why?" Junior asked incredulously. "If you don't mind my asking."

Michael stammered about enjoying the pictures and stories but mostly being drawn to the books themselves—the way they sat uniform on the shelves; their sturdy, vibrant spines; their vivid covers; their beauty as singular objects. His words gradually gained traction against his sentiment, and he said the books helped him forget himself and his life, at least for a while, and that just being in the same room with his collection made the world seem understandable and orderly. He had never voiced his love for his collection before, and he felt buoyant for having done so. When he started to say more, however, Junior held up his index finger and said, "Hold that thought." Then he typed out more words. "I've never liked kids' books, to tell you the truth. In my opinion, they set up unrealistic expectations that the world is fair or makes sense, which only does harm." Junior poked one key, then another. "This is just a summer job for me, between semesters at the University of Wisconsin." *Click. Clack.* Junior scowled at the typewriter. "I'd rather die than do this for the rest of my life."

Sensing someone behind him, Michael turned to see Oswald Knoll standing in the doorway, dressed as the Lone Ranger. Michael had hovered near the man at the gathering of the Great-Men Club, but had lacked the courage to approach him. Oswald removed his mask and watched his son with disappointment. Then he turned to Michael and asked if he could help him. Michael introduced himself, and Oswald shook his hand with vigor and smiled with deep delight.

"I'm up here with my wife," Michael explained, feeling giddy. "We're taking a little vacation."

"Well, bring her in. Is she waiting in the car?"

"She's resting at the lodge," Michael said, "so I came by myself."

Oswald showed Michael around the darkened plant with its silent machines, introducing him to a few employees rushing home for the weekend, but mostly reminiscing about the glorious years, at the height of the Depression, when Whitman was selling more than a million Big Littles a month. "The comic strips would come from the syndicates," he explained, "and it would be up to our editors and artists to take the material and make it fit our format. The artists would clip out the individual panels from the strips, and then they'd get busy covering up the word balloons with white paper and either making new backgrounds or finishing up the backgrounds already there—basically, doing whatever they had to do to make the necessary alterations as invisible as possible to the reader. Based on the word balloons, the editors would write up the stories. It was anonymous work, and I'm sure the comic-strip people thought there was no artistry to it, but there's art in taking something that already exists and making it new—or at least putting something of yourself into it. And there was a beauty and substance to the books themselves that no Sunday paper or comic book could ever replicate."

Trucks stood parked near the shipping bay, and the warehouse shelves were crammed with pallets of books. Michael imagined the bustle of the thirties and wished he had been there back then. He wished he was Oswald Knoll, who was telling him that the editors and artists also produced original titles for Whitman, although these never sold well and their characters—like Sombrero Pete, Kay Darcy, and Winsie Atkins—never caught on with the readers.

"In my early years," Oswald said, "I used to walk around after work and rummage through the garbage, looking for whatever I could find: dummy copies, original artwork, first drafts, you name it. I thought all of it was far too important to simply discard, which is what the artists, editors, and layout men often did."

Michael knew Oswald had some old books and an almost limitless amount of information, but in the dozen letters the man had sent in the past year, he had never mentioned this detail.

"What happened to all of it?"

"Oh, I still have everything," Oswald said. "I've got copies of every book, piece of artwork, contract, memo, and photograph I ever gathered up. I saved whatever seemed significant, and everything did."

"I'd love to see it all sometime."

The heels of Oswald's cowboy boots clicked on the concrete floor of the warehouse, then thudded softly on the carpet as he and Michael strolled in silence past empty offices. Michael imagined himself as a younger Oswald, prowling these hallways like a thief or explorer, finding treasure after treasure. He imagined Oswald handing over his entire collection to him.

"Where do you keep everything?" Michael asked.

"At my house."

"I'd really love to see what you have. It would mean a lot to me."

"I know it would."

Michael's heart raced the way it did whenever he found a book he'd been longing for or received a thick, padded envelope from Oswald, or whenever he approached a new girl in Lyons, knowing she would be his in a matter of minutes. All of these moments freed him from his own bleak company and briefly made his life feel epic.

"My wife's not expecting me back for a while," Michael said. "Maybe I could follow you to your house, and you could give me a quick tour. I wouldn't stay long."

"I'm afraid I have plans tonight, Michael."

"Couldn't you spare ten minutes? Five? Just five minutes, and then I'll go."

They stopped outside Junior's office. Oswald seemed to listen for a message in his son's typing.

"Shit!" Junior shouted, and then yanked paper from the typewriter.

Oswald sighed and said, "I suppose I could give you a quick look."

Michael's heart grew dark as he drove behind Oswald and Junior. He pictured Sara alone at the lodge, closed off in the bathroom with every right to be angry—more right to be angry, in fact, than she even knew. If only she had seen him drive to Lyons a few months after their son's death and cruise slowly up and down Ogden Avenue, disgusted with himself but more alive than he'd felt in nearly a year; if only she had seen him do the same thing the next month, and then the next week, and then stop at a tavern one week later and ask the bartender where he could find a girl. If only she had seen the girl, with her sticky bouffant, electric-blue eye shadow, and surgery scar across her belly; if only she had seen the one after that, and the next one, and the others. If only she had seen all of that, she would know how furious she should be.

Ella Cinders and the Mysterious House. Fighting Heroes Battle for Freedom. He thought he should call Sara from a payphone, tell her where he was headed, and promise to be back as soon as possible. Other than Oswald, she was the only one who understood what Big Littles meant to him. *The New Adventures of Tarzan. Og, Son of Fire. The Phantom and the Girl of Mystery.* Or he could call her to apologize and promise that things would get better. *Tom Mix Plays a Lone Hand. Tom Swift and His Magnetic Silencer.* But words had a way of forming and breaking apart inside him before he had the courage to release them into the world, so he kept driving and imagined Sara splashing around in the pool, flirting with the other men. *Wash Tubbs in Pandemonia. Zip Saunders, King of the Speedway.* She would be better off with a better man, he thought, and he would be better off in Lyons with criminals and whores and his books, with nobody to fail but himself.

Junior drove down a leafy cul-de-sac and eased up the driveway of a white wooden house. Michael followed.

The house was simple—the kind a child would draw as a face with windows for eyes, a door for a mouth, and a red triangular roof for a cap. Michael accompanied Oswald and Junior into the living room, its walls paneled in wood and covered with framed family photographs. Junior headed upstairs, and Oswald led Michael into a laundry room in the basement. He tugged a chain to turn on an overhead bulb and then shoved aside the washing machine to reveal a small hatch, with a handle and a dial, built into the cement floor. He spun the dial clockwise and counter-clockwise, grabbed the handle, and lifted open the door. A ladder led down into darkness.

"It came with the house," Oswald said, "so I figured I should put it to good use."

Oswald climbed backward down the ladder, stopping briefly to switch on the light. Michael followed. Soon they were in a bomb shelter's pantry, with shelves filled with canned food, toiletries, and *National Geographic* magazines. Oswald led Michael through the pantry, through a kitchenette, and into a sitting area with a love seat, two folding chairs, and a shortwave radio. Lace curtains hung in front of windows someone had painted onto the walls—false portals that overlooked mountains and a calm lake on one side, rolling farmland on the other. To the left and right were tiny, bare bedrooms. Ahead was a door, which Junior unlocked and opened. He flicked on a light and said, "Here it is."

Michael entered the room. Built into each wall were shelves laden with boxes.

"Take a look," said Oswald.

Michael felt numb with wonder, unsure where or how to begin. He ventured cautiously toward a box at random, and when he took it down from the shelf and removed its lid, the odors of carbon paper and old newsprint came to him. Kneeling, he felt like an archaeologist in a secret vault as he handled pristine copies of early Dick Tracy titles, along with rough drafts, rejected cover art, magazine ads, and contracts bearing Chester Gould's signature. He turned and looked up at Oswald, who was standing against the wall with his hands in his pockets, a wide smile on his face.

Michael moved on to a second box filled with more books in mint condition, to a third stuffed with contracts and drafts, to a fourth containing original artwork of Smokey Stover, Alley Oop, Secret Agent X-9, and Mac of the Marines. Michael's awe started to feel like enlightenment, or at least something more like understanding, and his collection suddenly seemed less significant, not simply because it was meager in itself, but also because it contained nothing original.

When Oswald explained that he really had to be going, Michael stood and asked, "Can't I just stay here while you go out?"

Oswald laughed. "I know what you mean," he said. "Sometimes I feel like I could spend all night down here."

"I'm serious," Michael said. "When will you be back?"

Oswald's grin left him. "Honestly, Michael, I really need to leave. I can't let you stay while I'm gone."

Michael's eyes roamed over the seven boxes he had investigated and the thirty more he hadn't, and his stomach and chest hurt when he imagined leaving them here. He turned again to Oswald. "How much do you want for all of it?" he asked.

"I'm afraid it's not for sale."

"Would you ever consider selling?"

Oswald sighed. "No, Michael. I'm sorry. It's not for sale and never will be. Now, I really do need to—"

"What about after you're gone?" Michael started to shiver. His eyes stung. He couldn't leave here with nothing. He couldn't head back into the world, into his life, empty-handed. "What happens then? Who will care for everything?"

"My son will."

Michael pictured Junior with his long ash and pimples, and he felt ill. "But he doesn't care," he said. "You heard him. He hates children's books."

Oswald folded his arms in front of his chest. "He's young. He'll change. He'll realize how important all of this is, and he'll learn to care for it."

"But what if he doesn't?"

"I'm sorry, Michael, but we really need to head out right now."

"But what if he doesn't change?" Michael stared at Oswald—the Lone Ranger, unmasked—and he wondered how such a great man could be so foolish. "I'd care for all of it more than he would. I'd care for it more than anybody."

Oswald placed a strong hand on Michael's back and guided him out of the room. "It doesn't matter," he said, as he locked the door. "You're not family."

"Family?" Michael said. The word tasted sour in his mouth.

"Family," Oswald said with a smile.

They climbed out of the bomb shelter and walked through the house. Oswald put his arm around Michael's shoulder and thanked him for coming to visit. Michael felt unwelcome and unwanted, but comforted by the weight of Oswald's arm and the calm in his voice. When he had been deposited on the driveway and Oswald had left with a handshake, Michael trudged to his car like a beaten fighter heading to his corner. A mile away from Oswald's house, he parked in a cul-de-sac, switched off the engine, and observed his hands holding the steering wheel, wishing he could live locked away in Oswald's bomb shelter. He tried to remember all he'd seen there—all the glorious pieces of the past that Oswald had saved and preserved—but the details were already leaving him. He thought he should cry for the loss he felt, but since he didn't know how to do that, he simply started the car and took a slow way back to Sara.

MEDIOCRE HEROES

1971–1976

1.

JUNIOR FELT LIKE A FOOL. HE WAS A MAN ON THE VERGE OF THIRTY, WITH a wife and two children, and here he was in the bathroom of his cramped apartment, putting on an Aquaman costume. He pulled the orange and green bodysuit up over his thighs, underwear, and torso, and he slid his arms through the sleeves. When he saw himself in the mirror, he sighed. His hair was thinning. He had bags under his eyes. He had never inherited the muscular physique he'd been promised as a child by his father. For years he had contemplated, but never bothered, asking people to call him Oswald or Ozzie or O.K., or at least something other than Junior. He'd spent his life not bothering, and where had it gotten him but back to where he'd started?

He quietly lifted the toilet tank's lid, gently set it upside down on the floor, and removed the plastic bag he'd duct-taped to the rough underside. Sitting on the toilet, he reached into the bag, removed a joint, and lit it. He inhaled, held the smoke for a count of five, and then exhaled. He wondered if he had made a mistake in agreeing to replace his father in sales and promotion. He'd had it pretty good a few years ago, playing drums with Up With People—knocking out cheery beats, grinning at crowd after crowd of bored teenagers, and feigning belief in the group's faith that humankind's ills could be eradicated through a blend of personal purity and capitalism. On tour, he refrained from drugs, booze, gambling, and girls, but on breaks in Madison he caught up on all the indulgence he'd been missing. In two years with the group, he visited twenty-eight states and the District of Columbia, performed on the steps of the Capitol, and shook the hands of

Walt Disney, John Wayne, and Pat Boone. Then, in Boston, he slipped up with Sharon, a new backup singer he'd been eyeing for months; a chaperone caught them in bed together, and soon they were sent off to Milwaukee with one-way tickets. They came to know each other better on the trip west and soon made their way back east, to New York City, where they were quickly humbled by the fact that their success with Up With People elicited only ridicule in the music world. Junior felt like an outsider everywhere he went: too square in one scene, not square enough in the other. He had trouble finding work and even more trouble keeping it, thanks in part to his growing interest in the horses down at Aqueduct. When Sharon became pregnant, they married. Their savings dwindled. Weary and broke and two months shy of having a baby, they took a Greyhound to Racine, where Junior asked his father if there was any work at the publishing plant.

As he smoked his joint, Junior listened to Trey throw one of his toddler tantrums in the living room and Sharon say, "Hush, hush" and then, "For God's sake, will you be quiet?" He looked down at his midsection, which was little more than a cushion of flab. Aquaman didn't have a spare tire around his middle, or a bulge at his crotch that was big enough to be noticed but not big enough to be admired. He didn't smoke hash and sell a little on the side, or blow twenty bucks taking Notre Dame, those overrated losers, to cover the spread against Purdue. And he didn't have trouble getting out of bed most mornings. Then again, Aquaman didn't have a family to support, bills to pay, or an inferiority complex. Junior ran his palms over his costume, which was patterned to resemble scales, and he thought how nice it would be if he were a fish.

He heard a knock on the bathroom door.

"Daddy," Ann pleaded, "I have to pee."

Junior inhaled, held the smoke, and exhaled.

"In a minute, sugar. Daddy's busy."

"But I have to go real bad."

Junior closed his eyes and imagined himself underwater. It was quiet there, and all around him swam other people dressed like Aquaman. Some were the size of guppies and others the size of whales, but all were serene, just floating around with no responsibilities and all the water and food they needed. They were like astronauts on a space walk, lost in the highlight of their lives, not worrying that soon they would be back on Earth with no words to express the letdown they felt as the weightlessness faded in their hearts.

There was a louder knock on the door. Junior's heart stopped, then resumed its wary beat.

"Junior," Sharon said, "Ann really needs to pee."

"I'm busy."

"Doing what?"

"Thinking about my performance this afternoon."

"Well, Ann's about to wet her pants, so it would be nice if you could think somewhere else." Sharon said nothing for a couple of seconds and then whispered, "And spray the air freshener. I don't want her asking any more questions."

Junior took one last drag, pinched out the lit end, returned the joint to the bag, and taped the bag to the toilet lid. When he stood, the room swirled around him.

Twenty minutes later, he was driving the company truck toward Milwaukee with his father beside him. The hash was really kicking in now, and as Junior stared blankly ahead at the open road, he pondered whether a man named Junior could ever make his own way in the world. As long as he was called Junior, as long as his very name implied subordination to another, he would always be known more as his father's son than as a man in his own right. But rather than annoying or depressing him, as it usually did, this conclusion simply made him think that in two months his parents would be living in a Florida condominium, where at some point in the future they would most likely die. Once they were dead, he figured, he might not mind being called Junior.

"I have something important to tell you," his father said.

Junior's eye caught sight of cows grazing in a field. If he could not be a fish, he wouldn't mind being a cow, he thought, just as long as he could be a cow that wouldn't get eaten. He glanced at his father, who was turned sideways in his seat. The old man's good eye was on him.

"You all right, Junior?"

"I'm fine, just a little tired. What do you want to tell me?"

"I've been working out the figures, and I've discussed it with your mother, and we've decided to take the house off the market and sell it to you and Sharon—if you want it, of course. We don't have to discuss money now, except to say that we'll knock down the price so you can afford it. We'll still have more than enough to live on."

The words moved viscously though Junior's brain, but eventually he scooped them all up and understood what his father was saying.

"And I'd like you to have my collection."

"You want me to take care of it for you?"

"I want you to have it."

Junior's heart thumped like the footsteps of a lumbering giant. "But I'll ruin it somehow. You know I will."

"I don't want to hear that kind of talk, Junior. Look at Sharon. Look at the kids. Anytime you've had a big responsibility, you've risen to the occasion. This won't be any different."

Junior thought he should express his gratitude, but it was hard to have such a decent man for a father, and to feel blessed and indebted at the same time. His father reached into the briefcase between his feet and pulled out his old Bell + Howell movie camera. He checked the batteries and loaded a film cartridge. Since Junior had left production and joined sales and promotion a month ago, his father had followed him around from appearance to appearance with the camera. Junior hated being scrutinized, but he had neither the heart nor the courage to ask his father to stop.

They exited the highway, drove along a few suburban streets, and eased into the parking lot of a large shopping mall. Junior parked the truck in a space far from the entrance.

"I know it's hard sometimes to put on the costume and play the part of one of these heroes," his father said. "I did it for too many years not to know how tiring it can be, especially with obligations at home."

A bird soared high overhead, and Junior thought: a bird; he wouldn't mind being a bird.

"But it's important to remember that these kids today need you— probably more than ever before. They watch men fly to the moon and don't grasp how monumental it is; every day they see something that was previously unreal become just another real thing. How can they look at the world around them and not think that man's highest purpose is to conquer unreality? That the best thing they can do with their imagination is destroy more of life's mysteries? It's up to those of us who work in the world of the imaginary to reach out to these kids and let them know they don't have to solve mysteries or prove anything. We have to show them it's all right to imagine and wonder and dream and believe in things that aren't real, and to be contented enough to let these things stay undiscovered and unreal."

Junior felt weepy. He wanted to love his job as much as his father had, but he knew he couldn't. He hated children's books. He hated sales and promotion. The costumes were humiliating, the vendors and store buyers were pests, and the letters from children and collectors did nothing but irk him.

"Do you follow what I'm saying, Junior?"

"Sure," he said.

"I don't want to tell you how to do your job, because I think you're doing great, but I want you to remember that when you step out of this truck, you are Aquaman. If you say or do something out of character, you could destroy a trust, built up through the books, that Aquaman, though unreal, absolutely exists."

Junior looked straight ahead, sensing his old man's good eye on him. It was simply a matter of time before he would let his father down.

"You sure you're all right, Junior? It's like you're not quite yourself today."

Junior knew his father was right. He was not quite himself today. He'd never been quite himself. He stared out at the asphalt, which shimmered in the heat like an ocean of black water, and he told himself he was Aquaman.

2.

PADDY SAW THE PACKARD ON THE WAY TO DEKALB. IT SAT DULLING IN the sun, at the corner of a rural road and a dirt driveway curving toward a farmhouse. Leaning against it was a sign: FOR SALE—AS IS—$200. Paddy stopped and inspected the Packard from behind the wheel of his tow truck. The car was a boattail speedster, from either 1929 or 1930. Its back window was missing, and a crack had split the front one into three unequal sections. Stuffing sprouted from the seats. The headlights had been smashed. The vehicle's body was weathered but not beyond hope.

An hour later he stood beside a hospital bed. Rabbit Dunne lay under the covers like a discarded marionette, tubes and wires rising from his arms, nose, neck, and torso. His muscles had withered away. His skin was ashen.

Sunlight filled the private room, as did the odors of urine, antiseptic, and chicken soup. Beneath a television broadcasting a baseball game, a muscular young man with a Fu Manchu and black sunglasses sat stoically in a chair. He'd frisked Paddy just moments before.

"Who's the gorilla in the corner?" Paddy asked.

"He's my doctor," Rabbit said in a raspy voice. "A specialist."

"What's his specialty? Being ugly?"

Rabbit's eyes closed and opened weakly. "Nobody from the old days comes to see me. After all I did for them, those piece-of-shit nobodies just leave me out here in the country to die alone." He smirked. "You're the last person I expected to come."

Paddy cleared his throat. "What is it you have, anyway? Cancer of the asshole?"

"Bowel cancer."

"That's right. I knew it was something like that."

"All I did in my life," Rabbit said, his eyes nearly shut, "and I can't even take a shit anymore. Isn't that pathetic?"

"Either that or funny." Paddy glanced back at Fu Manchu, then to the television, where a man was singing that weekends were made for Michelob. "Look, I can't stay long," Paddy said as he turned back to Rabbit. "I just wanted to let you know that as of yesterday, Union Auto is mine—paid in full, you son of a bitch. Did Georgie tell you?"

Fu Manchu rose from his chair and placed a heavy hand on Paddy's shoulder.

"It's all right," Rabbit said. "Let him have his moment in the sun."

Fu Manchu returned to his chair.

"I wanted to celebrate but wasn't sure how," Paddy said, facing Rabbit. "Then it struck me. Why not visit my old pal Rabbit? If I'm lucky, I'll get to watch him die."

Rabbit breathed hard. "I'm a businessman, Paddy. I did what I did because I could. And now you did what you could. We both could have done a lot worse."

"Yeah, well, speaking of business, I've got more than I know what to do with. And you're out here in the cornfields, dying of asshole cancer. Funny how things work out."

"It is funny."

"Well," Paddy said as he patted Rabbit's hand, "Gotta go. Just wanted to share the good news with you."

On his way out, Paddy tipped his hat to Fu Manchu. When Rabbit called his name, he turned around.

"I've got some news for you, too."

"Yeah?" Paddy said. "What is it?"

"I took a dive."

"What?"

"That time you beat me. I took a dive."

"Fuck you."

"Think about it, Paddy. All the money was on me, and I needed cash, so Red and I had some guys place bets on you at the last minute. I made a nice chunk of change that night."

"You're lying."

Rabbit shrugged. "Believe me or don't believe me. I couldn't care less."

Fu Manchu stood and faced Paddy, his eyes hidden behind his sunglasses. If he were a young man, Paddy thought, he'd take out this big clown in ten minutes, tops.

Rabbit laughed. "You know what your problem is, Paddy? You always think you're one step ahead when really, you're two behind."

"Fuck you, Rabbit."

Rabbit raised his hand in a weak wave. "Fuck you too, Paddy."

Paddy drove toward home, replaying in his head his victory over Rabbit nearly half a century ago. It *had* been a victory; nobody could take that from him. He'd put Rabbit on his back, and here they were, decades later, with Rabbit on his back again and Paddy still a winner. His customers often called him a magician and a genius, and although these compliments told him nothing he didn't already know, he enjoyed hearing them. And now the station was his. In a strange way, he was glad he'd paid twice for it: first by writing rent checks and then by buying the property outright. It offered proof of how much harder he worked than most people, and how stacked against him the world had always been.

When Paddy saw the Packard again on the way home, he jammed on the brakes and pulled into the farmhouse driveway. He got out of his tow truck and popped open the Packard's rust-eaten hood. He could rebuild the engine and bring it back to life, and he knew a man who could make the body look like new. After he'd been at the vehicle for ten minutes, a man with ruddy cheeks puttered over on a riding mower. About Paddy's age, he had a potbelly and stubby fingers. His overalls were smeared with what looked like mud but might have been manure.

"This pile of junk's not worth more than a hundred," Paddy said.

The man disagreed and went on about what a great vehicle it had been and still was. He spoke with a lilting accent. Probably a Dutchman, Paddy thought, from a long line of Dutchmen, stuck living on a farm. As the man talked about how sturdy the car had been since he'd bought it used in 1954, Paddy strolled a few feet to his tow truck, unlocked the passenger door, and opened the glove compartment. He pulled out an envelope containing five twenty-dollar bills, which he kept on hand in case of an emergency.

"The car's not worth more than a hundred," Paddy said. He handed the envelope to the Dutchman, who opened it and flipped through the bills with a dumbfounded expression.

A few minutes later, the Dutchman set two shot glasses on the kitchen table and filled each nearly to the lip with rye. Paddy picked up one glass; the Dutchman picked up the other. They clinked their glasses and downed the liquor, and the Dutchman poured another round. He took a second drink and said, "Now, let me find the title." He left the kitchen and soon returned with a shoebox, which he set on the table and opened. He flipped wordlessly through papers inside the box.

"Ah," the Dutchman said. He passed an old black-and-white photograph to Paddy. It showed a hard-looking woman in a long dress—a real country girl, Paddy thought, as sturdy and nearly as attractive as a plow horse. "My wife. Right after our wedding."

Paddy nodded and handed back the snapshot. Although he hadn't met a Dutchman in years and couldn't quite remember what they were supposed to be like, he thought this man was typical, as far as they were concerned: sentimental, simple, not exactly in a hurry.

"And this," the Dutchman said. He passed another picture to Paddy. It was of the Packard. "This is from 1958, I believe—right before the accident."

Paddy handed the photograph back to the Dutchman. He could tell the man wanted to say more, but he didn't want to hear it.

"Only accident I ever had in my life."

"That so?"

The Dutchman nodded.

"Otherwise, I had a spotless record. No parking tickets, no moving violations. Not a mark against me, except for that accident." Paddy had customers like the Dutchman: men and women who made vague references to financial or personal troubles, clearly hoping he'd play the role of priest or bartender for them. "I suppose I should tell you what happened, seeing that you're buying the car."

"I'll have to rebuild her anyway," Paddy said, "so what do I care about some old accident?"

"No, I should. It's only fair."

"I really don't care what happened."

"I was driving home from a bar late at night." The Dutchman gently returned the photo to the box. "I'm not a man with many vices, but drink has always been one, I'm sorry to say. Anyway, I was a couple of miles from home when all of a sudden I hit something. I assumed it was a dog or a deer, so I didn't even bother to slow down. I was too tired and drunk—figured I'd fall asleep if I stopped."

Paddy slowly drummed his fingers on the table and stared at dirty dishes in the sink. The Dutchman downed his third shot.

"The next day I heard they'd found a young man alongside the road, dead." He pulled the keys and the title from the box. "He was drunk—a hitchhiker, probably, or a hobo. Got hit by a car—by me—and headed for a ditch, where he bled to death."

"Any other problems with the car?"

"I didn't drive the car after that, just hid it in the garage and let it rust away for years." The Dutchman started blubbering. People like him were poison, Paddy thought. "I never told anyone—not even my wife—about what had happened, but I always sensed that people knew. This is a small town. People know. If he hadn't been a stranger, they would have arrested me for sure." The Dutchman signed the title and then passed it, along with the keys, to Paddy. "I wished it had been me that was hit."

Paddy wanted to tell the Dutchman that after he fixed up the Packard, he'd be more than happy to come back to the farm and run him over as often as he liked. But he held back his thoughts, stood, and headed outside. As he hitched up the Packard, he remembered that he used to dream of killing people until he killed Old Kevin. After that, he no longer wanted to kill anyone, though sometimes he hoped that his fist would land just right, or his car would swerve just so, and he would take another person from this world. But those were a young man's dreams, and now death didn't seem like such a big deal—it was certainly nothing to be feared or craved or dwelt on for too long. When he had the car hitched up, he shook the Dutchman's hand.

"Do yourself a favor and forget about that dead man," he said as he got into his truck.

"What do you mean?"

"The man you killed—forget him. He's dead. You're alive. That's the way things were meant to be, so that's how they are."

"But what happened was my fault. I'm responsible."

"But it's done."

"It's never done. Every day it's not done."

"Well, that's your fault. You'd be better off if you just forgot all about him."

The Dutchman stared piteously at Paddy. His face twitched. "How can I forget him? Every day I think of him."

Paddy shrugged and said, "Suit yourself." He started the engine and rumbled away, slowed by the Packard he was pulling.

Paddy arrived home shortly after nightfall with a bag of takeout and a bottle of scotch. Sitting on the living-room couch, he ate chop suey, sipped his liquor, and wondered who else he could tell about his good fortune. Yesterday he had bragged to Willie about buying the station, and tomorrow he would ask him to help bring the Packard back to life. Over the next few weeks, he would casually announce his new status as a property owner to some of his regulars, and he would show off the Packard to the few who knew something about cars. They would be impressed and would congratulate him, but they weren't here now, as his heart thumped with the need to brag. He picked up the phone and dialed his son's number. Upon hearing a busy signal, he set the receiver in its cradle. He poured himself another drink and lifted the glass.

"To Paddy Halligan," he said, and downed the scotch.

A few drinks later, he picked up the phone and dialed his son's number again. Still busy. He slammed down the receiver, then lifted it and dialed seven numbers at random. A man answered on the third ring.

"The place is mine," Paddy said, and then hung up.

For the next fifteen minutes he dialed random phone numbers, sometimes getting through to a person and sometimes not. Whenever he did, he told the bewildered listener his news and immediately hung up. He tried his son's number again. This time it rang.

"Hello," a woman said.

It must have been Michael's wife. He couldn't recall what she looked like, but he remembered she was a doll.

"Where's that husband of yours?"

"What?"

"Your husband—where is he?"

"Who's this?"

Paddy regarded his hand, which lay flat on his thigh. He was proud of his hands. They'd given him so much and continued to serve him well; they'd taken back what others had stolen from him.

"Tell him the place is mine."

"What did you say?"

He poured another drink and downed it. He thought the world would be a better place if there were more men like him, men who knew when to build and when to destroy and had the ability to do both well.

"I said, the place is mine. After all these years, it's mine. Tell him that for me."

"I'm sorry. You must have the wrong number."

Paddy chuckled. "This is Michael Halligan's number, right?"

"Who is this?"

"And you're the pretty little wife, right? I've seen you, you know. I've seen you shopping. I've seen you going into your house. I'll always remember falling into you on the train; it was a real treat."

"If you don't tell me who you are, I'm calling the police."

"All right, honey, settle down. Just tell him it's mine, all right? Union

Auto is finally mine—no thanks to him."

"Who is this?"

Paddy shook his head. Stupid people were like cracks in the street: every day there were a few more. You could ignore them, smooth them over, or jackhammer them into dust, but they just kept coming, making things rough for people with places to go.

"It's his old man," he said. "Who the hell did you think it was?"

"His father?" She paused. He thought how strange it was that this woman he'd never met was his daughter-in-law. "But I thought you were dead."

Paddy laughed. "Do I sound dead to you?"

At five-fifteen the next morning, Paddy woke on the floor of his bedroom. The overhead light was on. Crumbs were pressed into his cheek. He tried to push himself up but stopped when the room spun. He tried to reassemble the previous night but couldn't recall what he'd done after talking to Michael's wife. He gazed across the floor at hairs woven into the rug. The area under the dresser, which was little more than arm's length away, was especially dirty, littered with cobwebs, coins, dead bugs, and clumps of dust. As Paddy stared at the squalor, he noticed a piece of paper dangling from the bottom of the dresser. He crawled toward it and pulled it free. It was a check for a hundred dollars, made out to "Cash," from the account of Dr. and Mrs. Thornton D. Twitchell of Evanston, Illinois. Bits of dried tape still clung to the corners of the check, which apparently had been stuck to the dresser's underside. Paddy sat up slowly and leaned back against the side of his bed. The room swirled as he focused on the check's date: August 31, 1934. Two weeks before Elizabeth's death.

⳾MICHAEL COULDN'T HELP BUT FEEL THERE WAS SOMETHING DIVINE about his Big Little Books. How else to explain discovering *Tailspin Tommy and the Lost Transport* on a busy downtown sidewalk, untrampled and complete, as though it had been set there by the hand of God? Or stopping at a drugstore in Warrenville and finding seven books that had been sitting unsold, according to the proprietor, for more than twenty-five years? Or attending an auction of an old Kresge warehouse and encountering eighteen unopened shipping cartons of Big Littles, which he had then bought with an opening bid of only fifty dollars? How to explain all of this, except to factor in something beyond human under-standing?

And how else to explain the letter he had received from Junior, inviting him to Racine to buy Oswald's collection?

Michael parked the Econoline van he'd rented for the day, walked across the street to Oswald's house, and rang the doorbell. He took a deep breath, trying not to dwell on the hundred-dollar bills he was carrying: five in his right shoe, five in his left, three in each pocket, and the rest in his wallet. Three thousand dollars in all. Above him, clouds hung thick and low, like smoke from an imploded building.

Junior answered the door in a white T-shirt and jeans and invited Michael inside. He was nearly bald, with pockmarked cheeks and tinted glasses. The aroma of cigarette smoke surrounded him.

"You probably weren't expecting to hear from me, were you?" Junior said as he shut the door.

"I wasn't."

"That's the best way to live—not expecting anything. It's when you start expecting things that life goes to hell."

Junior waved Michael into the muggy living room. The walls were still paneled with wood and decorated with family portraits, but the room was less welcoming than Michael remembered. The drapes were pulled shut. A couch, a corduroy recliner, and two threadbare chairs were all aimed at the console television. Michael wondered if Junior lived here with his parents.

"Misery is all about expectations," Junior said. "If you expect a plateful of shit and you get a plateful of shit, well then, there you go. But if you expect strawberry shortcake and then get a plateful of shit, you're going to be pretty miserable. You know what I mean?"

"I think so."

"You brought the money, right?"

"I brought the money."

Junior grinned. "Want a beer?"

With Junior in the kitchen, Michael wandered around the living room, glancing at family pictures. After his previous visit here over a decade earlier, he had continued to write to Oswald Knoll, who had responded with brief letters that were polite, businesslike, and never accompanied by gifts. In response to Michael's questions about *Trouble in the City of Dreams*, he had merely written, "It was an attempt to feature several of Whitman's heroes in one book, and to promote the Century of Progress exhibition. In the end we had to withdraw it because of legal issues related to the use of existing characters and the appearance of a new character." Then, two years ago, Oswald had sent a letter saying he was retiring and would be replaced by his son. Michael had written a note of congratulations to Junior and then letters inquiring about specific books, but Junior had never written back until a month ago, when he had extended his surprising offer: his father's collection for three grand in cash.

Junior returned with two bottles of Point beer and handed one to Michael, who was looking at a pair of framed photographs atop the television.

"My kids: Ann and Trey." Junior picked up the photo of the boy and handed it to Michael. Inside the frame, a child about four years old, with freckles and sandy hair, grinned excitedly. "Right from the start, everyone called him Trey because he's the third Oswald Knoll. I resisted for a while and called him Ozzie, but eventually I gave in." Michael quickly did the math and figured out that his own son, had he survived, would have been twelve. "Apparently, nobody wants us to have identities of our own."

Michael carefully set the picture in its place and sat on the couch. Junior kicked off his flip-flops and fell back into the recliner. With a quick yank of its wooden handle, he thrust himself into a nearly supine position. The two men drank, and to break the silence Michael asked, "How is your father?"

"He's fine—been living in Florida with my mom for two years now."

"Does he know you're selling the collection?"

Junior laughed and then, in a mock-authoritarian voice, said, "Parents, it's ten o'clock. Do you know where your children are?" He took a swig of his beer. "He gave the collection to me, so it's mine." He swept his arm like an orchestra conductor. "All of their old crap is mine."

Michael drank and thought that if he had been Oswald's son, he would have moved the collection to a vault, insured it, and made certain it stayed in the family forever. At the thought of family, he pictured Sara, who in recent years had taken to exercising with Jack LaLanne each morning and going for long nightly walks by herself, her body growing leaner and stronger as his softened.

A few years earlier, on a Saturday afternoon in early autumn, Michael had overheard a conversation between Sara and her sister. They were sitting at the kitchen table, unaware that he had come around to the back of the house for a rake. He stood beneath the open window.

"Any more talk of trying again?" Michelle asked.

"Don't you have to have sex for that to happen?" said Sara.

"Never, huh?"

"Hardly ever."

Michael waited and listened. He considered heralding his presence by coughing or dragging the rake through the leaves.

"I was thinking the other day that this is how nuns must feel," Sara said. "The celibacy, the silence, the long hours with nothing to keep you company but your own thoughts. I hated it for so long—you know that. I fought and fought against it, but a couple of months ago I decided to give up and accept it. Now I don't mind it much. I really don't. It's only when he's around that I'm unhappy."

"Do you love him at all?"

Michael listened for an answer but didn't hear one, and as he sat drinking beer with Junior, he wondered if Sara was happy now that she'd left him.

Suddenly, Junior shot forward into a sitting position. He stared at the front door, where the girl from the photograph said, "Hi, Daddy." She was about six years old, with straight brown hair, and she wore shorts, tube socks, and a pale blue T-shirt emblazoned with the word *Warriors* in yellow. Darting up the stairs, she shouted, "I forgot my present for Grandma."

A woman entered the house. She had sad brown eyes and a sun-burned face.

"I figured you'd be halfway to Madison by now," Junior said.

"We were about forty miles away when Ann realized she forgot her present." She glanced at Michael, then back at Junior. "Aren't you going to introduce us?"

"Oh, sure. Yeah, of course," Junior stammered. "Sharon, this is Frank. He's new at work, so I invited him over for a beer." Junior looked at Michael, though he didn't quite make eye contact. "Frank, this is my wife, Sharon."

Michael shook Sharon's hand but wasn't about to speak.

"That's Frank's van out front," Junior said. "He rented it to move some stuff. I'm going to help him."

"Where are you moving to?"

"Who, me?" asked Michael.

Sharon laughed. "Is someone else moving?"

"Across town, over on Superior," Junior said quickly. "It shouldn't take us too long."

Ann ran down the stairs with the present, and Junior accompanied his wife and daughter outside. Michael sat with his beer and let out a sigh.

A week and a half earlier, he had returned home from work to a quiet house. At first he thought nothing of it. Sara worked at a shoe store on weekday afternoons and was out most evenings at community classes: pottery, watercolor, photography, and Italian. But when he went upstairs, he discovered that most of her clothes were missing. Her suitcases, jewelry, and makeup kit were gone as well. He called out her name and raced from room to room until he saw his old notebook on the middle of the dining-room table. For years he had meant to get rid of it, but since returning to Lyons he had been faithfully adding to his list of women. The rest of the time, he kept it hidden in a box of Big Littles.

For an hour he sat at the table, heavy with embarrassment and regret, but as he went about fixing dinner, he grew resentful of Sara for having looked through his personal things. After eating, he drove to Lyons, which grew seedier by the day, with strip club after strip club, biker gangs roaring up and down Ogden, and prostitutes gathering in twos and threes on the corners. He spied them, knowing some but not others, and picked up a petite brunette wearing a tube top and hot pants. As usual, Michael saw the imperfections once the girl climbed into the car. Her skin was sallow, her fingernails were bitten down to the quick, and she seemed spaced out on something.

Sitting beside her on a motel bed, he claimed his name was Mike Steele. "My wife just left me," he said, his muscles tense with anticipation, his heart agitated and empty.

"That's crazy." She kicked her legs like a girl sitting on the edge of a pool. She was so young, and Michael felt certain she was a runaway. "Why the hell would she do that?"

Keeping his eyes on the dingy yellow carpet, Michael started to tell her about Sara's finding the notebook. Almost immediately, the girl interrupted him.

"You're not one of those creeps, are you?"

"What do you mean?"

"I mean the kind that just wants to talk, or who tries to turn you on to Jesus or something but still gets off on being here."

"No, I'm not that kind of creep."

"Then what kind of creep are you?"

Upon returning home, Michael sat at the dining-room table and flipped open his notebook to add the girl to his list. Following number 346, he saw Sara's handwriting:

> Michael,
>
> Obviously I'm hurt and sad and stunned, but that should go without saying, shouldn't it? I thought all day about what to write and finally decided it wasn't worth writing much at all. There's too much in this notebook already.
>
> I will return for my things and at some point get a lawyer. I don't quite remember how divorces work, exactly, but I guess it will come back to me.
>
> By the way, when you were out last night, your father called to say that Union Auto is his. I assume you know what this means.
>
> Apparently he is alive, too, and of course you knew this as well. It was his call that made me snoop in hopes of understanding you better, and it was snooping that led me to this notebook.
>
> Is this the one you said you used for your dreams? That's what I was hoping to find.
>
> Sara

Michael flipped through the pages, backward in time from girl to girl, wondering what had happened to them all. How many were dead? How many were happy? He found the entry for Sara (number 269) from two months before their wedding. Sara had crossed it out so hard with a pen that the paper was torn. Michael flipped forward, moving toward the handful of pages left to fill, and immediately following her note he jotted down the details for number 347.

Junior came back inside without his wife and daughter, clapped his hands once, and said, "All right. Let's get down to business."

After handing over the cash, Michael followed Junior to the basement, his heart pounding as though it could beat its way right out of his body. Over the last several years, Michael had discovered that other publishers, including Dell and Fawcett and Saalfield, had come up with their own books modeled after Big Littles, and although he picked up these titles whenever he could, all he truly collected were Whitmans. He was only eighty books short of a full collection, and in just a moment he would own everything and more. Junior climbed down the ladder into the bomb shelter. Michael followed. In the room with fake windows, Junior pointed to fifteen boxes stacked in the corner.

"There it is," he said. "Feel free to take a look."

Michael stared in disbelief at the boxes. He felt ill. "That can't be everything."

"It's everything."

"But I was here before. I remember what I saw. There's no way all of it could fit into these boxes."

"Well, this is all that's left. This is what I'm selling."

"What do you mean, 'all that's left'?"

"I sold a few things here and there to make some quick cash, but this is most of it."

"Who did you sell them to?"

"You're not the only one who collects these things, you know. There's a few of you guys around the country who have been writing to my dad and me for years. *Where can I get this book? Where can I find that one?* My dad helped because he was one of you, but I never had any time for it."

Over the years Michael had met collectors of coins, stamps, magazines, and more, but he had never encountered another collector of Big Littles. He had never suspected his hobby was anything less than unique.

"I can call off the deal, if that's what you want. There are plenty of other guys who would rush up here in a heartbeat for a shot at this."

Junior reached into his pocket, took out the wad of money, and extended it to Michael.

"But it's not fair." Michael focused on the door to the room where he'd seen Oswald's collection years earlier.

"Fair?" Junior slipped the cash back into his pocket. "Since when is anything fair?"

"But you said you'd sell me your father's collection."

"I did, and I am. This is my father's collection."

Michael stepped quickly to the door. He tried to turn the knob, but it was locked.

Junior laughed and said, "Come on. Don't act like this."

"Where's the rest? What did you do with it?"

"I left it for my kids."

Michael glared at Junior, not sure what to believe. The man was obviously a liar.

"I'm serious," said Junior. "I may be a fuckup, but that doesn't mean I'm completely irresponsible. I need some cash right now, but my kids need something for the future. This is what I worked out."

Michael's eyes darted between the locked door and the boxes. He took a deep breath and reasoned that he could always come back for the rest. Junior was probably involved in something illegal. If he needed cash now, he would need cash later.

"At least tell me you didn't sell *Trouble in the City of Dreams.*"

Junior shrugged. "Is it rare?"

"Yeah."

"Then it might be gone. I'm not really sure."

After Michael checked the boxes to make sure they included objects from Oswald's collection, he and Junior hauled them in shifts, first up to the basement, then up to the living room. Michael went outside and backed up the van to the front door. The sky was as ominous as it had been earlier that day, as if a storm could break at any moment but probably wouldn't.

"Isn't it strange to think of the things you do in life?" Junior said as he and Michael carried the boxes out of the house. "You look back at yourself as a kid, and then you look at who you are now, and you think to yourself, *Man, what the fuck happened?* One day you're riding your bike around, pretending you're flying a rocket ship or driving a race car, just for the fun of it, and the next thing you know, you're an adult and the only reason you imagine shit is because your problems are too much to bear."

Michael carefully set a box in the back of the van. "Sounds like you enjoy making up worries for yourself."

"It does?" Junior loaded the last box and laughed. "Well, you're probably right. But that doesn't make my worries less real, now does it?"

Michael slammed the van doors shut. His haul was bountiful, worth more than three thousand dollars; each item was far better than anything he had previously owned. But he couldn't fight off the bitterness he felt. What he hadn't received seemed worth so much more than what he had.

"Will you do me a favor?" Junior asked when Michael had climbed into the driver's seat and closed the door. "Will you shake my hand and wish me luck?"

"Why should I wish you luck?"

"Because I'm not lucky."

Junior offered his hand through the open window. Michael scrutinized the hand and thought that Junior was hardly unlucky. He had a wife and children, he had Oswald Knoll for a father, and until today, he'd had a bomb shelter filled with everything Michael wanted. If Junior wanted to know what unlucky looked like, he should have poked around in Michael's memories and learned the meaning of the word.

"Come on, Michael, just a handshake and a word of luck."

Then again, someday Junior would need more money and would go looking for someone to buy the rest of the collection. So Michael shook Junior's hand, smiled as sincerely as he could, and said, "Good luck."

4.

Sara drove slowly past Union Auto for the third time and glanced at the garage, hoping to see Paddy Halligan rise up from behind a bumper, wiping his hands with a rag. She could fill up, head west, and reach Saint Louis tonight, as long as it didn't snow. Then tomorrow: Joplin, Tulsa, and Oklahoma City. Her trunk was stuffed with belongings, the divorce was final, and Santa Fe was a long way away. She passed Union Auto again and looped through Western Springs like a bird that had lost her flock but hid her fear with graceful flight. All her life, she had lived more or less with others: her parents, Art Malone, Michael Halligan. A few months ago, after leaving Michael, she had run off to her sister's guest bedroom. Now she would move in with a second cousin in Santa Fe, but this time only temporarily. She had money in the bank, clothes on her back. In New Mexico, people had once lived in caves dug into cliffs, and if they had survived there, then she could, too.

Sara returned to Union Auto and pulled into the lot. She parked her car beside the gas pump and rolled down her window. An old black man greeted her, and as he pumped her gas, Sara stepped out of the car. She'd passed Union Auto so many times that she had almost memorized the building's façade. There was something exhilarating about standing in front of the station, on the property, and viewing the world from here. When she asked the man if she could use the bathroom, he pointed to the station.

In the garage, a yellow sports car lay dead on blocks, its four tires off to the side. *The Devil's workshop*, Sara thought with a smile, recalling that train trip with Michael so many years earlier. After using the bathroom, Sara glanced behind the sports car and a large rack of tools, hoping to find her father-in-law. She looked behind the counter, but no one was there. Then she saw a door propped all the way open, a wedge of wood for a doorstop. With sweat on her back, she edged past the door and entered a tiny living room, where she saw a green couch with tattered arms, and a coffee table upon which sat a large bowl filled with peanuts. Sara made her way past the furniture to a tall bookcase with framed photographs and keepsakes on its shelves. She looked at pictures of a man—Michael's father, she assumed—at various stages of life. Young: posed for a fight, in boxing gloves and trunks. Middle-aged: standing in front of Union Auto. Old: behind the wheel of a fancy antique car. Sara's eyes passed over bottle openers, matchbooks, and key chains with the brand names Esso, Ace High, Wolf's Head, and Havoline, and settled on a photograph of a baby in a white gown. Sara picked up the photo and wondered if the child was Michael. She found it hard to tell with babies; with their moon-faces, spittled chins, and dazed stares, they all looked similarly beatific and bland.

"Can I help you?"

Sara turned to face her father-in-law, who stood in the middle of the living room with his sleeves rolled up above his elbows. Thick veins snaked down each of his forearms. In his right hand, he held a root beer bottle by its neck.

He pointed the bottle at Sara. "What are you doing in my house?"

"The man outside said I could use the restroom."

"Does this look like a restroom to you?"

"I got lost, and then I saw this photograph of a baby from across the room and had to take a closer look." She held up the frame. "Your son, I assume?"

"Put the picture down."

"I was just wondering, that's all." She looked down at the photo. "I lost a son several years ago."

"I'm trying to be nice here."

"I used to be angry about it and think about what should have been and what was taken from us, and about all the things I could have done better. My husband, Michael, acted like it never fazed him, but I think he never got over it."

"I'm warning you."

"The doctor prescribed me something for morning sickness, so I took it. I didn't know it would cause such awful problems. Nobody knew it would—not back then, at least."

"Lady, put the picture down."

"People told me it was for the best that my son died right away, that God was showing mercy by preventing him from dying horribly later on. At first I didn't believe them, and then I did, but now I don't know what to believe and don't really think it matters much either way."

"Put my goddamn picture down right now."

Sara placed the photograph where it had been on the top shelf, in a space outlined with dust.

"I don't know why you can't tell me if that's your son," she said. "It was just a simple question."

Paddy stepped quickly toward Sara, and she stepped left to avoid him. He tossed his empty root beer bottle onto the couch and seized her by the upper arms. The hand that had held the bottle was cold against her skin; the other was warm and sweaty. Suddenly he hoisted her over his shoulder, his arms wrapped around her thighs. She did not resist, did not squirm or scream, and as he carried her out of the room and through the garage, she tried to imagine Michael here as a motherless boy. Poor Michael, that sad little coconut. He had been broken years ago, and his sweetness, which she'd wanted so much to taste, must have spilled out and spoiled.

Her father-in-law set her down outside in front of the old black man, who stared at her with alarm.

"How much does she owe, Willie?"

"Four dollars and ten cents."

Sara reached into her pocketbook and fished out the money, which she placed in Paddy's palm.

"You're lucky I'm a nice guy." He glared at her. "If I see you here again, I'm gonna call the police. That's all there is to it."

"What will you tell them?"

"I'll tell them to arrest you."

"Well, just make sure you give them my name. It's Halligan, like yours. It's one of the few things I kept when I divorced your son."

Sara drove away from Union Auto with the needle on full and wondered how far the gas would take her. Daytime in Santa Fe made people feel more alive than they'd ever felt, she had heard, and nighttime made them feel peaceful. She could hardly wait to get there, could hardly wait even for Amarillo and Gallup and all the towns along the way. She pictured Michael, thinking she could have done more for him and he should have done more for her, but as she headed south past steel mills and paper mills, the traffic starting to bottleneck and the sky turning sulfuric, she whispered to him an apology and a few words of forgiveness, wishing him no ill, and then, at last, she released him.

5.

AFTER SELLING OFF THE HOUSE AND SETTLING UP WITH SARA, MICHAEL moved to an apartment in Lyons. It was where he belonged, he felt, and within days he was able to sleep through the sirens and motorcycles and fights outside his window. He had a well-stocked savings account, an unlisted phone number, and a bird's-eye view of the action on Ogden Avenue. In his spare time he bought old books, magazines, newspapers, baseball cards, toys—every trinket and doodad that was worth something— at garage sales and church bazaars, and then sold them for a profit to antiques stores and collectors he'd come to know through his travels. He kept some of these items in a storage space half a mile up the road, along with his portion of Oswald's collection and his own books, which now included at least one copy of every title except *Trouble in the City of Dreams*. He always had a few of his books in his apartment, and at night he lay in bed and read them. Occasionally, while trying to fall asleep, he hugged a pillow and tried to remember the feel of Sara's body.

He failed to encounter anyone else who collected Big Little Books, though he met several people who amassed comic books and comic-strip art, one of whom sniffed at Big Littles, claiming that the way Whitman Publishing had hacked up the strips of Alex Raymond and Milton Caniff amounted to nothing short of desecration. After that, Michael kept his collection to himself and did little to make friends with other collectors, many of whom struck him as elitists, mere hobbyists, or oddballs anyway. Michael found it easy to imagine that they lacked his commitment and pure intentions, and that they failed to respect what they collected as much as he respected his Big Littles.

As the months passed, Michael realized he could pay his bills solely with income from selling memorabilia, so he walked into his office one morning, typed up and turned in a letter of resignation, and left without a party or a gold watch to send him on his way, and without saying goodbye or thanks to men he'd worked with for more than a quarter century. After that, he started each day by walking up the street to make sure his collection was safe, and he filled most of his remaining hours by combing the classified ads for buried treasure, trekking from estate sale to junk shop like a soldier in search of bounty, and selling off what he'd found to a growing legion of collectors who were as desperate for what they coveted as he was for Big Littles. Sometimes he went days without speaking to anyone, and with greater frequency he talked in his head to Sara or his mother about the mundane details of his life. He often thought about the things Junior had denied him, and after writing several letters to the man and not receiving a single response, Michael called Whitman Publishing and was told that Junior had left town months ago and no one, not even his family, knew where he was. Afterward, on a few occasions, Michael drove up to Racine, parked near Oswald's old house, and waited in vain to see if Junior had returned.

A year after Sara left him, Michael looked up Aunt Mae's listing in the phone book. A week later, on the fortieth anniversary of his mother's death, he drove to Oak Park, feeling awful and alone, and knocked on his aunt's apartment door.

"Who's there?" she called out.

He answered her, and half a minute later she slowly opened the door a few inches and stood in the gap she'd just made. She was older and grayer, just past sixty, but otherwise she was her same brittle self.

"Can I come in?" he asked.

"Of course." She swung open the door. "You've always been welcome here."

Michael entered the living room, which was as cramped and cluttered as her old place and filled with the same furniture and tchotchkes, the same smoky odor, the same faces of Jesus on the wall.

"You're looking old," Aunt Mae said. The angles of her body had sharpened over the past thirty years.

"I'm forty-seven."

"You look older than that."

Michael shrugged.

"Time isn't kind, is it, Michael?"

"I guess not."

"Sit down," she said. "I'll fix you some coffee."

Michael sat at the table, in the center of which stood a blue flowered creamer and a tarnished silver dish filled with sugar lumps. He remembered the creamer and dish from decades ago and remembered it used to bother him that they didn't match. But now they looked to him like a set, as though years together had made their pairing natural.

"Nobody respects age anymore," Aunt Mae said as she entered the room with two cups of coffee. "There used to be a time when people like us were valued for their wisdom and experience, but nowadays there's no appreciation at all." She set the cups on the table and sat across from Michael. "I've smelled practically every perfume that's come along in the past forty years. I know their names, their scents, and what their bottles look like, but does that carry any weight in the world? Am I valued for what I know? Of course not. Who gets the raises and promotions and better schedules? I'll tell you who: all the lovely young hotshots who spend their time gossiping about matters that should be kept private and thinking that the world's only as old as they are." She poured cream and plopped sugar into her cup. "I know the bosses want to get rid of me, and one of these days they'll do it."

She picked up her cup with both hands and sipped her coffee. She hunched tensely forward, as if closing in on herself.

"And don't think you men shouldn't shoulder most of the blame. Rather than come to me—who could tell you a thing or two about the best perfume to buy, who could teach you something about taste—you go to the cute young girl who doesn't know anything about anything."

It was good to be here, he thought; it was reassuring to know Aunt Mae hadn't changed much. Her misery comforted him.

"Are you married?" she asked.

"No."

A siren blared outside the window, and Michael was glad for the distraction. Their kiss sometimes still came to him as he watched a late-night movie or woke in the morning, although at this stage of their lives, they were more like distant cousins than aunt and nephew, and this thought made Michael feel a little more forgiving of them both.

"I'm glad you decided not to marry, Michael. The fewer people you come into contact with in the world, the better. Everyone on television these days talks about broadening horizons, but I think there's something to be said for having narrow horizons—or no horizons at all."

For a second he thought he should mention Sara, but he knew better than to get too close to his aunt.

"So, tell me about yourself, Michael."

"I live in Lyons, in an apartment. I worked for an accounting firm downtown until recently, when I retired. There's not much to say other than that."

She asked what he did with his days, and he said he bought and sold objects from the past. He earned only half as much as he had as an accountant, but he didn't have to drag himself downtown or answer to anyone.

"I've wondered about you over the years," she said. "I figured you never got too far from here."

"And I figured you hadn't moved at all."

"I only moved because they tore down my building. I wouldn't have left otherwise. I had everything I needed where I was."

They sipped their coffee. The clock sounded like a tapping foot.

"You know what today is, don't you?" Michael said.

"It's Saturday," Aunt Mae said.

"But it's more than that."

"I don't think so, Michael. It's just a Saturday like any other Saturday."

"But today—"

"Michael, listen to me. I've prayed about this many times over the years, and I've learned that forgetting is one of the greatest gifts God has given us. It's like sleep: without it, we would fall apart." She sipped her coffee. "I read somewhere that in heaven, you learn everything you never knew, but I think in heaven you forget everything you ever learned. Doesn't that sound more like heaven to you? Wouldn't you be happy to have your thoughts and memories wiped away for good, and to get the chance to start over without having to worry about anything? I don't know about you, but for me, that would be heaven."

Michael downed the rest of his drink and looked into his cup. The liquid had left a kind of sludge in its wake.

"Well, I should probably be going," he said as he stood.

Aunt Mae wrung her napkin in her hands. "Will you be back?"

"Probably."

She reached her hand across the table, but she came nowhere close to touching him.

"I want you to come to Mass with me tomorrow." Her hand was bony and bare, tiny and trembling. "Will you do that?"

"You're not going to ask me to become a priest, are you?"

She laughed and pulled back her hand. "Don't be ridiculous," she said as she crossed her arms in front of her chest. "Why on earth would I want you to become a priest?"

6.

PADDY SAT BEHIND THE WHEEL OF HIS PACKARD AND LET HIS EYES WANDER from the three-story Queen Anne on his left to the stately elms and maples that surrounded it. It was October, but few leaves lay on the vast, manicured lawn, as if every few hours a crew of angels or laborers descended upon the yard and carefully removed anything that had dared to fall there. Paddy told himself he belonged here, that wealth was nothing to genuflect before. He was calm. He was purposeful. He was well prepared for what he had to do. He had bathed vigorously this morning, excavated grit from under his fingernails, and donned his best suit and overcoat. He knew from the Evanston white pages that someone named L. Twitchell lived here, and he assumed from his occasional reconnaissance that the elderly lady who came and went in a Lincoln Town Car was the Lydia Twitchell who'd signed the check he'd been carrying in his wallet for more than a year and a half.

Paddy rang the bell and adjusted his suit. The woman he'd spied several times answered the door in a white silk blouse, black slacks, and pearls. She was so gaunt, and her skin was so thin, that he saw the pulse in her neck and blue veins splayed at her temples.

"May I help you?" she asked.

Paddy cleared his throat and introduced himself, but then forgot the explanation he had rehearsed. He imagined Elizabeth. Even though he'd done his best over the years to obliterate her from his mind, she kept returning.

He removed the check from his wallet and handed it to the woman. "I wondered if this was yours," he said.

She removed glasses from her pocket, put them on, and examined the check for half a minute. "Where did you get this?" she asked.

"It was in my house. I wanted to know how it got there."

She returned the check to him. "What did you say your name was?"

Paddy told her his name and returned the check to his wallet.

"My name is Lydia Twitchell," she said. "Would you care to come in?"

Paddy followed her into the living room, which had white carpeting from wall to wall, transparent plastic on every cushion, and walls adorned with paintings of ships in choppy water and tranquil country homes. He sat in a paisley chair. Mrs. Twitchell sat on a sofa halfway across the room from him.

"You were Elizabeth's husband, I assume."

Paddy gripped the arms of the chair. For decades he had resigned himself to not fully knowing the circumstances of his wife's death, but the check had stirred up anger and unease within him. It had made him crave explanation.

"How did you know her?" he asked.

"I felt so terrible when she died," Mrs. Twitchell said impassively. She sat on the edge of the sofa with her back rigid and her hands folded in her lap. "It was such a tragic loss."

"How did you know her?"

"We belonged to a group called the Society for Sacred Possessions."

"What the hell was the Society for Sacred Possessions?" he asked.

"Please don't curse in my home, Mr. Halligan."

Paddy glowered at Mrs. Twitchell. He could have snapped her in two without working up a sweat. She had no right to know something about Elizabeth that he didn't.

She sighed and said, "The Society was a cause. I guess today they'd call it a movement. It had to do with the spirituality of possessions and providing for everyone." She pursed her lips and looked askance, as if trying to glimpse something she'd lost. "I don't remember much more than that, I'm afraid. There was a time when the Society was vital to me, when I could hardly make a decision without calling it to mind, but life kept moving. My kids grew and had kids of their own, my husband passed away, and many things that used to upset me ceased to be a bother. Now I can barely remember anything about the Society."

"What was the check for?"

"I'm a philanthropist, Mr. Halligan; I give money to worthy causes. As far as the Society for Sacred Possessions was concerned, I used to give my checks to Elizabeth, who in turn gave them to Eddie. What he did with them, I never asked."

Paddy rubbed the armrests with his palms. His arms longed to hit something or someone.

"Who was Eddie?"

"Eddie Kowal," she said. "He was our leader, though Elizabeth was much closer to him than I was. I assume he never received the check you have because of what happened to her."

"What do you know about what happened?"

Mrs. Twitchell stood and walked primly to a sturdy wooden bookcase at the far end of the room. "I don't know anything except what I saw in the paper," she said as she scanned the shelves. "I did not know her well at all— we never had any conversations of a personal nature—but she seemed to be a woman of exceptional resilience." Mrs. Twitchell pulled down a scrapbook and handed it to Paddy. "Perhaps you will find this helpful."

The scrapbook was filled with short newspaper clippings about protests, rallies, and public disturbances, interspersed with full-page flyers that tallied the group's grievances, issued their demands, and called the masses to action. The fervent words reminded Paddy of his old motivational booklets; they shared the same certainty, the same desperation. He flipped the pages, not sure what to make of Elizabeth's secret life, not sure if he should ignore it or hunt it to the death. Finally, he came across several short newspaper stories from 1938 chronicling the arrest and conviction of Edward A. Kowal, of 6320 South Rhodes, for breaking and entering and inciting a riot.

"Is this Eddie character still around?" Paddy asked.

"I'm afraid I lost touch with the Society long ago."

Paddy thanked Mrs. Twitchell for her time, and when he stood, he felt invincible, as though the Society's demise proved his own strength. As he walked out the front door and down the walkway, he thought that with a few breaks he could have become a philanthropist himself. He could have owned a fancy house and bedded proper ladies like Mrs. Twitchell. Repeating in his head the address for Eddie Kowal, he slipped behind the wheel of his Packard.

A week later, Paddy stood in front of a dilapidated six-flat at 6320 South Rhodes. The paint was cracked and peeling, and two windows were covered with plywood. The front door was gone. The neighborhood was crowded with colored people—or whatever colored people were called these days. Blacks? Afro Americans? Negroes? Minorities? They were always clamoring for something, Paddy thought, always complaining, always burning something up and marching, and then, sure enough, some politician would cave and give them whatever they wanted. The following week, another one would show up on the TV news as a reporter or walk around La Grange as if he owned the place. Down the block, children ran around and tossed a football, a group of young men loitered by a car, and a couple dressed in colorful African gowns glided down the sidewalk. This was the city where he had grown up, this was a neighborhood he had frequented, and yet it felt to Paddy like a foreign country. Some people would have been afraid to be here, he figured, but he had boldly driven through the neighborhood in his tow truck and nobody had said a word to him. He'd employed Willie for more than fifteen years now, and the two of them, Paddy felt fairly certain, got along as well as any two people in the world. They ate lunch together sometimes, talked baseball and football, and as a team had transformed the Packard from a heap of rust into a work of art. They'd collected parts from vintage-car restorers and installed them whenever work was slow; they'd had the exterior sanded down and painted crimson; they'd had the interior reupholstered in black leather. When the car kept dying in fourth gear, they'd narrowed the ignition point gap. When the problem lingered, it was

Willie who had thought to replace the breaker arm and valve springs, thus fixing the problem for good.

Every white man in the world could have lined up and asked to drive the Packard, and Paddy would have waved them away, passed the key to Willie, as he occasionally did, and said, "Take her for a spin."

Paddy stepped through the open doorway and knocked on one of the two first-floor apartments. He was probably wasting his time; if alive, Eddie had most likely fled this neighborhood decades ago. A young black woman in a T-shirt and jeans answered the door.

"I'm looking for a man named Eddie Kowal," Paddy said. "Do you know if he lives here?"

"You looking for the landlord?"

"I don't know."

"His first name's Eddie. I don't know his last name."

"Do you know where he is?"

She pointed upstairs and said, "All the way up, right above me."

Paddy climbed the two flights, feeling composed and commanding, as if he were hunting down men for Rabbit Dunne again. Hardly even winded, he knocked on the door. He heard a rustling on the other side, and a man's voice barked, "Leave a note. You know the arrangement."

"Are you Eddie Kowal?" Paddy said.

"Slip it under the door."

"I want to talk to you about Elizabeth Halligan."

There was more shuffling. It sounded like a mouse skittering inside a wall. "Go away," the man said.

Paddy opened the door, but the chain kept it closed. He shouldered the door once, then twice. On his third attempt, the chain easily tore free from the doorframe, and Paddy stumbled into a fetid apartment. He covered his nose with his hand and looked around the room. There were towers of old newspapers, mountains of books, and piles of empty pop bottles, cereal boxes, cookie tins, and aluminum cans. In the middle of it all, in a chair at a small desk, sat a man with a thick gray stubble and scraggly hair. He held a book and bore a stoic expression.

"I always knew you'd come," he said.

"Yeah?"

Eddie set down his book. "Be sober, be vigilant," he said, "because your adversary the Devil, as a roaring lion, walketh about, seeking whom he may devour."

"You don't say." Paddy uncovered his nose and realized he could tolerate the smell without retching.

"You don't frighten me," Eddie said. "The Devil has been stalking me my whole life in the form of the police, the bankers, the government, these people around here. It makes no difference that now he comes through you."

"Don't flatter yourself," Paddy said as he closed the door. "I didn't know who the hell you were until a few days ago."

The apartment had a faint movement and quiet rustle to it, as though the junk were twitching with life. Paddy looked closer and saw roaches scurrying amid the squalor.

"He came through your son, but I defeated him."

"Michael?"

"He came into this room and sat on that couch there, decades ago." Eddie pointed, but all Paddy saw was a mound of trash. "After accusing me of unspeakable activity with his mother, he assaulted me—no doubt in your honor."

Paddy tried to assemble all he was hearing and fit it together with what he knew and what he'd wondered.

"If you've come here to kill me, then kill me," Eddie said. "If you've come here to ask me questions, then ask them."

Paddy stared at Eddie and found it hard to believe this filthy recluse had been a leader of anything, or that Elizabeth had ever followed him.

"How did you know my wife?"

Eddie cleared his throat and said, "Imagine living here. Imagine living in this neighborhood with these people. You were outside. You saw them. You see the way they live. They have no respect for possessions, no appreciation for the sanctifying power of things. I've tried to speak to them, but it's like talking to a pile of bricks."

"Did you lay a hand on her?"

"I laid both hands on her," Eddie said coolly, "but only to embrace in the spirit of Christian fellowship—unlike you, who did what his basest desires demanded."

Paddy made a fist with his right hand. Sometimes the urge to hit a man came on like lust or hunger. When it did, he would work on a car and the urge would vanish, but banishing an urge was not the same as satisfying it. A starving dog will sit when ordered to sit. He'll do it a hundred, or two hundred, or a thousand times, but then finally he will rise and snarl and get his meat any way he can.

"Our love was of another kind," Eddie said.

"Oh yeah? What kind was that?"

"It was sacred, not physical."

Paddy laughed. "In other words, it was nothing," he said, feeling victorious. But then suddenly he felt sick and beaten to think the baby had been his.

"You look like your son, you know that?" Eddie said. "You should have seen him. Puffed up with anger, he made fists like you're doing now."

Paddy tried to imagine Michael fighting for his honor, but the picture wasn't clear. He studied Eddie, who was babbling now about his ridiculous group and all the persecution he'd had to face in his life. Paddy knew he could kill the man within ten minutes, and that if the police bothered to investigate, they would simply pick up some neighborhood thug at random and pin the rap on him. There had been a time in Paddy's life when he would have welcomed such a scenario, but now, with the odor of decay starting to get to him, he simply backed out of the room and left the building amid the racket of Eddie's raging about the Devil.

7.

☙ PROJECTED IN BLACK AND WHITE AGAINST THE WALL, THE LONE RANGER drew his pistol and fired all six shots into the air. Smoke rose in spurts from the barrel and then quickly vanished into the gray sky. He returned the gun to its holster and grinned at the thirty or so boys who had gathered around the stage, waving cowboy hats and cap guns in a salute to their hero. The Lone Ranger's pants and shirt were smartly creased and spotless. His boots gleamed like freshly spread blacktop. He gesticulated and spoke, but because the eight-millimeter film was silent, Oswald had no way of knowing what his younger self had been saying that afternoon at the Wisconsin State Fair. It was 1976 now; in the movie on the wall, it was always June of '48. Oswald lay down on his side on his brother's sofa. The springs lacked restraint, and the lumpy stuffing was starting to escape through a tear, but the couch was comfortable enough. Over the past two nights Oswald had adjusted to sleeping here, just as he'd adjusted to sleeping alone over the past nineteen months and eight days. If someone were to smash his head with a brick all night, he thought, he would probably adjust to that, too.

The Lone Ranger crouched at the front of the stage, where he picked imaginary grass from an imaginary prairie and tossed the blades into a faint imaginary breeze. Suddenly he stopped what he was doing and glanced around, as if trying to spot rustlers or runaway stallions. His hand hovered over his pistol for a few seconds but then returned to yanking out phantom grass. As he watched his former self, Oswald knew his words that afternoon nearly three decades earlier had no doubt been sincere, and his advice had most definitely been useless. He probably had warned the children against lying and cheating and had promised them a bright future in exchange for their best efforts and good behavior. *Don't listen to him, boys*, Oswald wanted to shout at the wall. *Don't believe a thing he tells you.* Thirty years ago, he had felt certain the future held nothing but betterment, especially for his family, but tonight, as with several hundred previous nights, he had the choice of falling asleep either to the memory of Louise dying in bed beside him or to the image of his grandson Trey lying comatose in a hospital bed.

The movie played on, and the Lone Ranger strutted around, talked, and tossed books to the crowd. When the remaining foot of film snapped loose from the feeder reel, Oswald watched the celluloid crawl forward like a dying man in a desert and then disappear into the projector. He looked at the wall, where the Lone Ranger abruptly vanished, replaced by a rectangular patch of light. Oswald reached over to the projector propped on a book on the coffee table. He rewound the film, boxed it up, and ran another movie. The Lone Ranger appeared on the wall in colors so rich, they looked unreal. The footage was from May 1970, at a carnival in northern Illinois. The crowd was smaller and less enthusiastic than before, and the Lone Ranger was thinner, less muscular, a little fatigued. He ambled back and forth and rarely grinned. Now, thanks to his daughter-in-law's stories, Oswald knew that drugs, worry, and depression were what had made his son so lifeless, but at the time he had simply believed that all a man needed to find his way in life were encouragement and something to cherish, and so he had told Junior to add more energy to his performances. Now, watching his son six years later, just after midnight in his brother's spare room, he suddenly found himself appreciating Junior's lethargy. Oswald had told his son so many times to let himself become the characters he portrayed and to act enthusiastic for the children, but now it seemed to him that these two pieces of advice contradicted each other. As the Lone Ranger traveled from mayhem to mayhem, crime to crime, he saw good people murdered and robbed; whether he was sleeping by a campfire or riding into town on Silver, he had to stay alert to ambush. He wouldn't have faced the world with a grin and good cheer. He would have faced it as Junior had, and probably still did, wherever he was: as if his life were a burden he had never wanted.

Louise was gone forever, and Trey would never be well; there was nothing Oswald could do for them. But it was still possible that Junior was in the world somewhere, simply not wanting to be found. All Oswald had of him were some old childhood items, photographs, and film footage. He knew the movies by heart—knew that in a minute his son would call up a boy from the crowd and show him how to steady a pistol by resting the barrel on his forearm, knew Junior would hand a book to the boy, knew the film would run out shortly thereafter. Wherever he went, no matter which sibling or cousin or friend or daughter invited him to stay out of sympathy and concern, he took his projector and films with him. During the day he watched family gatherings, summer vacations, and Christmas mornings with his hosts, laughing and crying over Louise and Trey. At night, alone, he watched himself and his son.

He had talked big over the years about accepting defeat, but losing half your vision was not the same as losing half your family. It had been his responsibility to protect his wife, his children, and his grandchildren, and at this he had failed. When it came down to it, he had been a great boxer but only a mediocre hero. Even on the old, rickety stages, in the tight, sweaty costumes, he had been less than impressive. He had long imagined himself a brave and peaceful man, but he had been most gifted at violence, which had arisen from a fear of defeat. It was Junior—a man who had fled his family when he was needed most—who had played the better, truer hero.

The film clicked free of the reel and was dragged steadily and slowly through the projector. On the wall, Oswald's son—a coward, a hero, the Lone Ranger—disappeared in a flash, just as he vanished every night.

8

IN THE HEART OF A CROWD WAITING FOR A PARADE ALONG BURLINGTON Avenue, Paddy sat perturbed in a lawn chair. After months of hype, the bicentennial was finally upon La Grange, with fire hydrants painted up as Uncle Sam, men dressed as founding fathers, and American flags hanging from practically every shop window and bicycle handlebar. Even Paddy had joined in the festivities by arranging his red, white, and blue cans of motor oil into the pattern of Old Glory. In the distance, a marching band turned a corner and approached with the rapid clacking of drumsticks on metal. The drums came in, and then the brass. The crowd cheered. Paddy cringed. He found no pleasure in twirled batons, Shriners, and fresh piles of steaming horseshit. Worst of all were the street closings, which ensured that no car could drive up to Union Auto until two in the afternoon.

A policeman ambled toward Paddy and said, "Looks like you've got the best seat in the house."

"Wouldn't miss this for all the money in the world," Paddy said, unable to force a smile. He knew he should know the name of the cop, a regular customer, but the wire between the world and his memory no longer charged the way it once had.

"Sorry about you losing business today," the policeman said. "I know it's rough."

Rough, Paddy thought; nobody knew the word as well as he did. Who could even pretend to know it that well?

As the musicians approached, the policeman jogged into the middle of the street and eagerly waved them his way. At the head of the band, a girl strutted in knee-high boots, thrusting her baton in the air. She was dressed like a showgirl or a hooker, Paddy thought—all sequined and leggy and unabashed.

On previous Independence Days, Paddy had opened the station as soon as the parade had ended, and then he'd stayed open late in hopes of recouping his losses. This year he refused to fight. He had given Willie the day off and put up a sign saying, UNION AUTO WILL BE CLOSED JULY 4TH IN HONOR OF THE BICENTENNIAL AND ALL OUR BRAVE HEROES. People would come looking for gas, and they'd be out of luck, but they would read the sign and know what an honorable man he was.

The Lyons Township High School marching band passed in their blue and yellow uniforms, doing their best to destroy "You're a Grand Old Flag." Village officials came next, followed by a Cub Scout troop, Little Leaguers, Brownies, a fire engine, and clowns tossing lollipops and Bazooka bubble-gum to the crowd. Next was a Mercury Cougar chauffeuring the bicentennial queen, who wasn't much to look at, in Paddy's opinion. A group of children dawdled by in colonial garb, and creeping behind them was a Cadillac convertible with a gray-haired man waving to the crowd from the backseat. The Caddy passed slowly. Draped on its side was a banner:

CHAMPION CADILLAC WELCOMES A TRUE CHAMPION
—OSWALD "HARD KNOCKS" KNOLL—
BOXING LEGEND! LA GRANGE NATIVE! UNDEFEATED!
HARD KNOCKS SEZ: "CHAMPION KNOCKS OUT ALL COMPETITORS' PRICES!"

The car inched past Paddy. Oswald Knoll waved listlessly to his left and his right. Paddy's skin tingled; a throbbing filled his head. He was tired of being kicked in the nuts by the world. Hurriedly he stood and folded up his chair. As he shoved through the crowd, he thought it would be nice if someone knocked Oswald Knoll down a notch or two, but Paddy knew the world didn't operate that way. The blessed kept getting blessed. The cursed never caught a break.

Inside his locked garage with his Packard, Paddy felt safe. The car made sense to him in a way nothing else did. When he turned it on, it turned on. When he turned it off, it turned off. And on the rare occasions when it broke, all he had to do was fix it. He had brought it back from the dead, after all, so who could possibly know it better?

Paddy sat in the driver's seat. He wanted nothing more than to take the Packard out on a highway or a country road, feeling regal as common cars passed him slowly or honked in appreciation. Outside, another band marched by, blasting "God Bless America." Paddy turned the key, and the car roared to life. It breathed, not as well as it must have when it first came off the assembly line, but better than any other vehicle its age. He closed the car door but still heard the marching band. Then he rolled up the window and heard nothing but the hum of the Packard.

He remembered those nights in Rabbit's garage, alone with a fleet of Packards, and how at home he had felt there. Now Rabbit was dead, and who could say what had happened to his Packards? They had probably been scrapped during the war, or shipped off to a garbage dump, where they lay rusting under other rusting cars. It was the same with everything, Paddy thought. The best parts of life vanished before the worst. The body surrendered its strength before its weakness.

Paddy closed his eyes. He felt exhausted. He felt weak. He would rest here for another minute, listening to the Packard. Then he would go inside and fix some lunch. He would forget about Oswald Knoll, Elizabeth, Eddie, and Michael, and all the times he'd been wronged.

His head nodded forward. Startled, he opened his eyes.

"I'm here," he said. "I'm awake."

The Packard breathed on, steadily, effortlessly. Paddy's grip on the steering wheel loosened. The speedometer held steady at zero. A little quiet once in a while wasn't so bad, he thought. He'd earned it. He deserved it. Just a quick break, and then back to work. To work, to work—always more work. He closed his eyes, and for a fleeting moment felt at peace.

9.

"IT'S HARD TO HOLD A SERVICE ON A WEEKDAY EVENING," SAID THE proprietor of the funeral parlor, glancing at his watch. "Especially during a holiday week, with the weather so hot."

The ceremony was to start in a few minutes. With the exception of Michael and Aunt Mae, nobody was there.

"If people wanted to be here, they would be here." Aunt Mae scrutinized the funeral parlor's chapel with its plastic crucifix and plywood podium. She scrunched her face, clearly finding the room lacking in sanctity. "But who wants to come to the funeral of a criminal?"

Michael and his aunt sat in the chapel with the urn, rows of unoccupied chairs, and a priest he had found by calling local churches and getting the best deal he could.

"Of course he wanted to be cremated," Aunt Mae whispered. "He always had to do things his way—even if they were wrong, which they usually were."

The priest quickly read a few passages from the Bible and spoke about the need to keep the deceased in one's heart and mind. Aunt Mae cried softly, but Michael felt nothing but vague wonderment that his father had been so reduced as to fit inside an urn.

When the ceremony was over, Michael paid the priest fifty dollars, and the priest handed over the urn as if he had been holding it for ransom. Michael didn't mention that the police suspected suicide.

"Do you know that when I was a girl, I used to look up to your father?"

Aunt Mae said as they walked into the humid afternoon.

Michael walked along beside her, his father's remains under his arm.

"When he and your mother were first seeing each other, he used to bring me candies, which was nice, although lots of people bring gifts to children, especially when they want to make a good impression with an older sibling. But he didn't do it to make himself look good. He never made a big deal out of it or gave me the candy in front of anyone, and he never seemed upset that I never thanked him. He just brought it to me, and I appreciated it, even though I never showed it."

"I never knew that."

She cleared her throat. "Well, don't go crying about it," she said. "As far as I can tell, it's the only good thing he ever did in life."

The next day Michael walked along La Grange Road past a hobby shop, hardware store, and ice-cream parlor, glancing at the directions he had scribbled on the corner of a newspaper. He turned right into a narrow alley, the walls of which were covered with psychedelic murals. The alley opened into another, wider alley, this one crowded with garbage cans and weeds. Michael ascended the first set of stairs he encountered, which switchbacked up the rear of Beautiful Day Records.

At the top of the stairs, Michael knocked on a metal door bearing a copper plate that read: CARL MORETTI, ATTORNEY AT LAW. A few seconds later a man opened the door briskly and said, "Michael Halligan," as though he were answering a trivia question.

"Carl Moretti?"

The man thrust his hand forward and said, "Bingo." As he vigorously shook Michael's hand, he said, "It's a shame about your old man—an absolutely God-awful fucking shame." Moretti was about fifty, the same age as Michael, with a thick black mustache and an aroma of Old Spice. His shiny lime-green tie, which was nearly as wide as it was long, resembled a napkin tucked into his collar.

Michael sat in a folding chair in front of a wooden desk, which was bare except for a blotter and a pen. The walls were decorated with the kind of vacation posters one might find in a travel agent's office, with waterfalls, white-sand beaches, and happy Hawaiian girls with hibiscus flowers in their hair. Standing beside Michael, Moretti slipped a business card from his breast pocket. With a magician's flourish, he held it out to Michael between his index and middle fingers.

"If you ever need legal assistance, keep me in mind," he said. "Promise?"

Michael took the card and said, "All right."

Moretti squeezed his shoulder. "Promise?" he said, more seriously than before.

Michael looked up at Moretti, whose stare was as strong as his grip. "I promise," he said.

Moretti smiled and gave Michael's shoulder a good whack. He walked past his desk and sat in his brown leather chair.

"Your father was a great man, Michael, a truly great man," he said. "And I don't say this idly. I say this with the utmost sincerity I can muster. Truthfully. If you want bullshit, go to a rodeo. If you want straight shooting, come to Carl Moretti." He put his hands behind his head, revealing yellow armpit stains. He rocked back and forth in his chair, which squeaked in time to his movements. "I'm a car nut. You know how some people are health nuts? Not me. I'm a car nut. You know any car nuts, Michael?"

"Not really."

"Well, I want you to imagine the biggest car nut you can, and then multiply him by twenty. That's how much of a car nut I am. You get what I'm saying?"

Michael nodded.

"Your father was the best fucking mechanic I've ever met. Bar none, Michael. Bar none. He had a black guy who worked for him who, between you and me, was a little better with engines, but pound for pound, your old man was the best. If he was a doctor and I needed someone to do brain surgery on me, I'd get on the horn to him as fast as I could. He was the Frank Sinatra of engine repair, Michael. The Babe Ruth of transmissions. That's how great he was. You catch my drift?"

"Sure."

"I'd been going to him for years, when one day he asks me to write up a will for him. Will I write up a will for him? Won't I!"

Moretti leaned forward with great velocity, like the sprung arm of a mousetrap. His forearms thudded the blotter.

"Look, Michael, we're both busy men here, so I'm not gonna waste your time reminiscing over good times, no matter how good they were." Moretti opened his desk drawer and pulled out a manila folder, which he tossed onto his desk. "Bottom line is, all of it's yours. Congratulations."

"All of it?"

"The station, the cars, the bank accounts. Everything. Well, he gave his tools to the black guy. But otherwise, my friend, it all goes to you. Your father was looking out for you, Michael. He was upholding a father's duties to his family until the bitter end, which for him, sadly, was death. All we've got to do is sign some forms; then I give you the keys and account numbers, we settle up what I'm owed, and I file a few papers. Zip, zip, it'll be over before you know it."

"Okay," Michael said, feeling like a bug on its back, legs flailing.

"But one thing," Moretti said, removing a white business envelope from the folder. "Your father left you a letter and asked that I read it to you." Moretti waved the envelope at Michael. "Okay by you?"

Michael nodded. His pulse quickened. Moretti ripped open the envelope and unfolded a piece of paper with writing on both sides.

"Hello Michael. Long time no talk to," Moretti read. "Well, what can you do? What's done is done. I'm not going to apologize, and I don't want you to apologize, because there's no room for apologies in life. But what I will say is that I started out with nothing and made something of it, and now all of it belongs to you. How about that, huh? Isn't that something?

"I don't ask that you do anything with it. Sell it, keep it going, burn it down. It's yours now and I'm dead, so what do I care? But I am your father, and if you owe me anything, it's listening.

"I know things about you that you probably didn't know I did. I know about Eddie, and I know you know about him, even though I don't know how you do. I know what you did to him, and I appreciate you for defending the family honor and sticking up for your old man. Quite frankly, I didn't think you had that sort of thing in you, but I'm not above admitting that I might have been wrong about something here and there.

"I also know about your son and your wife, and what can I say about that? Life is rotten at the core—but you probably figured that out a while ago." Moretti flipped over the piece of paper, cleared his throat, and continued: "When it comes down to it, I'm proud of all I've done, even if I shouldn't be, and you should feel that way about yourself, too. There's no use in worrying about what you should or shouldn't have done. And there's no use in not getting what you want from life if you can.

"Sincerely, Patrick Halligan, Owner, Union Auto Repair and Gas."

Moretti folded up the letter and handed it to Michael.

"No way he offed himself," Moretti said. "Not a chance. I don't give a shit what the evidence says. Your old man was one scrappy son of a bitch if there ever was one. He wouldn't have gone out like that."

Michael opened the letter and read through it, wondering how his father had known about his life and developed the misconception that he had defended the family honor. As he skimmed and signed various documents, he grew surprised at how little his father had saved during his lifetime, and that he'd bought the station only a few years ago.

"Yeah, I'm a real car nut," Moretti said. He rocked quickly in his chair. "It's my passion, I guess you'd say."

Michael signed a piece of paper and slid it to Moretti. "Is that so?"

"That is *absolutely* so." Moretti pulled another envelope from the folder, set it on the desk, and tapped it with his finger. "Now, I want to show you something here, Michael."

In the envelope were a check from Moretti to Michael for five thousand dollars and a piece of paper on which Moretti had figured out his fees for service, as well as the estimated value of the old Packard Michael's father had owned, plus the costs of maintaining and insuring such an expensive car, plus the realistic price a person could expect to fetch for it—not to mention the intangible fact that Paddy had passed away in the vehicle in question.

"What you're saying is, you want the car," Michael said.

"A win-win proposition, if you ask me." Moretti grinned. "Now, don't get me wrong. I'm not being callous here. I miss the old man. We all do. What the hell—I'll say it: I loved the guy—not in a funny way, mind you, but in a respectful sort of way, much as you probably did, if you really think about it. I love the Packard, too, but it's just a thing, and what's a thing compared to a person? Nothing, that's what. Not a damn thing." He leaned back. "But still, when someone passes on to the great beyond, what's left of us but things? That's all we've got left—and that sure as shit is something, isn't it?"

Michael examined the numbers, which seemed to add up for the most part, although Moretti was surely lowballing the car's value and overestimating its upkeep. Moretti clicked the end of his pen. Michael had no need for the car, but he took his time, pleased by Moretti's anxiety, an anxiety of yearning that he had so often felt himself. It was always a relief to see it in others.

After signing the Packard over to Moretti, Michael walked half a mile to Union Auto with a feeling of weightlessness, as though everything in the world—including him—were hovering in its usual place, ready to rise and float into disarray at any moment. He felt invisible to those around him, just as they seemed unreal to him.

He made his way across the gravel parking lot, past the dented gas pumps, and to the garage door, which he unlocked and lifted, nearly expecting to see his father standing there with a wrench in his hand. A familiar odor—gasoline and oil mixed with his father's sweaty exertion—greeted Michael, and he felt melancholic, wishing he could both travel back in time and completely forget his past. The Packard was gone; Moretti, being forward-thinking, had parked it at his house for safekeeping. The old counter and chairs were still there, as were racks of tools and cans of oil, which had a haphazard look to them, as if their owner had merely stepped out for a moment and would soon return—which, Michael suddenly realized, was happening at this moment. He was the owner. This was his return.

The living room and kitchen had changed little. Most of the furniture and appliances had been there in 1941. Michael looked at the few photographs his father owned—several of which he hadn't seen in thirty-five years but that he recognized instantly. They were all of his father: in front of Union Auto, inside Union Auto, as a young boxer, as a boy, as an infant in a white gown. On the wall, in a frame, as it had been decades ago, was a snippet of cloth, brown with John Dillinger's blood. Michael's old bedroom, too, had hardly changed. The surfaces had been dusted and his Big Little Books had been removed, but otherwise the room was as he'd left it. His old clothes still hung in the closet and filled the dresser drawers.

Michael sat on the bed and then lay down, and as he wondered what he should do with this old place, he drifted across the thin surface of dreaming. To his right, he heard weeds rustle and a dog bark in the alley; to his left were the sounds of the street. He sensed someone was in the house, searching for something, and so he rose half-asleep and went looking for who was there. He made his way to the living room but found no one.

A few minutes later, he carefully descended the unstable wooden staircase to the cellar. He walked halfway across the dirt floor, pulled the long overhead chain, and watched a mouse scurry and then disappear under the boxes, crates, and suitcases shoved against the far wall. Michael approached a stack of boxes, opened the top one, and meticulously removed tax returns, receipts from Union Auto, invoices, and finally his father's old motivational booklets, which were probably worth a few bucks altogether. After putting back the items, Michael lowered the box to the ground. The next box, as far as he could tell after quick perusal, contained his father's canceled checks and bank statements. Michael picked it up and set it on top of the first box.

Michael dragged over an old wooden chair and sat at the third box as if sitting down to a meal. He brushed off the box, which was a little warped and sagging, twice as big as the previous two, but smaller than the footlocker underneath it. He lifted the four cardboard flaps, peered inside the box, and was startled to see his old Big Little Books, their pages brittle and yellow, their covers bent and crushed. He pulled out the books one by one and flipped through the pages, trying to catch the memories darting in his mind. There was the time Uncle Red had stopped by with Martha and she'd removed Michael's splinter; there had been a Big Little involved, but as hard as Michael concentrated on his old books and tried to remember, he couldn't recall which one it had been. There was the morning a man had come by with a gun and held up his father; the evening his father and he had sat silently in the basement, waiting for a tornado that had ended up missing La Grange; those nights at the White Crow; those days of doctoring his father's numbers. Recollections arose indistinct and blurred into one other, as did people from back then: the man down the street who ran the drugstore, the beat cops who came by for their kickbacks, all those numbers runners. What was the name of the black one? Miller? Nelson? Mason? *Mason*. That was it. But a name wasn't a face; it wasn't a memory of the man, or the man himself.

Michael tossed aside the Big Littles that were ruined beyond hope. He set the others gently on the ground. When he had a dozen good books, he loaded them into his arms and carried them upstairs. He set them on the kitchen table and returned to the basement, where he kept digging through the box. Some of the pages had been eaten away by mice or bugs; some had nearly disintegrated. They all emitted a musty odor. He knew these titles and covers by heart—he owned better copies of each book—but seeing them in this box and knowing they had been his as a boy made them seem new again. He fished out the back half of *Hal Hardy in the Lost Land of the Giants*, then quickly found the front half. He held the halves together until they made a whole, and then he set the broken book aside. They were all here. Flash Gordon. Popeye. Barney Baxter. He found *Gang Busters Step In* and pulled it from the box, but about a quarter of its pages were missing, mingled with hundreds of other loose sheets. Rummaging again, he took hold of a piece of paper larger and thicker than the rest. He laughed. It was his report card from fifth grade: all A's, except for a B in History. He reached in and found other report cards, academic awards, a certificate commemorating his confirmation. He dug all the way to the bottom, where he found a photo of himself in eighth grade, holding a diploma and shaking the hand of a priest he did not recognize. He pulled out pictures of his grade school classes and snapshots of himself as a boy with his father, with Aunt Mae, with Uncle Red—but none of himself with his mother.

Michael looked around the basement. In the light of the bare bulb, dust swirled. He approached the loose stones in the wall, and as he slid them from their places, he found them lighter than he remembered. He reached into the dark hiding space, all the way to the far wall, his fingers encountering cobwebs and dead bugs and then a few pieces of paper. He picked one up. A photograph—he was sure of it. He pulled it out and wiped off the dust. It was a picture of a woman standing on the stoop of an apartment building. Her face had been scratched out by something—maybe a coin, maybe a pocketknife. Michael stood under the light and looked carefully at the picture. He had never seen it before, and though he assumed it was of his mother, he wasn't certain. He set the photo on the chair and reached again into the darkness. He pulled out a small stack of pictures, ten in all, and hurried upstairs to the kitchen table.

The photographs were of his mother, and in each one her face had been obliterated—scratched out, inked out, or cut away until there was nothing left but a ragged, crude hole. Michael felt ill. His hands shook holding the desecrated images. Here he was now, in a snapshot as a boy, standing with his parents at the World's Fair in front of a sign that read: YESTERDAY—TODAY—TOMORROW. He and his father were intact, just as they had been that day: Michael squinting; his father with his hands in his pockets and his hat so low, its brim covered much of his face. Standing between them, his mother wore a dark print dress and held a bonnet in her left hand. With her other hand, she shielded the sun from a face that had been cut away. The three of them stood in a row, not touching each other, the shadow of the anonymous photographer spread out before them. Michael set the pictures on top of his Big Little Books, stood, and said, "Well." He waited for more words to come forth from him, to soothe or educate or save him, to crush or kill him, but none did.

10.

᪥As they had almost every Sunday since reuniting two years earlier, Michael and Aunt Mae attended Mass, ate brunch at the International House of Pancakes, and then drove around the Chicago area, investigating estate sales, church bazaars, and flea markets. Michael disliked Mass, which did little but remind him of his failings, and he often sensed his aunt was growing tired of the sales, but neither of them complained too much. To please her, Michael had the heat in his Chevy Nova on high and the vents aimed her way. He removed his gloves and wool cap, but he was still burning up in his overcoat. Aunt Mae was drunk again, and, as always, she tried to hide the scent of alcohol with an excess of perfume. As they drove through Brookfield, she offered up tepid gripes about the chilly weather, the traffic, and the inappropriate attire of various churchgoers, though mostly she sat silently and stared out the side window. Michael was quiet, too, keeping his thoughts to himself, just as he kept his life as hidden as possible from her. He never invited her to his home, never mentioned her intoxication, and never suggested she see the collectibles store he was building to replace Union Auto.

"Here we are," he said as he parked in front of a bungalow. "You coming with me?"

"I'll stay here as long as you keep the car running. I'd prefer not to freeze to death, if it's all the same to you."

The home belonged to a family of circus performers, a fact the classified ad had emphasized, leading Michael to expect something extraordinary

from the estate sale. But as he moved from room to room, he grew disappointed by the family's ordinariness. They owned the same things as
everyone else: the same dishes, the same silverware, the same Mitch Miller
albums, the same James Michener books, the same bedspreads and lamps
and towels and paperweights and ashtrays. Michael was about to give up
on finding anything special when he came across a box of snapshots, which
were being sold for a penny apiece. Mixed in with images of birthday parties
and baptisms were a man with his head in a lion's mouth, a woman in
midflight from one trapeze to another, a gathering of clowns. A man walked
a tightrope in one photo and played golf in another. The contortionist, when
not twisting himself into a pretzel, stood smiling in front of Mount
Rushmore. The ringmaster sunned himself on a beach. As he sometimes
found himself doing at sales, Michael searched for his mother in the
snapshots, hoping she might show up as a passerby in someone else's life.

Photographs in hand, Michael returned to the car. The day had the cold,
damp feel of a washcloth resting on the edge of a tub, yet Michael wished
he could stay outside longer. Aunt Mae sat expressionless in the passenger
seat, staring out the window.

"Did you find anything?" she asked when he opened the door.

"Just these." He handed her the pictures.

A few months earlier, after a year and a half of attending sales with
Michael, Aunt Mae had finally made her first purchase: four half-empty
perfume bottles and a handful of snapshots. Two Sundays later, she had
bought more of the same. Since then, she had acquired dozens of fragrances
and hundreds of photographs, and on a few occasions Michael had bought
some for her, too.

They headed north on Mannheim, passing hot dog stands, taverns, and
used-car lots. Michael eyed a run-down warehouse and imagined its dark
interior filled with a Big Little collection far surpassing what Oswald Knoll
had assembled. Michael remained vigilant and hopeful about the possibility
that he would someday come across an abandoned store, godforsaken shack,
attic, warehouse, or basement containing forgotten treasure. At estate sales
and collectors' conventions, he had heard stories of men who had nearly

fallen to their knees in prayer upon finding lost recordings of Bix Beiderbecke in the back of a dead man's closet, letters from Abraham Lincoln in a bank vault, Lou Gehrig's uniform beneath attic floorboards.

"Why do you collect snapshots?" Michael asked Aunt Mae.

"I guess I've always been curious about what kind of person sells pictures of his family," she said. "Decent people pass on what they have to their children. They don't just sell private things as though they mean nothing."

"What kind of person collects them?"

"I don't collect them. I like to look at them, that's all—look at them and imagine who these people are. That's not a crime, is it? Last I heard, it's not a crime to wonder what other people's lives are like."

"I didn't say it was."

The air in the car dried Michael's eyes, cracked his lips, and left him feeling weary. He was often tired lately, especially after a long day transforming his father's old shop. Sometimes he didn't have the energy to check on his books; sometimes he couldn't be bothered with the girls on Ogden Avenue.

"Is it wrong to imagine that one person is a murderer and another is a saint?" Aunt Mae waved a photograph at him. "Just because I've had a dull life, does that mean I'm not allowed to do that?"

"Of course not."

"Because if anything, I'm entitled to my dreams more than most people."

Michael knew all about dull lives and dreams, and he knew about frustration. More and more people were collecting Big Little Books, and one of them in California had formed a group of fellow enthusiasts and now sent out a regular newsletter. Michael rarely associated with these other collectors, but he belonged to their group and read their newsletter enough to know they each owned less than he did, though not by much. The members' chumminess and mutual encouragement made him feel excluded, and whenever he read about a conversation one of them had had years ago with Oswald, he felt wounded. He opened each new issue in fear of discovering that one of them had found *Trouble in the City of Dreams*.

Michael drove west and merged onto the Tri-State Tollway, Aunt Mae asleep beside him. Cars crept and changed lanes with ample warning and unnecessary caution; their prudence irked him, made him drive aggressively. He had planned to visit an estate sale off the Gurnee exit and then take Aunt Mae home, but his thoughts were on Racine, which he had visited half a dozen times since making the deal with Junior three years ago. On each visit, he had seen Sharon and Ann, Junior's wife and daughter, but he had done nothing but sit in his parked car and watch them. Michael saw the sign indicating that the Gurnee exit was a mile ahead. Then he saw the exit. Then he passed it by.

With Aunt Mae still asleep beside him, Michael drove through Junior's old neighborhood and turned onto Junior's old street. In front of Junior's old house was a moving company's truck. Michael parked his car across the street. Leaving the engine running and the heat on, he exited the car and hurried to the truck, feeling bewildered and anxious. Two burly men carried a sofa out of the house, loaded it into the truck, which held just a few boxes and a recliner, and then lumbered back to the house. Inside the open garage, Junior's daughter jumped rope.

"What's going on?" Michael asked as he approached her. "Are you moving?"

The girl kept jumping rope. She wore a heavy green sweater and jeans. Her hair was in pigtails.

Michael realized he had been rash and foolish to approach her, so, as calmly as he could, he asked, "Is your family moving, Ann?"

"How did you know my name?" she asked. "I didn't tell you what it was."

"I met you once before, remember? I was a friend of your dad."

"Do you know where he is?"

"I'm afraid I don't."

Michael told himself to stay calm, be patient. "Is your family moving?" he asked again.

"Trey's not moving because he's still in the hospital. And my dad is still away."

"But you and your mom are moving?"

"Yeah."

The jump rope slapped the cement at a slow, steady pace.

"What's your name?" she asked.

Michael started to say his name but then recalled that three years ago Junior had introduced him as a coworker by the name of Frank, or maybe Fred. Ann stared at him with eyes that seemed neither too suspicious nor too trusting, but insistent on getting an answer.

"My name's Fred," Michael said. The moment the name left his lips, he knew he had guessed wrong.

The door leading from the garage to the house opened. Sharon appeared in the doorway. She crossed her arms, glared at Michael, and asked, "What do you want?"

"His name's Fred," Ann said. "He's a friend of Daddy."

"Why are you here?" Sharon kept her eyes on him. "Why are you talking to my daughter?"

"I was asking her if you were moving." Michael turned and pointed to the truck, as though its existence proved his sincerity. "I worked with your husband—before he left. He was a good man."

"Do good men leave their families? Do they run off with their son in a coma?"

"I mean, he was good to work with. He helped me move into my apartment."

Sharon unfolded her arms and placed her hands on her hips. Unable to face her stare, Michael turned toward the movers, who trudged across the front yard with a desk between them.

"The day my husband left, your name was Frank, not Fred."

"My name's Fred," he said. "You must have remembered it wrong."

"I asked Junior's coworkers about you, hoping you might know where he was. His note was so vague, and I thought if I could just get ahold of him, he'd come back. As far as I knew, you were the last one to see him. So I asked and asked, but nobody knew who you were. Would you mind telling me why that is?"

Michael's face flushed, and no adequate lie came to him.

Sharon turned toward her daughter and said, "Ann, go inside."

The girl continued to jump rope. "I don't want to."

"I'm not in the mood, Ann. Go inside now."

Ann sighed dramatically and stopped playing. She dragged the jump rope along the ground as she sulked past her mother and into the house. Sharon approached Michael.

"Who are you?"

"I already told you. I'm Fred. I worked with your husband." Michael tried his best to seem confident and calm, but neither trait came naturally to him.

"Is it about gambling? Is it about drugs?" She stopped a few feet in front of him. "Because if you're looking for drugs, you've come to the wrong place. And if my husband owes you money, there's nothing I can do about it. I have no idea where he is. As far as I'm concerned, he doesn't exist anymore."

"It's not about any of that. It's about the Big Little Books. I want to buy them."

The door from the garage to the house opened again, and Oswald Knoll appeared. Michael could tell from his arms and shoulders that he was still a powerful man.

"What's going on, Sharon?" Oswald asked.

"This man claims to be a friend of Junior, but he's not sure if his name is Fred or Frank."

"We weren't really friends," Michael said, trying to avoid looking at Oswald, hoping the old man didn't recognize him fifteen years after their meeting. "I worked with him for a couple of days. He helped me move, and then I never saw him again."

"He wants to buy the Big Little Books—or what's left of them."

Oswald came closer and stood beside Sharon. "Who told you about them?" he asked.

Feeling chastened, Michael tried to think of a way to explain who he truly was and what he wanted, to come clean and ask forgiveness from Oswald Knoll. He opened his mouth to speak, but stopped when he heard a commotion behind him. Aunt Mae staggered up the driveway.

"What's going on, Michael?" she called out. "Where are we?"

"*Michael?*" Sharon said.

Michael approached his aunt and grabbed her by the arm. He shushed her, but she kept asking where she was and what was happening. She reeked of perfume.

"Excuse me, ma'am," Sharon said as she pointed at Michael, "could you please tell me who this is?"

Aunt Mae glanced at the woman, then at Michael. "Is this a trick?" she asked. She reached her hand to Michael, who took it in his. She faced him with a helpless expression and shook like a feverish child. "Michael, what's happening? Things aren't right. They're not real."

He told her that everything was fine, but she sobbed and leaned into him. When her shaking finally subsided and her breathing was steady and deep, he told her to tell Sharon who he really was.

"His name is Michael Halligan," Aunt Mae said defiantly. "Who on earth are you?"

"I thought you looked familiar," Oswald said. "I just couldn't place you."

Sharon turned to her father-in-law. "You know him?"

"You could say that."

Sharon threw her hands in the air. "Then you deal with him. I have too much going on right now to waste my time playing games."

As Sharon stormed back into the house, Oswald dragged over a chair the movers had left on the lawn. Michael guided Aunt Mae to the chair. She sat, and Michael told her they would soon be on the road.

"Will your mother be all right?" Oswald asked a moment later.

"She's not my mother," Michael said.

The movers carried boxes up the ramp leading to the back of the truck. The metal rattled under their feet.

Oswald sighed. "So, you had dealings with my son?"

"He called me here three years ago. He sent me a letter, and I came."

"Did he sell you part of the collection?"

"He told me he'd sold part of it to someone else," Michael said. "Another collector you used to correspond with." He sensed from the silence and Oswald's watchful eye that the great man expected him to say more. "He wanted me to buy the rest of it, and he showed it to me, but he asked for more than I could afford," Michael lied. "While we were talking, your daughter-in-law and granddaughter came home. Junior made up a story about my being a guy who worked with him, and I went along with it; I didn't know what else to do. When they had gone, he and I haggled a bit, but he wouldn't budge on the price. I left empty-handed, and that was the last I saw of him." Michael felt surprised, but not displeased, by his ability to lie to Oswald. It gave him courage and drained away some of the humiliation and nervousness he felt. "I've come up here a few times, wanting to ask about buying the rest of the collection, but I never knew how to approach your daughter-in-law. I figured she'd be suspicious."

"You figured right."

Oswald smiled. The movers clattered back down the ramp.

"Did my son say anything else about who he sold the other items to?"

"No," Michael said. "Just what I told you."

"Because I'd like to talk to that person."

"So would I."

"I'd like to tell him how much the collection means to me and my family. I'd appeal to his better nature and ask him, as a favor to me, to return it. I'd offer appropriate compensation, of course: whatever he paid, plus a certain percentage."

"Well, I don't know who has it."

"I'd tell him that what's left of the collection is being held for my little granddaughter. Either she'll come to cherish it, as I hope she will, or she'll sell it. It'll be up to her when she turns eighteen."

Michael gazed down the street, with its sturdy trees and simple homes. He wished he had grown up here and lived here now.

"And I assume Junior didn't mention anything about where he was headed."

"No, he didn't say anything about that."

Oswald sighed and said, "I'm sorry about my son, Michael. I'm sorry he caused all this trouble. I wish there was something I could do."

Michael faced Oswald. "You could show me what's left of the collection."

"I don't think so, Michael. Things are chaotic in there, and we still have lots of work to do."

"I've never forgotten that time you showed me everything," Michael said, feeling something close to honesty inside him. "It was like I was seeing something sacred." He shook his head. "I know it sounds ridiculous, but it's true. Do you know what I'm talking about?"

The movers trudged back with another load. The clouds held back the sun. Michael felt on the edge of tears.

"I know what you're talking about," Oswald said. "If anyone does, it's me."

Three footlockers sat side by side in the back corner of the living room. The rest of the room was cluttered with cardboard boxes and furniture, including a love seat where Aunt Mae sat waiting. Oswald removed keys from his pocket and unlocked each footlocker. He and Michael sat on adjacent boxes.

"I'd tell you to be careful," Oswald said, "but if anyone knows how to handle this stuff, it's you."

The objects were as Michael remembered: dummy books, sketches, contracts, and artwork similar to what Junior had sold to him. They were so well preserved that they had hardly yellowed, and their scent was only vaguely musty.

"This is all that's left," said Oswald. "It's such a shame."

Michael handled the artifacts delicately, setting them on the floor when he was done with them, retrieving more, inspecting them, trying to memorize their features.

"How is your collection?" Oswald asked.

"Just fine."

"Complete?"

"Almost."

"I always admired your dedication. I always knew you'd stick with it."

Hunched forward, Michael moved from the first footlocker to the second. He wished he had a notebook so he could write down all he saw; then later he could look at his notes and remember.

"My son never quite knew how to take on a responsibility and see it through," Oswald said. "It's an awful thing for a father to say, but it's a fact. I don't think he ever saw it as a privilege to have people depend on him."

Michael stopped examining the objects, but he could not bring himself to look at Oswald. He glanced at Aunt Mae, who was starting to nod off, and then at the movers, who came in for more boxes, not exactly in a hurry.

"My grandson has been in a coma for nearly four years." Oswald did not speak for half a minute. Michael stared at the footlocker, knowing he shouldn't look through it right now. "I think Junior just couldn't take it anymore."

"I'm sorry," Michael said. "I don't know what to say."

"You don't have to say anything."

Michael waited for some indication that he could return to the collection, but he didn't know what that would be. Out of the corner of his eye, he saw Oswald as hunched over as he was, both of them like men in confessional booths.

"Still, I have my daughters and other grandkids, and Sharon calls me Dad despite what my son did to her, which means more to me than anything."

Michael turned his head slightly. Oswald's head was bowed, his elbows on his knees, his veined hands hanging down. When Oswald sighed and sat upright, Michael sat up, too.

"How is your family, Michael? You're married, right?"

"I *was* married," Michael said, thinking everything would have been fine if Oswald and he had been father and son. "It didn't work out."

"Any children?"

"No," Michael said. "We never had any children."

They sat side by side without a word, looking at artifacts that promised so much. *Mysteries! Thrills! Adventures!* Michael felt protected by the silence. *Fun! Comedy! Laughs!* He imagined the two of them sitting like this for hours.

"Oh well, I should help Sharon with the packing." Oswald stood. "You just let me know when you're done, and make sure to give a holler if you need anything."

After watching Oswald pass through the archway leading to the dining room, Michael returned to the second footlocker. As he slowly investigated its contents, his thoughts jumped from Oswald's grandson to his own son, to his mother, to his father, and to Sara, but then he focused again on the objects before him and let them sweep his memories aside. He moved on to the third footlocker and, about halfway through it, saw *Trouble in the City of Dreams*. He caught his breath. The copy was in mint condition. On the cover a rocket ship flew in the air, passing from a smoke-choked city into one that was shiny, clear, and clean. Michael gingerly picked up the book, which had a soft cover and was thinner than most Big Littles. He glanced around the room. Nobody was there except Aunt Mae in the love seat. Quietly, quickly, Michael slipped the book into his overcoat pocket, put on the coat, returned the other objects to their rightful places, and closed all three footlockers.

It took several seconds to wake Aunt Mae, but eventually she stood. Michael led her toward the front door.

"Are you leaving already?" Oswald called out. He entered the living room and approached Michael.

"I need to get my aunt home. She isn't well."

"I'll be the judge of my own health," Aunt Mae protested.

Oswald put his arm around Michael's shoulder and accompanied him to the front door. Aunt Mae kept pace at Michael's other side.

"Although the circumstances weren't the best, I'm glad you came by," said Oswald. "It was nice to see you again."

"I appreciate all you've done for me," Michael said, feeling forgiven by Oswald's arm around him. "I've always respected you."

Fifteen minutes later, in the car, on the tollway, Aunt Mae said, "I didn't like those people. They were loud and rude, bossing me around like that, keeping us there so long. That man didn't even shake my hand when we left, like I was nobody to him."

Michael stared ahead. Oswald undoubtedly would discover the book missing, and the crack in his heart would stretch out a little further.

"I hope they at least gave you what you came for," Aunt Mae said. "Did they give you what you wanted, Michael?"

The sun was slipping down. In Michael's coat pocket, *Trouble in the City of Dreams* sat hidden and alone.

"They didn't give me anything," he said.

"That's not right," Aunt Mae said. "You and I deserve so much."

PRESERVATION
2003–2004

1

THE CLOCK STARTED BEEPING AT SIX IN THE MORNING. MICHAEL REACHED over, turned off the alarm, and lay back in bed with his eyes closed. The radiator hissed out its heat, but its labor was no match for the wind, which sliced through the gaps between the window and its frame. Winter, though in its final days, seemed determined to kill whatever it could before passing. To hold off the fright that often rushed through him upon waking, Michael imagined that during the night he had been transformed into a man other than himself: robust, young, and easy with life, with straight white teeth, a thirty-one-inch waist, and a beautiful young woman beside him, twirling his chest hair with her finger. He held on tight to this fantasy, but the aches in his joints and muscles reminded him what was real. With a sigh, he opened his eyes to a dark, blurry room. He grabbed his glasses from the bedside table, and when he put them on, the room, though still dim, became clearer. The television sat, as always, on its portable stand at the foot of the bed. Cedar bookshelves filled with his best Big Littles covered the far wall. Now crossing fully into waking, Michael began to fear that during the night someone had broken into his home or into Yesteryear, his collectibles store, and stolen his possessions. He worried that a corroded wire somewhere had sparked a fire that within minutes would consume his house and his shop. He pushed himself up from the mattress and slipped on his robe and slippers. Outside, the alley lamp shut off in anticipation of the sun.

Michael switched on the overhead light and examined his books, which were wrapped tightly in Mylar and set snug in his shelves, which he'd had custom-built twenty years earlier. These were his best thousand, most of them in mint or near-mint condition, assembled in alphabetical order. Satisfied that nothing had damaged them overnight, he opened his closet, pushed aside his clothes, and crouched before his safe. He turned the dial right, left, right, and opened the door. Inside were seven thousand dollars and the best items from Oswald's collection, including *Trouble in the City of Dreams*.

When Michael had first read the book in 1976, he had been greatly disappointed in it. The story was nothing but a long, tiresome advertisement for the Century of Progress, in which none of Whitman's best heroes, including Buck Rogers, ever appeared. Instead, the book featured several lesser characters: Dan Dunn, Ace Drummond, Tom Beatty, Jack Swift, and a Buck Rogers knockoff named Rip Nelson, whom Michael had never even heard of, let alone seen. Within the first few pages, they came together to search for a villain, nicknamed the Meddler, who wanted to shut down the fair. But then, over the next two hundred pages, the convoluted plot seemed designed not so much to convey a suspenseful story as to find excuses for the heroes to pass by the fair's attractions and extol the virtues of General Motors, Aunt Jemima, Radio Flyer, Firestone, Kraft, Quaker Oats, Boeing, Goodyear, and Wilson & Company Meat. A few pages before the end, the gang caught the Meddler, a man wearing a Vandyke beard and a tight three-piece suit, who, when federal agents dragged him away, protested that progress would destroy the world. Onlookers laughed at his naïveté, and the lesser heroes, their work done, relaxed with mugs of Cocomalt. The book was an embarrassment and an insult to every other Big Little ever produced, Michael thought, and its sole virtue was its novelty for featuring the one and only appearance of Rip Nelson.

For nearly fifteen years, Michael had possessed the only known copy of *Trouble in the City of Dreams*, although nobody, with the likely exception of Oswald Knoll, knew it. At conventions and in the pages of the Big Little Book Club's national newsletter, collectors speculated about whether the mysterious book still existed or had ever existed, what was contained in its pages, and if and when it would be found. Michael followed these debates with silent, nervous pride, and though he occasionally felt an urge to reveal what he owned, he didn't want people clamoring to see the book or pestering him with questions about when and how he had found it. He worried, too, that Oswald would come looking for it, or that the police would knock on his door and arrest him for the theft, but neither Oswald nor the police appeared. Then, in 1991, a collector who owned one hundred books at most found a copy in his late uncle's steamer trunk and was subsequently treated like Christopher Columbus. Two years later, a copy appeared in a Minnesota farmhouse, and another in the boiler room of a Cleveland grammar school. All in all, seven copies had surfaced since Michael had stolen his. Each was valued near two thousand dollars. Given its condition, his copy was worth twice that amount.

After closing the safe, Michael plodded to the kitchen, where he made sure the dials on the old Wedgewood stove were switched off, the pilot lights lit, the refrigerator closed, and the back door locked. Then he headed to the living room, half of which served as a place to sit and read or watch TV, with a coffee table, couch, recliner, and 27-inch Sylvania. The room's other half resembled library stacks, with locked file cabinets and three long rows of bookshelves filled with nearly two thousand Big Littles and the items he'd bought from Junior. Michael loved how fragile his books had become, and how their vibrant colors had faded, but as he passed his collection now, he wondered what the point of all his effort had been. As he had done countless times in recent years, he immediately brushed aside these doubts and unlocked Yesteryear's door. Upon entering the back of his store, which had once been his father's garage, he flicked on the light switch and saw that nothing had been harmed during the night.

Michael passed bookcases and file cabinets stuffed with magazines, comic books, pulp novels, postcards, albums, and eight-tracks. Two decades earlier, he had marked the shelves and cabinet drawers with masking-tape labels, but the past was forever expanding, and the bits of tape, which had grown brittle and curled at the edges, no longer matched what they had once identified, and the ever-growing stock of memorabilia now left barely enough room in the store for customers. Rising in unsteady towers from the tiled floor were cardboard boxes filled with Hardy Boys, Nancy Drews, license plates, toy soldiers, and Barbie dolls. Atop the file cabinets sat milk crates overflowing with beer bottles and buttons, and here and there were rusted coffee cans crammed with matchbooks, swizzle sticks, playbills, and pressed pennies. Movie posters that had once hung outside the great cinema houses of Chicago leaned against walls adorned with neon beer signs and pockmarked metal advertisements for Wrigley's, Modox, and Moxie. From the ceiling, yellowed newspapers wrapped in plastic hung on ornament hooks, exclaiming stories of war, championship, assassination, and scandal; they turned slightly, almost imperceptibly, each time the door opened or closed or someone passed beneath them.

Near the front of the store, Michael sat on a stool behind a glass display case that held the rarest items he had for sale, including a baseball card autographed by Babe Ruth, Civil War insignias, and the signatures of five former presidents. He leaned forward on his elbows, cash register on his left, front door in front of him. Jimmy Stewart. Marlon Brando. Rita Hayworth. Black-and-white movie stills were pinned to the wooden door like badges on a Boy Scout's chest. John Wayne. Clark Gable. Greta Garbo. They looked out at the world, as proud and predictable as demigods, softly lit and superior to the mere mortals in Aunt Mae's anonymous snapshots.

Michael had been the last person to see his aunt alive—ancient, deaf, and incoherent—just four months earlier, on Thanksgiving morning. He had spent most of those final days at the hospice, waiting for her to die and half expecting something significant in her passing. In the end she went quietly, while Michael had turned to the television to watch an enormous inflatable Underdog soar above the streets of Manhattan. When he turned back, he saw her face centered on the clean white pillowcase and wide-eyed, as though death had come as a shock after all. Since then, Michael had spent much of his time feeling terrified. He went to bed feeling terrified he would never wake again, and when he woke each morning in the same old bed and the same old body, he felt terrified of the day that awaited him.

Michael was one of the first to arrive at the 25th annual Century of Progress convention, a two-day event at the Hillside Holiday Inn, just a few miles north of La Grange on a patch of concrete bordered by a landfill, the Eisenhower Expressway, and a nondescript former movie theater that had recently been converted into the Progressive Life-Giving Word Cathedral. He found his assigned table, spread out his wares—which consisted of unspectacular souvenirs such as postcards, commemorative coins, key chains, and playing cards—and wandered past the other tables to chat with fellow dealers he'd come to know over the years. He sought the unique and unusual among what they were selling, but found nothing he hadn't seen a hundred times before. The main problem with the past was its finiteness, he believed; a person could rummage through it for something previously undiscovered, but at some point he had to acknowledge that there was nothing left to claim.

At ten o'clock the doors opened, and after the initial rush of thirty people, the crowd merely trickled in. Michael sat behind his table and watched attendees amble around the room. There were grazers, who liked to peruse and handle old things but always left empty-handed; investors, for whom all that mattered was price; and purists, who cared nothing of cost, their longing obvious in their eyes. There were old-timers wanting to reminisce, amateur scholars looking to lecture, and a few who defied easy classification, including a petite young woman with an enormous duffel bag slung across her slightly bowed back.

At noon, Michael covered his table with a blue plastic sheet and ate lunch in the lobby restaurant. His Monte Cristo was cold, his fries limp. Outside the smudged window, traffic raced by on the Eisenhower. On the way back to his table, he stopped at a room adjacent to the convention hall. Inside stood about fifty folding chairs set in rows, and at the entrance was a signboard listing special events for the weekend. That afternoon featured several former World's Fair employees speaking about their experiences on the job, an architectural historian lecturing about art deco, and the debut of a new video history of the Century of Progress. The next day promised two university professors discussing the economic and cultural impact of the fair, a live auction, and "home movies of Century of Progress appearances by famed boxer Oswald 'Hard Knocks' Knoll, presented by his granddaughter Ann Knoll."

Michael stared at the last line. Over the years he had wondered what had happened to Ann Knoll, and whether she had kept or sold the rest of her grandfather's collection. As for Oswald, Michael often felt guilty about stealing the book from him and on a few occasions had considered writing an apology to him in care of Whitman Publishing. Then, a few weeks after Aunt Mae's death, Michael had opened the *Chicago Tribune* and read an obituary for Oswald, who had died of natural causes at the age of ninety-four and had been preceded in death by his wife, Louise, and his grandson, Oswald III, and was survived by "two daughters, six grandchildren, five great-grandchildren, and possibly a son."

Michael asked the woman staffing the check-in area if she knew Ann Knoll. The woman shook her head and referred him to another woman, who referred him to a man, who led Michael to the man who had organized the event.

"Sure, I know Ann Knoll," the man said. "I guarantee you've seen her."

"I have?"

"You can't miss her. She's the gal hauling around a giant duffel bag."

As he waited on customers, Michael watched for Ann. He saw her across the room, then lost her, then found her and lost her again. The crowd dwindled. By three-thirty there were more dealers than attendees, and Ann was nowhere to be seen. Michael turned away from his table and started to box up his wares. Hearing someone behind him, he turned and saw Ann Knoll. She was ringed and bangled, with wavy brown hair that looked unwashed, and she wore an old green mechanic's coat and a pair of faded jeans held up with a seatbelt studded with old bottle caps, its buckle bearing a Chrysler logo. She dropped her duffel bag to the floor and picked up a 1934 World's Fair guidebook.

"You can have that for ten bucks," Michael said. "Or five."

Her hands were slender, almost bony. Her cheeks were sunken.

"But it says fifteen on the cover."

Michael shrugged.

"Are you always such a tough bargainer?"

He smiled. "Not always."

"Well, it's very nice of you," she said as she set down the guidebook, "but I'm afraid it's still too steep for me."

Michael watched her study the merchandise and thought she appeared younger than the thirty-odd years she must have been. He tried to imagine what she looked like under her clothes, but her getup was so formless, he couldn't find the curves to use as an outline. Michael had touched only one naked woman in the last decade, and that had been Aunt Mae just a few years ago. Living with him by then, she had slipped in the tub and broken her hip, and it had been up to him to lift her out of the water, dry and dress her, and take her to the hospital. Over the next year, before moving her to a nursing home, he grew used to helping her bathe, dress, and wipe as she complained about the way he did things or apologized for being such a burden. He had hated most of his time with Aunt Mae, but ever since her death he had missed her. Her injury had made him feel useful, and now he wondered what purpose he served other than buying and selling unwanted things and living anonymously amid his books.

"I knew your grandfather," Michael said.

Ann looked up at him. "Pardon me?"

"Your grandfather was Oswald Knoll, right?"

"Yeah."

"Well, I knew him. He and I wrote back and forth about Big Little Books."

"No kidding. What's your name?"

"Michael Halligan."

She looked away, concentrating hard, and Michael felt uncomfortable knowing she was pondering his name, trying to solve the mystery of who he was. When she bit her lower lip, he tried to remember what she had looked like as a girl jumping rope, talking about a father who had left her, but there was nothing in his mind but the vaguest of recollections.

"I'm sorry, but I've never heard of you. My grandfather rarely talked about his life."

Michael felt relieved. As far as she knew, he might have been an honorable man.

"I was sorry to read about his death. I hope he wasn't in too much pain."

"It was Alzheimer's, so it wasn't pretty, but at the end I don't think he felt much of anything."

Michael watched her browse halfheartedly through his things. He imagined her selling the rest of Oswald's collection to him, saying it was wonderful to meet someone who had truly known and respected her grandfather. When she said she had to be going, Michael picked up the guidebook she'd looked at moments ago.

"You can have this," he said as he handed it to her. "For Oswald Knoll's granddaughter, it's free."

She thanked him. With the guidebook in her hand, she crouched down, picked up her bag, and heaved it over her shoulder.

"I'd love to talk to you about my grandfather," she said. "There was so much about him I never knew."

At eight-forty the next morning, Michael sat alone at a table in the lobby restaurant. He skimmed the menu, ordered coffee, and glanced nervously at the hotel entrance in hopes of seeing Ann, who was already ten minutes late. He'd not slept well. In bed he'd imagined her listening to his plea for the rest of Oswald's collection and handing it over out of respect for his worthiness. He'd imagined giving her advice about one thing or another, and having her appreciate his wisdom. He'd imagined her naked beneath him. To settle his nerves and try to sleep, he'd closed his eyes and attempted to determine the number of hours he had been alive. With some difficulty he was able to multiply his seventy-five years by 365 days, but when it came to determining the number of leap years and how many days he had waded into year seventy-six, his mind faltered. The numbers scattered. He tried again, failed again. Frustrated, he rose from bed and went into the room that had been his father's and then his aunt's. The room contained a twin bed, a table, a lamp, and a dresser covered with empty and half-empty perfume bottles. The drawers were filled with hundreds more, along with his aunt's old clothes, which he'd not yet had the heart to sell or discard. Michael opened the closet door. Hanging before him were more of his aunt's clothes, including dresses that had been draped in plastic dry-cleaning covers for decades. On the floor were her shoes, a large box of snapshots, and his father's old stack of *Man of Leisure* magazines. When she'd first moved in, Aunt Mae had complained about the magazines, but after that initial complaint, she had said nothing, and on a few occasions Michael had found her passed out with an issue or two at her side.

Michael grabbed a *Man of Leisure* at random and lay down in bed with it. These timeless, two-dimensional women had long ago replaced the girls of Lyons, the town having swept out its vice fifteen years earlier. He had heard rumors of where the hookers had gone, but feeling less lust and more shame than he once had, he didn't follow them. Instead, he let himself be satisfied with the women in his father's magazines. Barbi. Brooke. Amber. Terri. Leaning back in the bed, he looked at girls locked in time and pose, forever young and outdated, and he touched himself until he closed his eyes and fell asleep with Ann Knoll on his mind.

In the hotel restaurant, Michael glanced at his watch. It was nearly eight-fifty. The waitress refilled his mug and asked if he was sure he didn't want to go ahead and eat. He ordered breakfast, and a few minutes later she returned with his pancakes. As he ate, he silently cursed Ann. He had been friendly to her, he had given her something for free, and she had repaid him by standing him up.

At nine-ten, when Michael was nearly finished with his pancakes, Ann hurried to his table, apologetic and breathless. She wore the same clothes as she had the day before.

"I'm sorry I'm so late." She dropped her bag to the floor and sat. "Have you been here long?"

Michael nodded.

"Did I miss my chance to have breakfast with you?"

"No," Michael said, "that's fine."

Over his many years of buying and selling, Michael had come to sense vulnerability in others. Ann certainly seemed vulnerable—probably poor, maybe even hungover or high. He imagined her selling Oswald's collection for far less than it was worth.

After ordering an omelet and coffee, Ann pulled a notebook and pen from her bag and said, "So, could you tell me some stories about my grandfather?"

Michael told her about his correspondence with Oswald Knoll and the meeting of the Great-Men Club. She asked a lot of questions, scribbled notes as he spoke, and once stopped to say he reminded her of her grandfather: quiet, thoughtful, obviously committed to the things he loved. She rarely paused to eat or drink, but when she did, she attacked her breakfast as though she hadn't eaten in days.

"Did you ever meet him?" she asked.

Michael mentioned the first encounter: the Lone Ranger outfit, the bomb shelter, her grandfather's refusal to sell.

"After that," Michael lied, "I never saw him again."

"From what I understand, he was pretty lively when he was younger, but about all I remember is him being sad and disappointed." Ann closed her notebook and capped her pen. "After he got Alzheimer's a few years back, all he wanted to do was watch old home movies on the television. For the first couple of years he understood he was the one playing the characters on the screen, but he couldn't remember why he'd ever dressed up like that. Then he started to think the characters had been friends of his. He was living with my aunt in Jacksonville, and she kept trying to explain that he was watching himself, but he thought she was crazy. 'That's not me,' he'd say. 'How could that be me?' He'd tell her, 'That's Flash Gordon' or, 'That's Tarzan.' He knew the name and all sorts of details about every single character, and he thought they were as real as any of us." Ann sipped her coffee. "I was moving around a lot back then, so I only saw him a few times a year. But when my aunt got sick a couple years back, she moved him into a nursing home, and I headed down to Florida and took on the responsibility of visiting him. He spent his days watching TV shows and getting more and more frustrated and angry, thinking the people on the screen were in the room with him, telling him things that made no sense."

"Whatever happened to your father, if you don't mind my asking?"

"He left when I was seven, supposedly because he felt responsible for an accident my brother had—but I never quite believed it. That was just an excuse for him to quit his family."

"Did you ever hear from him?"

"He sent a couple of letters early on."

"That's it?"

"We moved, so who knows what happened? Maybe he had a change of heart. Maybe he came back and found us gone. Since my mom died ten years ago, I've sometimes thought I should track him down and tell him, but then I think, *why bother?* He made his decision to stop being my dad, so why should I try to be his daughter?"

Ann finished off her omelet and wiped her mouth with a paper napkin.

"Did you know my father, too?" she asked.

"Not really."

"Same here."

When she grinned, Michael thought that maybe they could get to know each other. She could come to him with her problems, and maybe he would have some good advice for her. It wasn't impossible.

"I corresponded a few times with your father. In one of his letters he mentioned that your grandfather had given him the collection."

Michael fidgeted with the paper napkin on his lap. They were new friends here, just having a casual conversation. She would say something, then he would say something, and after a little back-and-forth he would make an offer, almost as an afterthought.

The waitress topped off their coffees and laid the bill face down on the table. Michael immediately grabbed the piece of paper. Nobody could accuse him of being less than generous.

"To be honest, all that comic-strip stuff never interested me." Ann took a drink. "I know you collect it, but to me it never held any appeal. I always figured the real world needed all the attention we could give it, so why waste time with imaginary ones?"

Michael twisted his napkin around his index finger and asked, "What happened to the collection?"

"I saw it a few times when I was little, but after my mom and I moved, it just sort of disappeared. Then, a few days after my eighteenth birthday, my mom took me up to the attic, unlocked three footlockers that were against the far wall and buried under boxes and clothes, and showed me all that old stuff. 'This was your grandfather's and then your father's,' she said, 'and now it's yours.' I looked through it, but it meant nothing to me. I was eighteen, about to go away to college, and I was convinced that all my thoughts were brilliant. The only things I wanted to do were hang out with my friends, smoke pot, and consider all the ways I was going to make my mark."

"So, what happened to the collection? Do you still have it?"

Ann rolled her eyes. "Oh, no. Definitely not."

"Where is it?"

"It's gone."

"Gone where?"

"I don't know. The air? The ground? I burned it up until there was nothing left."

The napkin was wound so tightly around Michael's finger that his fingertip felt numb. His breath caught in his throat.

"What can I say? It wasn't a good age for me. My dad was missing, my mom and I were fighting most of the time, and inside me was this awful pain because of my brother's death. I hated everything, especially if it had to do with my family, so getting a bunch of useless junk was the last thing I needed. It was like a final insult from my father, like, *Hey there, sweetie. Sorry about everything. Here's some crap you don't want.* So one night I was sitting around the house with friends, and we got to talking about it. My mom was a nurse; she was working late at the hospital. I started telling a story my grandfather liked to tell, about a guy who drew one of the comic strips, and how he got so disgruntled that he burned up everything he'd ever done. For Grandpa the story was pure tragedy, but for me and my friends, what the guy had done was a great act of rebellion, or liberation, or something—the total annihilation of his past. It didn't take us long to decide that I needed to do the same thing." Ann shook her head. "At the time, it seemed like such a profound and symbolic act. And it *was* incredible in a way—gathering everything up, driving out to the woods with some beer, and then torching it all."

Michael watched the surface of his coffee quivering. Ann's story had to be untrue. Oswald's collection shouldn't have vanished so easily.

"My mom said I was an idiot to destroy something that would be worth good money someday, but I didn't care. Or at least I told myself I didn't. What I'd destroyed was mine, so what business was it of anyone else? But as the years passed, I realized I'd broken my grandfather's heart. He never said a word to me about it, but the older I got, the more I understood how devastated he must have been. Then later, when he was too far gone to accept my apology, it dawned on me that even though I had owned all that stuff, it had belonged—I mean truly belonged—to him." Ann cleared her throat. "I still feel bad about doing that to my grandfather. I feel like I owe him something, even though he's dead—or maybe especially because he's dead. I owe him some kind of tribute or penance. Anyway, since you knew him, I thought you might have something of his: an old letter or picture, anything. I was hoping you might give something of him to me."

Michael strangled his napkin beneath the table. He looked up from his coffee and glared at Ann.

"You want me to give you something?"

"It would mean a lot to me if you did."

"And what about things that mean a lot to me?"

Ann eyed him with a puzzled expression. "I'm sorry, Mr. Halligan. I don't follow what you're saying."

"Why did you destroy all those things?" His voice and body shook. "How could you do that? What gave you the right?"

Ann stiffened her back and inched toward the edge of her seat. "I'm sorry, but I don't understand—"

"Why didn't you sell it to someone who deserved it? Who would have cared for it?"

Michael tore the napkin in two and tossed its remains onto the floor. He stood and fumbled through his wallet. He threw a twenty on the table and glowered down at Ann, who seemed more stunned than scared.

"Do me a favor," he said, "and don't talk to me anymore about your goddamn family."

*

Michael tried to ignore Ann for the rest of the morning, though he often found himself watching her move from table to table and chat with others. He was glad to be rid of her, glad to be done with the entire Knoll family.

At noon he ate lunch in the lobby. When he returned, the guidebook he'd given Ann was resting on his chair, along with some money—his change, he assumed, from breakfast. He pocketed the cash and set out the guidebook for sale, and as he surreptitiously watched Ann appear and disappear amid the crowd, he tried to cling to his anger, tried to hate the very sight of her, but found he couldn't. By the middle of the afternoon, he even felt a little relieved that at least nobody else would ever own the rest of Oswald's collection.

At three-thirty, he covered up his table and made his way to the entrance of the special-events room. Half of the chairs were occupied, and a man tinkered with a projector. At the head of the room, Ann stood in front of a screen.

"And so he traveled around the Midwest, playing the various characters that appeared in Big Little Books, which led him to the Century of Progress," she said. "He and his coworker filmed four of their trips. The movies are about five minutes each."

The lights dimmed, and the projector started. On the screen appeared a pickup truck with a wooden flatbed and WHITMAN PUBLISHING—RACINE, WISCONSIN printed on the door. The camera panned the truck for several seconds before Oswald Knoll suddenly appeared on the screen, wearing a Buck Rogers costume. What Michael saw collided with what he knew, and he realized that the Buck Rogers he had seen as a boy might have been Oswald Knoll. From the flatbed, Oswald gestured to a crowd of children like a swashbuckler in a silent movie. The projector whirred. When Oswald began to act out a scene that involved much jumping and gesticulating, laughter rippled through the room. The movie suddenly switched to passing buildings, then cut to crowds on the midway, the sky ride, boats on Lake Michigan. Again Oswald appeared in the back of the truck. The camera stayed on him for a few seconds, then scanned the exuberant children, and finally zoomed in on a young woman holding her forearm in front of her face, shielding her eyes from the sun. She stood a little behind the crowd, her dress blowing against her body. When she lowered her arm, Michael saw that the woman was his mother. Her image rushed over and through him, and a great pounding started in his heart.

"Apparently, the cameraman had his eye on other things," Ann said.

The audience laughed as the camera lingered on his mother's bemused face and then slowly panned her body from head to toe and back again. She looked over her shoulder, then turned and walked offscreen. The camera swung around to Oswald, who held up a book, which he eventually threw to the crowd. The children jumped in delight and jostled each other for the book, and then another book, and then another. Transfixed, Michael searched for his mother and himself in the footage, but the children were moving too quickly and the camera was sweeping wildly. The film ended abruptly. The audience applauded.

Light-headed and shaken, as if jarred awake from a fever dream, Michael hurried to the bathroom, where he sat in a stall, taking deep breaths until his dizziness passed. He returned to the special-events room, where Oswald appeared on the screen as Dick Tracy. Michael watched him spin his pistol and tip the brim of his hat, but his thoughts were on his mother: how young she had looked, how doomed she had been. When the final movie ended, the lights turned on and the crowd cheered.

"Thank you for coming," Ann said as she stood. "It means so much to me to share a little bit of my grandfather with you."

As the audience filed out, murmuring pleasantly, Michael loitered at the back of the room and watched Ann shake hands and chat with others. When the room was nearly empty, she walked back to the projector and gathered her films, her eyes briefly meeting his. He approached her as she was kneeling on the floor, cramming the movies into her duffel bag.

"I'm sorry about earlier," he said.

"Did you get your money and guidebook?"

She knelt on the bag and zipped it shut.

"I got them."

She stood and swung the bag over her shoulder.

"I was hoping to talk to you about your home movies."

She hurried past him, out the door, and down the dim hallway to the hotel lobby.

"I was wondering what it would cost to buy one of them from you," he said as he caught up with her. "I'd give you a fair price."

She stopped and turned to him. "You have a lot of nerve, you know that?"

"This is important."

"You know something? I take back what I said at breakfast. You're not like my grandfather at all."

She started walking briskly again, and Michael struggled to keep pace with her.

"I need one of your films." With each step, he felt himself break apart and scatter a little more. "You have to believe me."

"And I'm sure you deserve it, too. I'm sure you deserve it much more than I do."

She stormed through the lobby and out the front doors. The day was frigid, but the sun was bright in the west. Beyond the parking lot, cars flew by on the expressway. Ann looked all around, as if she were trying to make sense of bad directions.

"That woman in the first movie you showed," Michael said. "She's my mother."

Grief swelled quickly and powerfully inside him, and before he knew what was happening, he was weeping. He covered his eyes with his hands, and the world around him vanished. Eventually he got control of himself and faced Ann, who lowered her bag to the ground, reached inside it, and pulled out the canister containing the movie. She held it out to him.

"Here," she said. "It's yours."

"What do you want for it?"

"I don't want anything," she said. "Just take it."

Michael took the film. His body calmed; the world returned. "But I have to give you something for it," he said. "It's only fair."

"It's not about buying and selling, or about what's fair. Why can't I just give it to you because I want to?"

"Because it's worth something."

"I don't mind."

"Well, then, because it's yours."

"Not anymore, it isn't."

"Isn't there something you want? Isn't there something you need?"

She sighed. "Do you really want to know what I need?"

Michael nodded.

"I need something to eat and money to get me to Racine. Can you give me those things? Would that make us even?"

2.

LIFE WAS A SERIES OF TRANSACTIONS, ANN THOUGHT, A CONTINUAL adjustment of values and negotiation strategies, an ongoing assessment of strengths and weaknesses, and then deal after deal after deal. For years she had tried to live outside this daily commerce, but all it had done for her was put her on the losing end of each exchange. Even now, as she sat in a pizza joint across the street from a cemetery just south of the Holiday Inn, she felt like a loser. Michael Halligan had her movie and his mother, and what did Ann have besides two slices of mushroom pizza and a Sprite?

"Al Capone is buried there," Michael said between bites. He pointed out the window. "Along with almost every dead bishop from the Chicago archdiocese."

Ann gazed at the graveyard, which seemed to stretch out forever on the other side of light Sunday traffic. The sun would soon set into it.

"Have you ever heard the story of the Italian bride?"

Ann turned to Michael, not sure how much to trust him. Over the years she had lived with so many people in so many different off-grid housing cooperatives, eco-villages, Catholic Worker houses, and activist havens that she considered herself a quick judge of character. But Michael Halligan, with his temper and his tears, was a mystery.

"I haven't," she said, feeling exhausted.

"The story goes that there was a young Italian woman who died in childbirth in 1921 or '22. Her family dressed her up in her wedding gown and buried her right out there in Mount Carmel cemetery." He wiped his greasy fingers on a paper napkin and sipped his Coke through a straw. On the wall behind him hung pennants for what must have been local high school teams: Panthers, Pirates, Friars, Crusaders. "Right afterward, the girl's mother started having horrible dreams where her daughter came to her, saying she wasn't really dead. The mother had these dreams for years and years, and they upset her so much, she asked the church and then the state for permission to exhume the body. Finally, six years after the girl's death, they dug up the coffin, which was starting to rot. When they opened it, they discovered that the girl was dead, but that her body hadn't decayed at all. Neither had her gown."

Ann imagined a young woman in a casket, as dainty and indifferent as a doll. Two years ago she would have called such preservation a miracle, but now it seemed to be nothing more than a hoax or a natural reaction to something in the earth.

"I don't believe you," she said.

Michael blushed and looked down at the crumbs on his Styrofoam plate. "I'm not saying it's true," he said. "I'm just saying it's a story—but there *is* proof."

"Proof?"

"Before burying her daughter again, the mother took a picture of the girl in her coffin and put the photo in glass on a new headstone. The picture is out there. I've seen it."

Ann looked out at the cemetery and imagined thousands of bodies underground, millions worldwide—all of them perfectly preserved, beautiful, useless. For years she had conjured her brother's decomposing body, and then her mother's, both buried in Racine, and these thoughts had driven her to a transient life of adopting one faith after another: in Buddha and Jesus, in indulgence and denial, in the country and the city, in social commitment and withdrawal from society.

"And over there," he said, pointing out the window and down Wolf Road, "is Queen of Heaven, where they used to have visions of the Virgin Mary."

"You know a lot about cemeteries, Mr. Halligan."

He laughed nervously. "My parents are at Mount Carmel, and my aunt and son are at Queen of Heaven. Other than that, I don't know anything special."

"Do you visit them a lot?"

"Hardly ever."

The radio played a peppy cover version of a sad song from the eighties, which itself had been a remake of an older tune.

"I've been thinking—I probably have some letters from your grandfather. I'm sure they don't reveal much about him, but if I can find them, you can have them."

"I'd like that, Mr. Halligan."

"Call me Michael," he said. "When you say, 'Mr. Halligan,' you make me think of my father."

After passing strip malls and subdivisions, Michael's van rumbled over train tracks, pulled into a gravel parking lot, and came to rest in front of a building with peeling yellow boards and a green roof that seemed ready to collapse. The name Yesteryear was printed on a splintered plank above a display window.

Ann grabbed her bag from the back and followed Michael to the front door. After unlocking a series of locks, he opened the door, accompanied her into the store, and turned off a burglar alarm. Ann had never seen so much junk in her life.

"You have a lot of stuff."

"Thank you," he said.

As Michael carried boxes from his van into Yesteryear, Ann squeezed her way down the aisle with her bag. The air felt dried out, as though history was little more than the simple desiccation of life. The sheer volume of things made her wonder how the store didn't fall in upon itself.

After returning with the final box, Michael led her through a door at the back of the shop. She had learned long ago to quickly assess her surroundings whenever entering a new place. She identified escape routes, checked that the windows weren't barred, looked for potential weapons to fend off attack, and left at the first inkling of concern. These rules had made her feel safe in the dozens of places she had lived, but she doubted she would need them here.

Michael left for a moment and returned with a twenty-dollar bill and a train schedule. After explaining that the Burlington Northern would take her from Stone Avenue to Chicago's Union Station, where another train would surely take her to Racine, he told her to make herself at home. He opened one of his file cabinets, and as he rummaged through his papers, Ann wandered around his home until she reached a bedroom decked out with frills and Catholic curios. She dropped her bag to the floor and picked up a dusty bottle of perfume from the collection atop the dresser.

"They belonged to my aunt."

Ann set down the bottle and turned to see Michael in the doorway.

"She used a lot of perfume, huh?"

"She drank it sometimes—when there wasn't any liquor handy."

Ann nodded. Michael was a sad man, though not as sad as the various addicts, orphans, victims, immigrants, and otherwise impoverished people she had met over the years.

"She lived with me for fifteen years, and then I put her in a home. She died around the same time as your grandfather."

"I'm sorry."

Michael opened the top drawer of the dresser.

"Help yourself to her clothes if you need any. Or feel free to rest awhile."

"Thank you," she said, wondering just how needy she looked.

"I'm going to keep looking for your grandfather's letters." Michael inched out of the room. "Give a holler if you need me."

Ann locked the bedroom door and removed her coat, happy to be alone. Over the past two weeks she had made her way from Jacksonville to Chicago through shared rides and hiking and Greyhound, spending each night with a former housemate or friend, or friend of a friend living in some kind of community. New Tribe Eco-village. Wild at Heart Artist Sanctuary. The Eden Project. Gaia Grove. Quixote's Farm. Koinonia. Last night she had stayed with six young women at a place called Magdalene House, an old brownstone with a backyard organic garden on the west side of Chicago. The women were all social-justice volunteers, eager and pacifistic and just a year or two out of college, and with them she had cooked and eaten sweet potato–bulgur stew. They washed their dishes in cold water, burned candles instead of electricity, and fertilized their garden with their own hair and waste and menstrual blood. After dinner they talked, and soon the discussion turned to the topic of pain, as it was likely to in such settings. One of the women claimed it was important not to love or hate your own pain too much, because if you did, it would atrophy and thus never grow into anything beneficial. Another disagreed, saying a person had to hold tightly to her pain and lift it up for the world to see, because pain, at the very least, was what kept people accountable to each other. Ann had trouble staying awake during the conversation, and when one of them asked what she thought, she said, "About what?"

"About anything."

"I don't know," she said. "I'm all out of thoughts, I'm afraid."

In the morning the women whispered and stepped lightly around the house as Ann teetered between sleep and waking. After she rose from the futon, already a few minutes late for breakfast with Michael, they helped her pack and sent her on her way with hugs and a slice of pumpkin bread.

Ann sometimes found it hard to believe she had spent so many years living in community with others, when what she wanted mostly now was solitude. In his last few months, her grandfather had lost the ability to speak. She used to visit him, and together they sat as silent as monks, although every so often she told him things about her life that she'd never told anyone. When visiting hours ended, she inevitably dreaded returning to shared meals and chores, discussion groups, and calls to action.

She searched through the dresser drawers, finding more perfume bottles and old-lady clothes. Then she opened the closet door to find more clothing, *Man of Leisure* magazines that struck her as more quaint than pornographic, and a box of old snapshots. She grabbed a handful of the photos and sat on the bed with them. There was a boy on a bike, a soldier, two girls with batons, a man with a baby, a girl with a birthday cake, a family at a park. Ann envied Michael for having such a large family and so many friends and acquaintances. Over the years she had known thousands of people, but felt that none had truly known her.

Ann woke to the sound of knocking. The room was dark and unfamiliar, and it took her a few seconds to remember where she was.

"I found the letters," Michael called.

She sat up slowly and switched on the lamp on the bedside table. She hoped she hadn't missed the last train downtown.

Michael knocked again and said, "I also found a projector, if you want to watch more of your movies. I turned it on. It still works."

When she entered the living room, Ann saw a projector resting atop a stack of boxes and aimed at the wall. She sat in the recliner, groggy from her nap, and Michael handed her a small bundle of letters held together with twine.

"You can have them," he said.

"Are you sure?"

"Of course I'm sure."

He loaded the film she had given him into the projector, and together they watched her grandfather at the Century of Progress. When the movie neared its final scene, Michael stood and approached the image flickering on the wall. His mother appeared and then disappeared.

"Were you close to her?" Ann asked as Michael rewound the film.

"She died when I was seven, so I don't remember her all that much."

Michael ran the movie again and again. Each time his mother appeared on the wall, he drew close to her. When the film ended for the fourth time, Ann asked, "Do you mind if I play one, too?"

Her brother, Trey, raced around the backyard in a red cape and a superhero costume. On his chest was the letter T. He climbed onto the picnic table and leaped to the grass. He swung back and forth on the swing and then let his body take flight. Upon landing, he fell forward to his hands and knees, stood up, and ran again.

"My brother loved my dad's costumes," Ann said, "so Dad got him a superhero outfit. Trey used to wear it everywhere and made everyone call him Super Trey."

Her brother ran and jumped, weaved crazily.

"One day we were visiting my dad at work, where Trey could wear the costume and nobody would laugh or look twice. I don't know how we did it, if it was something we'd planned or if it just happened, but we made our way to the roof."

She had said these things aloud only once before—to her silent, demented grandfather—but in this strange, dark house, at an unknown hour, she felt safe and free to speak.

"I can remember jingles and sitcom episodes from when I was a kid, but I can't remember what happened then, except that Trey was up there on the roof with me one second, and the next second he was gone. I don't know if he tried to fly or if he fell or what. All that's left of that time is a blank, like I completely annihilated those days in my mind."

Super Trey was inside now, eating macaroni and cheese at the kitchen table, buttered Wonder bread on the side. His feet kicked back and forth, several inches above the floor.

"From what everyone told me, they found me sitting on the roof, hugging my knees to my chest. It was days before I said a word." As she watched her brother and herself on the screen, Ann could not remember exactly how she had gone about obliterating her memories, but the sense of her determined, desperate attempt to forget still lingered inside her, as lonely and proud as the last of a dying people. "I should have protected him, but I didn't."

Back outside, Super Trey ran and ran until the film ended.

"He was in a coma for five years. My mom and I visited him practically every day." Ann stood and rewound the film. "The nurses would cut his hair and trim his nails, and we would talk to him about TV shows and the Green Bay Packers, but he never said a word, never moved except to breathe. He just lay there, getting older, until one day he died without warning."

Ann removed the reel from the projector and returned it to its canister.

"Are you homeless?" Michael asked.

"Not really."

"Are you broke?"

"Almost."

Michael walked to his bedroom and returned a minute later with a small book, which he handed to her. "Here," he said. "Take it."

The book was called *Trouble in the City of Dreams*, and although she didn't recognize it, she knew it was a Big Little. When she started to open it, he told her to stop. He took it back and opened it slowly until the front cover formed a ninety-degree angle with the rest of the book. "You've got to be very careful," he said as he closed the book and then opened it again, slowly, gently, emphasizing the delicacy of his movements. He demonstrated his simple actions twice more and then handed the book to Ann, who carefully turned the pages.

"This book belonged to your grandfather," he said, not quite making eye contact. "I stole it from him."

As Michael talked about collecting, and buying some things from her father, and stealing *Trouble in the City of Dreams*, Ann tried to remember meeting him as a girl, but nothing came to mind.

"The book is yours," Michael said. "It's been yours the whole time I've had it."

Ann didn't really want the book, didn't know what good it could do her. It couldn't feed or shelter her. It couldn't bring back her family or soothe her panicked, searching heart.

"And now that the book is yours," Michael said, "I want to buy it from you."

"Come on, this is silly." She extended the book to him. "I appreciate the gesture, I really do, but seriously, just keep it."

"But I want to buy it from you."

"You don't have to do this, Michael. I forgive you for stealing the book, and I'm sure my grandfather forgave you, too. Just think—if you hadn't stolen it, I would have burned it up with everything else."

"How about I give you five thousand dollars for it?"

"What?"

"Six thousand?"

"This is ridiculous."

"Seven thousand? Could you use seven thousand dollars?"

She was crying. "Why are you doing this?" she asked.

"I don't know," he said. "Just please let me do it."

She could tell from the way he stared at her that he needed her to accept his offer. It was the kind of look she had seen in the fervent newcomers to whatever mission or activist group she belonged to, and in the broken people who came to them for help and never got better.

"Okay," she said. "Thank you."

He took the book from her and went into his bedroom. A few minutes later he reappeared and handed her a plastic grocery bag filled with hundred-dollar bills.

"Do you mind if we watch some of the other movies?" he asked.

Silently, they watched films of her family from her grandparents' wedding to the time she was a girl: holidays, vacations, parades, school pageants, and simple afternoons at home. After the tenth movie, Ann looked over and noticed Michael slumped to the side, asleep against the sofa's arm. She rewound the film, turned off the projector, and pulled the train schedule from her pocket. In the kitchen she found a wall clock and saw that the time was ten minutes to eleven. In fifteen minutes, the last train would leave Stone Avenue for Union Station. There was no more for her in Racine than anyplace else in the world, but it was as close to a home as she had. With Michael's money, she could rent an apartment, buy some furniture, and look for work. She could track down people she used to know and ask them what they remembered of her life.

She tiptoed past Michael, stopping briefly to gather up all of her films except the one she'd given him. She went into the dead aunt's bedroom and stuffed the movies, the money, and the letters from her grandfather into her duffel bag, and picked up the snapshots she'd looked at earlier. The images were both familiar and new to her, and they made her think there were echoes between people in the way they posed. Given the right light, even lifelong enemies could cast identical shadows. She set the pictures back in the box in the closet, put on her coat, and sprayed some ancient perfume onto her neck.

After writing a short note to Michael, she slipped through the kitchen and out the back door with her bag on her back. Spring would arrive in a few days, but it would be weeks before it no longer felt like winter. When the crossing gates clanged, Ann hurried around the side of Yesteryear and toward the arriving train, faithful that the future would be better than the past.

3.

YESTERYEAR SAT HUNCHED AND BOXY, TWENTY FEET BACK ON A CORNER plot that people had once called a prairie and now called prime real estate. The building tilted more to the west than it ever had, though the lean was less an indication of its weakness than a sign of its strength for having endured nearly seven decades. Because of harsh winters, acts of vandalism, acts of God, and the simple decay of age, there was little reason such a rickety place should have lasted as long as it had. In the home behind the store, Elizabeth Halligan shielded her eyes from the sun. She lowered her arm, and soon Oswald Knoll appeared in a Buck Rogers outfit, only to be displaced by a crowd of children, who jumped and grabbed until the screen turned blue. Soon Oswald appeared again, and then Elizabeth, and then children who were now either elderly or dead, until there appeared a bright blue that signaled both the end and the beginning.

Michael hit Stop on the remote control and rose from bed. It was four in the morning, and he had been awake for nearly an hour. In his pajamas and robe, he made his way to the kitchen, where a sealed envelope lay on the table. He sat and picked up the envelope, which contained a letter he had written a week ago but had not yet mustered the courage to send to Ann.

A month after she had slipped out of his house—nearly a year and a half ago now—a postcard from her had arrived, saying she had found a studio apartment in Racine and a job as an aide at a nursing home. Michael had converted the movie of his mother to video and had it copied onto seven tapes. He stored one tape beside his television, one in a cardboard box in the living room, one behind the counter in his store, and three in his closet safe. He mailed the seventh video to Ann, along with a note of thanks for remembering him. Since then they had exchanged letters or phone calls every few weeks, which was never soon enough for Michael. Whenever too many days passed without contact, he worried that something awful had happened to her, or grew resentful with the feeling that she had forgotten him, or feared that she had decided to return to a transient life. But then a card or letter would arrive, or the phone would ring, and his body would relax in appreciation.

Two months earlier, she had invited him up to Racine for lunch. Without hesitation, he accepted her offer and drove north. She looked healthier than before, though her attire was still grungy, and she gave him a long, heartfelt hug that made him want to cling to her for hours.

"Other than my aunts and cousins and a few of my mom's old friends, nobody remembers much about me from when I was a girl." They shared a table in a quaint little sandwich shop overlooking Lake Michigan. Michael stared at the water stretching out forever, and he imagined it was an ocean. "I got so sick of asking people about my life that I recently started asking them about theirs. It's weird—I used to be so driven to help people, but I'm not sure I ever really heard and saw them as well as I should have. I think I'm just figuring that out now. Do you know what I mean?"

"I think so," said Michael.

Over tomato soup, Ann asked him about his mother and his father and Sara, and he answered her honestly about most things, but not everything. He couldn't bear for her to know the worst parts of him. When the check came, he insisted on paying for lunch, but she insisted harder, and as they parted they promised to see each other before the end of the year.

Michael picked up the envelope from the kitchen table, stood, and stepped outside into the early morning. The sky was dark, crisp, and still. Nobody was on the street to see him as he walked along in his robe and slippers, like an escapee from an asylum, past a realtor's office, a coffee shop, a boutique for dogs. A bird cawed crazily somewhere overhead, and Michael wondered if the creature was lost or had been abandoned, or if it had simply confused night with day. He stopped and looked up at streetlights, trees, and buildings but couldn't find the source of the call that echoed all around him.

Once he was dead, everything would belong to Ann. She could do whatever she wanted with the store and his money, but she was to save the Big Littles. He wouldn't hear a word of protest about it from her. He started walking again and soon reached the post office, where he opened the hatch to a mailbox and sent the letter on its way.

Back at home, Michael picked up the remote control, hit Play, and lay back in bed, wishing he knew what had happened to everything and everyone he'd ever lost, wishing they'd all come back to him. His mother covered and then revealed her face. She was breaking apart, becoming more fragmented with each viewing, more and more an assemblage of black-and-white specks and less the person she'd been. Michael scooted to the edge of the bed and inched his face toward her. Up close she was nothing but little illuminated squares, but when he put his fingertips and then his lips to the screen, and the static kissed him back, he felt a hum and a flicker of life.

ACKNOWLEDGMENTS

I am indebted to many people for supporting me as I wrote *Dream City*. I especially extend my gratitude to the late James A. Michener, whose remarkably generous gift to the University of Texas provided me with financial support during the writing of this novel; my classmates at the University of Texas for being talented writers, insightful readers, and generous peers; Jim Magnuson, Marla Akin, and the rest of the Michener Center staff for creating such a hospitable environment; Steve Harrigan, Elizabeth Harris, Tony Giardina, and (once more) Jim Magnuson for their excellent advice; Joy Williams for championing this book when it needed a champion; David Bradley for forcing me to raise my standards and become a better writer; the faculty and staff of St. Albans School, especially Malcolm Lester and Paul Piazza, for giving me the time, space, and financial support to write the first draft; Tom Boyle, whose collectibles store, Yesterday, fed my baseball card habit when I was a kid and served as my initial inspiration for what would become *Dream City*; William O'Rourke for being the first person to tell me I could write fiction; and Buzz Mauro, David A. Taylor, Robert Williams, Josh Deutchman, and Kate Blackwell for their early encouragement, and for reading as well as they write.

Big thanks also to Kim Witherspoon, my agent, for believing in my work and finding a good home for my book; Julie Schilder, Kim's assistant, for her insightful edits and thoughtful guidance through the publishing process, and for being nearly as invested in the novel as I was at times; and the folks at MacAdam/Cage Publishing, especially Kate Nitze, Khristina Wenzinger, Scott Allen, and David Poindexter, for embracing my novel so enthusiastically, offering wise advice for improving it, and putting up with my assorted anxieties.

In the course of writing *Dream City*, I consulted many books, articles, and websites. I tried to stay as true to the facts as my research and patience allowed, but I didn't let the truth stand in the way of the story. I am grateful to the authors of the various works I consulted, especially Larry Lowery, president of the Big Little Book Club and editor of *The Big Little Times* newsletter. Everything I got right about Big Littles was because of the newsletter; his book, *The Collector's Guide to Big Little Books and Similar Books*; and his website, www.biglittlebooks.com. Everything I got wrong (or made up, as in the case of *Trouble in the City of Dreams*) was because of me.

In addition to the sources listed on the copyright page, I want to acknowledge text excerpted from the following: *Black Silver and his Pirate Crew, with Tom Trojan* (author and artist uncredited); *Gang Busters Step In*, written by Isaac McAnallay and illustrated by Henry E. Vallely; *Grandmother's Prophecies* fortuneteller card by Mike Munves Corp.; *Hamlet* by William Shakespeare; *Official Guide Book of the World's Fair of 1934*, published by A Century of Progress International Exposition; *Official Guide: Book of the Fair 1933*, published by A Century of Progress; "Too-Ra-Loo-Ra-Loo-Ral (That's an Irish Lullaby)," lyrics and music by J.R. Shannon; and "Uses of Great Men" by Ralph Waldo Emerson. Additional thanks to the artists, writers, editors, and others who produced the Big Little Books and comic-strip characters mentioned in *Dream City*.

Thank you to Mari, Bruce, Fionn, Annalee, Bairbre, Melinda, Biff, Mary, Marybeth, and the rest of my family and friends for always being supportive of my writing and for continuing to care how the novel was coming along, year after year.

My deepest gratitude goes to my parents, William and Nora Short, for providing me with unlimited love and support, and for being the most heroic people I know; my daughter, Elizabeth, for inspiring me every day and reminding me that many things are more important than writing a book; and mostly Stephanie, for her enduring patience, encouragement, editorial brilliance, and love.

ABOUT THE AUTHOR

BRENDAN SHORT is a graduate of the University of Notre Dame and the James A. Michener Center for Writers at the University of Texas. His stories have appeared in several literary journals, including *The Literary Review* and *River Styx*, and have been nominated for a Pushcart Prize. A former writer in residence at St. Albans School in Washington, D.C., he lives in the Chicago area with his wife and daughter. *Dream City* is his first novel.